A DEATH IN THE KEYS

A DEATH IN THE KEYS

A Key Largo Diving Story

Thomas Simmons

Copyright © 2021 by Thomas Simmons

All rights reserved. No part of this work may be
reproduced or transmitted in any form by any means,
electronic or mechanical, including photocopying and
recording, or by any information storage or retrieval
system, without permission in writing from the author.

ISBN 9798532233171

Independently published

This is a work of fiction and none
of the people depicted in these pages
is an actual person, living or dead. So even
if you really, really think I'm writing
about you or someone you know, I'm not.
Seriously.

Cover design: Lisa Fowler

For the gang at SFS.
I love you guys!

Chapter 1

Kaitlin was already beginning to struggle by the time Davey got to her, which was a bad thing. Struggle can lead to panic and panic can kill you underwater.

Davey turned around just in time to see her jerking the right shoulder of her buoyancy control vest in the narrow passageway behind him. Her alternate-air regulator hose was hung up on a bracket that jutted out from the wall of the shipwreck. Instead of stopping to locate and solve the problem, she was tugging at her vest and trying to swim forward.

With two quick fin kicks, Davey got to Kaitlin and signaled her to stop moving. She looked up at him and he saw the eyes, the big eyes, the eyes that said, "I'm getting ready to panic. *Here I go!*"

He repeated the "STOP" signal more emphatically.

Then he reached behind her right ear and pushed the hose back and away from the bracket.

Kaitlin felt it release and moved forward a bit, unhindered.

Davey made the "OK" sign and Kaitlin returned it, almost petulantly.

Now she felt criticized and he could tell that it was almost as annoying as getting hung up in the first place. Maybe more. Davey mimed clapping his hands, meaning "GOOD WORK," to ease the sting but she was still angry with herself.

And by extension, she was angry at Davey, too.

Behind Kaitlin, Davey could see her brother, Matt, her mother, Shelli, and her dad, Bill, hovering in the water column, waiting.

Davey signaled "SLOW" and swam forward toward the doorway 50 feet away, careful not to raise silt from the floor beneath them.

Just outside the superstructure, he turned to get a picture of each of them swimming out through the doorway. The picture everyone wants.

"Look at me! I penetrated a deep wreck!"

Kaitlin came out, quickly faced the camera and waggled a "HANG LOOSE" hand signal. No pout on this girl when there's a camera present. That's her Instagram picture tomorrow. *For sure.*

Matt came out, pretending he didn't even know there was a camera. Joe Cool. Shelli popped out flailing her arms in an ineffective breaststroke--*no matter how many times I tell her it just slows her down,* Davey thought, shaking his head.

He got a nice picture of each, hoping the focus stayed sharp. Sometimes the pictures blurred because the camera couldn't tell where to focus. Or maybe the low light at 80 feet down caused the blurring. Water was funny stuff.

Davey waited for Bill, holding the camera very steady. The others hovered above the deck behind Davey.

And he waited.

But Bill didn't come out.

Fifteen seconds ticked by, seemed like a lifetime.

Shit!

This was Davey's worst nightmare come true: a missing diver. *Inside a deep wreck!*

He swam to the passageway and looked inside. The space was heavily silted back where Kaitlin had gotten hung up. Davey didn't see Bill anywhere and he couldn't see daylight at the other end through the silt.

Did Bill turn back? Did he make a wrong turn? Go out the side?

Shit!

Davey turned to the other three and signaled "STAY WHERE YOU ARE. *STAY!*"

He swam down the passageway, looking into each side room for Bill. The silted area stretched for about 15 feet. The passageway was clear on the other side.

Davey swam through the silt. Still no sign of Bill.

Davey exited at their original point of entry and Bill wasn't there either.

They had briefed for this before getting into the water but that was meaningless. People didn't pay attention to briefings. They nodded, they smiled, but they didn't actually listen and learn.

Shit, shit, shit!

Davey swam outside the wreck and back to where the other three were hovering. They'd stayed where he'd told them to stay, which was a minor miracle in itself; thank God for small favors.

He signaled they should all follow him and headed for the mooring line. That's protocol: if we get separated, we meet back at the mooring line.

That was in the briefing. That's what he'd told them to do.

When they got to the mooring line, Bill wasn't there.

Davey checked everyone's air. They had all started with a full 3,200 psi in their scuba tanks.

Shelli and Matt had 1,700 psi remaining. Kaitlin only had 1,200 psi but that's because she'd gotten anxious when she was hung up.

If your heartbeat goes up, you use more air. Simple biology.

Meanwhile Bill was nowhere to be found and that wasn't good.

The *USS Spiegel Grove* is a 510-foot dock landing ship that was sunk off Key Largo in 2002 as an artificial reef. It's an immense wreck. Most people are stunned by its size the first time they dive it.

When it was scuttled, the charges went off wrong and the ship flipped over and landed on its side. Three years later, Hurricane Dennis came along and turned the ship right side up. A 510-foot ship, 130 feet down.

You want an example of the power of nature, let that sink in.

There are seven mooring lines on the *Spiegel*. Davey always made sure his divers took a close look at the line they came down and where it tied off on the ship, so they could find and identify it for themselves if they got separated.

They all had plenty of air and there were 12 minutes of No Decompression Limit (NDL) time left, the time allowed at a given depth before a diver enters decompression, which adds risk factors beyond the recreational diver's equipment and certification.

But the clock was ticking.

They were supposed to start their ascent up the line with 1,000 psi or five minutes NDL time whichever came first. That's what Davey had briefed.

Fat lot of difference that made now.

Plus, Davey didn't know how the situation was affecting Bill; he might be huffing through his air if he was feeling anxious. He knows he's supposed to meet us at the mooring line but it's a huge ship.

Can he find it on his own? Does he know where he is on the wreck? Why the hell didn't he stay put?

Going up any mooring line is better than running out of air or making a free ascent but Davey liked his divers to stay together where he could keep an eye on them.

If he didn't have all his divers in sight, he'd lost control of the situation. He needed to regain control.

And the clock was ticking.

Visibility on the wreck was about 50 feet today and suddenly Davey spotted Mark, one of the other instructor/guides, looming into view, leading his group up to the mooring line from the stern area.

And there was Bill, swimming alongside him.

How the heck did he get…? Doesn't matter. *Huge fucking relief!*

Davey signaled for Bill's air pressure. Bill checked his gauge and casually raised one finger, hand forward, then four fingers, hand backwards: 1,400 psi. Cool as a cucumber. No biggie.

The man was Zen.

Davey didn't care how much air or NDL time they had left at this point; it was time to end the dive before something else went wrong. Davey gave the "thumbs up" signal: head for the SURFACE. He put his hands on the mooring line and signaled the others to do the same.

Mark started his group on the mooring line right below Davey's.

Hand over hand, one foot per second. Maximum depth was 80 feet so at 40 feet they held for a minute and did a Deep Stop, off-gassing some excess nitrogen from their body tissues.

Everyone was cool.

When a minute was up, they headed up the line to 15 feet where Davey stopped the group for the standard three-minute safety stop.

Casually, Bill gave Davey the OUT-OF-AIR signal, drawing his flat hand across his throat.

What the hell!

Davey presented his alternate-air regulator to Bill, who made the exchange as if the two of them did this all the time.

Total Zen. *Yeah, thanks, breathing is cool. I like to breathe.*

Davey checked Bill's SPG and it was at zero. Davey still had over 1,500 psi so there was no problem with air supply, but still. What the hell happened to Bill's 1,400 psi? Did he mean one plus four: five, which is nuts? Or did he just misread his gauge?

Bill's an Advanced Open Water diver; he's supposed to know this stuff.

Mark signaled Davey from below on the line: you OK? Davey nodded, returned the OK sign. Yeah, we're fine. SNAFU. Situation Normal: All Fucked Up.

Bill was bobbing and weaving like he was listening to a playlist on ear buds.

Davey counted down the three minutes on his dive computer. Then he signaled everyone to check their own computers. Bill indicated he was done by sweeping his hand across his dive computer; Kaitlin, too; Sherry followed suit.

Matt was still showing time on his safety stop.

Ten seconds later Matt was all done and Davey gave the "thumbs up" signal and led them to the surface. They moved slowly and carefully, since Bill was on Davey's air and had to stay close or Davey's alternate-air regulator would be pulled from his mouth.

When they broke the surface, Davey told Bill, "Orally inflate your BCD. Then put your snorkel in your mouth."

The waves were two to three feet at the surface. Not too serious but there was current and they needed to do this right.

Matt came up, then Kaitlin and Shelli.

"That was so *awesome!*" said Matt.

"I'm so pissed about my alternate getting snagged!" Kaitlin was pouting again. Shelli pushed her mask up and rubbed her eyes.

"Okay, guys, *guys!* Keep you regs in your mouths. Shelli, put your mask back on. Fully inflate your BCDs and keep a firm grip on the granny line. There's current."

"I still can't believe…"

"*Kaitlin,* put your reg in your mouth. Inflate your BCD."

The current was less than one knot but that's still too strong to swim against. The waves were crashing over their heads and they had to get back to the ladder at the stern of the dive boat without floating away.

Like to Miami.

Again, nothing new. Davey had to baby-step every group at this point in the dive.

"Hand over hand. Hold tight to the granny line."

The granny line was a rope from the mooring ball to the dive platform at the stern of the dive boat. In strong current, divers hold onto the granny line to keep from being swept behind the boat and, literally, out to sea.

Five feet from the ladder, Davey stopped Bill.

"Take your fins off and hand them to me. Then grab the ladder with both hands before you put your feet on the bottom step."

Davey had to give Bill credit: he followed directions like a champ.

Davey handed Bill's fins up to Javier, the Jamaican mate, and Bill climbed the ladder. Javier grabbed Bill's tank stem and escorted him back to his seat, stretching a restraining bungee cord over his regulator's first stage.

Javier wore a buff over his head to keep the sun from scorching his scalp. He was more of a Harry Belafonte-type Jamaican, with short hair and light caramel skin. His voice was like music, easygoing and melodic, never raised or harsh.

Kaitlin reached for the ladder and Davey pushed her back. "Fins first," he told her. "Don't let go of the granny line."

If Bill was good with directions, Kaitlin was the exact opposite. Everything Davey told her pissed her off. She struggled to get her fins off and Davey grabbed them before they slipped out of her hands and sank.

To the bottom, which was 130 feet down.

Kaitlin was still on the ladder when Matt handed Davey his fins and pulled himself toward the boat.

"Stay back," Davey warned. "Never get under another diver on the ladder. If she falls, her tank lands right on your head."

Davey could see Matt working out that image in his mind.

Shelli made it to the ladder, climbed two steps, spat out her regulator and started to take off her mask.

"No, no, Shelli, *darlin'*," sang Javier in his lilting Jamaican chant. "Keep you mask on you pretty face, keep you regulator in you mouth. So you fall back in the water, you still a diver!"

Shelli got frustrated and let go with one hand to replace her mask, nearly falling back into the ocean. Javier grabbed her tank stem and pulled her back up.

"I got you, Shelli, *honey*," he cooed. Javier was mellow personified. "Here we go now." He walked Shelli back to her seat and wrapped the bungee cord around her tank to secure it as soon as she sat down.

Davey climbed onto the dive platform and headed back to his seat. He was tall, just under six foot three, yet he moved easily in the heavy scuba gear even with the dive boat rocking in the waves. He had arrived at a point in life where he was neither young nor old but somewhere in between. He was tan and fit by virtue of being a working dive instructor and he was easy going by nature though sometimes uncooperative divers tended to put that to the test.

Now it was time for some positive reinforcement.

"So… great dive guys! How'd you like the *Spiegel Grove?*"

"It's awesome," repeated Matt.

"It's so big," said Shelli.

Kaitlin was deciding whether she was still pissed or not so Davey gave her a little nudge in the right direction.

"Kaitlin, great job not panicking down there. I was really impressed."

Big smile. Now that she'd been complimented, she was all for agreeing she'd had a good time.

Bill was just grooving to the beat. Davey looked at him in wonder: ignorance is bliss.

"You gave me a bit of a scare," Davey said, evenly. *Did you listen to any of the briefing? At all?* Davey thought to himself behind his guest-services smile.

"I couldn't see," Bill said happily. "So I swam out the side."

But you didn't come to where we were! And you didn't go to the mooring line! You got outside of the wreck and then you did everything wrong! Davey wanted to shout.

"And then I got confused. I might have gotten a little lost."

And you might also have totally misread your air gauge, too, you moron!

Davey smiled at Bill. "You did great, man. Great dive, everyone."

There was no point in losing his shit on Bill at this point. Everyone was back on the boat. Making Bill feel bad now would just put a damper on the dive and reduce the size of Davey's tip later.

Mark's group got on board without a hitch. BCDs filled, masks on, regulators in mouths, fins off. Like good little soldiers on parade.

Where's the justice? Davey thought, shaking his head.

Kaitlin and her family weren't bad divers. Far from it. They were pretty typical of the guests Davey guided: certified divers who didn't get to dive that often. Folks who lived inland, away from any good diving opportunities, got certified on vacation put a few dives in their log, and then only dived once a year or every couple of years.

Their skills never became intuitive and each dive trip was a re-learning experience.

Bill, Shelli, Matt and Kaitlin had about 20 dives apiece. They were competent underwater but didn't have a lot of reserve to handle the unexpected. On a shallow reef dive, there was no problem. But a deep wreck offered a whole lot more risk factors to be considered.

For Davey, deep wrecks were a harrowing experience. He loved diving them but being responsible for other divers at 80 to 100 feet was sometimes a daunting task. He'd dived with this same foursome on Molasses Reef the day before and felt good about their skills.

But taking them through that long passageway had been a mistake. Davey made a mental note to himself. Never again.

While Javier cast off the mooring line, Davey headed up to the flybridge, away from his guests, for a little restorative privacy.

Captain Di was at the helm, lips pursed, eyebrows knitted. He was checking the surface around the boat for divers' bubbles before engaging the props. His face was lined with consternation, his natural expression when his mood hadn't been mellowed by alcohol.

Di, short for Diogenes, liked that the flybridge was separated from the passenger deck. Guests annoyed him. He'd drown them all like a bag of cats if it wouldn't cost him his captain's license.

Di was a big man, barrel-chested with heavy limbs and a corona of inky black, curly hair dotted by swaths of gray. Boat captains in the Keys don't wear uniforms, but Di always wore his Greek fisherman's hat on his head, which gave him a quasi-official look.

"That's it," Davey said. "From now on I'm not taking groups larger than two through the passageways."

"You crazy," Di answered. "Why risk even one? Or take them all and leave them inside."

"I had a missing diver for five minutes."

"Scary, man."

"Longest five minutes of my life."

"Certified diver, right? Not a student? So, he's on his own."

"When he's in my group. I'm responsible."

Di looked at the bow and frowned.

"Javier, where's the ball!"

Javier pointed to the left. "Port bow."

Di reversed the engines to get clear of the mooring ball. He turned to starboard and moved the boat forward, slowly.

Javier coiled the bow line and clipped it to the railing. He tapped his head with his fist--ALL GOOD--and moved back toward the passenger deck.

"You got 'em all on board, right?" said Di.

"Yeah, they're all back and happy."

"Then count your blessings. Scuba Doo lost one today on the *Benwood* wall."

"*What!* You're kidding!"

"No joke. Especially no joke for them."

Davey looked casually around the dive site as he absorbed this information.

There was only one other dive boat on the *Spiegel Grove* this morning. It was at the bow ball: a 40-foot Corinthian catamaran, *Reef Rider*, with about 30 people onboard.

Di keyed the radio mic. "Reef Rider this is Calypso. Go to 18."

Di turned his radio dial to channel 18. The captain of *Reef Rider*, a tough old buzzard named Rocky, came on. "Hey Di, what's up?"

"You double dipping the Spiegel this morning?" Di asked.

"Roger that," Rocky replied.

"You hear about Scuba Doo?" Di was still checking the surface for diver's bubbles as he slow-walked *Calypso* off the dive site.

"Yeah, bad news, huh?" What he meant was better them than me.

"Ruined someone's day," Di agreed.

"Let me know what you hear. Be safe," Rocky said by way of signing off.

Di switched the channel back to 16, the Coast Guard channel, and pushed the throttles forward.

Since *Reef Rider* was doing a second dive on the *Spiegel Grove,* the divers would sit on the boat for a one-hour surface interval to off-gas excess nitrogen before going back underwater. Davey's boat, *Calypso,* was scheduled to head over to the *Benwood* wreck, a shallow site, for their second dive of the morning.

No surface interval required.

Calypso was a Delta 38-foot, monohull, custom dive boat with twin diesel engines. It was rated for 24 passengers but rarely carried more than 18, including crew.

The white fiberglass decking gleamed in the bright sunlight. The brightwork sparkled. All the dive boats were washed with soap and fresh water at the end of each day so the salt wouldn't corrode the aluminum and cake on the surfaces.

"How do you lose a diver on the *Benwood* wall?" asked Davey, rhetorically.

The *Benwood* wall wasn't really a wall at all, more of a slope. About 50 yards east of the *Benwood* wreck, the sea bottom angled down from 45 feet to 90 feet.

Caribbean islands have walls because they are mostly ancient volcanoes, mountains that rise straight up from the sea bottom. But the Florida Keys are on a shelf, which gradually descends to the east in tiers until it reaches the bottom of the Florida Straits.

The *Benwood* wall was just a deeper tier of sand and coral.

"They call the Coast Guard five minutes ago. Seventeen divers go down, 16 divers come up," said Di, laconically

Davey shook his head in wonder. His day was looking better and better. "There are no overheads there. No swim-thrus."

"Been over an hour and twenty since they went in."

"What do they do now?"

"They wait. For the Coast Guard. Rescue diver already went down. He find nothing."

"That sucks. We still going to the *Benwood?*" Davey asked.

"Oh yeah, with a million fucking Coast Guard there? That's just where I want to be," answered Di. He snorted.

"I'm going over to Mo," Di continued. Mo is short for Molasses Reef. "See if you can lose one of your divers at Mo."

"Very funny. You're a riot. You should do stand-up, Di." Davey shook his head in wonder. "I still don't see how you can lose someone on the *Benwood* wall."

"Bringing everyone back. It's over-rated."

"How many in the group with lost the diver?" Davey asked.

"No idea. Everything I know, you already know. We hear all about it at Bubble Talk later. Maybe some even true." Di whistled a desultory tune.

Bubble Talk was the name given to the informal chatter among scuba professionals at the various Happy Hours around the island. It was rarely a source of reliable information, mostly just rumors and gossip.

"One out of 17. It's not so bad." Di faced into the wind and smiled happily.

"You know what you are, Di? A misanthrope, that's what," said Davey.

"A what you say…?"

"Misanthrope. Someone who doesn't like people."

"Come on, you just made that up."

"Nope, it's a real thing."

"A *missing trope?*"

Sometimes Di's lingering Greekness got in the way, even though he'd been in the U.S. for more than 45 years.

"Close enough."

Di laughed and for a moment Davey thought he might actually break into song.

"Missing trope. *That's me!*"

At least Bill had come up with the rest of them; there was that to be happy about. Davey's day hadn't been nearly as bad as someone else's day had been.

He wondered who was the poor son-of-a-bitch leading that group.

Chapter 2

Near accidents are a daily occurrence in recreational scuba diving. People misjudge their air, underestimate the current or lose control of their buoyancy. There's even the odd burst eardrum, mild decompression sickness or an occasional ride in the deco chamber.

But actual deaths are rare.

Of course, the Scuba Doo incident was technically still a "missing diver" but no one held out any real hope that the diver would be recovered alive at this point. If that were going to happen it would have happened by now.

So, this was a dead diver. The nightmare of every dive shop in the world. This was the dice coming up craps, the short straw, the stone in the snowball.

Among dive professionals, a little shiver runs down every spine when a diver dies and in the rush to find out what happened, truth is often a secondary consideration. So that was the essence of Bubble Talk on the night of the accident.

No one in Key Largo actually believed what they heard at Bubble Talk but they acted as if they did and passions often ran high.

"I heard they lost sight of her and she never surfaced with the group," one instructor said over his beer with great conviction.

"Totally wrong," said another with equal certainty. "It was a man and he swam away from the group. Everyone saw him go but they couldn't catch up to him."

"I'll bet it was a drug recovery," insisted a third. "Someone cut a bale loose when they were interdicted by the Coast Guard and the diver put a float bag on it and surfaced at another boat. Square grouper. I'd put money on it."

After a short silence, the first instructor insisted, "That's the *dumbest* thing I ever heard."

"No, it's not." Then after a moment. "*Why?*"

"Because if they had a second boat, why go out on a commercial dive boat in the first place and attract attention."

That prompted some rapid rethinking.

"Could be a distraction," offered the drug theorist. "Get people looking in the wrong direction."

"*Stupid.* Just plain stupid," snapped the second instructor with finality and the third instructor sulked but didn't argue.

Each said a silent prayer of gratitude that the lost diver hadn't been on their boat and, what was even more important, they all ordered more drinks before Happy Hour ended.

There were almost as many bars as there were dive shops on Key Largo. But for Davey and Captain Di, Get Shorty's was the go-to place to relax and unwind after work because it was less than a half-mile from where *Calypso* docked.

Get Shorty's tiki bar was a popular spot among other local dive pros for a number of reasons but the big one was Ladies Night on Tuesday evenings. Women drank for free from 6:00 to 7:00 PM.

Free drinks were restricted to rail liquors, jug wine and draft beer but that didn't matter one bit. A line of people filed in at six o'clock, like shoppers on Black Friday, and at seven o'clock on the dot they left the place as if it were on fire.

Unless they were already drunk. And most of the time they were.

For the guys who had girlfriends, this was a cheap date. For single guys, it was a target-rich environment.

"Davey Jones, you magnificent *missing trope!* Buy me a shot," bellowed Di. "Or I buy you a shot."

Di was already hunched over the bar when Davey walked in.

"You know I don't drink shots, Di," said Davey. The irony of having the name David Jones and working in the dive industry had long since worn off for Davey but Captain Di never got tired of it.

"I know. Don't make no sense to me but whad'ya gonna do?" Di mused.

Jorge, the bartender, brought Davey a draft beer. Davey nodded at Di and Jorge brought him another Captain & tonic. Jorge was tall and broad, and looked like a muscle builder but he was always calm, a gentle presence. Still, nobody felt like testing him.

Davey acted like one of the guys when he was at Get Shorty's but, in fact, he was a careful drinker. His limit was three beers. Three beers took the edge off the day and allowed him to relax. But it wasn't enough to let in the "background noise," those hidden demons that were always lurking, waiting to overtake him anytime he dropped his guard.

Di polished off his old drink, picked up the new one and touched his plastic rim to Davey's. "Here's to us and all who's like us!"

"Damn few," said Davey, by rote.

"And they're all dead!" Di swallowed about half his drink in one gulp. He still wore his Greek fisherman's cap. It had nothing to do with being a captain; it had entirely to do with being Greek.

Get Shorty's was located on the bayside shore of Key Largo, overlooking Blackwater Sound. A few coconut palms dotted the shoreline but mostly the view of the sunset in the evening was unobstructed. A tiki-thatched roof covered the bar while the patio-dining area was open to the elements.

On any given night, the place attracted every category of local denizen. There were the dive professionals, of course. But many non-diving retirees also lined the bar. Some had been on the island for years, arriving back in the day when

Key Largo was still a cheap place to live. They were a grizzled bunch, growing old gracelessly and stanching their lifelong disappointments with cheap drinks.

Also in evidence were the more recent retirees, the ones who had money and boats. There weren't a lot of them––their group tended to favor the more upscale spots on the island–– but they were easy to spot: they were the ones wearing jewelry and ironed shirts, and they expected constant attention from the wait staff, which they rarely if ever got.

"What do you hear about the lost diver?" Di demanded. "Anything?"

"I just got here. You already know more than I do from this afternoon," Davey responded.

"I'll tell you what happened. The husband *kilt* her, that's what happened." It was Binky, who sat to Di's right, clearly working his fourth or fifth Happy Hour cocktail but that was nothing unusual. Binky was one of many local characters.

He probably cut quite a figure when he came to Florida from Michigan back in the 80s, with his sun-blonde hair, sculpted features, then in his mid-30s, lean and tan. Sporting a sexy two-day growth of beard, like Don Johnson in *Miami Vice*.

But that was 35 years ago.

Time and alcohol hadn't been kind to Binky. He still saw himself as a member of the dive community but he was no longer employable. He lived on Social Security, which was barely enough to keep him in cocktails. And pretty nearly anything he said was taken to be false or misinformed, even though he always sounded sure of himself to the point of belligerence.

His sun-blonde hair was dyed now, streaked and straggly, his eyes hollow, rims red. The stubble wasn't sexy anymore, just patchy and unkempt.

Over the last 35 years, Binky had failed to learn there are no cute, old drunks. And it didn't seem to have occurred to him that Binky was no name for an old man.

"You know that?" Davey asked. "I mean for a fact?

"Sure, I do," replied Binky with authority. "I mean it stands to reason. It's always the husband that done it."

"So, you don't know," said Di, unkindly. "You don't even know if there was a husband."

"You don't even know if the diver was a woman," Davey added.

"I do, too," insisted Binky. "That I *do* know." There was a pause. "Stands to reason. I mean, who's more likely to have an accident, man or a woman? And what's a woman like that gonna be doing diving without her husband?"

"A woman like what?" Davey asked.

"How the hell do I know!" Binky exploded. "A woman who goes diving down at 90 feet and gets herself *drownded!*"

Binky seemed satisfied that he'd closed the subject.

"Well, that was a waste of time," said Di, disgusted.

"Not really." Davey smiled. "At least we have one scenario we can positively rule out."

Di signaled Jorge who brought him another drink and Davey another beer.

"Diogenes, tell me where is your lantern?" The voice had a lilting, Norwegian accent. "Are you finding yet your honest man?" asked Roald.

No one had noticed that Binky left; no one ever noticed when Binky left. So, Roald slid deftly into the seat on Di's right, now vacant.

"Honest man!" Di spat. "I gave up trying. The closest I came was Davey here and he don't drink shots with me so I can't even look at him."

"One beer, please," Roald said to Jorge. He looked questioningly at Davey, who shook his head.

"Not even worth explaining," Davey said.

24

Roald was about 28 and looked like a Norse god. He'd gotten his instructor development training in Malaysia, kicked around the Philippines a bit, then Hawaii and landed in Key Largo about six months ago.

Every woman who saw him suddenly wanted to learn scuba. He was good with students, a little by the book but that wasn't uncommon among newer instructors.

The other instructors at Dive World got bent out of shape because there were a lot of requests for Roald, which screwed up the rotation. But generally, he was liked and respected.

"What are you hearing about the lost diver?" Roald asked.

"We hear fuck nothing!" Di roared. "Binky here says…"

Di looked around. "Where did he go?"

Binky was nowhere to be seen.

"Well, who cares what he says anyway," Di said derisively. "It's never true."

Di looked around the bar, half hoping Captain Rocky would be there at Get Shorty's since Rocky was always a good source of information, both true and speculative. But Di didn't see his grizzled face in the crowd.

Only Captain Carly offered a brief wave from across the bar, sandwiched between two tourists who had their backs to her. Carly was the woman captain of *Deep Seas*, the dive boat for Key Largo Divers.

There weren't that many women captains in the Keys and the good old boys still weren't sure how they felt about them. Actually, they were pretty sure how they felt about them, they just weren't sure they were allowed to say it anymore.

Di energetically waved Carly over. She smiled, picked up her beer and started toward them.

"Make a hole," Di ordered as Carly arrived. She gave each of the men a brief hug, not because they were especially close friends or anything but just because the Keys are a huggy place.

And no woman ever missed the chance to hug Roald, even though Carly had a live-in boyfriend.

Carly's long curly hair streamed over her shoulders. It had blonde streaks but underneath the color was dark chestnut. Like most young people in the Keys, she didn't fuss much over her appearance and the result was an attractive, natural look.

Of course, a pretty girl is a pretty girl. That's just how it is.

"What are you hearing about Scuba Doo?" Di asked eagerly as Carly sat in the seat Roald made available for her.

"Aside from they lost a diver today, nothing," Carly answered.

"How are we hearing nothing about this?" Di asked rhetorically.

"I tried to get Clemson on the radio but he never picked up," Carly offered. Clemson was Scuba Doo's boat captain.

Davey said, "He might have been a little busy."

"Yeah, I'd be busy, too," said Di. "Putting White-Out on the manifest over the lost diver's name. No Coast Guard. No report. You were never here." The manifest was the list of passengers and crew onboard. The Coast Guard required a manifest on every commercially operated vessel.

"I text Clemson a couple hours ago and get no answer," Di reported solemnly. No one was surprised; Clemson had a history.

Most of the first mates in Key Largo knew he had a beer bracer in the morning before going out just to calm his nerves from the night before. One time he'd actually shown up too drunk to drive the boat and the tour had to be cancelled. The owner's wife made up a story about the waves being too high but no one was fooled. No one, at least, who knew Clemson.

After any diving incident, the Coast Guard gives every member of the crew a "piss test" as soon as the boat docks. It didn't take anyone more than a second to realize that Clemson would have been in his car driving like a bat out hell before the mooring lines were even taut.

"Who is owning Scuba Doo?" Roald asked.

"That's Jerry," Di answered. "Jerry Delblaine."

"Why is no one calling him? Wouldn't that be the best way to know what is true?" Roald asked innocently.

Davey raised his eyebrows. Carly looked away, shaking her head.

"Great idea!" roared Di. "Perfection itself. We just call Jerry on the worst day of his whole fucking life and ask him to recite every terrible detail for us."

Roald looked a little sheepish.

"So, then we can gossip maliciously behind his back!" Di finished, wide-eyed. He slid his phone over to Roald. *"Here. You make the call."*

Roald looked at the phone as if it were a venomous snake. There would be no more suggestions to call Jerry.

Everyone in the scuba community liked Jerry. Scuba Doo was one of the older dive shops on Key Largo and Jerry was one of the most respected Course Directors on the island. He'd taught many of the local dive instructors who now enjoyed senior status.

Most people thought he was generous but foolish to keep Clemson on as Captain. No other dive shop would have touched Clemson but he and Jerry were old friends and Jerry didn't desert old friends. He was like that.

"What do you think happened, Davey?" Carly asked.

"I have absolutely zero information," Davey said with a smile.

"That never stopped anyone," Carly answered.

"Could've been anything. I had a close call on the *Spiegel* today," Davey offered.

"Close call!" Carly laughed. "Nobody's interested in a close call, my friend. There's red meat on the table!"

"Makes me nervous even to talk about it," Davey said. "Could have been any of us. There but for the grace..."

"Amen to that," Di raised his glass.

A certain solemnity fell over the group for a moment. They all knew it was serious, even though their default position was gallows humor.

But whenever an accident of any kind happened there was a ritual to be observed. First, it was imperative to know exactly what happened even if some of the details were simply guessed at. Then it was time to place blame. "Oh, he should never have done that!" or "I can't believe he didn't guard against such and so!"

Finally, at the moment of truth, it was time for the uninvolved to convince themselves that such a thing could never happen to them because they were always alert to exactly the thing that had gone wrong. Which, of course, was completely bogus. Because any one of a hundred things could go wrong and when something did it was almost always random and totally unexpected.

"Who else is here who might know something?" Carly asked, looking around. She stopped short when the only other dive professional she saw was Captain Kenny who drove a Corinthian for Silent Ocean. Kenny was Carly's ex-boyfriend.

Carly quickly looked away but their eyes had met and now Kenny was staring sullenly in her direction. He was in his mid- to late-30s, only about 10 years older than Carly, but middle age was descending on him in unflattering ways. No more tight abs and bulging biceps. The gun show had left town as muscle turned to fat. And the slight suggestion of jowls was reshaping his lower jaw.

"Would he know anything?" Di probed, cautiously.

"First time for everything," Carly answered, and she made a face. There's an old expression among the men in the Keys: You don't lose your girlfriend; you lose your turn.

The way Kenny was looking at Carly indicated he might still be waiting for his turn to come around again but no one who knew Carly shared his optimism, even partially.

Carly had been quite young when they met and Kenny was still at the top of his game. It had been through his initial encouragement that she'd sought and obtained her captain's license. Then almost immediately he'd exhibited a keen sense of competition with her and the relationship turned sour.

The break-up hadn't left either of them with a good feeling about the other. Kenny was convinced that Carly still owed him her affection, a debt to be paid. Carly felt, correctly as it happened, that Kenny would never accept her as his equal and so their future together was a non-starter.

As her star rose in terms of respect among the dive community, his fell in almost exact correlation. He hadn't lost his turn. He had, in fact, lost his girlfriend.

"Let's talk about something else," Davey suggested. "All this lost diver stuff makes me edgy." He was halfway through his second beer and he was feeling worse, not better. He knew he had to be careful.

"What should we talk about?" Di demanded. "Why you don't drink shots with me like a normal person?"

"Let's talk about you," Davey deflected deftly. "An idealistic young Greek who comes to this country in search of what, exactly? Fame? Fortune? A better hat?"

"That's not a good story," Di responded. "I don't wanna tell that story."

"But I want to hear it," Davey answered.

"I would be interested, also," Roald chimed in. "It is the story of Odysseus, yes? With many adventures along the way."

Carly smiled. She had an enchanting smile. It wasn't like she was hitting you with her high beams the way some pretty girls do. There was nothing forced or pushy about her smile. It just engulfed you in an Edenic aura of amity and happiness.

Few men could resist Carly's smile.

"You want *my* life story" Di reposted. "What about you? We know fuck nothing about you. You sit there all quiet and get nosy about other people."

Carly turned toward Davey. Roald looked hopefully.

Davey looked at their expectant faces. He was hearing faint rumblings of the background noise.

"Not much to tell, really. I came down on the midnight train from Georgia," Davey said sincerely. "I had a life-long desire to work with Greek immigrants and your name kept coming up. So here I am. And that's my story."

"See! *That*," spat Di. "That's what we get from you."

"It's a good story," said Carly with another smile. "I laughed, I cried, it became a part of me."

Di dismissed Davey with a wave of his hand.

"What's a good story?" asked Theo, joining the group with a broad smile. He pulled up a stool and put his beer on a hightop near the bar.

Theo worked as a mate on *Ocean Spray,* the 46-foot Newton operated by Diving Adventures. He was Divemaster working on his instructor's rating. Theo was young and dewy-eyed. He brimmed with enthusiasm. He still regarded the scuba industry in general as an ambitious and worthy career choice.

"What are you hearing about Scuba Doo?" Di challenged Theo, changing the subject abruptly.

"Oh, *lots!*" responded Theo, flush with the conversational advantage of having no critical filter whatsoever. "I heard the Coast Guard was up at Scuba Doo grilling Jerry for hours."

Di shook his head.

"No, that's wrong. The Coast Guard conducts the search. The police maybe."

"Yeah, could have been the police," Theo responded brightly, as he thoughtfully twisted a dreadlock.

"What else?" Davey asked just to keep the conversation away from him.

"It was a couple from Cleveland," said Theo. "Here on vacation."

"Students? Certified divers?" asked Di.

"No one knows," Theo said, as if he'd been asked the meaning of life.

"What do you mean no one knows?" Di answered. "Someone knows! You just don't know."

"Well," started Theo, defensively, "I've heard it both ways."

"Young? Old?"

"Young… I think. Boyfriend, girlfriend."

"Which one went missing?"

"Him. *No, her!* It was definitely her."

"This is worse than knowing nothing," said Di, disgustedly.

"It's exactly the same as knowing nothing," Davey corrected.

Theo was unfazed by the criticism. He was just happy to be among other members of his chosen tribe.

Over the next half hour, a spirited discussion determined that the lost diver was either male or female, young or old, certified or a student who was diving with a friend, husband, wife or, possibly, a neighbor.

The diver was either local or from someplace else.

Davey finished his third beer.

"I have to go," he announced. "See you guys later."

"How can you leave now, just when we're starting to get somewhere?" Di was getting a little drunk and Davey didn't want to debate the point.

"I have a thing. You can tell me all about it tomorrow."

"What thing?" Di demanded.

Davey nodded his goodbyes to Roald and Carly. "Theo, thanks for all the brilliant insights."

Theo raised his hand for a high five. He was big on high fives.

Davey reluctantly slapped Theo's open palm.

"Buy me a shot! Or I buy you a shot," Di tried vainly.

"Later," Davey said. He paid Jorge for three Happy Hour beers and Di's rum tonic, and gave him a five-dollar tip.

Then he walked out into the warm night air and left the background noise behind him.

Chapter 3

"Are you sleeping with my Mom?"

Davey looked at Abigail. She had the direct, penetrating gaze that only the 12-year-old daughter of a single mother can pull off.

Abigail's long, dark hair hung in pigtails over her shoulders. She was big for her age and strongly built. But there was already a hint––just a hint––that she'd grow up to be a stunning young woman someday. Something about the eyes.

Davey smiled. He never tried to bullshit kids. Waste of time. They see right through you.

"Your Mom and I are neighbors. We're friends."

"Friends with benefits?"

Like a dog with a bone, this girl.

"Just regular friends," Davey promised. "What do you know about friends with benefits?"

"I know stuff," Abigail insisted. "I listen."

"They talk about that at school?"

"Lots of places. I listen everywhere," she insisted.

"Me, too. I'm a listener," Davey agreed.

"Yeah? You…? I can see that. I can totally see… ," Abigail nodded. *"Hey*… you changed the subject."

"I'm having a conversation," Davey replied.

"But that's not what we were talking about," Abigail insisted.

"If I was sleeping with your Mom, would I be here babysitting you while she's on a date with another guy?"

Abigail pursed her lips. "That's fair," she conceded.

"Thank you, my little Savonarola."

"What's a Savonarola?"

"He was a Florentine monk during the Renaissance. Google it," said Davey, with a smile.

"Hunh," snorted Abigail, not entirely happy about being a Savonarola, whatever that was.

She sat back on the ratty couch.

Abigail's mom, Bethany, was a waitress at Pompano Grill. Her apartment was pretty dreary but waitresses didn't make much money and when they were single moms like Bethany, it was even harder to make ends meet.

The Bayside Bungalows were furnished slums for paupers, a two-story, concrete row of twelve tiny apartments with a view of the scrubby trees that lined Route 1 at Mile Marker 105. Mostly, they were transient housing; two months was the average tenancy.

The decor might be best described as Spartan warrior. There was a couch and chair, both from Goodwill, two shelves, which were boards on cinder blocks. A defeated light fixture hung from the ceiling above the coffee table.

In a corner of the living room was what passed for a kitchen: a sink and stove with very basic cooking implements and some dishware. Plus, an old plastic and aluminum breakfast table with four chairs. Two small bedrooms off to the right shared a tiny bathroom.

Bethany had done her best to cheer things up with some brightly colored fabrics tacked on the walls and some scented candles here and there. Nothing fancy.

Every spare dollar Bethany earned went for decent clothes for Abigail and whatever school supplies she needed. Those were the priorities. Whatever was left over... well, there wasn't anything left over. Ever.

Davey and Bethany had been neighbors for about a year, which made them the most permanent residents of the building. He liked her. For a woman who'd been bounced around a bit, she hadn't developed a hard shell and a suspicious nature.

There was still an optimistic little girl in there, which sometimes caused problems of its own.

Waitresses meet a lot of new people, get a lot of offers. But a lot of them are pretty crude. Guys who think they've bought the waitress with their meal.

Bethany was trusting by nature, which meant she was often disappointed. When that happened, Davey's was the shoulder she cried on.

The one amenity in the apartment was a 40" flat-screen TV, a DVD player and a small collection of movies, which stood on the makeshift bookshelves. Davey had sold the whole set to Bethany six months earlier for $50; he told her he was replacing his old stuff with a new set.

But the truth was he'd bought everything at K-Mart and thrown away the boxes so Bethany wouldn't see that they were new.

No 12-year-old kid should be without a TV and some decent entertainment.

"You should eat your pizza while it's hot," Davey suggested.

"I like Pizza Village," said Abigail, defiantly.

"This is from Upper Crust. It's better," said Davey.

"Says who?"

"Says the guy who bought the pizza."

Abigail pulled a slice onto her plate and regarded it with suspicion. "Pepperoni and mushroom? Who gets pepperoni and mushroom?"

"Same guy," announced Davey.

Abigail took an experimental bite. "It's pretty good, I guess." Then she tucked into it like she'd never seen food before. Davey smiled and took a slice.

"You think I should mind my own business, don't you," Abigail said with her mouth full of pizza.

"No," answered Davey. "I think who your Mom dates *is* your business to a degree. But I think you should talk to *her* about it. And maybe with a little less attitude."

"Now you're gonna tell me about all the sacrifices she makes for me." Abigail polished off the pizza crust as if it were her favorite part.

"Making sacrifices is her job as a Mom. But she also has a right to a life of her own. And she deserves your respect."

"Hunh," said Abigail, taking another slice of pizza as if she were selecting a book to read.

"You sure you don't have homework?" Davey asked.

"Did it at school," Abigail insisted.

"I always hear about kids with hours of homework. Hours and hours. But not you."

"Done."

Abigail was a top student, smart as a whip. She got straight A's, including Algebra Honors, and she played on the volleyball team. This was not a kid who needed to be ridden hard.

"You want to watch a movie? I got *Frozen II* if that's not too girly for you." Abigail scrunched up her face.

"I'm all for Girl Power," said Davey.

Abigail picked up the remote, pressed a few buttons and the TV came to life. Cinderella's castle filled the screen. Davey grabbed another slice of pizza.

"I like you, Davey, you know?" said Abigail.

"Thanks, Abby. I like you, too."

"Abigail, never Abby."

"I like you, too, Abigail-never-Abby."

The movie started and Abigail sat back on the couch.

"So maybe you and my Mom-- "

"--Now there," Davey interrupted, "is where I'm going to tell you to mind your own business."

• • •

When Stasie was four years old, she asked, "What happens to us when we sleep, Daddy?"

She was tucked into her bed, with Davey lying on the covers beside her while she went to sleep, the way they did every night.

"Nothing happens. We just sleep. Our bodies rest."

"But I dream I'm in different places. Magical places."

"That's your brain, imagining things. You're still right here in bed."

"How do you know? You're asleep, too. Maybe we all go to different places."

"We don't. We stay in our beds."

"But how can you be sure? If you're asleep, too?"

"Because I've watched you sleep when you were dreaming."

"The whole time?"

"Not the whole time. But long enough to know you didn't go anywhere."

"It seems like we do. It really does."

"We don't. We stay safe in our beds. Now go to sleep honey-bunny. I'll stay right here till you do."

"'Night, Daddy. I love you."

"Goodnight, Stasie. I love you, too."

• • •

Bethany got home around 10:30, pushed the door closed and leaned heavily against it, as if monsters were fighting to get in from the other side.

She was a good-looking woman, petite and well formed, with longish auburn hair that she wore up most days in a ponytail but tonight it swept across her shoulders like a shiny, red wave.

She wore a bright batik wrap-around skirt tied at her waist below a scoop front top, which clung to her slim body and made her breasts bulge.

There was an ankle bracelet that Abigail had given her, which was really just colored string twined together with a few beads.

Bethany had long legs for a small woman. Long enough to reach the ground; Lincoln would have approved, Davey thought to himself. She looked beautiful all dressed up for her date.

But right now, she was as mad as a snake.

She dropped her purse on the table with a *thunk* and went straight to the refrigerator to pour a glass of wine.

"How was your date?" Davey asked, innocently.

"Oh, it was *wonderful!*" Bethany spat out the words. "I think I might marry this one. *Definitely.*"

"Sorry," said Davey. They'd been here before.

"What is it with men, anyway? I mean, for Christ's sake!"

"I don't know. I missed the last few meetings."

"That's it, make a joke. Do you have any idea what it's like to be a 35-year-old, single mom?"

Davey didn't answer. Bethany looked straight at him.

Finally, Davey said, "I can't help feeling that's a trick question."

"Let me tell you about this guy! *A class act.* Of course, he assumes I'm going to sleep with him because, after all, I'm a waitress."

Bethany raised her glass in a mock toast.

"Then he finds out I'm a single mom, and *oh boy*, now he has the gall to suggest that we start the evening's festivities with a blow job. Says he can go all night after one of those. Says I'll be glad I did it."

Bethany refilled her wine glass.

"There wasn't anything to drink at dinner?" Davey asked.

38

"I was being demur. What a waste of time that turned out to be!" Bethany carped.

"So, you declined his generous offer…" Davey prompted, knowing it was best to get all the poison out.

"Yeah, so then he's mad, right? Says what do I think I'm waiting for, seeing as I'm a little past my sell-by date and I'm dragging a kid along behind me."

Bethany stopped and looked directly at Davey. Davey looked back at her, and she melted. "He seemed so nice when he asked me out. All 'I-bet-you-already-have-a-boyfriend' and everything. And he was cute."

She blew a strand of golden red hair away from her face.

"I'm like a bad joke. Here I am with the perfect man sitting right in my apartment and I'm bitching and moaning about the losers I go out with."

Bethany looked at Davey. He was handsome, older than she was but not by a whole lot. His light brown hair was flecked with gray, his features still rugged, his body slender and sculpted, his arms muscular. But the thing about Davey that always got to her was his silly, crooked smile. It just said, "Nothing's wrong. You can do this."

Whenever she was around him, she felt better, stronger.

Davey knew what was coming next but he didn't say anything.

"God, I hate myself sometimes!" She put down her wine glass and hugged her arms tight around her body, facing the wall.

After a moment, she turned to Davey.

"Can I…? I mean, do you mind…?" Bethany stammered.

Davey stretched his arm out and patted the back of the couch. Bethany jumped in next to him and snuggled up close. Davey dropped his hand to her shoulder and she rested her cheek on his chest.

They sat for a minute without talking.

"Am I being a total bitch? I mean, you know, sitting here with you like this when I've with just been out another guy?"

"Are you using me, you mean?" Davey said with a smile.

Bethany poked Davey in the ribs a little harder than she intended.

"You're fine. We're friends; it's okay. Maybe it'd be different if I'd asked you out or something."

Davey knew it was a mistake the moment he said it. Bethany sat up like a shot and straight-armed him against the couch.

"And that's another thing, *God damn it!* Why haven't you ever asked me out?" Davey could see where Abigail had gotten her penetrating look.

"I'm your babysitter. You don't want to date your babysitter. You'll end up in the tabloids, like the Kennedys."

"*Bullshit!* The tabloids."

"*National Enquirer. Star.* The ladies at the grocery store will be laughing over your life story. *Schadenfreude.*"

"Oh, I'll give you *schadenfreude.* Don't pull your big words with me, Buster."

"It's German. All German words are big."

"It's total crap! You're deflecting."

She snuggled back against him with a snort.

"I mean, I can see it, if you don't like the package. If you're not attracted to me, just say so and-- "

This time Davey pushed Bethany away. "--Don't be stupid," he scolded. "You're First Prize, Bethany. The gold ring. Don't *ever* let anybody make you think you're not."

"It's a brass ring," she pouted.

"In your case, it got upgraded."

He let her slide back into him and squeezed her shoulder with his hand. He thought about kissing the top of the head but decided against it.

"I still think you're deflecting," Bethany complained.

"Just trying to protect your reputation, that's all," Davey asserted. "You know how mean the ladies at the grocery store can be."

They sat without talking for what seemed like a long time. Finally, Bethany sighed.

"You can be really full of shit sometimes, you know that?" Bethany said.

"Yeah," Davey answered softly, "I know."

Chapter 4

It was still early in the day and Dorothy was already shaping up to be a real piece of work.

"My son is autistic. You knew that, right?" Dorothy said.

Actually, until that moment, Davey hadn't known. It didn't make any difference, really. Timbo could either learn the skills or he couldn't. Like any other student.

Still, it seemed unusual to have signed up for a mother/son Discover Scuba Diving course without asking in advance if Timbo's autism was going to be an issue.

People were funny sometimes.

"I didn't but that's okay," answered Davey. "We'll figure it out as we go along."

The day had started out like any other, which is to say it was chaos from the get-go. Davey arrived at the shop before the owners, Kate and Katherine, and filled the rinse buckets down on the dock next to *Calypso*.

He liked to be the first one there, when everything was calm and quiet. It was a good way to start the day.

Kate and Katherine drove in 20 minutes later, already deeply involved in an argument.

"I'm not taking three non-swimming snorkelers on North North Dry Rocks," insisted Katherine. "Take them yourself if you're so gung-ho. I'll be shop girl today."

"You're only saying that 'cause you think it's easy to be shop girl," Kate spat back at her half-sister. "You couldn't handle half of what I do every day. *Not half!*"

Kate and Katherine were unlikely siblings. Katherine was tall and slender, sensuous for her age except that her manner was brusque when it wasn't modified by vodka. Kate was short and round. Her squat figure accentuated by short brown hair framing her moon face.

Their dad had opened Captain Dan's Dive Resort back in the 70s.

Daniel Cruikshank was never actually a captain. He was never actually a certified diver either, let alone an instructor, as he liked people to believe.

A life-long ne'er-do-well, Captain Dan had only one real passion in life and that was drinking. He took it seriously and applied himself. Which pretty much eliminated any chance of his becoming a captain or a scuba instructor.

But he'd spotted a trend with scuba and he'd gotten in early.

Scuba diving was just starting to catch on in the mid-70s, the way skiing had done in the early 60s. There was room on the ground floor and Captain Dan grabbed his chance.

Property in Key Largo was comparatively cheap in early the 70s. It was still too downscale for the *arrivistes* up north. But the diving on the Key Largo reefs was actually a lot better than the diving in Miami. So, it was really only a matter of time.

A little shop on one of the canals, a compressor, some inventory, some tanks and a bunch of second-hand gear was the basic buy-in. A boat--nothing fancy, just a six-pack-- made it a going concern.

He made money right from the start.

Successful for the first time in his life, Captain Dan didn't let it go to his head. He invested in only two things: expansion and alcohol. First, a bigger boat; then a bigger shop. He added 20 guest rooms in 1985, which made Captain Dan's a full-service dive resort.

Sensibly, he never added a restaurant. He knew instinctively that he and his drinking buddies would just put it right out of business.

Kate and Katherine were half-sisters from different mothers, neither of whom had stuck around for long.

Giving them the same first name was indicative of Captain Dan's particular sense of humor. If he'd had a third daughter, he liked to joke, he'd have named her Katherine as well and called her Kitty to complete the litter.

Captain Dan took decent care of the girls and made sure they got an education but aside from that he was a curse from God. The girls worked in the dive shop from the time they were kids and pretty soon they were running the place because their father no longer could.

After Captain Dan wrecked his third car driving drunk, the locals started to call him Captain Crunch. The magistrate made it pretty clear he'd never have a driver's license again, so Captain Dan figured he'd outsmart them all and he got himself a Moped, which didn't require a license.

It wasn't strictly legal since not having a license and having had your license taken away are two different things in the eyes of the law. But the local cops turned a blind eye.

At least he would only kill himself, they reasoned.

No one thought Captain Dan would last more than a couple of months on the Moped but to the total bewilderment of everyone, he never had another accident.

Not even a slide and fall.

The man led a charmed life from that moment on.

Eventually, nature took its course and Captain Dan succumbed to his alcoholism in 2005. He weighed about 95 pounds at the time and his liver was as hard as the limestone bedrock of the Florida Keys.

The girls inherited the dive center, which was worth a pretty penny by then. Katherine immediately saw it as an opportunity to cash in her chips and follow the family calling; she'd learned from her father to love alcohol.

There was only one problem: the Will. Captain Dan's Will left everything to his girls in common, *as an indivisible interest.* In other words, neither one of them could sell their share outside of the family partnership.

They could sell the business outright, both shares together, but neither could sell her half-share independently.

Except, theoretically, to the other sister.

When Kate and Katherine had, at one time, talked price, they were more than a million dollars apart between what was asked and what was offered.

Kate had no incentive to be generous. Or even reasonable.

She definitely wanted to keep the place. Running the dive center was the only job Kate had ever had and she was afraid to go out on her own. It was a big, scary world out there but at Captain Dan's Dive Resort, she was the Chief Goddess and Ruler Bitch.

Try to find that job title in a nine-to-five.

The sisters had always been competitive toward one another, bordering on actual hatred. So, the fact that this arrangement only sharpened their native hostility toward one another came as a surprise to no one. Everyone assumed it was Captain Dan's final joke from the grave.

On quiet evenings, when the gentle breezes blew through the thatch palm trees and the setting sun limned the clouds over Blackwater Sound, Dan's old drinking buddies swore they could hear him laughing about what a great trick he'd played.

"He was some piece of work, old Dan," they'd say, and nod sagely over their beers. "Yup, he was *that!*"

"You know it'd be really nice if you'd ever *do* something around here," barked Kate. "Like getting your captain's license. That would save us a bundle!"

"I'm not getting any captain's license, that's for *damn sure!*" snapped Katherine, older by two years but under Kate's thumb since Kate had turned 10.

"Carrying tanks, smelling like diesel fuel. No thank *you!* Not to mention Di. Whad'ya gonna do, throw him under the bus?"

"When did I adopt Di? *Huh?* When did he become my responsibility? He's a grown man. He can get another job."

Both Kate and Katherine were dive instructors, still active and insured, but both preferred to stay off the boat, if possible. Kate didn't trust anyone else to run the shop and Katherine, her father's daughter, didn't like pitching decks on general principles.

Kate turned to Davey.

"You've got the two DSDs in the pool this morning."

"I'm just pulling their gear now."

Mark walked in the shop at just that moment and Katherine pounced.

"Mark, you've got three non-swimming snorkelers on the boat this morning," she announced.

"That's cool. Bring 'em." Nothing fazed Mark.

"Load 'em up with pool noodles and let 'em bob around on the surface like corks," Katherine suggested.

"Actually, I may start them out one at a time just to see how they do," Mark answered, stroking his chin thoughtfully.

"You do whatever you want, honey, just take 'em out and bring 'em back. The rest is up to you."

Katherine walked back to the repair bench to hide for a while. She liked being around her tools and there was vodka in the freezer next to the ice trays, which was comforting.

The rest of the dive shop had dive equipment for sale on the walls and logoed apparel hanging from racks scattered around the floor area. There was a TV and DVD player in the back, and folding chairs leaning against the wall, for classroom instruction.

Mark considered his morning task cheerfully. It really didn't matter what you threw at Mark, he always handled it like a boss. No one ever had a bad time with him and many wrote glowing tributes on TripAdvisor, calling him out by name for special praise.

New customers walking into the shop asked for Mark by name.

Mark was in his early thirties and buff--frankly, there weren't that many overweight dive instructors. His short curly hair was nearly blonde, which accentuated his deep tan and pale blue eyes.

He'd been diving since his early teens and never even considered a different career. Diving was Mark's life. He'd be a Course Director one day, no doubt about it.

Shortly afterwards Greg arrived, a little late as always. Greg was a question mark, as far as Kate was concerned. He passed every random urine test the Coast Guard required of him but he always seemed a little stoned.

Greg was a free spirit, at least that's how the people who liked him described him. Others had less charitable characterizations. He wore his hair long and put it in a ponytail when he was diving. Every outfit he wore looked as if he'd slept in it.

Greg rarely seemed totally focused but he also never got even a little bit rattled. He was totally cool, man.

"Greg, you've got a family of four divers on the boat. Dad's Advanced Open Water and the other three are Open Water only," said Kate.

"Right. Any gear?" asked Greg.

"Full gear. Everyone."

"Cool."

Meanwhile, there was Dorothy and Timbo to deal with. Dorothy had just made her little autism announcement while Timbo was in the bathroom. Timbo was 14 but tall for his age, and lanky. Dorothy was in her 40s, slight of build and tightly wound. She didn't give the impression she was a single mom but there hadn't been any talk of Timbo's Dad, either.

Davey pulled gear for both of them and he was ready to get started.

The thing about Discover Scuba Diving is that it's flexible. It's not a certification course, so the skills don't have to be "mastered." The instructor has a lot of discretion about how much DSD students need to learn and how well they need to learn it.

Safety and fun. Those are the benchmarks. Show them a good time and bring them back alive.

After Dorothy and Timbo had watched the tutorial video, Davey brought them outside to assemble their dive kits.

"This is an air tank, also called a cylinder, or a bottle," said Davey, with his hand on the tank stem. "The average tank is 80 cubic feet, which means the air in this tank would expand to 80 cubic feet if it weren't under pressure."

Timbo looked at the tank with wonder. Davey picked up one of the vests. "This is your BCD, or Buoyancy Control Device. The strap fits over the tank, like this, with the tank valve opening pointed toward the vest."

Davey fitted the strap over the tank and snapped the buckle tight.

"About a third of the way down the tank is where you want to set the strap. Like I've done here."

Davey picked up one of the regulators, holding the first stage in his hand. "This is your regulator. It has four hoses coming off the first stage. Two of them have mouthpieces. Those go on your right-hand side. The third hose is your low-pressure inflator and the fourth goes to your submersible pressure gauge, or SPG. They go on the left."

Davey fitted the first stage over the tank stem, positioning the hoses right and left, and tightened the adjuster knob.

"Not too tight. The air pressure, which is about 3,000 pounds per square inch, will create the seal. If you crank it too tight, you'll never get it off."

Timbo was laser-focused on every word. Dorothy, on the other hand, looked as if she'd just been asked to defuse a nuclear bomb.

Timbo wasn't Davey's first autistic student. He'd had two before and they'd each reacted differently. The first one, Paul, simply couldn't do it. He got confused then frustrated and Davey, regretfully, had to tell his Dad it just wasn't going to work.

The second one, Arthur, did every task perfectly but had trouble remembering sequences and multi-tasking. He'd add air to his BCD at the surface even when he wanted to descend. If you got him to clear his ears when he was descending, he'd forget to adjust his buoyancy and slam into the bottom of the pool like a depth charge.

When he was adjusting his buoyancy, he'd forget to swim.

Davey considered the situation carefully and brought Arthur's Dad into the pool as his dive buddy. He explained what he wanted him to do.

"Arthur can manage all the tasks individually but he can't do them in combination. You're going to need to manage his task loading and you need to do it proactively, so you'll miss a lot of the dive. Your wife will lead, Arthur will follow her and you'll manage Arthur. That's the only way this is gonna happen."

It worked like a charm. Arthur and his Dad functioned like one diver. And the boy got certified, conditionally, but certified.

Where Timbo was going to fit into the mix remained to be seen but it was apparent even at this stage that Dorothy was going to be a hot mess.

"These three items together are called your dive kit," said Davey. "Now, there are your tanks, regulators and BCDs. Let's see you assemble them. I'm here to help."

• • •

When they got in the pool, Davey hoped for the best but prepared for the worst. Baby steps, he reminded himself.

They started in the shallow end where it was four feet deep and it would be possible to stand up if someone panicked.

"So, what we're going to do," Davey said calmly, "is we're going to lie on top of the water with our faces down, and we're just going to float and breathe through our regulators. Float and breathe. Let's do that for 30 seconds."

Timbo did it without a hitch. Dorothy thrashed around a bit, struggling to keep her balance, but she made it work, more or less.

Where things really went south--where things always go south--was when they got to mask clearing.

"Okay, I'm going to show you a magic trick," said Davey. "I'm going to show you how to get water out of your mask *while* you're underwater."

Dorothy chortled. "I don't see how that's possible."

"It's not only possible, it's easy," said Davey.

Yeah, right.

"Okay, watch me," Davey instructed. "I'm going to let water in my mask by opening the top, just a little. See? And then I'm going to press the top of the mask against my forehead with my fingertips, lean my head back, breathe in through my mouth and out through my nose. *In* through my mouth and *out* through my nose. It'll probably take two breaths."

"Well, I don't see how that can work," Dorothy protested.

"It works, trust me," said Davey. "It might help to know how it works."

Timbo nodded; he was fascinated. Dorothy frowned.

Davey said, "Okay, you're blowing air into your mask through your nose. The air rises to the top, where it can't get out. So, the air pressure forces the water out the bottom. With your head tilted back, the water runs right down your cheeks and out of the mask."

Timbo smiled like a Cheshire cat. Dorothy looked puzzled.

"Now, here we go. We're going to kneel down on the bottom and I'll demonstrate the skill. Then I'll ask each of you to do it individually. Not both of you at the same time, okay?"

Davey put his hands out, palms up, to show them how he'd indicate it was their turn to do the skill.

"Ready, here we go." They sank to the bottom of the shallow end on their knees. Davey let water into his mask from the top, filling it about halfway. He took his hands away so each of them could see the water in his mask.

Then he pressed the top of his mask to his forehead with his fingertips, put his head back, and blew air out through his nose. Half the water was gone. He breathed in through the regulator, repeated the process and all the water was out of his mask.

He took his hands away so they could see his empty mask. OK, Timbo? Timbo returned the OK sign and Davey could see he was smiling. Timbo thought this was cool.

OK, Dorothy? Nothing but confusion on her face but she returned the OK sign.

Here we go.

Davey indicated for Timbo to clear his mask. He did everything but tilt his head back and got out almost all the water. Davey mimed clapping. He held Timbo's neck and tilted his head slightly backwards. Timbo breathed out through his nose again and the water was gone.

High five, Timbo! Davey could see the joy in his face.

OK, Dorothy, your turn.

For about five seconds, she did nothing. Then she started hyperventilating and getting herself in a state. Abruptly, she seized her mask as if a possum had just landed on her face and flooded water into it.

Next thing, she was standing up in the pool.

Davey indicated to Timbo to stay kneeling right where he was. The more time he spent underwater, the more natural it would become.

Davey stood up. Dorothy was still highly agitated.

"I swear to God I thought I was going to drown!" she exclaimed.

"No one's going to drown. You'll get this," Davey cooed reassuringly. "Here's what you did."

Davey explained that most people, not just Dorothy, had a problem with this skill because they tried to breathe in through their nose, which was, of course, surrounded by water.

The trick was to breathe *out* through your nose but then *in* through your mouth, through the regulator, because that's where the air was. So, let's try that.

They knelt on the bottom of the pool and Davey demonstrated the skill again. He indicated for Dorothy to try it. Once again, she started revving herself up into a near panic. Davey grasped her hands and held them.

He signaled for her to SLOW DOWN. Calm. No hyperventilating. Nice and easy. OK, now try.

Dorothy put her hands on her mask and let a little water in. So far so good. No big eyes. No panic. She held the top of her mask to her forehead, tilted her head slightly back, breathed out through her nose...

And then she was standing up again.

When Davey got to her, she was choking and sputtering and on the verge of tears. "It's okay, we're fine. You're going to get it. It's okay. Nothing to worry about."

"I can't do this! I just *can't do it!*" A lifetime of unfair expectations and disappointment throbbed plaintively behind her words.

"Actually, you came very close that time. You're almost there," said Davey. Now it was the time for his instructor discretion to kick in. Don't keep doing what isn't working. Find something that does work.

"So, here's what we're going to do right now. We're going to swim a couple of lengths of the pool underwater. Just so we get the feel of scuba diving. No more skills, just swimming. Sound good?"

Dorothy nodded, and even put on a brave little smile.

When it came to the swimming part, Dorothy was like an otter.

• • •

"How'd things go in the pool?" Kate asked when Davey got back to the shop.

"They'll be fine. I told them to grab some lunch and meet me back here at 12:30."

"So, you're taking them out on the boat this afternoon?" Kate confirmed.

"Yeah, Mom's got some issues but Timbo's a superstar," said Davey. "How did Mark do with the non-swimming snorkelers?"

Kate raised her hands to the heavens and gave Davey a look of undiluted amazement. "From what Di texted me, Mark's had them swimming around the boat like a pod of dolphins. I just don't know how he does it."

Davey laughed, "He's got the magic touch. I'm going to go pull the tanks for the afternoon boat." Davey checked the manifest, counted tanks, and headed down to the dock.

Davey, Timbo and Dorothy; that was six tanks. Greg's family of four was diving again in the afternoon. That was 10 more. Mark had two walk-ins from this morning, so that was six more. Twenty-two tanks.

Plus, two captain's tanks. Spares, in case someone needed a rescue, but no one talked about that. However, the captain's tanks were still on the boat from this morning.

So, 22 new tanks in all. Davey pulled them out of the closet by the dock and gauged them to be sure they had at least 2900 psi. Two tanks each for two shallow reef dives.

Back to the dock by five o'clock.

Over at Get Shorty's by 6:30.

Life is good.

Chapter 5

Di was typically holding down the bar at Get Shorty's by the time Davey arrived because washing the boat with Javier took less time than filling all the scuba tanks and restocking the rental equipment.

Greg never came to Get Shorty's that anyone could remember. Everyone just assumed he was at home staring at his hands with drugged wonder by the light of a lava lamp. And Mark hung with a different crowd at Barracuda's, which was down island on one of the canals. Javier didn't mix with the crew during off-hours.

Binky was a regular fixture at Get Shorty's, of course, although he came and went like an island breeze.

"Buy me a shot," yelled Di when Davey entered. "Or I buy you a shot."

"At least you're consistent," Davey answered, shaking his head as Jorge brought him the first of his three beers.

"I heard something," Di hunched toward Davey conspiratorially.

"About what?"

"You know that woman? The one they lost at the *Benwood* wall the other day?" Di wore a serious, almost mournful, expression.

"I didn't even know for sure it was a woman," Davey answered.

"It was a woman," Di pulled ruminatively at his chin. "They found her body up by Carysfort Light.

"*Huh*," said Davey. "I wonder if we'll ever know what happened."

"I already *tolt* you what happened—" Binky started, but Di cut him off mid-sentence.

"Shut the fuck up, Binky!" Di barked.

Binky looked wounded to the core.

"So, we know for a fact it was a woman," Di said solemnly. "The Coast Guard reported the recovery."

"Already *tolt* you that," said Binky sullenly, mumbling under his breath so Di wouldn't hear.

Roald approached with a young, exotic looking woman clutching his arm with both hands. "We have news," he said happily as they sat at the hightop. "You will be wanting to hear this."

Di couldn't take his eyes off the woman, who was wearing a low-cut sundress at least a size too small.

"This is Renata," Roald said by way of introduction. "Her roommate used to date the brother of the Scuba Doo first-mate."

"So, we're practically hearing this from the source," Di said, without apparent irony.

"Exactly," Roald affirmed, vigorously nodding his head.

"The dead diver was a woman," Renata said gravely.

"We already know that," Di answered.

"Apparently it was a husband-and-wife dive buddy team," Renata continued.

"We heard that, too," said Di, moving on.

"We also heard every other possibility," Davey added, thoughtfully.

"Yes, but now we are knowing for sure," said Roald, with obvious pride in the woman sitting next to him.

"How big was the dive group?" Di probed.

"What'dya mean?" asked Renata, frowning.

"Seventeen divers on the boat. How many groups? How big was the group that lost the diver?" asked Di.

"Were they being guided or were they on their own?" Davey added.

"I don't understand what you mean," Renata looked to Roald for help. She hadn't expected to be interrogated.

"Dudes, what's up?" Theo hoisted himself up on a barstool, happy as always to be among comrades. This time no one returned his high-five and he reluctantly had to put his hand down.

"We're hearing about the dead diver," Di said, shushing him.

"Man, I already told you all about that," Theo said brightly.

"You told us every possible version," Di said impatiently. "Which tells us nothing!"

Theo looked a little downcast by the criticism.

"Now, we're hearing the facts finally. Maybe," Di added thoughtfully.

"Yeah but, I don't understand your question," Renata complained.

"Okay, just tell us what you know," said Di, patiently. "Tell us everything you heard."

"Well, this is what I was told…" Renata started.

Davey saw Katherine approaching out of the corner of his eye but not in time to make an effective, evasive maneuver.

"There you are; look at you!" she said, circling her arms around Davey's neck and swinging around him from back to front until she was pressing her body against his chest.

Katherine was just at that point in her inebriation where women as well as men take it for granted that they are irresistibly sexy.

She pinched Davey's ass for a quick second. Not a big, invasive grab, just a little "Hi! It's me!"

"You're not a half bad looking fella, Davey Jones. I mean that."

Davey tried to step backward and away but Katherine had a surprisingly strong grip on his shoulders.

"No one says 'fella' anymore Katherine, unless they're in a revival of *Oklahoma!*"

Katherine slapped Davey's chest and laughed much harder than the joke deserved. She had a cigarette laugh that went with her gravelly voice. "You're quite a card, you know that? A real card."

For someone who was aging poorly and took no care of herself whatsoever, Katherine was still an alluring woman. She was thin and shapely, with blonde highlights in her hair and a nice flat tummy that she generally showed off by tying her shirttails up above her waist.

The woman had learned her social graces from her father, so Davey figured there was room for a little forbearance. But he was still careful around Katherine; she was like an unexploded bomb.

"What I don't get--maybe you can explain to me. But what I don't understand is how you and I... you know, never..." Katherine pumped her fist and raised her eyebrows.

"You're too much woman for me, Katherine. It's pure survival instinct on my part."

Katherine rubbed her breasts against Davey's chest and breathed hot, boozy breaths in his ear. The others just watched, the same way you watch a train wreck. Renata still had her mouth open but no sound came out.

Davey stood immobile like a statue.

"You have to remember we work together, too," he added. "Think how complicated that would be."

"*Hunh,*" Katherine snorted. She had a pretty high threshold for embarrassment but they were getting dangerously close to it now.

She took her arms off his shoulders and patted Davey's cheek, playfully. "You can really be full of shit sometimes, Davey Jones, you know that?"

"So, I've been told," Davey shrugged. "See you at work tomorrow."

Katherine waved over her shoulder without looking back.

"Make good choices," Davey added but Katherine wasn't listening.

"Wow, that was random," said Theo, scratching at his dreadlocks.

"Never, *ever*, say no to pussy," said Di in a reproving tone. Then he looked at Renata, who turned suddenly pale.

"I apologize," Di said quickly. "I speak my mind."

"Seriously?" Davey asked, "You want that kind of crazy in your life?"

"There are principles involved," Di announced, with a dismissive wave. "Some things are sacred."

"I can get her back here. Tell her you're quite a card."

"Don't joke about things that are serious," Di said, with finality. "There, I've said my piece."

But apparently, he hadn't because in five seconds he was back on the subject again.

"What're you, Davey, 38, 39?" asked Di.

"Forty," Davey answered.

"So, you in your prime, *man*. You come here from nowhere, what, five years ago? Nobody knows from where. Nobody knows nothing about you," Di mused.

"People with past lives they want to talk about tend to keep living them," said Davey.

"Good-looking guy, smart, I think sometimes, except when I see you turn away pussy. So why you don't want to live a little?" Di looked at Davey with raised eyebrows.

"I'm happy the way I am," Davey answered.

"No one is happy alone," Di pronounced, decisively.

"You're alone," said Davey.

"When is the last time I tell you I'm happy," Di shot back. "You don't drink shots. You don't fuck." Di glanced quickly at Renata.

"I apologize for my crudeness. *Again.* All men are swine."

He turned back to Davey. "What kind of life is that for a young guy like you?"

"I'm diving every day. I'm teaching. I get to change people's lives."

Davey signaled Jorge for another beer. He looked seriously at Di.

"The boy on the boat today. Autistic. No one expects him to succeed. No one expects *anything* of him. He did great today. He'll probably end up getting certified. I opened up a whole new world for him. Tell me, what's better than that?"

"Opening up new worlds *and* getting laid. That's what's better," Di said flatly. He shook his head. "You gonna let me die of thirst here, you motherless bastard?"

Jorge was already on it.

"We would like more drinks also, please," Roald said to Jorge.

"So where were we before Davey here upset the nature of things?" Di asked grumpily.

"We were hearing about the diver," Roald answered with a nod toward Renata.

"Right. *Right.* What did you hear? From your friend?" Di asked.

"Her roommate," Roald corrected, helpfully.

"Yes, yes we know," Davey nodded.

"Her roommate who dates the brother of the first-mate--"

"--*We got it!*" Di held his hands up to heaven in supplication. He breathed in, slowly. "What did you hear?" he asked softly.

"Many things," answered Roald. "And some cannot be true together so we are not trusting so many of those. But that's natural, *yah?* That's Bubble Talk."

"Just assume half of what you heard is complete bullshit," asserted Di. He was starting to slur his words.

"Well," Renata took her cue. "It was a husband-and-wife team taking an advanced diving course--"

"Advanced Open Water?" asked Davey.

"*Yeah.* Yeah, that's it," said Renata, pointing her finger at Davey. "So, they went down for this dive and the wife never came up."

Renata sipped her drink through the straw, as though there was nothing more to be said on the matter.

"They were taking a class?" Di pondered.

"Yeah, Advance Open Water. Like he said."

"That means they were in the water with an instructor. Do you know which instructor?"

"How would I know that?" Renata asked, honestly perplexed.

"I thought maybe," Di was holding back his frustration with extreme effort, "your roommate might have told you."

Renata shook her head. "Nope. She didn't tell me that, *for sure.*"

"Okay. Okay," Di answered patiently.

"I don't think she even knows, to tell you the truth," Renata added, ruminatively. "I doubt she knows any of the instructor's names."

"Fine. That's fine. Very helpful. Do you know how big the class was?" Di measured every word.

"See, that right there is where you're losing me. I don't know what that means." Renata shrugged.

"How many people in the class," Davey answered. "There were seventeen people on the dive boat. How many of them were in this class?"

Renata looked at Davey like he was an idiot.

"All of them," she said with a shrug, as if that could be the only answer. "They were all in the same class together."

Davey and Di looked at one another. "One instructor and sixteen students," Davey said, shaking his head.

"You're sure?" Di asked, pointedly.

"Yeah," said Renata, with just a touch of sarcasm. "One big class. I'm not stupid, you know."

"Wow!" said Davey, pursing his lips.

"It had to be Jerry," Di said, regretfully.

"It is not so good, *yah?*" Roald agreed.

"Why, what's the big deal?" Renata wanted to know.

Di slapped the bar with his hand. *"God damn,* I knew it. Sooner or later. It had to happen."

"And none of the others were instructors?" Davey asked. "Divemasters? Anyone helping with the class?" Roald shook his head in wonder. Renata looked at him.

"Why is that a problem?" she asked.

Davey whistled. "One instructor with 16 students on a deep dive. That's... brave."

They sat in silence, absorbing the information.

"It was only a matter of time," Di said, sadly. "Everybody knew this would happen."

"But why? Why only a matter of time?" Davey probed.

"Jerry's wife is a greedy bitch. She wants volume, more certifications, more divers. So, she sells courses on Groupon," Di explained. "With the discount, plus what you pay to Groupon, there's no profit unless you take big groups."

Davey didn't know Jerry well; they'd met, talked a bit at the annual instructor's meetings. He seemed like a decent guy, smart, earnest, serious diver.

But this was ludicrous. *Sixteen students!*

"He is so far out of standards, you can't even see them anymore," Roald observed.

Standards are the rules established by the certifying agencies, PADI, NAUI, SDI, and SSI. In Key Largo most of the shops were PADI or SSI. Standards covered things like the allowable number of training dives per day, depth limitations, and age restrictions.

And, of course, instructor/student ratios.

"I am not feeling comfortable if I have even six that I'm leading," Roald said. "I'm looking out a little bit over the sand for rays or turtles, then look back, 30 seconds, no more, I see four divers not six and some bubbles far behind. In 30-, 40-foot visibility, it happens very often."

"Yeah, it does," Davey agreed. "Particularly at the *Benwood*." The *Benwood* site was known for less than wonderful visibility.

Sixteen students! One instructor! It was beyond imagining. Like galloping a horse through a minefield!

This was worse than everyone's worst nightmare. It was the mother of all worst nightmares. The grandmother of all worst nightmares.

It should never have happened.

Davey said, "Standards limit you to eight students per instructor. He'd have needed a second instructor to stay in standards. And even then, *man,* that's a cluster fuck! Anything can go wrong."

Of course, it was an advanced course so they were already all certified divers. But still. That didn't matter.

Nothing mattered except the outcome. And Jerry was out of standards. Way, way out.

"I would be so afraid to do that," Roald said, haltingly. "What will this do to his reputation?"

"That's not his biggest problem," said Davey. "His biggest problem is that his insurance won't cover him. He's on his own."

"That's right," said Di, fingering his glass, not thirsty anymore.

"What are you saying about insurance?" asked Roald, suddenly alert.

"If you're out of standards, your liability insurance doesn't cover you when there's an incident," Davey explained.

"They can do that?" Roald asked, nervously.

"They can and they do," Di answered.

"But if you pay to have insurance," Roald was still stuck on this point. "I'm sorry but what is the purpose if they can choose not to protect you? I think that seems very unfair."

"Insurance is conditional. They'll cover you if you operate within standards," Davey explained. "But if you're out of standards, you're not insured."

"How can anyone take such a chance?" Roald wanted to know.

"Most people don't," Davey answered.

But there was something else that bothered him, something he couldn't quite put his finger on. A voice in the back of his head.

Divers don't die because they're out of standards. So, why did this diver die? Why wasn't anybody asking that question?

"Most people aren't married to a greedy bitch that sets them up to take a fall," Di announced.

"Sixteen divers," Davey mused. *"Shit!"*

"Well," Di said definitively. "That's life for you. Davey turns down pussy. And Jerry's gonna get fucked."

They raised their glasses together but no one was laughing.

• • •

"Where do we go when we die, Daddy?"

"What makes an eight-year-old even think about a thing like that?"

"I get curious. I wonder about things."

"I don't know, Honey. Different people believe in different things. No one knows for sure."

"Do you believe in Heaven?"

"Not really. But I could be wrong."

"If there is a Heaven, I wouldn't want to go there if you're not there."

"Don't worry, Sweetie. If I'm wrong and there is a Heaven, I'll be right there with you."

"Even though you don't believe in it."

"Yes, even so."

"How do you know that?"

"Because otherwise it wouldn't be Heaven, would it?
"Are you sure?"
"Yes, go to sleep now."
"Promise?"
"I promise."

If I'm wrong, he'd said. If I'm wrong... He'd never hoped so hard to be wrong.

Chapter 6

"I don't like nicknames," said Patricia, decisively. "They're harmful; they're diminutive."

It was one of the fundamentals of their relationship that Patricia always considered her opinion to be the final word on any subject, especially about things that concerned Anastasia.

Of course, a lot of mothers feel that way but it was strange in Patricia's case because Davey was the nurturing parent; he spent significantly more time with their daughter than Patricia did.

Davey was an ER nurse--yes, yes, he'd heard all the jokes about him doing a woman's job--but he liked being a nurse. He'd never wanted to be a doctor, not that medical school was ever a financial possibility for him.

Plus, he was a damn good ER nurse. The charge nurse put him on the worst cases, which at a Level 1 trauma center, tended to make even hardened, healthcare providers weak in the knees.

He worked mainly evenings and night shifts, but he still got up in the morning to make Anastasia breakfast and get her off to school. Davey did the parent/teacher conferences, the school plays, the soccer games, you name it.

Davey was a great Dad.

Patricia was a top litigator on partner track at Hamilton, Overstreet, Patterson in downtown Rockford, Illinois and she rarely got home before Anastasia's bedtime.

Most mornings, she was out the door by 6:30 AM. Weekends she spent a lot of the time closed up in her home office.

Rockford was a typical middle-American city located just northwest of Chicago. It was founded in the early nineteenth century as a manufacturing town and was modestly prosperous, as were its citizens.

Its claim to fame, if it had one, was that a young lawyer named Abraham Lincoln had come there in 1855 to defend John H. Manny and the Manny Reaper against a patent suit brought by Cyrus McCormick.

Lincoln won in court and today there are literally hundreds of families in Rockford claiming to own a chair once sat in by the famous rail-splitter. If even half of the claims are true, for a young lawyer on the move, Lincoln spent a lot of time sitting down.

All of Rockford's residents were steeped in Lincoln lore. Civic pride demanded it.

"She likes it when I call her Stasie. Anastasia's too big a name for a little girl."

"My father hated nicknames," Patricia continued, as if Davey hadn't spoken at all. "He wouldn't allow them. He had some very definite ideas about raising children, I can tell you, and I think it's fair to say his judgment has been pretty well vindicated."

Patricia was an outwardly modest person. She would never brag or boast about herself openly but she usually found a way of getting there.

"My father was an abusive drunk," Davey riposted, believing this an effective argument for nature over nurture.

Patricia smiled indulgently and placed her hand lightly on Davey's cheek. "I know," she said tenderly. "That's exactly my point. Just think what you might have been if he weren't."

And there it was. The second underlying assumption in their relationship: that Davey was not fulfilling his potential as an ER nurse, while Patricia was exceeding hers as a rising-star litigator.

Privately, Patricia believed that Davey had excelled most conspicuously in marrying her. That was his moment of highest achievement. He was good at what he did and, heaven knows, he was a dedicated parent but the family's future depended upon her ambition and she took that role to heart.

Patricia was a striking woman in many ways. She was always perfectly put together and her sense of style suited her professional persona.

She was perhaps a little stiff, her Nordic platinum blonde hair pulled a tad too tight into a professional bun at the back of her neck. Her make-up a little severe and her crimson lipstick a bit like a red gash on her pale face.

But that was understandable. Patricia was a woman in a man's world. Completely within reason.

When they were dating, Davey had found Patricia's unquestioning confidence intriguing. After 10 years of marriage, he found it less so, even tiresome at times.

But none of that really mattered because Anastasia was the center of his universe. And there could be nothing wrong in a world with her in it.

The first time her bright little eyes met his in the delivery room, it was as if he'd been hit by lightning. Her toothless smile never ceased to delight him. Davey had done ninety percent of the diaper duty and actually seemed to enjoy it.

At sixteen months Anastasia started talking and the questions she asked, my God, what an imagination this child possessed! Anastasia and Davey talked for hours.

And because he never treated her like a baby, she never talked like one.

"You can't have the kinds of discussions with her that you're having," Patricia complained. "She's too young. She can't process it."

"She understands more than you think she does," Davey countered. "And when she doesn't, I break it down for her."

"You have to let her be a kid," insisted Patricia. "There's a right way to grow up and it's important for young minds to develop naturally, unforced."

"What does that even mean, let her be a kid? She *is* a kid," Davey said, shaking his head. "That doesn't mean she needs to spend her days wondering how the Tooth Fairy knows where she lives. Kids don't care about the Tooth Fairy unless we tell them to, and then a few years later we tell them we lied. How is that good?"

Patricia never wavered in her parenting beliefs or, for that matter, in her certainty that she was right. But she often gave up arguing simply because she had other things to do. So, she let Davey have his way for now, confident she could remediate as necessary when Anastasia got older.

She never doubted that she could do this effectively even though her relationship with her daughter was theoretical at best.

One single day in his life as a father stood out in Davey's mind as a seminal event. He'd taken Stasie with him to the grocery store and they got out of the car to cross the parking lot.

Stasie wasn't a kid to run into traffic; there was no danger of that. But as they walked out from behind their car, she put her little hand in his without being asked and he held it, her little hand in his big one.

In that moment, Davey became God astride the universe, a protector, an invincible defender with awesome and ultimate responsibility. "I trust you, Daddy," the little hand said. "Nothing bad can happen to me while I'm touching you. I'm safe. I'm protected and safe."

It was that simple. And also, that devastatingly complex.

I exist to protect this child, to nurture her, to save her from monsters, real and imagined, to make the world safe for her.

And she trusts me unconditionally. She just assumes I can do all that. So, I must be able to.

I have to be able to.

Nothing was ever quite the same after that day. And many other days repeated and reinforced the same visceral feelings.

"I worry about Anastasia, as an only child, thinking she's the center of the universe," said Patricia one day, apropos of nothing.

"She doesn't. And she never will. She's a great kid," said Davey, unconcerned about any potential flaw in his cherished daughter.

"But you treat her that way. You set the example," Patricia insisted. "It may come back to haunt us when she gets into the upper grades and needs to interact effectively with her peer group."

That was how Patricia talked, like a textbook on parenting. Davey finished folding Stasie's laundry and put the basket outside her bedroom door.

It was nine o'clock, almost time for his shift to start. Patricia had just gotten home and Stasie had been asleep for over an hour.

"She's 12 years old," Davey said, with a smile. "She's humble, curious, smart and caring. Everything a 12-year-old should be. You worry too much."

"Well," Patricia said with pursed lips, "someone has to." And with that simple statement she again usurped the prerogative of parent-in-charge in spite of the fact that she was absent most of the time.

• • •

"You can't go in there," said, Millie, the charge nurse, putting her hand on Davey's chest.

"I have to! I can help!" Davey begged.

"You can't help. You're not allowed in there and you know that."

"I need to help my daughter!" Davey said miserably.

"Listen," Millie grabbed Davey's shoulders and looked straight into his eyes, "I've got my best team in there. They're doing everything possible for Anastasia. But as soon as you go in there, someone has to stop helping your daughter and deal with you. You know that."

Davey did know that. He knew Millie was right, he just couldn't accept it.

"You know that!" Millie repeated.

"There has to be something I can do," Davey insisted.

"There is," Millie told him, gently. She pointed toward Patricia, pacing in the waiting room, frantic, near tears except that she wasn't a crier.

"You can go help your wife. She needs you now."

Davey turned, looked back at the trauma room where his daughter was fighting for her life, then walked over to Patricia, pacing, agitated.

"It wasn't my fault," said Patricia, almost as if she were repeating a mantra.

"No one is saying it was," Davey said softly. He tried to hug Patricia but she pulled away, needing to keep pacing, trying to escape the guilt she felt.

"It was a drunk driver running a red light," said Davey. "It had nothing to do with you."

An F-150 pickup truck had T-boned Patricia's car on the passenger side. Patricia and Anastasia had just left a restaurant where they'd had a rare mother/daughter dinner together.

When the ambulance arrived at the ER, Davey had no idea it was Stasie on the gurney. Her head was wrapped in bandages, there was a lot of blood, one leg was in a splint. The EMT was reciting the circumstances of the accident and the patient's vital signs when

Davey saw Patricia step out of the ambulance, clutching Stasie's book bag.

And then he knew.

That was his daughter. That traumatically injured patient, that poor little bloody body, was his Stasie, his responsibility, his reason for being.

"We should get someone to look at those contusions on your forehead," Davey said to Patricia.

"I'm fine. I don't need anyone looking at me," Patricia insisted.

"I know you're fine but let's be sure," Davey said.

Two policemen stood by the pickup truck driver in another exam room. He was young man, about 25. A doctor was drawing blood for a BAC test. The kid had a few bumps and bruises but nothing serious. He was sitting on a bed, handcuffed to the bedrail.

He was crying.

"Two glasses of wine, that's all," said Patricia, miserably.

"What?" said Davey, suddenly confused.

"Three at the most. And I didn't even finish the third one," Patricia stated flatly.

"Wait. Stop talking!" Davey interrupted. He looked over at the policemen, whose attention was entirely devoted to the pickup truck driver. The man was wiping his nose on his sleeve. He looked at the officers with pleading eyes, trying to convince them he was sorry.

"Patricia, look at me. You need to be quiet. No one is blaming you. This was not your fault. But you need to stop talking, now!"

Patricia looked at Davey and nodded silently. For the first time ever, she actually did what he suggested. She obeyed. She accepted his judgment.

She was quiet.

An alarm sounded in the room where they had Stasie. Two nurses rushed in with a crash cart and pulled the curtain closed behind them.

"What was that?" Patricia asked, panicking.

"She coded," Davey answered miserably, wishing he didn't know.

"She coded?"

"Her heart stopped. They're restarting it now," Davey said. The professional in him had kicked in.

They heard the first defibrillator shock. Like a big, sudden "thud" as Stasie's little body jumped up from the gurney.

Davey heard the doctor call for an increased charge.

"They can do that?" asked Patricia.

"Usually," Davey responded. "The stats are good on defibrillation."

Davey heard the second "thud" and then the sound of the heartbeat monitor in Stasie's room. "It worked. They've got a pulse," he said, clinically.

Patricia had never felt helpless before so she had no idea how to act. She almost hugged Davey but then moved away to continue pacing. She couldn't... she didn't know... there was nothing in her confident life that had prepared her for this event.

The world she knew was gone. Just like that.

Davey heard the alarm again. Stasie had coded. Again.

And he knew deep in the depths of his soul that it was over. This time she wasn't coming back. Not enough blood pressure, too much internal bleeding, a traumatic brain injury... it could be a lot of things but it wasn't going to get better.

Stasie was gone. The center of Davey's world, his heart, his purpose in life, had ceased to exist.

Twelve years old and in the flash of a moment: gone.

"Where do we go when we die, Daddy?"

The grim-faced doctors came out of Stasie's room and walked toward Davey and Patricia.

We go to my emergency room, honey, where there's nothing I can do but watch you die. Nothing. I. Can. Do.

Davey knew these doctors. He'd stood with them on many occasions when they delivered this news. He knew it by heart. We did everything we could but her injuries were just too serious. We're so sorry for your loss.

But this time they were saying it to him, to Davey. This time he and Patricia were the grieving parents.

Even though she wasn't a crier, Patricia exploded into tears, pounding her fists on Davey's chest. Davey just stood there, no expression, no visible emotion--a statue--nothing could convey how he felt. He placed his hands on Patricia's shoulders while she cried.

"Do you believe in Heaven, Daddy?"

I hope I'm wrong. Oh God, I hope I'm wrong.

Chapter 7

The man who had killed Stasie was uninsured and driving on a suspended license. He wasn't a bad man. He'd never been in trouble before. He came from a good Rockford family and his remorse was very real.

Davey expected to attend the trial, to watch what happened to the person who had ended his world by running a red light drunk, but there was no trial.

The facts were not in doubt and the driver didn't dispute them.

"He pled guilty to involuntary manslaughter with a vehicle," the prosecutor told Davey. "His lawyer agreed to a deal with a sentencing recommendation."

The sentencing recommendation was 10 years in jail. Well, that was something, Davey supposed.

But the prosecutor seemed equivocal. Something she wasn't saying. She was an earnest young woman of about 25, which seemed awfully young for a case of involuntary manslaughter with a vehicle.

She had warm, caring eyes and an empathetic face but she was definitely not telling him something.

On the day of sentencing, Davey sat in the courtroom as the judge went through a litany of questions.

"Do you understand the charges against you and the plea you are making?" Yes. "You understand that by pleading guilty you are giving up your right to an appeal?" Yes.

It went on for nearly five minutes.

"As part of your plea agreement, you have agreed to allocute. Do you understand what that means?" Yes.

The young man related the events of that evening. He cried. He made no excuses for himself and never tried to ameliorate his guilt.

His license had been suspended for speeding tickets. He'd been with a group of friends. There had been beer. Lots of beer.

He knew he shouldn't have been driving. He wasn't the kind of person who hurt other people; he wasn't but now he was. He'd hurt someone. He'd killed someone.

It was clear he could barely comprehend the change that had occurred in his life in just a few terrible seconds.

Even Davey was moved by his remorse.

"Does the prosecution accept this allocution?" the judge asked.

"We do, Your Honor," the prosecutor stood up and stated, calmly.

"Then the court is prepared to pronounce sentence in this matter. The defendant will rise."

The defendant stood up.

"I have given a great deal of thought to this tragic event. I have reviewed the defendant's prior actions, family situation, and all available information to try and grasp what kind of person made these decisions that resulted in this child's death."

The judge shuffled some papers in front of him.

"There is a sentencing recommendation in place, which seems to me not to entirely fit the circumstances I have before me. Therefore, I have determined a modified sentence, which I believe serves the cause of justice more appropriately."

Davey sat up when he heard this. He looked at the defense table but no one seemed surprised or concerned. He looked at the prosecutor and saw the same lack of surprise.

"I hereby sentence you to a term of 10 years in a minimum-security facility of the state's choosing," the judge continued in an even tone, "with that term suspended in favor of a probationary period, which will cover the same 10-year term. Do you understand what that means?"

"Yes, Your Honor," the defendant answered. But Davey didn't know what it meant. What did it mean?

"If you are convicted of any felony, any repeat offense, during that entire 10-year term, you will be remanded into custody to serve the original sentence in its entirety, plus whatever additional sentence you receive on the additional count. Do you understand?"

"Yes, Your Honor," the defendant answered.

The judge continued. The defendant would be required to attend an alcohol-abuse counseling program. He would be required to speak to groups of teenagers just getting their driver's licenses to tell them what he'd done and how it had affected his life.

That requirement would last the entire term of his probation. For the next 10 years, he'd be allocuting to strangers to scare them into making better decisions than he had. He'd be reliving his crime for the next 10 years.

There was a hefty fine.

"So, he's not going to jail at all!" Davey shouted at the prosecutor just outside the courtroom after the judge gaveled the case closed. "He just goes on with his life!" Davey waved his arm, as if erasing an unpleasant memory.

The prosecutor was stoic. She couldn't let Davey see that she, too, disagreed with the sentence. "You need to calm down. You're still in the courthouse," she said but Davey couldn't calm down.

The defendant's family was prominent in Rockford. He'd been a star athlete in high school and college. His lawyer convinced the judge that a sentence of community service, which constantly subjected the defendant to a recitation of his guilt, would be more productive, and better serve justice than jail time.

"Being from a good family means he can drive drunk and kill my daughter! *And get away with it!*" Davey slammed his fist against the window frame next to him, rattling the venetian blinds. A dozen people turned to look.

"Seriously, you can't act like this," the prosecutor urged. "The bailiffs will come for you."

Davey wanted to hit something or someone. Badly.

His ears were pounding. He could barely see. Since Stasie's death there had been times he could barely stand the noise inside his head, it seemed so overwhelming.

"Because I'm the dangerous one! I'm the one who needs to be punished!" Tears ran down Davey's cheeks. *"Not the guy who killed an innocent 12-year-old girl!"*

The prosecutor looked at Davey as if deciding whether or not he might become violent. Fifty feet away, one of the bailiffs was making the same evaluation.

"He's getting off! And in a year or so, it will be as if she never existed at all." Davey was in agony. "He won't ever be held accountable for what he did."

The prosecutor was sympathetic, but remained unemotional.

"If he went to jail, would that bring your daughter back?" she said, touching Davey's arm.

Davey turned and left without answering.

• • •

Patricia never recovered from the night of the accident. She had crossed a bridge and couldn't get back. Her world of unquestioned self-confidence was gone, irretrievable, a distant memory.

She began to drink more. It was only wine so it seemed harmless enough but it was never just one glass anymore, or even two.

Davey knew he should do more for her, knew he should reach out, try to be there for her. But the huge hole in the center of his heart prevented him from helping anyone, including himself.

He threw himself into his work, which could absorb everything he had to offer. Every life saved was a small, if transient, victory. But the satisfaction was short-lived. Nothing brought Stasie back.

Nothing made his world whole.

And the losses affected him emotionally as they had never done before. He learned to hide his emotions but they were still there, eating at him from the inside.

Sometimes his head was pounding, as if the beating of his heart would crack his skull. He called it his background noise. He learned to control it, or at least adapt to it. When he felt it coming on, he'd stop what he was doing and look for a safe place to hide.

He was often short of breath, as if someone had punched him in the solar plexus. Sometimes it just came over him in a wave. One moment, he would feel fine, almost normal. And the next moment, he could barely stand.

After a couple of months, Patricia was no longer on the partner track at Hamilton, Overstreet, Patterson. A month later, she was no longer employed by the firm.

When Davey came home late at night or in the early morning after his shift, he'd find an empty wine bottle on the counter. Sometimes, there was another one in the trash.

They rarely saw one another during waking hours. And when they did, it was perfunctory; they were like zombies. One day Davey came home and Patricia was gone. She'd just vanished.

All of her clothes and personal items had been removed. She'd taken nothing from the house itself. Not even family pictures.

A week later, having had no word at all from Patricia, Davey decided to call her parents. He had not seen or spoken to them in the six months since the funeral.

On that sad day, he and Patricia had stood next to each other, not touching, as the little coffin was lowered into the earth.

Her parents stood apart, comforting each other but not their daughter.

"Robert, it's Davey," Davey managed to say when Patricia's father picked up the phone. It was difficult. He knew her parents had never really approved of their marriage, or of him.

"I know who it is," said the voice at the other end.

"I'm trying to find Patricia," Davey stammered. "She left… actually a while ago… and I don't know where she is. I'm worried. Is she with you? Has she contacted you?"

"Who?" demanded the voice.

"Patricia. Your daughter."

"I have no daughter." He hung up.

And that was that. The world-renowned authority on parenting had disowned his own daughter.

Davey felt a pang of sympathy; he felt sorry for Patricia. It was a new and strange emotion for him.

Three months after Patricia left, Davey received a registered letter in the mail. The postman woke him up; he had to answer the door and sign for it.

Shuffling back into the kitchen in his bathrobe, Davey pulled the official-looking document out of its envelope. It was from a lawyer in Kenosha. It was a signed, notarized quitclaim to Patricia's interest in their house; her equity was made over to Davey.

A handwritten post-it note from the lawyer simply stated, "Please make no attempt to find or contact my client."

The next week was kind of a blur. He went through the motions; he did his job. But gradually, Davey came to the realization that there was nothing keeping him in Rockford. Nothing at all.

He edited the family scrapbooks, keeping only the pictures of himself and Stasie, or Stasie alone.

He put the house on the market and it sold in three days. Nice neighborhood, good schools, lots of space to raise a family. He sold all of his furniture in a yard sale. Anything that didn't sell he simply left out on the sidewalk.

He packed his clothes and his memories into his Ford Escape and drove to Key Largo, Florida, where he became a scuba instructor.

That was five years ago.

Chapter 8

"What do you hear about Scuba Doo?" Kate asked one morning.

"Not much so far," Davey answered. "It was a woman. They were students taking Advanced Open Water. Large group, way too big."

"What's Bubble Talk saying?" Kate wanted to know.

"Some people say it was bound to happen," Davey answered.

"Jerry liked to teach those big classes," Kate agreed, shaking her head. "Seems like a big chance to take."

No one spoke in Jerry's defense. He'd taken an insupportable risk and had a bad outcome. That made him an outcast in the diving community.

But everyone was chilled by the accident. They all knew it could happen to anyone, any day. Maybe they stayed in standards. Maybe they were more conservative in their dive plans. But no one was immune to a quick and catastrophic turn of events.

There but for the grace of God...

"What about her dive buddy?" Kate probed.

"Lots of talk but it's tough to know what's actually true," Davey responded. "Other divers at the site saw the group following Jerry back to the boat. The lost diver's buddy was swimming alone at the end of the line."

"Why? Why not swim up to Jerry? Or stay back to find the missing buddy?"

"That's where things get confusing. There are a lot of versions but most of them sound made up. To be honest, it feels like everyone is so focused on Jerry that no one's really investigating how the poor woman died."

"You've got a private Open Water student in the pool this morning and on the boat this afternoon and tomorrow morning," said Kate, effortlessly reverting on to her own self-interest.

"On it," answered Davey, who had already pulled the gear.

• • •

"We'd like to thank you for choosing Captain Dan's Dive Resort but for the next three to four hours, the name to remember is *Calypso*," recited Davey, giving the boat safety briefing to three snorkelers, five certified divers and his private Open Water student, all of whom were eagerly listening to information they would almost immediately forget.

Mark and Greg helped Javier cast off from the dock. Davey did the briefing most days since neither of the others liked doing it.

"*Calypso* is a Coast Guard certified vessel and we have a variety of safety devices on board to deal with emergencies, although we do not anticipate needing any of them today."

Most people who came out to dive the reefs didn't spend a lot of time on boats. So, it was ironic that the first thing the Coast Guard required of all operators was to terrify their guests with the litany of things that could go wrong. Davey always tried to underplay the danger while meeting the legal requirement to inform passengers.

"In the V-berth, that's the lower section of the vessel behind the bow, we have 24 adult and six child life preservers.

If you see Captain Di sneaking down there and putting on a life preserver, it's probably a good idea to follow his lead."

Everyone smiled.

"In the unlikely event that we hit an iceberg today and become Key Largo's newest wreck, there are float-away life rafts on the roof above my head that will automatically deploy. You'll find Captain Di and First Mate Javier hanging onto them filling out their résumés. Find a spot next to them. An electronic beacon will automatically notify the Coast Guard of our GPS position and they will come to our immediate rescue."

Davey's student was a woman from Northern Virginia. She was in her mid-30s, single, cute, and she had already shown herself to be a good student. The pool session had gone extremely well and she listened to Davey's briefing as if it were received wisdom.

Her name was Rachel; she was a senior executive for an IT firm in Herndon, Virginia, a "Beltway Bandit" as she called it. She carried herself with calm assurance. She made sure Davey knew she was in Key Largo for a one-week vacation.

Rachel planned to do more diving once she had earned her certification and it was clear that she already had her eye on Davey.

The briefing covered fire extinguishers, man-overboard rings, first aid, emergency oxygen, and how easily the marine head could clog if anything other than human waste were flushed in it.

"Every member of the crew is EFR, certified in case there is an emergency, which there won't be," Davey announced with a reassuring smile.

Greg was leading the snorkelers today and Mark was guiding the five certified divers. Soon they'd be giving their own briefings to their groups but Davey still had two more subjects to cover.

"Getting off and on the boat," Davey stated in a clear voice. "If you remember nothing else I've said this afternoon, remember this."

Davey explained that they'd be jumping in off the dive platform attached to the stern of *Calypso*. Getting in the water was easy: gravity. Anyone could get *into* the ocean. But getting back on the boat could be tricky.

"If there are waves, this vessel will rock from bow to stern. The ladder, which is hinged, will rock up and down with significant force."

Davey explained that everyone needed to hold the current line attached to the stern of the vessel while they took off their fins, and grab the ladder's side rails with their hands before putting their feet on the bottom step.

"If have your feet on the ladder before your hands grip the rails, and the stern rises up on a wave, you'll do a backward somersault. Not good." Everyone smiled.

But if he weren't there in front of the ladder to prevent them from doing it at the end of the dive, at least half of them would try to do exactly that.

"Captain Dan's is proud to be a Blue Star operator. Blue Star is a program of NOAA, which has jurisdiction over the National Marine Sanctuary here on the Florida Keys." Davey explained that the Florida coral reef system is the third largest barrier reef in the world and informed the guests that although only one percent of the ocean was composed of coral reefs, 25 percent of all marine species lived on the reefs.

The briefing lasted about 20 minutes and if anyone ever retained more than one single fact it would be a minor a miracle.

As *Calypso* cleared the Marvin D. Adams Waterway and headed for the mangrove forest to the east of Largo Sound, each of the dive instructors huddled with their group to offer a specific briefing for their individual tours.

"Dives one and two are pretty easy from a skills standpoint," Davey told Rachel. "You've already done everything in the pool and for most of the time, we'll just be swimming around having fun."

Rachel's wide, doe eyes never left Davey's face. She was wearing a bikini and hadn't put on her wetsuit yet. Her skin was pale––it was still early spring in Virginia––but her body showed all the hard work she put in at the gym. She was well put together and she knew it.

"Thanks to God I work in a business where all the women wear bathing suits," Di had said on more than one occasion with genuine appreciation.

"We'll start at the bow, using the mooring line as a down-line for our descent," Davey continued. "Hand over hand, equalizing our ears every foot or so."

"I don't think I need a down-line," Rachel said. "I'm comfortable doing a free descent."

"I'm sure you are," Davey answered, "but the down-line is a requirement for Dive 1 and Dive 2. It's a standard."

"Okay," said Rachel, but she clearly was looking to challenge herself. Davey knew exactly what she must be like at work.

"We'll be heading for Winch Hole on Molasses Reef," Davey continued. "A wooden ship grounded on the reef in the 1880s and the crew tried to use the ship's winch to kedge the vessel off the reef. What they succeeded in doing was pulling the winch off the deck and now it's sitting in 30 feet of water."

Davey told Rachel what sort of marine life they might expect to see on the dive and sometime later, Javier gave the 10-minute warning for divers to gear up.

Rachel didn't need the down-line at all; she'd been right about that. Her comfort in the water was absolute. She did mask clearing and regulator recovery without missing a step. She got her buoyancy under control on the first try and off they went.

During the entire dive, Rachel stayed six feet to Davey's right, in view but not ahead of him. She'd listened to the dive briefing and remembered every word.

They came across a sleeping nurse shark in one of the sand channels, which awoke and swam lazily away as they approached. In the winch hole itself, a large green sea turtle swam right between Davey and Rachel.

Davey snapped a picture of the turtle with Rachel swimming just behind it. That would be a keeper. She'd show that one around the office.

Just before the end of the dive they came across a free-swimming green moray eel. Eels weren't uncommon but they generally stayed hidden under ledges or in holes in the coral, with only their heads or tails sticking out.

This one swam right in front of them with a black grouper swimming alongside while the eel searched for cover. It was an exceptionally rich dive.

"Why was that fish swimming with the eel?" Rachel asked when they were back on the boat.

Davey said, "The two of them hunt together so the grouper protects the eel when it's out in the open."

"Fascinating," Rachel cooed, and she probably at least partially meant the grouper and eel partnership.

There are over 30 mooring balls on Molasses Reef. For Dive 2, they went to Aquarium, and although there were no large animals there, the water was filled with schools of angelfish, parrotfish, yellowtail snappers, Bermuda chubs, and sergeant majors.

Rachel did her mask-off and alternate air skills flawlessly. Davey ended the underwater part of the dive 10 minutes early and did all the surface skills at one time.

"For tomorrow morning," he said when they were back on the boat, "all we have is CESA and navigation. They're tough skills but you'll have no problem, I'm very confident."

Rachel seemed very confident, too.

CESA was the Controlled Emergency Swimming Ascent. The theory was that if you ran out of air and your dive buddy wasn't close by, you could still ascend from 30 feet or less at a safe speed without holding your breath, which could cause injury.

Davey considered the CESA to be a waste of time. Any diver, he reasoned, who hadn't kept track of their air pressure and didn't stay close to their buddy wasn't likely to avoid panicking and blasting for the surface when their air ran out. Just wasn't going to happen.

Ascending rapidly from depth is one of the worst mistakes a scuba diver can make. Rapid expansion of the excess nitrogen in a diver's bloodstream due to reduced water pressure at shallower depths can result in Decompression Sickness (DCS), also called the Bends. And, the rapid expansion of the air in the diver's lungs, particularly if they hold their breath, can lead to barotraumas, which are lung injuries that can possibly even cause fatal air embolisms.

Most serious injuries in recreational scuba diving relate in one way or another to coming to the surface too quickly.

"Help me understand the whole excess nitrogen thing better," Rachel asked Davey. "I mean, I get it but I don't entirely get it."

"Okay, let's start from the beginning," Davey said. "The air we breathe is about 78 percent nitrogen." Rachel nodded.

"Our bodies can't metabolize nitrogen so our body tissues just absorb it according the pressure of our surrounding environment. The air pressure at sea level is 14.7 psi, which we call One Atmosphere."

"I get that part," said Rachel.

"Now let's say we're diving at 30 feet of depth, which is nearly two atmospheres of pressure. Twice the pressure as on the surface. So, the pressurized air we're breathing has twice the nitrogen molecules per breath. Now, our bodies start absorbing the additional nitrogen into our bloodstream and tissues."

"Okay…" Rachel was tentative. This was where it got confusing.

"Nitrogen is a gas." Davey continued. "Now, let's imagine a soda bottle. Soda is carbonated. But if you look at it when the bottle's unopened, there are no bubbles. Because the gas is under pressure and that holds it in solution with the liquid."

"Makes sense," said Rachel.

Rachel was pulling off her wetsuit. Her trim, lithe body came into view as she rolled down the neoprene covering. She stepped out of the wetsuit and smiled up at Davey.

"What happens when you open the soda bottle?" Davey asked.

"The bubbles come out!" Rachel said brightly.

"Because you've released the pressure that was holding them in solution. Same thing with nitrogen in your body. If you release the pressure too quickly, the gas comes out of solution and forms bubbles. And that's decompression sickness or DCS."

"Oh," said Rachel, conjuring a troubling image.

"That's why you come up slowly from depth, so the excess nitrogen can osmose through your lungs as you exhale in reduced pressure, the same way it was in-gassed through your lungs as you increased pressure by going below sea level on your dive."

Di had turned on the water pump for the fresh water shower. Davey adjusted the water temperature before handing the showerhead on its flexible hose to Rachel.

Rachel smiled at Davey the entire time she was moving the shower stream across her body. She smoothed back her short, brown hair, scrubbed her tight little abs with her free hand and pulled away each side of her bikini bra as she rinsed off her breasts.

She didn't care who else was looking but she certainly hoped Davey was, and was suitably impressed.

Later, Davey and Rachel sat in the sun on the stern bench during the ride back through the mangroves. Snowy egrets perched on the tree roots in search of the small fish that were hiding there in profusion. A single majestic osprey perched on a branch of one of the highest treetops, waiting, watching.

Rachel stretched her body like a cat and asked, "So, what do you do for fun around here?"

Davey smiled back at her, made sure Greg and Mark were out of earshot, and then softly answered, "I'm probably not the best person to ask. I'm married."

• • •

Get Shorty's was pretty full that evening even though it wasn't Ladies Night. Davey came straight off the boat, unshowered, still wearing his bathing suit, rash guard and buff.

The bar at Get Shorty's is bisected by an aisle through the middle, which allows people to walk past the bar into the patio dining area overlooking the Sound.

Di, Roald and a group of Bubble Talkers were over on the right side, clustered next to the corner by the aisle. Davey was about to join them when he saw Jerry Delblaine, the infamous Jerry, owner of Scuba Doo, at the far-left corner near the band, all alone.

The whole bar was packed but there was a free zone around Jerry, as if he had a contagious disease. Even the tourists seemed to avoid him. Davey looked from Jerry over to the dive group, laughing and talking, but never looking at Jerry, as if he weren't even there.

Jerry stared sadly down at his beer. He was in his mid-fifties, a fixture in the dive community at Key Largo. He was one of the first and best full-service dive operators on the island.

Everybody liked Jerry. At least, they used to.

But tonight, he huddled over his drink and rarely looked up. When he did, he moved his head in a constant arc to avoid eye contact with anyone who might be looking his way, took a deep breath and cast his sad eyes back down at his beer.

Davey slipped in beside him and Jorge placed his first of three beers in front of him.

"You ain't worried you'll catch what I got?" Jerry said, without looking up at Davey.

"Take my chances," Davey answered, quietly.

Jerry was silent for a long time and when he spoke, it was the voice of a beaten man.

"I haven't been out in public since… well, you know," Jerry said sadly. Davey nodded. The band was playing an old Kansas song, Carry On Wayward Son.

"I thought it might be nice to get out of my own head and see some friendly faces," Jerry continued. He smiled ruefully. "That's not the way things turned out."

The two men were silent for a minute. Finally, Davey spoke.

"Accidents make everyone nervous," he said. "It's not about you. It's just they don't know how to behave under the circumstances."

"You're Davey, right? Work up at Captain Crunch?" Jerry asked. Then he quickly added, "I mean Captain Dan's. No offense. Old habit."

"None taken," answered Davey. "We get that a lot."

Jerry nodded. He looked up and swung his gaze around the bar again.

"I was the first Course Director on Key Largo. At least 10 of the people here tonight went through my IDC." Instructor Development Course. "They owe their careers to me. Not one of them even came over and said 'Hello' tonight."

"Like I said, they're nervous," Davey replied.

"Then there's you. You don't owe me nothing," Jerry said.

Davey shrugged. "I like to be close to the band."

Jerry laughed, sadly. He offered his hand and Davey shook it.

Jerry's sandy hair was thinning and turning gray. He wore it close cropped, as most dive instructors tend to do. Long hair is a nuisance when you're diving.

"You're an enigma, you know that. People talk about you. No one knows where you came from, what you did before this. You keep to yourself. No one can figure you out."

"People talk about everybody." Davey spread his hands. "My life is an open book."

Jerry let out a short laugh. They were quiet for another minute.

"Funny thing is, she booked that class, you know, Henni did. She booked it. And now," Jerry stopped to take a long sip of his beer, "now she's making like it's all my fault. The whole thing."

Henni, short for Henrietta, was Jerry's wife. She was not highly thought of among the dive community. Nice looking woman but with a mighty bad attitude. She never hung out with the rest of the dive professionals and, frankly, no one missed her.

"How's she doing that?" Davey asked.

"Taking me to court for half ownership of the business, separate, in her own name, claiming I put her equity at risk," Jerry said, miserably.

Jerry looked at Davey for the first time. "Is that fair? I mean, I'm asking, is that fair?"

"I wouldn't know," answered Davey. "Seems kind of cold."

"Cold," Jerry snorted. "That's the word, all aright. Cold."

He took a drink of his beer.

"Guess I won't be going out for drinks much after this. Just makes it that much harder." Jerry looked up at Jorge and signaled for another Happy Hour beer. Jerry looked at Davey.

"You're still young. Maybe life ain't run over you yet like a big goddamn Mack truck. But watch out. Your whole life can change in an hour? In a minute. Just like that!" Jerry snapped his fingers. *"Boom!* Everything you had is gone."

"What're you gonna do?" Davey said, with forced casualness. His heart was suddenly thumping. He felt the background noise rising up inside him.

Jerry responded. "Guess I'm waiting for the other shoe to drop."

Jorge placed a beer in front of Jerry and he took a big gulp.

"Shop's closed. Insurance all cancelled; I can't book a tour. Can't even take the boat off the dock till this is over. Only thing I know for sure, I'll never instruct again."

He looked at Davey and smiled a sad smile.

"I miss diving, you believe that? I miss it. There's a kick in the head for you. And all the folks who used to be my friends, they're gone. Everyone thinks I killed that poor woman."

Davey looked Jerry straight in the eyes and said, "Not everyone." He was feeling a tingly sense of vertigo, just a little, behind the eyes.

"Why didn't he stay with his dive buddy and surface? That's what we briefed" Jerry mused. Davey shook his head but didn't answer.

"She was his wife, for Christ's sake!"

Jerry took a long pull on his beer.

"Why didn't he let me know she was missing right away? When we were still all gathered in a group?"

Davey had no answers for Jerry and the discussion was bringing back old feelings that welled up inside him and made him anxious. Old wounds reopening, clutching hands reached out from the past.

That nagging little voice in his head.

Davey's heart pounded.

Jerry continued, "My lawyer thinks he'll sue. Even though he and his wife were certified divers. Even though I briefed them chapter and verse."

"We both know the briefings don't make a bit of difference," Davey said sadly. "The only thing that matters is the outcome."

Jerry nodded, slowly. The same Sword of Damocles hung over every dive instructor's head.

Davey's vision was narrowing. He felt slightly dizzy and a little sick. It was happening again. The background noise was getting worse. He had to get out of there, fast.

He tucked a ten-dollar bill under his plastic beer cup and stood up. Jorge was busy and Davey didn't want to wait for his tab.

Davey put his hand on Jerry's shoulder.

"Anytime you want to dive, bring your gear over to our shop and come out on *Calypso*. No charge. You'll join my group," Davey said.

Jerry looked surprised.

"I can just imagine what Kate will say about that."

"This doesn't involve Kate. You're my guest. Di will back me. I'm serious. Anytime. You can dive whenever you want to."

Jerry looked at Davey, his eyes red with fatigue and beer. "Thanks. And thanks for..." he indicated Davey sitting next to him and shrugged.

"You're not alone. I know it feels like you are but you're not," Davey said.

"Yeah, we'll see." Jerry wiped his nose on his sleeve.

"Come dive with me. I'll be disappointed if you don't," Davey said.

As Davey walked through the aisle between the bars on his way out, Di called out to him in a heated whisper.

"Davey! *Davey!* Come here, what's happening? What did he say?"

"Ask him yourself," Davey said peremptorily and he strode quickly toward the parking lot with his heart pounding in his ears.

· · ·

When Davey got home, Bethany and Abigail were just leaving their apartment. Bethany gave Davey a nice smile and Abigail bounced up right in front of him.

"Abigail, never Abby" said Davey, with a smile.

"Bonfire of the Vanities," Abigail pronounced victoriously. Davey laughed. "What?"

"Savonarola. He organized the Bonfire of the Vanities. All the rich Florentines burned their precious stuff as an act of contrition," Abigail answered.

"Yes, they did," Davey agreed, smiling.

"I looked him up. He was a crazy man." Abigail shook her head. "Didn't work out so well for him in the end."

"Nope. Didn't pay to cross the Pope in those days. Good for you!" Davey patted Abigail's shoulder.

Bethany was watching this little scene with amusement and confusion.

"So why am I Savonarola?" Abigail asked.

"Because you were questioning my morals," Davey answered. "And because I wanted to give you a project."

"We're on our way to get pizza, if you'd like to join us," Bethany invited.

"Pizza Village?" Davey asked.

"No, Upper Crust. It's *wa-a-ay* better!" Abigail chirped. "Come on, come with us! *Pleeeeze!*"

Davey squatted down so that his face was at the same level as Abigail's.

"How often do you and your mom get to go out for special dinner, just the two of you?" he asked.

"Not very often," Abigail answered, tentatively.

"Well, I definitely don't want to be a third wheel on a special occasion like that."

"What's a third wheel?" asked Abigail.

"You wouldn't be," Bethany protested. "Join us. It'll be fun."

"You two ladies have a wonderful time. I'll take a rain check." Davey stood up and walked to his front door.

"What's a *rain check?*" Abigail asked her mother.

"Google it!" Davey laughed and he went inside his apartment.

That night, Davey lay in bed with visions of Rachel rinsing herself under the shower and stretching her taut body in the sunshine. She hadn't been subtle, not at all. But he'd closed that door and the way he'd done it, it could never be re-opened.

"You blew that one, Davey boy," he thought to himself. "Yes, you did."

But did he really regret what he'd done? He just wasn't sure.

Chapter 9

Prepping *Calypso* was a mindless routine that Davey actually enjoyed. It started the day with a calm before the storm and allowed the impending chaos to build slowly and gently wash over him.

He began by starting the hose in the first of two rinse buckets. Then he opened the lockers to get the gear out. Twenty-two tanks, including the captain's tanks; 10 divers. Davey pulled the tanks.

He hauled *Calypso* in tight to the dock and cleated her; at night she rode out on longer lines. The ice cooler came off the seat and went onto the deck. The mask and camera buckets got secured along the centerline.

Davey started gauging the tanks while the first rinse bucket was filling. One bucket for masks, snorkels and regulators. A second bucket for BCDs, wetsuits and everything else.

The tanks needed 2,900 psi minimum for shallow reef dives. If they had less than that, they were given to crew, who generally used less air than guests. If they were below 2,500, Davey sprayed a little soapy water on the neck to check for leaks. Tanks with neck leaks went up to Katherine for repair.

Davey moved the hose to the second rinse bucket. He put a cup of bleach in the mask, snorkel and regulator bucket and a cup of lavender-scented soap in the BCD and wetsuit bucket.

At this point, Captain Di and Javier arrived and began lugging fuel cans down to the dock from the storage shed.

Davey left the boat to them and went up to the shop to wait for Kate and Katherine.

The two sisters were pulling into their parking space just as Davey arrived at the front door, arguing as usual. As they got out of the front seats, a tall, dark-haired man of about 35 climbed out of the rear seat on the passenger side.

"You can't just make these kinds of decisions unilaterally," Kate was complaining.

"Why not? *You do!*" Katherine riposted. The tall man stood quietly behind them, trying to pretend their argument wasn't about him. Kate unlocked the front door of the dive shop and headed to the alarm box to type in the code.

"Davey, who hired you?" Katherine demanded.

"Kate did," Davey answered and he quickly headed for the equipment rack to get out of the middle of whatever this was.

"You see," demanded Katherine. "You *see!*"

"That was different," Kate insisted. "We already knew Davey. He did his IDC in Marathon and he'd been working in Key Largo for over a year."

Davey picked out two regulators with computers in their consoles and hung them over his shoulder.

"Davey, say hello to our new instructor, Paolo," Katherine demanded. The tall man smiled and put out his hand. He was trim and looked buff. Longish curly brown hair framed his craggy face, making him look like a fashion-magazine model.

Kate rolled her eyes dramatically enough for people in Miami to understand what she thought of this impulsive hire.

"Hey, Paolo," said Davey, warmly. Paolo give him a firm handshake, maybe a little firmer than necessary.

"People really call you Davey?" Paolo asked in heavily accented English, "not David or Dave?" Europe somewhere, maybe Italy.

"That's what people call me," answered Davey and he headed for the side door.

"Why are you taking computer regs?" asked Kate. "We're on *Benwood* and French Reef this morning. You won't need computers."

"I've got two SDI referral students," answered Davey. "They have to be taught on computers. It's their standard."

"Oh… Okay, then," said Kate feeling at least that she had asserted her authority.

"Davey, Paolo will be taking Mark's group this morning. We gave Mark the day off," Katherine said, decisively.

"You mean you did," Kate interjected, pointedly.

"That's six divers," Davey observed. "Pretty big group for a first-time tryout."

"Six divers is no problem for me at all," Paolo said with a shrug. "I did much bigger groups in Kho Tao."

Kho Tao is an island in the Gulf of Thailand

"You worked in Kho Tao?" Davey asked, politely.

"I train there," answered Paolo. "Dive training capital of the world." That was true, at least in terms of volume.

"Okay, then," said Davey. "Let's get the tanks on the boat. I'll show you how we do things here."

"It's no problem for me," Paolo said confidently. "I have worked at many dive shops. One is not so different from the other."

Davey led Paolo down to the boat. Di had finished running up the engines and the deck hatches were back in place. Javier was filling the fresh water tanks for the shower.

"There's room for 10 tanks per side in the aft section," Davey told Paolo as he picked up two tanks. "We generally put guests aft and crew forward, unless we're totally booked."

Davey put two tanks in the racks on the port side. "I'll put my two students here with a space between their tanks. You can put two of your divers on this side and four on the starboard side."

Paolo grabbed two tanks and stepped aboard. He looked puzzled for a moment and then placed his tanks on the port side.

Ten minutes later, they had all the guest tanks in place with Davey and Paolo's tanks forward and the captain's tanks next to the V-berth. Davey loaded his dive kit from the equipment locker.

"You have your own gear?" Davey asked Paolo.

"Yes, everything," answered Paolo quickly, "But not here with me." Davey nodded, wondering how that answer was at all helpful.

"You'll need to pull gear for yourself out of rental," Davey told Paolo. "And when your guests get here, it's up to you to make sure they fill out their releases and to find out what gear they need."

"Doesn't shop staff do that?" Paolo looked surprised.

"Everyone helps but it's your responsibility," Davey answered.

Davey checked his gear: BCD, fins, booties, and weights. Masks and regs were kept upstairs. "Let's head up," he said to Paolo.

An eager young couple stood by the register. "Davey, this is Gregg and Leslie, your SDI students from Wisconsin," Kate explained.

"Great! Glad to meet you. I'm Davey. I'll be signing off on your training dives." Davey shook hands with each of them.

They were mid-20s and looked to be possibly newlyweds. Gregg had a full red beard and already thinning hair; Leslie had a toothy smile and big, Susan Sarandon eyes. They were both on the small side, under five ten.

Wisconsin gave Davey pause. Some of the inland shops did a great job of teaching up the through pool sessions, but not all of them. Some instructors took shortcuts since they knew they wouldn't be dealing with the open water dives.

Wait and see, Davey figured, wait and see.

Davey saw Katherine talking with Mark in the parking lot. Mark gestured angrily with his hands and stomped back to his car. He didn't look like someone who'd been called and given the day off.

"You don't know what size BCD you wear?" Davey heard Paolo's accented English from the back of the shop. "How do you dive?"

"Hang on a sec, okay," Davey said to Gregg and Leslie.

A middle-aged couple sat on the couch in the back of the shop looking up at Paolo with a mixture of embarrassment and mild annoyance. "Hi folks, I'm Davey," Davey said with a big welcoming smile. "You're Nicole and Herb, and you both need full gear today, right?" They nodded.

"That's right, Davey" said Herb, relieved. "We need everything."

Davey looked at Paolo. "She'll need an extra-small BCD and a medium wetsuit. He'll take a medium BCD and an extra-large wetsuit. They'll need to try on masks and fins out back."

"Medium BCD and extra-large wetsuit? It makes no sense," said Paolo decisively.

"Trust me, that's how our sizes run," said Davey, and to the couple he said, "Follow Paolo out to the equipment sheds behind the store and he'll get you all set up."

Walking to the front, Davey said, "Gregg and Leslie, let's get you guys set up with gear."

"We have our own masks and fins," Gregg offered. Not surprising. A lot of inland shops made students buy some of their gear as part of the course fee since they were losing part of their profit to the referral shop. It helped them with their bottom line.

"Perfect," answered Davey. "So, we'll set you up with the things you do need."

When Paolo's four other divers arrived, Davey made sure he met them first even though he was supposed to be helping his students.

They were two couples vacationing together: Tim & Carole and Dan & Alice. They were in their 40s and they were experienced divers. The first couple, whom Paolo had already geared up, had about 20 dives in their logbooks so all things considered it shouldn't be a tough group to lead.

Davey got the foursome geared up and brought everyone down to the boat. Paolo had his first couple sitting next to Davey's students.

"Let's put you four here on the starboard side," Davey said to the two couples. "If you like, we can set up your gear for you."

Both couples started arranging their dry bags on the front bulkhead, effectively indicating that they were happy to have their gear set up for them.

"Gregg and Leslie," Davey said to his students, "since you're doing training dives, you're required to set up your own gear. I'm here to help if you have a problem."

Gregg and Leslie nodded and started to assemble their dive kits.

Paolo stood with his arms folded and watched.

"Paolo, you can get started assembling your group's gear," Davey suggested. Paolo frowned and moved sullenly to starboard.

Captain Di watched Paolo with growing disgust. It was pretty clear he disliked the new instructor on sight.

"Javier, join me on the flybridge," he commanded and the two of them left the main deck for their private preserve.

Gregg and Leslie assembled their dive kits perfectly.

So far, so good. "Great job," said Davey. "Now for the most important part." Davey wrapped a restraining bungee cord around the regulator first stage on each of their assembled dive kits. "Always put the bungee cord over the regulator first stage to keep the tanks from falling when we're in choppy seas."

Davey looked over at Paolo's divers' tanks. He'd set up three so far. No bungee cords.

Davey started setting up the remaining tanks. "You'll want to get the bungees on those," he said to Paolo, indicating the tanks he'd already set up.

"Yah, sure," said Paolo, setting the bungees. "Most boats have the tall sleeves so no bungees." Not really, but whatever. And even if it were true, we don't so let's get with the program, Davey thought.

When they were finished, Davey saw that Paolo had one of the bungees set under the regulator so it couldn't be undone. "That diver's going to have trouble getting off the boat," he said, raising his eyebrows.

While Paolo reset the dive kit, Davey went forward to address the group. "Okay, I want everyone to inspect his or her own dive kit and make sure you have everything you need for a fun, safe dive. We're happy to assemble your gear but, as certified divers, it's up to you to check them out."

The six divers went back to their seats and started checking out their gear. Davey calculated weights for each of the divers and started placing them under their bench seats.

"I only need eight pounds," said Dan, looking at the weights Davey had selected for him.

"Were you diving a full wetsuit with eight pounds?" Davey asked with a smile. Dan pursed his lips. "No. Rash guard," he answered.

"Let's try the 14 pounds and if you feel over-weighted, we can adjust for the second dive." People were always under estimating their weights and that meant adding more lead after they were in the water, which was a pain.

The drive out to the *Benwood* was calm. Seas were low but when they got to the site, there was medium current from the southwest. *Calypso* moored on the starboard bow ball, so with the current it was hanging directly over the wreck.

"We're over the wreck," Davey told Paolo, "but the current might carry you northeast during descent. Head southwest and you'll find the hull."

"It's a wreck," said Paolo, with a shrug and a smile." You can't get lost on a wreck."

Davey had already briefed Gregg and Leslie on the ride out. Since they were students, Davey splashed in first and waited for them on the current line off *Calypso's* stern. Javier talked them through their giant-stride entries and everything looked good.

The sea bottom wasn't visible from the surface, which meant visibility was below 30 feet, not unusual for the *Benwood*.

Javier had rigged the granny line from the mooring ball so Davey and his students didn't have to swim against the current. Davey took Gregg and Leslie down the mooring line to the bottom and everything went well. They cleared their ears with no problems and seemed comfortable in the water column.

They did their mask clearing and regulator recovery skills on the sandy bottom, ducked down for a picture at the mystery anchor off the bow and spent the rest of the dive exploring the wreck's hull.

Schools of parrotfish, yellowtail snapper and chubs swarmed the deck of the *Benwood*. Gregg and Leslie stayed close together like good little dive buddies. They were totally comfortable in the water.

Like they'd been doing it forever.

A loggerhead turtle swam by right next to Leslie and Davey got a nice picture of the three of them. They rousted a nurse shark sleeping in the sand next to the hull. All in all, a great first dive.

During the ascent, they did a three-minute safety stop on the mooring line since they had been below 40 feet. High fives all around. These guys were going to be easy.

"Great work, you guys," said Davey, when they were back on the boat. "Nice trim, solid skills. We're going to have no problems. You'll do fine."

Gregg and Leslie basked in the compliment.

Dive training was an affirmative process for Davey. He always emphasized the positive and built confidence whenever possible. That way the corrective measures, when needed, seemed less like criticism and more like help.

Paolo and his group surfaced northeast of the dive boat and Javier had to swim out the 500-foot safety line (which crews call the Asshole Diver Retrieval Unit or ADRU) to bring them in. Once they reached the current line, they pulled forward toward the ladder.

Paolo was the first one out of the water and he walked directly over to his seat in the forward cabin to shuck his gear. Shaking his head, Davey slipped on his fins and jumped back in the water to help Paolo's group get up on the boat.

Javier clucked his tongue and sang reggae tunes softly to himself.

Paolo may have impressed Katherine (although not with his dive skills, most likely) but Davey didn't think much of him so far. Di stood and watched, disgusted.

"Let's start switching the gear over," Davey said to Paolo, who reluctantly complied. Gregg and Leslie switched their own gear as part of their Open Water course.

"What did you think of the wreck?" Davey asked Paolo's group.

"It was mostly debris," Dan said. "Okay, I guess."

"We saw so many fish around the hull," Leslie gushed.

"There was a hull," Herb asked, confused.

Davey looked at Paolo, who shrugged. Paolo's group had spent the entire dive northeast of the wreck site, where loose pieces of the wreck lay strewn about. Exactly what Davey had warned him against.

When *Calypso* arrived at French Reef, the current was still coming out of the southwest but it was not as strong as it had been at the *Benwood*. Javier tied up to the Sand Bottom Cave mooring ball and swung the ladder into the water.

"Put Paolo's group in first," Davey said to Javier. "My guys need to backward roll off the side."

"What? Why are you doing that?" yelled Di from the flybridge. He could hear anything, anywhere on the boat, when he felt like it.

Davey stuck his head around the side. "They're SDI," he said to Di. "They need to do two different deep-water entries."

To Paolo, Davey said, "French Reef is the hardest reef to navigate. Stay close to the mooring line. Come up to the surface and do a boat check if you get lost."

Paolo put his hand on Davey's shoulder and said, with more than a touch of continental condescension, "Do not worry about me, my little friend. I got this."

To hell with him then, Davey thought, and he got ready to lead his divers through Open Water Dive 2.

The area in front of Sand Bottom Cave, at 25 feet, was a perfect place to do the alternate air with ascent skill. Davey had briefed the skill on the boat and both Leslie and Gregg went through it underwater without a hitch.

Davey led them around the area and came across an eagle ray in one of the sand channels. Five minutes later, a Caribbean reef shark swam lazily by. Davey ended the dive at 30 minutes and did 10 minutes of surface skills before getting his divers back on the boat.

There was no sign of Paolo and his group.

"His group's bubbles headed down current at the start of the dive," said Di, grumpily. "I haven't seen any sign of him since."

"I already repack the ADRU," Javier said, solemnly.

Di just shook his head and looked at his watch. "Ten minutes from now, I gotta call the Coast Guard."

But five minutes later, seven little dots appeared on the surface about a half a mile to the northeast.

Di spotted them first. "There they are!" he pointed. *"Shit!"*

"They in deep water," Javier observed.

"Get us off the mooring ball," Di commanded. "You throw out the current line when I pull up next to them."

Leslie and Gregg looked at Davey with concern on their faces.

"Does this happen often?" asked Gregg.

"No, this is unusual," Davey answered, but then he smiled quickly to reassure them. "It's not a problem, though."

When *Calypso* reached the dive group, three of them had their masks on top of their heads, an early indication that this was a situation that could unravel quickly. At least Paolo had kept them all together; he'd done one thing right.

Javier threw the current line expertly; it landed right next to the group. Di killed the engines so the props weren't spinning.

"Grab the line and pull yourselves toward the ladder," Di commanded. Javier swung the ladder off the fantail into the water.

The seven divers grabbed onto the line. Paolo was nearest the boat and again he got to the ladder first. Di moved quick as a cat to cut him off, and he stood blocking the top step of the ladder.

"You stay in the water and help your group!" Di growled, acidly.

Paolo dropped back in the sea while his divers took off their fins and climbed the ladder, one by one. Di went back up to the flybridge and Davey helped Javier get all the divers back to their seats.

"You guys covered some territory," Davey said in an upbeat tone, trying to set the mood. "See anything cool?"

"I saw a couple of reef sharks," said Nicole, tentatively.

"Yeah, me too," said Herb.

"That's great," said Davey. "Probably because you were in deeper water."

"Damn, I missed them," said Tim, suddenly interested.

"Really, they swam right by you," Carole scolded.

Dan and Alice had seen a school of barracuda and pretty soon everyone was comparing their dives and laughing happily about the rescue.

"I think I got some good pictures," Alice chimed in, holding up her GoPro on a floaty. "Fingers crossed."

Paolo shed his gear sullenly and sat forward, next to the captain's tanks, by himself.

Javier secured the ladder and Di fired up the engines. They were headed home.

On the trip back, Davey briefed Gregg and Leslie about tomorrow morning's dives. They'd do navigation and Controlled Emergency Swimming Ascent (CESA) among other, less complex skills. Davey had no doubt they'd do fine and he told them so.

Then, since Paolo wasn't engaging with his group, Davey went over to recap their dive with them and keep them happy.

By the time he finished, Nicole and Herb were really bonding with the other two couples and they were all talking about where to have dinner that night. There was a lot of discussion about the sharks they'd seen and everyone seemed pretty excited about the dives. So, all good.

"Have some water. Stay hydrated," Davey suggested. "You've been working harder than you think you have."

Davey went up to the flybridge to see how Di was doing.

"He never steps foot on my boat again," Di spat, disgustedly. "I already texted Kate. It's done."

"He had a tough first day. I don't think he took it seriously enough," Davey offered.

"Maybe," answered Di. "And maybe he was smarter before Katherine fucked him stupid. It makes no difference. He never comes on my boat again. Period."

They were getting close to the mangrove channels. It was time for Gregg and Leslie to disassemble their gear. Davey headed below to supervise them.

As soon as the boat was tied up to the dock, Kate leaned over the wall above. *"Paolo!"* she cooed. "Come up to the office, please."

Davey watched Paolo slowly climb the stairs knowing that it meant he'd have to rinse and stow everyone's gear by himself. At least there was no afternoon boat scheduled so time wasn't an issue.

"Thanks for everything!" Davey turned and saw Gregg and Leslie were smiling up at him. "We want to get a picture with you."

"We think you're the best instructor we've had!" Leslie gushed.

"Well, I cheated. I used sharks and turtles to make me look good." Davey smiled.

Javier took Gregg's phone while he and Leslie flanked Davey, arms around his waist. "You guys came to me well-trained, which is the main thing. Your instructor in Wisconsin did a great job."

Javier handed Gregg back his phone.

"Thanks, Davey," said Herb, getting off the boat. "We appreciate everything you did for us." The other five nodded and all three men shook Davey's hand.

Nicole surprised Davey by giving him a quick hug. Then they all went up the stairs toward the shop.

Davey loaded the gear in the rinse buckets and hauled the tanks over to the fill station. He rinsed them off with the hose then handed the hose to Javier so he and Di could wash down the boat.

Javier and Di finished with the boat before Davey got all the tanks filled and the equipment re-hung. When he finally did get up to the shop, Kate was there alone.

"Some day, huh?" she said when Davey walked inside.

"It had its moments," Davey answered.

"The Bataan Death March had its *moments,*" Kate responded grimly.

She seemed quite subdued. It was obvious that Katherine had left with Paolo under not the best of circumstances.

"You got some tips here," Kate offered an envelope. "Paolo didn't get a share so it was a three-way split with you, Di and Javier."

Davey stuck the envelope in his pocket without counting it.

"Turns out," Kate continued, "that our friend Paolo is not an active-status instructor and his insurance is lapsed."

"Oh, shit," Davey exclaimed.

"Oh, shit is right," Kate responded. "Because if anything had happened today, we stood to lose the shop, the boat, the resort, everything. We'd have been royally screwed."

Davey pondered that in silence.

"*Did* anything happen today? That you saw? That could put us in jeopardy?" Kate asked.

"No, it was a cluster-fuck but everything turned out okay. We have no liability, so far as I can see," Davey answered.

Kate nodded thoughtfully.

"I gave that group of six a free tour on the afternoon boat tomorrow. They like you; they said so. I want you to guide them and make sure they leave here happy," Kate said.

"Yeah, no problem," Davey answered. "I'll finish Gregg and Leslie in the morning. My tomorrow afternoon is open."

Davey looked around the shop. It was quiet for a change.

"You sure you don't want Mark to take them? Everyone loves Mark."

"No, they know you; they like you. I want you to take them."

Davey nodded.

"Katherine go home?" he asked.

"She and Paolo left together. Not our finest moment," Kate answered.

Davey forced a smile. "She coming back?"

"Eventually, I suppose. But I better not see him again. Not ever. Not if he knows what's good for him."

Davey hated that he felt obligated to ask the next question.

"You need me to hang out, Kate? So, you're not all alone here?" Please say no. *Please, please say no!*

"No, you go on home. And thanks for all your hard work today."

Kate was silent for a moment. She seemed strangely vulnerable, which was a little creepy. "I depend on you, Davey," she said finally. "I really do. I hope you know how much."

"You've got a good crew, Kate," Davey responded, uncomfortably. "You can depend on every one of them."

"I know but I rely on you more than the others. I don't exactly know why, but I do," she said.

Davey didn't exactly know why either. He also didn't exactly know why it made him so uncomfortable to be talking with Kate like this, but it did. He couldn't wait to get out the door.

"Okay then, see you tomorrow," Davey said.

"See you tomorrow," Kate said and Davey left.

He hoped that things would be back to normal tomorrow; he hoped nothing had changed during this brief, uncomfortable exchange.

Davey's new life here in Key Largo was neat and tidy, just the way he wanted it.

But who knew how fragile it really was?

So, keep it simple.

And please, *please* don't let anything change.

111

Chapter 10

On days when he wasn't working, Davey tried to sleep late but he rarely made it past 7:00 AM before he just couldn't lie in bed any longer and had to get up.

When he wasn't at work, he didn't know what to do with himself. There was laundry, of course, but that was only once a week. And Davey didn't have a lot of outside interests. So, generally he found himself kicking around looking for something to occupy his time.

On this particular morning at 10:30 AM, he was out on the porch drinking his fifth cup of coffee when the phone rang. Davey assumed it was Kate calling about a walk-in booking.

"Hello," Davey said into his cell phone.

"Hey!" It was Bethany. "Are you at work?"

"Nope, I'm home. What's up?"

"I hate to even ask you…"

"Bethany, I'm home. I'm bored stiff. What do you need?"

"I'd do it myself but I can't get out of work. I wouldn't go out with Ben, the day manager here and now he's punishing me." Bethany sounded desperate.

"Stop beating around the bush. *Ask,*" Davey prompted.

"It's Abigail. She's at school. There's been some kind of problem and they called me to come to the assistant principal's office."

"You've got a family emergency and the manager won't let you leave?"

"He's being a royal prick. Says if I go, don't bother to come back."

"Okay, problem for another day. Tell me about the school thing," Dave said.

"They wouldn't tell me anything over the phone. Abigail is in the assistant principal's office. They need me to come there and I can't get away." Bethany sounded frantic.

"I'll be there in 10 minutes. Now listen. Are you listening?" Davey said.

"Thanks! *Oh God,* thanks so much!" Relief filled her voice.

"You need to call the school and tell them I'm coming instead of you. You need to tell them I'm not a family member but you've authorized me to pick up your daughter. Can you do that?"

"Yeah. Yeah, I can do that," Bethany said.

"It's very important," Davey stressed. "Otherwise, they won't let me into the school and I probably won't even see Abigail."

"Right. I understand," said Bethany. "I owe you. *Bigtime.*"

"It's no problem. I'm glad you called," Davey said, reassuringly. "Now call the school."

"I'll call them right now."

"Great. I'll see you when your shift is over."

Even with Bethany's phone call it took a while for Davey to get a visitor's pass at Key Largo School. The fact that he wasn't a family member caused great anxiety at the reception desk.

"You're not registered with us as someone who might come to pick up this student," the receptionist explained.

"I understand," said Davey, "but this is an unexpected situation and her mother called and asked me to come over."

Finally, after several phone calls within the school, he was cleared to go to the assistant principal's office. Abigail was sitting in the outer office under the watchful eye of a dowdy secretary.

Abigail looked scared but brightened a little when Davey entered.

"Hey, you okay?" Davey asked.

"Yeah, this is total —

"Don't explain. Not yet. Let me do the talking," Davey advised. He walked over to the secretary's desk. "I'm David Jones. I'm a friend of Abigail's mother and I'm here to see Mister Duplay."

"We weren't sure if anyone was coming," the plump woman said, dismissively. "It'll be just a few minutes. He's very busy today."

Davey sat down next to Abigail and waited. She started to speak a couple of times but Davey stopped her, indicating the secretary, who was pretending not to listen but clearly was.

The two of them sat in silence until a buzzer sounded at the secretary's desk. "You can go in now," she said, without looking up.

Davey and Abigail entered the inner office. Davey shut the door behind him. The little man with thick glasses and a failed moustache didn't get up to greet them but merely indicated two chairs in front of his desk. A desk nameplate identified him as Kenneth Duplay.

Davey extended his hand. "I'm David Jones, a friend of the family. May I call you Ken?"

"You may call me Mister Duplay," the little man replied. He didn't offer his hand. His pug nose and prominent front teeth gave him a distinctly rodent-like appearance.

Okay, so that's how it's going to be, thought Davey, as he sat down in one of the chairs.

"I had rather hoped Abigail's mother would come herself," Mr. Duplay said, disapprovingly.

"Abigail's mother is a single parent who works very hard to provide for her child," Davey responded. "She's at work and her manager wouldn't let her to leave."

"We see so little of her here at school," Duplay continued, "we sometimes wonder just how involved she is in her daughter's life."

"Are you a single parent, Mister Duplay?" Davey asked. He was starting to want to strangle this little twerp.

"Heavens, no," Duplay said with a dismissive wave. "My children are growing up in a stable, loving home environment."

Duplay stopped fiddling with the papers on his desk and looked up with the somber mien of a Supreme Court judge.

"This morning, Abigail was involved in an altercation with another student, a fight actually. The other girl is currently at the school infirmary." Duplay cleared his throat.

"It wasn't--" Abigail started to speak but Davey raised his hand to stop her.

"The Key Largo School has a zero-tolerance policy on violence. We take it very seriously. Very seriously indeed."

"I see," said Davey, cautiously. He wasn't sure what role to play here.

"Abigail is a good student, in spite of her mother's apparent lack of interest, but I'm afraid we have no choice in the matter. The prescribed punishment for this infraction is a one-week suspension, effective immediately. This will go on Abigail's record, of course."

Abigail crumpled like a rag doll at this news; she looked close to tears. Davey patted her hand, gave it a little squeeze.

"That seems excessive," Davey said in a friendly tone. "There must be some room for mitigation. I know this girl. She's not a trouble-maker."

"I'm afraid my hands are tied in the matter," Duplay stated, without any sign of regret.

"Suspended for a week? That seems very harsh," Davey said.

"We will see Abigail back in school next Tuesday. And I'll be watching her like a hawk from now on," Duplay added, ominously. "That is all."

Duplay ended the conversation with a wave of his hand and went back to the papers on his desk.

Davey waited for a sign that he could extend the conversation but none was forthcoming.

He stood up slowly and Abigail jumped to her feet beside him.

"That's it? No one wants to hear my side of it?" Abigail asked, frantic. Davey could see her eyes were welling.

"I know her mother will be very disappointed to hear this news," Davey said. "I wish there were some other way to handle things."

"Next time there's an issue, if there is a next time, I certainly hope Abigail's mother will consider it worth her while to come in person," Duplay said snidely without looking at Davey.

And that did it. Like a switch went off in Davey's head. Suddenly, everything just changed.

"Let me see your hands," he said to Abigail. She held up her hands and Davey turned them over, inspecting her knuckles.

Davey turned and stared Duplay dead in the eye until the other man looked away. "I assume the other girl is suspended also?" Davey said, pointedly.

"I'm afraid we see the other girl as a victim and Abigail as the aggressor," Duplay answered, curtly.

"What are the other girl's injuries?" Davey asked. "Why exactly is she in the infirmary?"

"I'm really not at liberty to discuss another child's—"

"—Is there some kind of report that I can look at? Describing the incident?" Davey interrupted.

"A report?" asked Duplay, as if stung. "There's no report. The matter has been handled. It's settled."

"That's just not going to cut it," Davey stated flatly.

"I beg your pardon—"

"—There's something wrong here," Davey said, walking back toward the little man's desk. "And I'm not leaving till I find out what it is."

Duplay looked up from his papers, suddenly defensive.

"Mister Jones, this meeting is over. I'm afraid I must ask you to leave my office. *Immediately!* Or else I will call security."

Davey's gaze was unwavering; he spoke very deliberately. "You say the matter is settled. But when I take it up with the Superintendent of Schools for Monroe County, I imagine he'll want to see some kind of report, don't you?"

Duplay blinked, as if a bright light had just been flashed directly into his eyes. "What did you say?"

"You accuse Abigail of starting a fight that sent another girl to the infirmary." Davey grabbed Abigail's wrists and held her hands out toward Duplay. "But there are no abrasions on her knuckles. No evidence of any fight whatsoever!" Davey challenged.

"I don't think you fully understand—"

"––I think I understand perfectly," Davey was adamant. "I'm going to tell you what I think happened."

"But... but you weren't there," Duplay stammered.

"Two girls got into it. Not a fight really, more of a tussle but one of your teachers had to break it up. So now someone has to take the fall because of your zero-tolerance policy."

Duplay looked like a trapped animal.

"Of the two girls involved, one is a popular girl with lots of friends and a parent who volunteers frequently at the school," Davey said in a measured tone.

"Mrs. Downey is certainly an active parent in the––"

"––The other girl is a smart loner with a single mom you disapprove of. Am I getting warm?"

"You are making a lot of assumptions and I frankly resent the implication that––"

"––I bet once we do a thorough investigation, we're going to find the other girl has been in altercations before. And she's gotten off every time. Whereas Abigail has never been in any kind of trouble."

Duplay took a handkerchief from his pocket and dabbed at his forehead. He blew his nose, loudly.

"You're covering for a bully because her mom chairs the bake sale, or something like that," Davey asserted. "And you're ready to punish Abigail because her home situation doesn't meet your narrow-minded, self-righteous standards."

"Our policy is absolute and my decision is final," Duplay stated, but he didn't seem as sure of himself as he had been before.

"I have no intention of accepting this punishment without a complete review of the incident, including witnesses. And I'm willing to pursue it at the highest levels of the school system," Davey stated simply.

Duplay stared blankly at Davey.

"You're way out of line," Duplay croaked, with as much authority as he could muster. "You have no standing--"

"--I've told you what I'm willing to do. What happens next is entirely up to you," Davey insisted.

The little man squirmed as if trying to shed an itchy skin. "It's true that Abigail is an exemplary student. And while I find your tone and manner uncalled for, I would hate to see her suffer needlessly."

It was an opening and Davey took it.

"She comes back to school tomorrow and there's nothing on her record. Or else I take this to the next level and make the biggest stink you have *ever* seen," Davey said quietly.

Duplay was silent.

"You get to choose. Right now," Davey added, sternly.

"I may be able to keep this off her record but she'll need to--"

"No buts!" Davey stopped him. "She comes to school tomorrow and that's the end of it. I need to be sure we're clear on that."

Duplay cleared his throat. He nodded. "I'm going to agree to that... for Abigail's sake. Not because you acted inappropriately."

Abigail's eyes were as wide as saucers. "That was *awesome!*" she exclaimed. Davey spun toward her and raised his index finger in front of her face.

"You don't speak right now," he said sharply. Abigail looked as if she'd been slapped. Davey turned back to Duplay.

"Do we understand each other?" Davey asked evenly.

"Yes, I believe we do," Duplay answered, totally deflated.

"I don't know about the other girl," Davey added, "but Abigail will apologize for her part in the altercation."

"Hey, why do I have to apologize when—?"

"Because when you get into a fight, you've stopped trying to think of a solution," Davey stated flatly. "And you, of all people, should never stop thinking." Abigail could tell from the look on Davey's face that this was non-negotiable.

"I–– I apologize, Mister Duplay," Abigail said contritely. "It won't happen again." The little man seemed more or less satisfied with the outcome. And he struggled to appear as if he was still in charge.

"I certainly hope not," Duplay said, solemnly, to Abigail. "We'll see you in school tomorrow, young lady." And with that, Davey and Abigail stood up and left his office.

"That was *incredible!*" Abigail shouted when they were in the parking lot. She jumped up, hugged Davey's neck and wrapped her legs around his waist.

"Thank you, thank you, *thank you!*" Abigail repeated into his ear.

"Okay, that's enough of that," Davey answered. "You're going to have to get down off of me."

"Why?" Abigail asked. "You're my hero!"

"You're a 12-year-old girl and I'm a grown man who is not a family member. We've had enough excitement for one day," answered Davey, with a reassuring smile.

The truth was, he didn't hate it.

Abigail dropped to the ground and held Davey's hand as they walked. Just like that. Her little hand in his big one.

Davey felt her warm little palm gripping his.

A million thoughts ran through his head simultaneously.

He stopped walking, uncertain of what to do next.

He looked down at Abigail, who was smiling up at him.

For a moment, time simply stopped.

Finally, Davey spoke.

"I think we should go to the Pompano Grill for lunch," Davey said. "I know someone who works there. She'll be happy to see you."

Abigail eyes got wide and her smile lit up her whole face.

Twenty minutes later, when they walked up to the maître d' stand at Pompano Grill, a dough-faced man holding menus greeted them with a fake smile. "Two for luncheon?"

Bethany spotted them from the far corner of the patio and stifled a scream. She ran over to Abigail. "Are you okay? I was so *worried.*"

"I'm fine, Mom," Abigail said, like nothing bad had happened. "You should of seen Davey! He was *amazing.*"

"Bethany, table 31 is signaling you," the maître d' interrupted, annoyed. "I believe you are still working this shift, aren't you?"

Bethany looked at the maître d', pursed her lips, hugged Abigail quickly and rushed back to her tables.

Davey watched this exchange carefully. He handed the maître d' a credit card. "There's a chance Bethany will try to pay my check. I don't want that to happen."

The maître d' regarded Davey inquisitively.

"And you are?" he asked.

"The guy buying lunch for two," Davey answered, sticking the credit card in the maître d's hand. "We'd like to sit as close to the water as possible."

"Follow me," the maître d' responded with poor grace. He led Davey and Abigail to a table next to the coffee stand. But before he could lay down the menus, Davey pointed to a table over by the rail overlooking the dock. "How about that one?" Davey asked.

The maître d' showed mild annoyance. "As you wish."

Abigail sat down and took her menu. Davey stood close to the maître d'. He was still feeling pretty good about how the meeting with Duplay turned out so he decided to take another turn at bat.

"I'm guessing you're Ben?" he said softly.

"That's right," Ben answered, suddenly defensive.

"From what I hear, you're standing on a MeToo land mine right now that could blow you sky high. Better watch out it doesn't go off."

"I'm afraid I don't understand," Ben said, opaquely.

"Sure, you do," Davey answered, and he took the menu from Ben's hand and sat down. "Please make sure my card goes on the check."

"I'll take care of it, sir," Ben said, with forced dignity.

Davey sat back and savored the way he felt at that moment. It was hard to describe but if pressed, he would have to say that he felt like his old self again. A feeling barely recognizable from a vague and distant memory.

It was a good feeling.

"What was that about?" asked Abigail.

Davey smiled over at Abigail. "What's good here?" he asked.

• • •

When Jerry showed up at Captain Dan's the next morning, Davey was surprised but pleased. No one else had arrived yet and Davey was filling the rinse buckets when Jerry came down the stairs lugging his dive bag.

"I'm glad you decided to go out with us," Davey said, shaking Jerry's hand.

"Not sure this is a good idea but you offered. So, I came," Jerry answered.

"Let's get your stuff aboard. I'm still setting up the boat," Davey said, taking Jerry's dive bag and stowing it under a guest seat.

Di and Javier came down the steps and Di stopped as if frozen in place. He stared at Jerry like he was an apparition.

"Jerry's coming out as my guest today," Davey said simply.

"Kate know about this?" Di asked.

"She will when she gets here. Meanwhile, let's make our guest feel welcome," Davey said. Di remained frozen for another second then he turned and walked back upstairs to get fuel cans.

"Hey, Jerry man, happy to see you, brother," Javier sang. "We gonna have fun today!" Javier went to the V-berth to retrieve the tool that opens the boat's fuel cap.

"You what?" demanded Kate, when Davey told her.

"I invited him," Davey repeated. "I'll bring the release form down to him but I need you to add him to the manifest."

"What am I, a charity now? How's this going to look?" Kate asked.

"Like you're a good person, Kate," Davey responded. "That's how it's going to look."

During the entire boat safety briefing, Mark and Greg stared at Jerry as if he had suddenly appeared in a puff of smoke.

Davey was leading a group of three certified divers and he introduced Jerry to them simply as an old friend out for a fun dive.

On the boat ride out, Davey took photos of the other guests, smiling, looking forward to their dives. This was a standard practice and the pictures would appear on the shop's blog and Facebook page. But Davey discreetly made sure that Jerry didn't appear in any of the images.

"It's bad luck, is what it is!" Di pronounced, wagging his finger at Davey. "You think that's silly but captains take bad luck seriously."

"It's not bad luck. It's kindness," said Davey quietly. "What if something happened on your boat? How would you want to be treated?"

But Di was not mollified. "You're tempting fate," he said, sourly. "You ask any Greek how good is it to tempt fate. *You ask!*"

Davey left the flybridge and re-joined his dive group.

The Christ of the Abyss statue is located at Key Largo Dry Rocks. The Cressi family, manufacturers of a popular line of dive gear, donated the underwater statue in 1965.

It's one of only three in the world.

The nine-foot statue stands on a five-foot, stepped base in 25 feet of water within the John Pennekamp State Park. The site is located in a Sanctuary Preservation Area, which is why the statue, now encrusted with coral, can't be cleaned.

Typically, the site is mobbed with snorkelers and other dive boats and the visibility is often less than 30 feet. But today was an anomaly. *Reef Rider* was the only other dive boat at the site with *Calypso* and visibility was at least 60 feet.

Davey swam his group to the statue and lined them up for the photo. He'd already told them not to touch anything because the statue is covered in fire coral, which can burn your skin.

Jerry stayed back; he didn't need a picture. He hung there suspended in the water column, perfectly horizontal, motionless, as only an expert diver can do.

Most guides lead their divers up the coral sand channels toward the dry rocks but Davey stayed clear of them today because they get shallow very quickly and there was a lot of tidal surge.

Instead, he headed southwest away from the statue and stayed in the deeper water. You could always find a moray eel or two at the site but larger marine animals were rare.

Which was why Davey stopped short when he saw three eagle rays swimming in echelon formation 10 feet in front of him. He signaled "STOP" to his dive group and they all held position.

Eagles rays are among the most beautiful of all marine creatures. Black on top with white spots, pure white on the bottom, they glide through the water column with minimal effort, their wings moving in slow motion, their bodies perfectly adapted to reduce resistance and conserve energy.

The three rays, two adults and a juvenile, swam majestically past the group, circled behind them once and swam out in front again, heading southeast. Davey shot video of the whole encounter, which included a long segment of his divers with the rays behind them.

In the uncharacteristically clear water, the experience was breathtaking. Making the rest of the dive, though still beautiful, almost anticlimactic.

"The video will be up on our blog tonight," Davey told his group when they were back on the boat. "You can download it. It's yours, free, for coming out with us today."

The three divers high fived and punched each other's shoulders.

Jerry sat silently with a serene smile on his face.

When *Calypso* got back to the dock and the other divers had left, Jerry rinsed his gear in the wash buckets. He was silent for a long time before he looked straight at Davey and said, "Guess this must be how it feels when someone tells you that you don't have cancer."

"Not a one-time offer, Jerry," answered Davey. "Dive with me anytime. Come out next week."

"Thank you." Jerry looked back at the boat, out the canal, and then up at the sky, as if he'd never seen any of them before.

He patted Davey on the shoulder and tried to stick a couple of bills in his hand. "No way," said Davey, pushing Jerry's hand back. "Your ride is free."

Jerry looked reflectively at Davey.

"You know, the irony is she was a much better diver than he was," Jerry said, as if Davey would know exactly what he was talking about. "He had more experience but she was the better diver. That happens sometimes."

"We hear a lot of stories," Davey answered. "Never know what's true."

"Well, that's Bubble Talk, right? Some things never change."

Jerry nodded, smiled, and hauled his dive bag up the stairs. Davey watched him disappear behind the wall before he joined Mark and Greg carrying the empty scuba tanks to the fill station.

Chapter 11

When Captain Dan decided to expand his empire by building 20 rooms adjacent to the dive shop in 1985, he followed his usual business practice: he consulted with his drinking buddies and then cut every corner possible.

In the event, fortune smiled on a series of bad decisions. One of Captain Dan's friends, Shor Prentiss, was a general contractor who had turned the operation of his business over to his son, Neil, so that he, like Captain Dan, could focus his energies on his true passion, which was alcohol.

Neil had found Jesus a few years prior to becoming the boss and, as part of his chosen ministry, he offered employment to industrious immigrants who couldn't find decent opportunities anywhere else. The result was a surprisingly respectable operation known for fair pricing, honest dealing, and quality workmanship.

Neither Shor, nor for that matter Captain Dan, could have imagined such an outcome.

It was also decided during an exceptionally long and self-congratulatory night at the bar that the services of an architect would be a ridiculous luxury. A better solution would be to hire Neil's structural engineer to design the buildings and avoid the *frou-frou* excesses of extraneous and expensive architectural design elements.

Taken together, these decisions resulted in a complex with the aesthetics of a military bunker, built in a squared-off horseshoe configuration around the dive shop. It was an austere but substantial bit of construction made of reinforced concrete.

A low wall fronted Route 1, Overseas Highway with a sign promoting Captain Dan's Dive Resort, complete with a fanciful picture of an imaginary, quasi-piratical Captain Dan. Access to the facility was achieved through a central entrance via a two-lane break between the two "L" shapes formed by the rooms, beyond which the dive shop was only somewhat visible.

The structure formed a protective cocoon around the parking lot, which served both room guests and divers. Patios and sundecks looked inward, toward the parking lot, with only the second story sundecks offering a view of the canal leading out to the bay.

The rooms were very basic and had been well maintained, but not upgraded, as Key Largo became more gentrified. Once again, a questionable business decision had conferred upon Captain Dan's a distinct niche in the marketplace.

While the rest of Key Largo was developing luxury resorts offering expensive accommodations, Captain Dan's presented a low-priced alternative and the rooms were in high demand for most of the year, even during the slow months of fall and winter.

Since his investment had been minimal, Captain Dan made money immediately. In fact, the profit from the rooms dwarfed the profit from the dive shop by a substantial margin. They were operated as two separate businesses, even though the rooms existed to funnel customers to the dive shop, though there was never any doubt about which was the dog and which was the tail.

A couple from Belize named Carlos and Lucinda, friends of Neil's construction foreman, were hired as handyman and housekeeper. However, it quickly became apparent that Lucinda, who had trained as accountant in her home country, knew much more about bookkeeping than Captain Dan.

Both Carlos and Lucinda had perfect English.

In spite of his many faults, Captain Dan was a fair, unprejudiced man who was always willing to exploit the vulnerability of a less fortunate person's station in life, regardless of their race, color or place of national origin.

He therefore altered his arrangement with Carlos and Lucinda so that they lived on premises rent-free, (which incidentally made them available basically 24-hours a day) and he added bookkeeping to Lucinda's mandate while Carlos handled reservations in addition to the maintenance.

This revised deal provided Captain Dan with a respectable profit for absolutely no work on his part. It also represented a welcome opportunity for Carlos and Lucinda, who in fact had never been to Belize in their lives, and instead had emigrated to the United Sates from Cuba in 1980 as part of the Mariel boatlift.

Managing a residential property with no supervision whatsoever allowed the couple to provide temporary shelter for family members and friends who continued to escape from Cuba on their way to Miami. Since the rooms were rarely one hundred percent booked, and Lucinda herself was the housekeeper, it was not difficult to shelter an occasional guest off the books with no one the wiser.

Carlos and Lucinda did not make money from the arrangement and would have been horrified at the suggestion that they could have done so. They were honest people and staunchly proud of it. What they were doing was simply a kindness to benefit refugees from a repressive regime, as they themselves had once been.

Their part in the Underground Railroad was short-lived, as it turned out. It ended abruptly when 10-year-old Katherine confronted a frightened refugee couple surreptitiously leaving their room early one morning.

"Hello, I'm Katherine. What are your names?" she demanded.

The couple looked at one another, petrified, as if they had been stopped by the dreaded G2, Castro's intelligence service. *"No... no English,"* stammered the woman.

Non-English-speaking Hispanics were not at all uncommon in Key Largo but they were not typically guests at Captain Dan's Dive Resort, especially ones wearing shabby clothing.

Later, Katherine innocently asked Lucinda about the guests in Room 15 and they became the last Cuban refugees to be sheltered at the hotel.

Even so, Carlos and Lucinda continued to enjoy their employment at Captain Dan's. And any guest of the property could be forgiven for assuming that they were actually the owners.

They were so ubiquitous, and worked so hard to make everyone comfortable and happy, it was difficult to imagine they were merely hired help. Which, nonetheless, they continued to be.

Captain Dan paid them less than they were worth, which was far more than they could earn anywhere else in the Keys, and everyone was happy with the arrangement. By the time Davey came to work at Captain Dan's, Carlos and Lucinda had been with the property for over 30 years and expected to remain there until their retirement.

The only anxious moment had come when Captain Dan died and the couple fretted that his two daughters might wish to take over management of the rooms. They didn't have to worry for long.

Katherine and Kate saw how much work Carlos and Lucinda did for relatively meager pay and never seriously considered replacing them. Carlos and Lucinda's jobs at Captain Dan's were as secure as any employment can ever be, and everyone was happy.

As for the resort itself, no one ever sent home pictures of Captain Dan's with the line, "This place is beautiful!" In fact, it was as homely as a maiden aunt.

But on a practical level, the design was inspired.

When Hurricane Irma hit in 2017, the protective configuration of the L-shaped structures, combined with the fact that the sundecks and patios faced inward toward the courtyard, protected the buildings from the most damaging effects of the storm and kept the dive shop tucked safely inside its protective cocoon.

Even the dive boat, *Calypso,* snug in its low canal, rode out the storm with no major damage in spite of the storm surge, which raised the level of the water to well above the dock but still below the elevation of the island at that location.

The minor repairs required in the aftermath were significantly less than insurance premiums would have been for adequate protection over the years, so Kate and Katherine continued their father's practice of living without such quotidian considerations.

Captain Dan's Dive Resort, much like Captain Dan and his Moped, seemed to lead a charmed life.

For the most part, Carlos and Lucinda were invisible to the divers who frequented Captain Dan's Dive Resort. They were quiet and self-effacing, and like many Latinos they were anonymous to the vast majority of visitors and residents in the Keys.

But since Davey arrived early every day, he often saw them and occasionally exchanged a few pleasantries.

"You work too hard," Davey said to Carlos one morning when the little Cuban was digging into the limestone bedrock with a pickaxe in preparation for planting some shrubberies.

"Good morning, Mister Davey," answered Carlos cheerily. "A little bit of work today but these hibiscus will look beautiful forever!"

Davey had offered to help Lucinda carry heavy loads of laundry up to the second floor so often, always being turned down with a demure smile, that he stopped asking. "Good morning!" he said brightly to the small figure nearly hidden behind a stack of folded sheets. "Good morning, Mister Davey," came the muffled reply. "Be safe on the water today."

Carlos and Lucinda were as much a fixture of Captain Dan's Dive Resort as the silly pirate sign on the highway.

That's how it had always been and nobody anticipated anything different in the future.

• • •

Leading snorkelers was much harder work than guiding divers. And like everyone else at Captain Dan's, Davey did both.

His snorkel group today was a family of four including two children aged four and six. The parents, Bill and Mindy, were eager for their kids to have the authentic ocean experience.

Four-year-old Caley slept all the way out to French Reef, which was generally a bad sign. Waking up from a child's dream in the middle of the ocean? How was that going to go down? The six-year-old, Matthew, stared at the horizon as the land receded in the distance and held onto the side railing with little white knuckles.

Davey expected problems in the water even as he gave them their briefing. Bill and Mindy had said they all knew how to snorkel but he still explained how to breathe through the mouthpiece and clear water from it. He knew having the kids wear fins was worse than useless; they wouldn't be kicking anyhow. He'd leave them off.

During the boat ride the kids were wearing life preservers, per Coast Guard regulation, and Davey decided to just leave them on when they got to the site. He'd try to get Bill and Mindy to accept pool noodles (even though they proudly proclaimed they were strong swimmers) because he needed them to be able to comfort and support the children in the water.

Once they were moored at the reef, near Christmas Tree Cave on French reef, Mark and Greg's divers splashed in first and then Davey led his group to the swim platform.

"I'll jump in the water and stay right in front of the swim platform. Bill, you're next. Tuck the pool noodle under your arms." Davey demonstrated. "Then Mindy. Then the kids can jump into your arms."

Davey did a giant stride off the platform. Bill sat with his feet in the water and pushed himself forward. Between the buoyancy of the wetsuit and the pool noodle, his head hardly went underwater at all.

Bill thrashed his way over to the current line and held on for dear life. "Wow, we're really out here, aren't we?" he panted. Two-foot waves rocked the boat gently and Bill rode their crests.

"Wow, *ha!* This is something," he said, nervously.

"Let's keep the snorkel in your mouth, okay Bill?" Davey said and Bill complied.

"Okay, Mindy, let's get you in the water." Mindy looked like she was about to jump out of an airplane. Or off a cliff. She sat on the swim platform, took a deep breath and pushed herself forward.

"Oh! Oh, no. I'm sinking!" she gasped, beating her arms on the water's surface. With a wetsuit and pool noodle, sinking was not really a possibility. But she had convinced herself it was happening and the water splashing in her face wasn't helping.

"Oh my God. *Oh my God!"* Mindy cried. Davey grabbed Mindy's arm. "Mindy, stop moving! Stop moving and *you'll float,"* he shouted.

He might as well have asked her to fly. Mindy was beating the water into a froth and taking large accidental gulps of the ocean as she edged closer to panic.

"Hold onto the current line. Over here," Davey instructed.

"I'm sinking!" Mindy insisted. *"I'm sinking."* She bolted for the ladder.

"Okay, okay," Davey reassured. "But we have to get your fins off first." Mindy wasn't stopping for anything. As she grabbed at the ladder Davey shucked off her fins so her feet could find the steps.

Caley and Matthew watched with wide eyes as their parents unraveled. Both of them held onto Javier's hands with blank expressions on their little faces.

How do you make God laugh? Make a plan, right? Wasn't that the old joke? Davey watched as his whole dive plan disintegrated.

Bill, meanwhile, was suddenly calm. Something about watching Mindy melt down had brought out his inner dude.

"What you wanna do?" Javier asked Davey. While Davey was considering how to play it, Caley piped up. "I wanna go in the water!" she keened, and she jumped up and down on the deck.

"Me, too!" enthused Matthew. "We want to go in!" They both jumped up and down.

Mindy had climbed onto the deck and was staggering around like a drunk. "I think I'm going to be sick," she cried.

"Go to the side, over there," Javier pointed to the break in the railing amidships, what the boat briefing referred to as fish feeding station #1. Mindy lurched to the side, quickly knelt and emptied her stomach into the ocean.

"We want to go in!" Matthew repeated.

"Now, *now!*" cried Caley.

Davey swam up to the platform. "Let's get you in first, Matthew," he said, looking up at Javier.

Still holding Caley's hand, Javier lifted Matthew by the arm and handed him down to Davey. Davey held both of Matthew's hands and pulled him away from the pitching boat.

133

Matthew was giggling uncontrollably. He wouldn't put his face in the water and his little feet were running a marathon below the surface but he was the happiest kid on the planet.

"Me! Me!" cried Caley.

Davey tried to hand Matthew off to Bill but Matthew wasn't having it.

"No, Daddy, no!" he cried, pushing Bill away. "Stay with Davey!"

It was just as well because Bill's dude façade was beginning to crack. Davey moved toward the swim platform.

"Hand her down to me," he called to Javier. The mate lifted the little girl up and passed her down to Davey.

Caley held onto Davey's arm with both hands and stuck her face in the water. He could hear her breathing through the snorkel, while she laughed and screamed at the fish.

"Hey, Matthew, try putting your face in the water, buddy, okay?" said Davey calmly. With one child on each arm, Davey moved back from the swim platform and positioned himself at the end of the current line, holding the float.

Bill was edging closer to the ladder. "I better go check on Mindy," he explained, halfheartedly. "Fins off!" Javier cautioned. Bill managed to remove his fins and pass them up to Javier, who took the pool noodle as Bill climbed the ladder.

Bill was on his way to Mindy when he suddenly lurched to the other side of the boat, fish feeding station #2, and projectile vomited into the sea.

Caley and Matthew, in spite of everything, were the happiest little snorkelers imaginable. They rarely lifted their heads out of the water and rode the small waves like lily pads riding the ripples on a pond.

There was no need to swim around. Davey held onto them at the end of the current line and they watched the reef below like a movie.

About 10 minutes later, Davey heard Di calling out.

"Divers, are you okay? Divers, are you okay?" A standard call to divers who have surfaced near a dive boat that's not their own.

A woman's voice answered, "You not our boat. This not our boat!" she said to her dive buddy.

The marine radio crackled to life. Davey couldn't make out the transmission but he heard Di respond, "Roger that."

Di called down from the flybridge. "I need the current line, Davey. Bring 'em in."

Davey held the line as Javier pulled it toward the boat. He handed the kids up one at a time, took his fins off and climbed up the ladder.

"Divers, grab the line!" yelled Di from the flybridge. Javier threw the line and it landed an arm's length from the two divers bobbing at the surface, a woman and a man.

"No, we goin' back to our boat!" the woman shouted back.

"Grab the line! *Do not descend!*" Di shouted, his fragile patience already fraying.

The woman had her mask on her forehead and her BCD only halfway inflated. Her regulator was out of her mouth and the waves were breaking right in her face.

The divers were from Carly's boat, a Corinthian catamaran named *Deep Seas*, that was moored 100 yards up current. There was no way in hell they were getting back to it.

The man was bobbing on the surface, fully inflated, regulator and mask in place, calm as could be. He grabbed onto the current line but the woman wanted to argue some more.

"I'm swallowin' water up here. I need to go under," she protested.

"Inflate your BCD. Put your regulator in your mouth. Stop talking," Di responded flatly. "Your boat is coming to get you."

"I'm a Divemaster. I know what to do," she yelled back.

"If you knew what to do, you'd be back on your boat instead of hanging onto my current line," Di shouted.

The radio crackled again with Carly's voice and Di grabbed the microphone. "We got 'em. But you come quick or I drown 'em myself." Davey hoped they weren't still on the Coast Guard channel.

"This is worse than if we was underwater," the woman complained. "Why you makin' things hard for us?"

"Your captain asked me to keep you on the surface so you don't get lost again." Di made no effort to hide the contempt in his voice. "She's responsible for you. Me, I don't care what happens to you."

Deep Seas arrived and tied up to the mooring line closest to *Calypso*. The mate jumped in with the ADRU, swimming quickly toward his divers.

"I don't need that. I'm gonna go under and swim to the boat," the woman protested when the mate arrived. The mate didn't answer. He just reached over and inflated her BDC, stuck her regulator in her mouth and made sure the man was holding on, too.

"Okay," the mate yelled, spinning his arm in a circle in the air. Back on *Deep Seas*, Captain Carly started rewinding the ADRU rapidly on a hand winch mounted on the deck.

Davey and Javier couldn't hear what she was actually saying but the woman diver complained every inch of the way until she was back at the dive boat. *"My, my, my, my,"* sang Javier. Davey smiled.

When they got to *Deep Seas*, the woman diver stopped on the ladder and turned to say something else to the mate, still on the line. "GET ON THE GODDAMN BOAT, LADY!" the mate yelled back at her.

Yeah, they heard that.

Davey's snorkel family was watching the scene with wide eyes and he decided it was time to get everyone back on a grace note.

"Never know what's going to happen on the ocean," Davey said with a smile. "Mindy, how are we feeling, better?" She wasn't really but she put on a brave front and smiled weakly.

"Bill, how about you?" Another brave smile. "Hey, Caley and Matthew, tell Mom and Dad what you saw underwater, okay?" Both the kids went to Mindy and started tugging on her arms, describing the fish they'd seen.

Davey handed them the fish ID chart but it didn't help really because what the kids were describing came straight from their vivid imaginations.

Greg's two divers surfaced and climbed aboard; Javier guided them to their seats holding their tank stems. Greg climbed up after them and headed for his seat.

Then Mark surfaced with his three divers.

"I need some help here!" he called out. That didn't sound like Mark. Davey looked toward the stern. *"Need some help here now!"*

A switch went off in Davey's head. He raced to the swim platform. Mark had a diver buoyant and rolled on her back. Her mask was off and her regulator wasn't in her open mouth. Her eyes were closed.

The other two divers held the current line.

"What happened?" Davey called out.

"Passed out. About 10 feet down. We were coming up and she lost consciousness." Mark wasn't moving the diver closer to the boat. He was visibly stressed and hadn't kicked into rescue mode.

"Undo her dive kit," Davey ordered. "We need to get her on the boat!" Mark tried to undo the clips on her harness but his fingers kept slipping and he couldn't open them.

He was losing it. And the seconds were ticking by.

One second, two... Davey jumped into the water. "Pull us in!" he called to Javier. To Mark, he said, "Hold onto the current line and the diver." Mark's expression was blank but he did what he was told.

Davey pinched the diver's nose closed and administered two "rescue breaths" mouth-to-mouth. He quickly unclipped the chest strap, both shoulder straps, the belt buckle, and ripped open the cummerbund while Javier drew them up to the boat.

Grabbing the ladder with one hand, Davey faced the diver and draped her arms over his shoulders. He grabbed the ladder with his other hand and climbed aboard: the ladder carry position. It almost looked like the diver and Davey were dancing.

"Get her dive gear," he called back to Mark. "Get the others aboard!"

Davey carried the diver forward.

"Everyone out of the way! Move the cooler!" Everyone cleared a path as Davey approached. Bill pulled the cooler out of the way.

Arms still around her shoulders, Davey unzipped the diver's wetsuit and pulled it down to her waist. He laid the diver down on the deck, head toward the stern, holding her head stable.

Davey gave two more rescue breaths and checked the diver's carotid artery for a pulse. Placing both hands on her sternum, he started CPR compressions.

One, two, three, four… staying alive, staying alive…

Whoever had figured out that the old Bee Gees song had the perfect beat for CPR? *Twelve, thirteen, fourteen, fifteen… staying alive, staying alive…*

"Everyone sit, please. I need plenty of room here." The divers and snorkelers moved back as if they had been pushed. Everyone was in a state of shock or near it, which made them compliant.

"Javier, make sure Di knows we have an unresponsive diver."

"He knows," Javier answered.

"Please confirm, okay?" Javier called up to the flybridge. On his 30 count, Davey gave two more rescue breaths mouth-to-mouth.

"Mark, I need the O2 kit." But Mark was frozen like a deer in the headlights. Stoned-pony Greg was the one who jumped up.

"On it," Greg said, and he headed for the V-berth.

Oh, oh, oh, oh… staying alive, staying alive.

Greg set the green box on the deck next to the unconscious diver. "I need it hooked up to the mask and set on 'flow'," Davey ordered. Greg started assembling the O2 rig. When he was finished, Davey said, "Check for color."

Oh, oh, oh, oh… staying alive, staying alive.

"Do what?" Greg asked.

"Check her nail beds and inside her lips. Tell me if you see any blue." Greg did a quick check. "I don't see any blue."

Davey placed the O2 mask over the diver's mouth and went back to compressions.

Oh, oh, oh, oh… staying alive, staying alive.

"Get the AED, please. On the wall in the V-berth." Greg jumped up and headed back to the V-berth. Give bystanders a job, Davey remembered from his training. They need an assignment to keep them busy and out of the way.

Mark needed a job. "Mark, have we got the diver's gear?"

"Yeah… Yeah, it's onboard." Davey saw the dive kit on the swim platform. "Let's secure it, please. Bungee it into the rack."

Mark moved back toward the stern. He grabbed the dive gear and secured it in place on the dive bench.

"I… I can't find her mask," Mark stammered, as if that were the real tragedy. "We don't need it, buddy," Davey answered. "All your divers onboard?"

Mark looked around. "Yeah, everyone's here."

"Di, what's our status?" Davey shouted up to the flybridge.

"Coast Guard is on the way," Di responded crisply.

"Thank you," Davey answered. She'd been down three minutes since he'd been working on her. Maybe three minutes before that.

Greg arrived with the Automated External Defibrillator, the AED.

"Set that up for me, please, Greg," said Davey, keeping the compressions going. "Take the stickers off the pads." Greg got the machine ready. Another minute had gone by: seven minutes down.

"Stick that pad just above her right breast," Davey instructed. He stuck the second pad on the diver's left side at the bottom of her rib cage. He sat back while the AED calibrated.

There was no human sound on the boat. Everyone was transfixed, all eyes on Davey and the unconscious diver. The AED's robot voice announced "SHOCK INDICATED. CLEAR."

The shock made the diver's body jump.

Davey checked the diver's carotid artery. "I've got a pulse!" he called out. "Mark, what's her name?"

"What…?"

"What's the diver's name?" Mark thought for a second. "Erin."

"Erin!" Davey slapped her cheeks lightly with the backs of his fingers. "Erin, can you hear me?"

Erin's eyes fluttered and opened. She tried to lift her shoulders but Davey pushed her gently down. "We got you, Erin. My name is Davey and you're going to be okay. Stay there, just stay down, okay?"

Davey checked the pulse in her wrist.

"She's conscious, Di. Where's the Coast Guard?"

"Thirty-five minutes out," Di called back.

Erin was trying to push the oxygen mask off her face. Davey pulled her hands away gently. "How fast can we get to Port Largo?"

"Twenty-five minutes," Di answered.

"Let's go!" Davey shouted, and then to Erin in a softer voice, "Stay with me, Erin, okay? You got this. Breathe deep, okay?" Davey demonstrated long, deep breaths.

"Javier, cast off the mooring ball!" Di shouted. Davey could hear Di on the radio, talking to the Coast Guard.

Javier ran to the bow and Di started up the twin engines.

"Mark, are you with me?" Davey called out.

"Yeah, whatdya need?' Mark was coming out of it.

"Call 911. Tell them we're bringing a near drowning victim to Port Largo. Have the paramedics meet us there."

"You got it." Mark answered. He went to the bulkhead and pulled his phone out his drybag.

Di firewalled the engines and *Calypso* headed for shore. Erin was trying to talk but she was still woozy.

"Don't talk. Just breathe. I got you," Davey cooed. "Greg, get me some life preservers from the V-berth."

"How many?"

"Keep bringing them till I say stop."

Davey rolled Erin gently onto her left side, holding the oxygen mask in place. As Greg handed him life preservers, he piled them behind Erin's back for soft support.

"Okay, that's enough."

Erin made a choking cough and some water came out of her mouth. She did it again and then stopped, breathing easier.

"That's good," Davey reassured. "Deep breaths."

Davey placed one of the life preservers under Erin's head as a pillow. He pulled the cooler back over and shoved it behind the life preservers to brace them.

Mark's other two divers were still strapped into their gear.

"Is she… is she going to be okay?" one of them asked, probably the boyfriend.

"Erin is going to be just fine," Davey answered. "Go ahead and get out of your gear."

Davey held up his hand as a warning. "Stay back, though. Let's give Erin plenty of room here, okay guys."

"They want to talk to you," Mark said, holding his phone to Davey's ear. Davey listened for a moment.

"Diver lost consciousness underwater. We administered CPR and defibrillated. She's on O2 and conscious now. I have a carotid pulse but no wrist pulse. I have no way of determining BP." Davey listened. "Yeah, we've done that."

"Erin, without moving your head, watch my finger." Davey said, holding his index finger in front of her face, moving it left to right.

"Pupils normal, eyes responsive. Breathing good. Color good."

Davey listened. "Twenty minutes. See you there." Davey nodded to Mark, who took his phone back.

"Thanks, Mark. Grab me a couple of towels, would you?"

Mark brought over the towels and Davey draped the towels across Erin's torso for warmth.

"Okay, Erin," Davey said with a smile. "We got a bumpy boat ride coming up." *Calypso* cut through the water at top speed, hitting an occasional wave with a hard *thump*.

When they got to Port Largo, the ambulance was waiting at the dock. Two paramedics loaded Erin onto the gurney, checked her vitals and interviewed Davey. Erin was able to talk now. Her blood pressure was in the safe zone. Two ribs were cracked from the CPR.

All things considered, an excellent outcome. "Good save," one of the paramedics said to Davey.

Mark was shaking his head. "I froze, man. I just fucking *froze*."

Davey looked straight into Mark's eyes. "You got her to the surface. You saved that woman's life."

"We... ah..." it was Erin's boyfriend and his buddy.

"Go with her," Davey pointed at the ambulance. "We'll have your gear for you at the dive shop. *Go!*"

"Thanks, man. Thanks so much!" The boyfriend pumped Davey's hand and the two men jumped into the ambulance. Mark and Davey stepped back onto *Calypso* and cast off for Captain Dan's.

On the ride home, Davey had only one thought on his mind: Today? *Seriously, this happened to me today?*

Chapter 12

Before Davey even walked into Get Shorty's, he knew he shouldn't be there. Not tonight. *Especially not tonight.*

But his adrenaline was still pumping and he was afraid if he went home and got trapped inside his own head, he'd go out of his mind.

The police had been waiting at the dock to impound Erin's dive equipment; they had to be told what to take but that was fair: why should they know? The Coast Guard was there, too, administering urine tests to every member of the crew onboard. All standard operating procedure. But still.

So, what could it hurt? A couple of Happy Hour beers, a little camaraderie, then home and safety. Ignore the background noise. Just push it back down.

The first person Davey saw was Carly. He sat down next to her and Jorge brought him his first beer. Carly leaned over and gave Davey a hug.

"Thanks for your help today," Carly said. Davey smiled at the memory. "They seemed like quite a pair," he answered.

"That they were," Carly agreed. "I wasn't going to let her back in the water but she just would not shut up. I had to let her dive again just to get her to stop talking."

"Wonder where she got her Divemaster rating," Davey mused.

"Heard you had an interesting afternoon after we left," Carly said, changing the subject.

"Oh, yeah... pretty standard EFR stuff," Davey said. Emergency First Responder was the training every dive instructor had to have.

"Not what I heard," Carly answered.

Davey shrugged. "Di's still doing paperwork for the Coast Guard. His favorite thing in the world."

Roald appeared out of nowhere and sat on Davey's other side. "The hero walks among us," he slapped Davey on the shoulder. "Very good work, my friend!"

"Innkeeper, one beer, please," Roald ordered. "And one drink for my friend, the hero."

"Guys, it was no big deal. Anyone on the boat could have done the same thing," Davey protested.

"If you say so," Carly said, with a doubtful smile. Davey looked up and saw that everyone at the bar was staring at him. Some raised their glasses. He didn't even know most of them.

This was getting bizarre. He could feel his pulse throbbing in his ears.

"Another rum coke," Carly said when Jorge brought Roald's drink. Carly was known to be able to put away a few drinks but no one had ever seen her drunk. She rode a fat wheel bicycle everywhere, so there was never a problem with driving.

Still, there were indiscreetly whispered rumors that she'd had a DUI and some of the other captains, all of them men, thought she should have her ticket pulled or be fired.

Her ex-boyfriend, Kenny, had started the rumor and he knew it was false because he'd made it up. Still, it had some passionate supporters. Such is life in the Keys.

"Can we talk about something else?" Davey complained. The background noise was starting to rise up inside him.

"Yah, sure," said Roald, "enough about Davey. Carly, let's talk about you. What do you think about Davey the hero?"

Six months in the county and he's doing comedy routines. What's next: Who's On First?

Jorge delivered a tray full of drinks to the bar in front of Davey.

Dimly, Davey became aware that there was a crowd of dive professionals standing around and behind him, some he barely knew, ordering drinks, joking and slapping him on the shoulder.

Davey was at the center of a party. A big party. This was tonight's Bubble Talk. And Davey was at the center of it.

"I been here more'n 30 years and I heard a maybe two saves!" Binky! When the hell did Binky get here? "Hell of a job, brother."

Oh God, Davey thought, now I'm Binky's brother.

"What up, guys?" asked Theo from somewhere behind Davey. "I'm hearing all kinds of crazy stuff."

"You shoulda seen him in action. Captain Take-Charge!" It was Greg. Greg was at Get Shorty's?

The group behind Davey was growing larger every minute. It was as if there'd been a memo.

Mark threw his arm around Davey's shoulders. Mark was at get Shorty's!

"You saved my ass," said Mark. "I fucking *froze*. This guy saved my ass!" He needed to stop saying that. He needed to quit blaming himself but Davey was too distracted by the Trans-Siberian Orchestra pounding inside his head to say anything to Mark or offer any consolation.

"Make a hole!" Di shouted as he pushed through the crowd, clearing a spot next to Davey. He enveloped Davey in a big crushing bear hug and kissed the top of Davey's head with a noisy smack.

"You know how much more paperwork I would be doing right now if that woman died? And I hate fucking paperwork!" Di roared.

Di sat down with a grunt and waved to Jorge.

"You gonna to let me pass out from thirst, you motherless fuck?" Di looked at Davey with his crooked grin. "Buy me a shot, or I buy you a shot! Oh, that's right, you don't drink shots. You don't fuck either, isn't that right?" Di draped his heavy arm around Davey's shoulder.

"What am I going to do with you, my son?" Di shook his head.

The background noise was drowning out everything else. Davey couldn't stop it. He looked at Jorge, who seemed far away, at the end of a tunnel.

The noise in Davey's ears was deafening.

"I'll have a Bourbon neat. And give it to me in a real glass, not one of those stupid plastic cups you give the tourists," Davey said, finally.

• • •

Davey woke up without opening his eyes. He was aware of a very bad headache. His mouth was dry and tasted like moldy cheese.

He smelled perfume.

Davey tentatively opened his eyes. Bethany was staring at him from about five feet away. Was he in her apartment? How did he get there? No idea.

"Good morning," Bethany said.

"That's your opinion." He moved his head a bit, looked around: he was in his apartment, his bed. He closed his eyes. "Am I dead?"

"Nope. But pretty close."

"You willing to finish the job? I can pay."

"There's a sick bucket on the floor next to you. Or I can help you get to the bathroom if you need to throw up."

"Terrific. I was hoping our relationship would level up to this."

Davey took a couple of deep breaths and opened his eyes again.

"I need to get to work," he said, halfheartedly.

"That's just not going to happen," Bethany answered, shaking her head. "I called you in sick for two days. Sleep as much as you can."

"Don't you have to be at work?"

"I got the day off. I don't know what you said to Ben but he's walking on eggshells around me now. Genuine Mister Nice-Guy."

Bethany had her hair in a ponytail. She was wearing a man's blue work shirt and shorts and even in his current condition, Davey could see that she was effortlessly beautiful.

"How long have you been here?" Davey asked.

"Stop talking so much. Get sick or go back to sleep. There's nothing else you need to do."

Davey closed his eyes and in less than a minute he was asleep.

There were parrotfish in his dreams. Blue ones, rainbows, stoplights. The manta ray from *Finding Nemo* swam by with his students riding on his wings. Davey was giving CPR to a shark, which turned into Stasie, who morphed into Erin. Her eyes opened wide in death.

"How long was I asleep?" he asked. It seemed five minutes later. "Three hours," Bethany answered.

"You been here the whole time? Don't you have stuff to do?"

"I'm reading a book," said Bethany. "You're interrupting me."

Bethany stood up and felt Davey's forehead. She adjusted his covers a bit and sat back down.

"Where's Abigail?" Davey asked.

"At school. It's a just little after noon."

"Did she see me... before?"

"No, she was asleep when you got home. We were both asleep when you got home. Sounded like shore leave in

148

Shanghai. Guess you decided to start drinking shots. See what you've been missing."

"Sorry. I didn't… I just… It's not that…"

Bethany walked into the kitchen. She came back with a can of Coke, opened it and handed it to Davey.

"Drink as much of this as you can at one time. The bubbles should burn your throat," she said. Davey raised himself on one elbow, took the can and drank as much as he could.

"Oh my God, that hurts!" he said when he put the can down.

"Now go back to sleep. We can play 20 questions when you feel better." Davey closed his eyes and was gone.

The next time he woke up the room was dark. He opened his eyes fully and blinked: it couldn't be. But it was. The sun was down.

It was night again.

He actually felt a little better. His head still throbbed a bit and there was nothing good going on in his stomach. But it was localized now. He didn't feel like his whole body had been run over by a truck.

He struggled into a sitting position and almost immediately regretted it. First, he was dizzy, then he was staggering for the toilet.

Davey got to the bathroom just in time. Steering the porcelain boat, that's what the frat boys called it, the drunk college kids that came into his ER dragging their unconscious pledges, certain they were dying of alcohol poisoning.

"He was just steering the porcelain boat and then he passed out on the bathroom floor!" they'd say.

In five minutes, he was sure there were no more fluids in his entire body. He pushed himself away from the toilet bowl and got up. He was leaning heavily on the doorframe when Bethany came in with a bowl of soup on a tray. She stopped when she saw him.

"That's going to make you feel a whole lot better, trust me," she said, putting down the tray on the bureau.

"What's that?" Davey asked, indicating the bowl of soup.

"Chicken noodle soup. I'm telling you, the Jews are really onto something with this stuff. Cures everything."

"You made me soup?"

"Get serious. I opened a can. You might want to think about rinsing out your mouth if you're going to enjoy this at all."

"I'm really not hungry."

Bethany looked at Davey with a determined expression.

"I know you think you're all better but I can still take you."

"You think?" he asked.

"Try me," Bethany said with a hard stare. Davey nodded.

"Meet you at the kitchen table," he said, and he went back into the bathroom to rinse his mouth.

When he sat down at the table a couple of minutes later, he wasn't the least bit hungry. But the rich aroma from the steaming bowl of soup stimulated his appetite and he started eating, slowly.

"How are you feeling, Davey?" Bethany's expression had softened and she was in full Florence Nightingale mode.

"Embarrassed. Ashamed," he said between spoonfuls.

"That's not what I mean. And you shouldn't be. There's no reason."

"I cost you a day of work and I'm going to pay you back, by the way. I'm dead serious," he said flatly.

"No way," she said quickly. "I'm taking two days off and I'll make up the shifts. I told you, Ben gives me whatever I ask for these days."

"You shouldn't be taking time off to look after me," Davey said.

"Yeah, 'cause you've never done anything for me at all," Bethany huffed, sarcastically. "Or everyone else you know, for that matter."

Davey took another spoonful of soup.

"I'm here because I want to be," Bethany said, finally. "And all those people who brought you home last night, drunk as they were. They wanted to make sure you got home okay. They brought your car this morning. They look up to you, Davey."

"Oh God, not you, too."

"Not because of that. They respect you. They care about you." She made a scrunchy face. "I even like you a little bit myself."

"This doesn't taste like it's out of a can," Davey said, taking another spoonful of soup.

"I put sherry in it. I'm pushing Michelin for a second star."

Davey smiled. "I still feel like an idiot," he said.

"You had a tough day. You did the hard stuff like a champion and then you crashed. Nothing to beat yourself up about."

Bethany's hazel eyes had little flecks of gold in the irises. Her blue work shirt made her eyes look blue. Why weren't men just falling dead at her feet? Good men? Nice men? It was a mystery.

"What does Abigail...?"

"I told her you had food poisoning. She wanted to come over but I wouldn't let her."

Davey nodded, well that was good at least. Bethany stared at Davey, pursed her lips. He was still wearing his bathing suit and hoodie from last night. Stubble was growing on his face.

"Who's Stasie?" Bethany asked in a quiet voice. Davey looked at her like he'd been struck.

"I'm not prying--I don't care who she is--that's your business." Bethany backpedaled as fast as she could. "It's just that you said her name. A lot. And it seemed like you were hurting pretty bad."

151

Bethany looked deep into Davey's eyes. "Is Stasie your ex?"

Davey looked at the empty bowl on the table. "She was my daughter. Anastasia. She died."

Bethany raised her hand to her mouth. "Oh my God. I'm so sorry. Oh Davey, that's terrible. I'm so sorry." Her eyes filled with tears.

"No, it's okay. I'm glad I told you," Davey said. "No one else knows. I never talk about it."

Bethany pulled her chair around so she was sitting next to Davey and he told her the whole story, about the night that Stasie died, the drunk driver, being in the ER when they brought her in and not being able to do anything to help his dying daughter.

It was as though a dam had burst inside him and the whole dismal, brutal truth of his life and Stasie's death spilled out.

"It happened on April 11th," Davey said.

"Yesterday was April 11th," Bethany gasped. "Oh, Davey. *Oh my God!*"

"I usually stay home. I sit by myself until it stops. I call it my background noise. It's gone the next day and I'm fine again."

He told her that he didn't trust himself to be anywhere that the background noise might overwhelm him. He stayed locked away in his room with the lights out.

"Last night, I just couldn't manage it," he said, sadly. "I couldn't stand to be by myself. I just couldn't face it alone."

So, he broke his own rule and went out. Went to Get Shorty's. Saw people. After that, what happened just happened.

They sat together, leaning into each other, quietly, feeling each other's warmth and soft breathing. Bethany put her arms around Davey's neck and rested her head on his shoulder.

They didn't say another word for more than an hour.

The next morning when Davey woke up it was already nine o'clock, which surprised him. But he felt better, much better.

He shucked off his old clothes and put on clean sweatpants and a T-shirt. When he walked into the kitchen, Bethany was sitting there.

"There's coffee. I'll make you bacon and eggs later but not yet. It's still too soon."

"How are you getting in and out of my place like this?" Davey asked.

"I have your keys, Sherlock." Bethany held up Davey's key ring. "I'll give them back to you when I've washed your sheets."

"You are not going to wash my sheets," Davey said firmly.

"Wanna bet?" Bethany challenged.

"I am totally back to normal and I can do my own laundry, thank you very much," Davey stated, flatly.

"You only think you're back to normal" she said, knowingly.

"I guess I oughta know how I feel," Davey asserted.

Bethany smiled at Davey. "How about some nice fresh oysters with ketchup and beans?"

Davey sat down, quickly. "Don't do that," he said, stifling a wave of nausea.

"You'll be better tonight. You won't be normal until tomorrow. I used to live with an alcoholic. I know how this works." Bethany handed Davey a mug filled with coffee.

"Now go out on the porch or go take a walk, just get out of my way," she ordered. Davey went out on the porch to stare at the view, which was mostly a trash-strewn yard overgrown with weeds.

Later, he went for a walk but stayed off the bike path where anyone might see him, especially someone he knew. Breathe in and out, slow and deep. Just like you tell your students. Feral cats peeked out from behind trees, looking to see if Davey had food for them. And when he passed Winn Dixie, there were free-roaming chickens in the woods, pecking at God knows what. Crazy. Wild chickens.

Bethany's bacon and fried eggs tasted like the food of the gods. No meal had ever been so good. As she cleared away his plate, Bethany said, "Now it's time for you to shower, shave and brush your teeth so you can rejoin the human race."

She was wearing shorts that showed just the bottoms of her buttocks and a tight top with a low neckline. Her ponytail swayed from side to side. Her movements were lithe and graceful after years of waitressing.

Davey leaned back in his chair. "I think I'll just sit here and watch you for a bit."

Bethany turned and raised one eyebrow. She lowered her chin and stared at Davey without saying a word. Eyes like lasers.

"Right after I clean up," Davey said and he headed for the bathroom.

The hot shower felt so good he just let it run. Two days of sweat, tears and bad memories washed right down the drain. By the time he'd shaved and brushed his teeth, Davey felt almost brand new.

He walked out of the bathroom with a towel wrapped around him and was surprised to see Bethany standing in the bedroom.

"Hello," Davey said. "Is this part of your care plan?"

"No, I'm finished taking care of you," Bethany answered. "Now, I'm just invading your space."

She stood by the door, keeping her distance. "Tell me about Carly," Bethany said.

"She's a boat captain. I hardly know her. She was at Get Shorty's last night," Davey said, wondering where this was going.

"The way she was helping you up the stairs, I thought it might be, you know, something more," Bethany mused.

"Who, Carly?" Davey was surprised. "She lives with her boyfriend on the other side of the cut. He's an instructor, too."

"Well okay then," Bethany said, looking at Davey appraisingly. He was slender and muscular. He didn't have the abs of a weight lifter but he was in good shape and it showed.

Bethany nodded, pursed her lips.

She walked slowly toward Davey. "So, I've been in and out of here a lot in the last two days," she started.

"I'll say," said Davey.

"And I want you to know that I have not been snooping. I respected your privacy," Bethany put her hands on Davey's bare shoulders. "For the most part," she added, softly.

"What's happening?" Davey asked.

"But I'm not blind and I couldn't help but notice that you've got a really old TV."

"I rarely watch. Not really a big TV guy." Davey didn't see where this was going at all.

"Which means the one I have was never your old TV. It's a brand-new set with a DVD player that you bought and sold to me for fifty bucks!"

"About that--" But Bethany had no intention of letting Davey talk.

"--You just did it. No one asked you to." Davey knew better than to interrupt now. Better to let her go and get it all out.

"So, here's my question. Did you mean it, what you said about me being First Prize and all that other horse shit?" Bethany asked.

"Every word," Davey answered.

"Then I'm through waiting for you to come to your senses. And I don't want to hear any more crap about tabloids. Or *schadenfreude*. Or any other nonsense you might make up and throw at me because this time I'm not taking 'No' for an answer, Davey Jones!"

Bethany pulled off her ponytail holder and shook her hair free. She stood up on her toes and kissed Davey lightly on the mouth. Her lips were soft and tasted slightly of citrus.

Too late, Davey realized he was fresh out of excuses.

"How can you not take 'No' for an answer?" he asked, halfheartedly. "What if I'm gay? What if 'no means no?'"

Bethany ran her tongue across her lips and kissed Davey again, this time with her mouth open and inviting.

"Are you gay?" she asked, as she pulled away.

"No," Davey breathed. She drew his head down closer to hers and kissed him deeply and for a long time.

"Are you saying no?" Bethany asked, her face an inch in front of his. She ran her hands down his chest and back up to his shoulders.

"No," Davey answered, softly. "I mean, technically, I did just say 'No' but I meant 'No, I'm not saying n—'"

Bethany placed her finger on Davey's lips and stopped him in mid-sentence.

"Davey," she whispered quietly. "Shut the fuck up."

Any further resistance was useless because now Davey's fingers were running through Bethany's silky, auburn hair and suddenly he was leaning over to pull her up to him, her legs wrapping around his waist as his towel fell to the floor.

They didn't crash into the walls. Nobody tore each other's clothes off or pushed dishes and glasses off a table. It wasn't like the movies.

They were quiet, searching. Davey stood there naked, slowly taking off Bethany's clothes. First her top then her bra. She pressed herself against him.

His hand moved down her sides, lightly touching her breasts, then he slid her pants and underwear over her buttocks and down her legs. She stepped out of them.

His hands went back up her legs, slowly. He kissed her stomach, her nipples, her lips. Bethany drew back the freshly washed sheet on top of the bed. She sat down in front of him and drew him down beside her, pulling the sheet up over them like a tent.

For the next half hour, there was no one else in the world, no world at all, no Key Largo, no Captain Dan's, no anything...

Afterwards they lay in each other's arms, not talking, just breathing. Bethany played with her fingers on Davey's chest. Finally, she said, "What are you thinking?"

"I'm thinking you have really big boobs for a short girl," Davey answered, with a smile. Bethany poked him in the ribs, hard.

"And you like to punch me a lot," Davey added.

"I mean about this, you know, us, what we did," Bethany probed.

"I haven't had time to think yet," Davey answered. "I may not even be capable of thought for several days. Could be a week."

Bethany kissed Davey's chest.

"It doesn't have to change anything, you know," Bethany said. "I know I pushed myself on you but nothing needs to change between us."

"You totally forced me," Davey said. "As soon as you leave, I'm calling Ronan Farrow."

"Are you done being a total dick yet?" Bethany asked, a little edge in her voice.

"I'm not sure," Davey said thoughtfully. "Might be a little longer."

Bethany stretched her arm across Davey's chest and hugged him to her, and then traced her hand down his belly and between his legs.

"It gets longer?" she asked.

"You don't think this changes anything?" Davey breathed.

"It doesn't need to," Bethany insisted. "I promise. We can keep things just like they were before."

Davey rolled toward Bethany and looked into her eyes. "Let's be honest, Bethany. It changes everything," he said simply. "Pretending it doesn't is how people fuck things up."

"I don't want... I don't want to lose what we have... our friendship," she said.

"Then we'll have to be honest with each other. So that what has changed between us doesn't change us."

"And that's it?" Bethany asked.

"Yeah, for now, that's it," Davey replied.

Bethany snuggled closer to Davey, resting her head on his chest. "I can do that," she said.

Twenty minutes later it was time to get ready for Abigail to come home from school.

Chapter 13

Davey knew his whole world had been blown to bits but he wasn't quite sure what that meant yet. Even filling the rinse buckets seemed different somehow. He'd woken up in another dimension.

"Hey Davey," sang Javier. "How you feelin', man?" He was coming down the steps carrying two heavy fuel cans. Di was right behind him carrying two more heavy cans.

"No man can learn to drink like me in one night," Di said, gruffly. "You got to work your way up to it if you want to be like the Greek."

"You won't be offended if that's not my ambition," Davey answered with a smile. He carried the hose onto the boat to fill the mask and camera buckets.

Di put down the fuel cans. "Hey, who's that cute girl came out when we brought you home? Where you been hiding her?"

"That's my neighbor, Bethany. And I haven't been hiding her. We're friends." Davey made it sound as casual as he could.

"If I were you, I'd be on that in a Mykonos minute," Di pronounced. "The little ones, they surprise you sometimes."

"Well, you're not me and more importantly, I'm not you," Davey answered, offhandedly.

Di stopped and looked at Davey, quizzically. "Hey, look me in the eye you phony baloney," he demanded. Davey tried to look at Di without really looking at him.

"You're hitting that! Don't bullshit a bullshitter. The Greek knows all!" Di raised his hands in benediction and leered ecstatically.

"Drinking *and* fucking!" Di put his arm around Javier's shoulders. "What happened to our little Davey?"

"Shut up, you reprobate," said Davey.

"Missing trope! I'm a missing trope," Di stated proudly. "Don't make me learn another big word."

"I can think of a number of new words to describe you," Davey said, dismissively.

Di pretended to wipe away a tear. "They grow up so fast!" he moaned, shaking his head, then laughing uproariously.

"I don't know how you put up with him," Davey said to Javier.

"I'm happy for you, man," Javier responded. *"Don't worry. Be happy,"* he sang lightly.

"I'm going to go check the manifest," Davey said with disgust. "You boys be careful not to accidentally spill fuel and set yourselves on fire."

Davey walked up the steps to the shop.

Kate was already there, which was unusual, and she was already busy, which was even more unusual. Davey turned the manifest so he could read it while Kate finished a phone call.

"We'll see you then," she said sweetly and hung up the phone. Kate stared up at Davey.

"Listen, Kate," Davey started, "Sorry about the last two days."

"Normally I'd have something to say about that but under the circumstances, I'm going to let it slide."

"Won't happen again," Davey promised, solemnly.

"Tuesday, I had to cancel all tours," Kate perused some folders and stuffed them into her file cabinet, slamming the drawer closed. "I didn't have one single crew member who was fit to go out on the vessel." Davey tried not to smile.

"You cost us money!" Katherine yelled from the repair bench. So, Katherine was back. Well, that was good, Davey supposed.

"Wednesday was a little better. I sent out a morning and an afternoon boat. But *you* weren't on either of them. And I had requests for you."

There were sixteen divers on this morning's boat; nearly sold out. Thirty-four tanks, including the captain's tanks. That was pretty high for midweek. Davey made a mental note.

"The thing is, you saving that diver made us look good." Kate wasn't used to giving out compliments and it showed. "Erin's boyfriend––was that her name, Erin?'

"Yeah, Erin," said Davey.

"Erin's boyfriend wrote the whole thing up on TripAdvisor. Can you believe it?" Kate shook her head. "Not the kind of publicity we usually look for. Five stars, though. He mentioned your name. And the fact that the paramedics told him unresponsive divers usually don't survive. Facebook, Yelp, Google, he put it on all of them."

"Oh God," Davey didn't like the sound of this.

"Our online reservations are blowing up. The phone's been blowing up," Kate said in wonder. "Everyone wants to dive with us. And they all want to dive with you!"

It was more of an accusation than an accolade.

"That's terrible!" Davey couldn't believe it.

"It's terrible that we're making money?" Kate shot back. "The rooms are sold out for the next month and a half. We're usually quiet in May. I may have to hire another DM."

"That's not what I'm saying," Davey said. "This is an accident waiting to happen. It's totally the wrong way to look at things."

"How do you mean?" asked Kate.

"You know those big companies that have the sign outside saying how many days since they had an accident?" Davey asked.

"Yeah, sure, so what's your point?" said Kate.

"So, what do you think that sign looks like the day after an accident?" Davey raised his eyebrows.

Kate's expression changed slowly, meaning she understood.

"Then I guess *you'll* just have to make sure we don't have any accidents," Katherine said accusingly, standing just outside her repair cubicle, her safe area.

So, holding a bit of a grudge are we? For Paolo? For rejecting her?

"I need to load this morning's tanks," Davey said and he grabbed the air gauge, turned on his heel, and left.

During the boat safety briefing as they were leaving the canal, when Davey got to the part about where the emergency oxygen was stored, one of the guests interrupted. "We don't need to know where it is, as long as you know where it is," the guest said with a smile.

All the others nodded in agreement.

"Coast Guard regulations require that I inform everyone where our safety equipment is located in the event of an emergency," Davey continued. "Which we don't expect, naturally."

Davey felt like he was a monkey at the zoo.

When the briefing was done, Davey turned things over to the individual dive groups. Mark and Greg started their briefings but all of their divers craned their heads around to hear Davey briefing his group. Eventually, Mark and Greg just stopped talking.

Davey didn't like the new paradigm. He didn't like it one little bit.

When they got back to the shop after the morning dive, Erin was there with her boyfriend waiting for Davey.

She smiled when she saw him.

"I didn't want to leave without coming to see you. I'd hug you but I can't raise my arms," Erin said, holding her ribcage tenderly.

"Sorry about that," Davey said with a small shrug. "It happens."

"Sorry?" gushed Erin. "What sorry? I'm here because of you. I'm breathing because of you. There's no sorry!"

"Saying 'Thank you' seems like such a small thing," her boyfriend added. "But it's all we got."

"And I will thank you forever, David Jones. As long as I live. *Thank you.*" She came forward, stopped, leaned up and kissed him. "Thank you, you wonderful, heroic man."

The boyfriend shook Davey's hand firmly and they got in their car and drove away. Davey waved. "Take care of yourselves!" he called out at the departing vehicle. "Come back and see us."

When he heard himself say it, it sounded incredibly idiotic.

Then Davey walked back in the shop and saw that Kate had a strange expression on her face, even for her. "So..." she started, tentatively, "Erin's boyfriend sent over a pretty big tip by Venmo. Normally, I'd split that among the crew but I think, in this case, it's safe to say he meant it to go to you, personally."

"I don't need a tip for saving someone's life," Davey said, shaking his head in disbelief. "My God, that's our job. It's basic."

"Well, you got one whether you need it or not," said Kate. "It's five hundred dollars, Davey. That's not nothing."

No, that was a lot. Even large families who spent a whole week on the dive boat didn't leave that much.

"Put it with the crew tips for the day," Davey said flatly.

"Seriously?" Kate asked. "It's a lot of money."

"There were five of us on the boat. Everyone played a role," Davey answered. "It was a team effort."

"Well, if you're sure--"

"--Can we...," Davey put up his hands in protest. "Can we just get past this?"

"Yeah, sure. It's done. In with the crew tips." Kate sat down at her computer, which ended the conversation.

• • •

It had been a really long day and when it was over Davey knocked on Bethany's door like a man selling insurance. She opened the door and smiled at him.

"Hey," he said, lamely.

"Hey," she answered. And they both stood there.

"I'm not sure I even remember how to do this," Davey said, finally. Bethany laughed strangely. "Me either," she admitted.

Davey leaned in and gave Bethany a quick kiss, like a cousin at Thanksgiving. It was over before she knew it was happening.

"Okay, that was nice," he said.

"Yeah, like you're picking me up for prom," Bethany answered, brightly.

"So... I came over as soon as I got off—"

"—You didn't have to do that. I mean, you could have—"

"—I just thought I should maybe check in and see what—"

"—I don't want you to feel you have to—"

"—It's just that..." Suddenly, they both stopped talking.

"You go," said Davey.

Bethany shook her head violently. "No, I want to hear what you were going to say," she insisted.

Davey tried to think of what he was going to say and couldn't come up with anything. "You know," he said, finally, "there's a good chance we may both suck at this."

Bethany started to laugh. "I know, right?" Davey leaned forward and Bethany jumped into his arms for a hug.

"That's better," she said. Davey inhaled deeply. "God, you smell good," he said.

"*Ooo,* so do you--" Bethany sniffed. "Actually, you don't. Came straight off the boat?"

"Forty minutes filling tanks in the hot sun," Davey answered.

"I can tell," she said, still hugging him tight. She pushed back and gave Davey a big kiss, then climbed down off him.

"So, I have a thought, if you want to hear it," Bethany said tentatively.

"Yeah, please, you go," said Davey, desperately.

"I think we should each do exactly what we would normally do if nothing had happened. Except, sometimes, we should do something we wouldn't normally do and we should do it together," Bethany said.

"When you say it like that, it sounds easy," Davey, smiling.

"I'm all for easy," Bethany agreed. "The hard stuff will find us."

"Okay, I think you're onto something there. So, normally, I'd go home and take a shower," Davey said.

"Which you need," Bethany agreed, nodding.

Davey turned to go, then turned back again. "What about...?" He nodded toward Abigail's room. "Are we saying something, or...?"

"Oh... no, no, no, no, no, way too early," Bethany shook her head vehemently.

"Totally," Davey agreed. "Way too early. Way, way."

"What would we even say?" Bethany asked.

"Exactly," Davey agreed, with an exaggerated shrug.

At that moment, Abigail's door opened and she bounded into the room like a bouncing Tigger and hopped into Davey's arms.

"Davey, Davey, Davey, *Davey!*" she cried happily. "I'm so glad it's you. I really wanted it to be you!" She clung to his neck like a python.

"Of course, she may have already guessed," Bethany said, thoughtfully. "Or been *listening at her door.*" The last part was a scold but it didn't have any noticeable effect on the 12-year-old.

Davey knelt down so Abigail's feet touched the floor and his face was on the same level as hers. He held her hands and looked into her eyes.

"I think that's the nicest thing anyone ever said to me. In my whole life," Davey said to her with a warm smile.

Abigail started to hug him again but he held onto her hands and kept her in front of him. "And I promise you I will always tell you the truth about what's going on between me and your Mom, okay?" Abigail mirrored Davey's solemn expression. "But you need to give us some time, is that fair? We need to know what we're doing. Because until we know what this is, we won't have any good answers for you. Does that make sense?"

"Yeah, I suppose," Abigail said, but it really wasn't what she wanted to hear.

"In the meantime," Davey continued, "I guess we'll be spending more time together and I'm really happy about that."

"Me too!" Abigail responded, smiling again.

"Now, how about you give your mother and me a little alone-time so we can figure out how not to babble like idiots. Okay, Kiddo?"

"Okay, deal," said Abigail. "But it's not Kiddo, it's not Sportsfan and it's definitely not Pumpkin. It's *never* Pumpkin. It's Abigail."

"Deal." Davey put out his hand and Abigail shook it. "Now beat it." And Abigail ran back into her room.

"You're so good with her," Bethany said, shaking her head.

"She's a good kid. Must have a great Mom," Davey answered. "I'm heading for the shower."

166

"We're having dinner in about an hour. If you want to join us." Bethany looked at Davey with a hopeful smile.

"No... I mean I do want to but I'm not going to," Davey tried to explain. "Look, this is all brand new. If I have dinner with you tonight, then it becomes why aren't I having dinner with you tomorrow night? And the night after that. And every night? I want to be sure we're setting the right expectations."

"You're right," Bethany agreed, nodding. *"You're right."*

"Can I come over around nine?" Davey asked.

Bethany raised an eyebrow. "For a booty call?"

"No," Davey answered. "It'll give me a chance to say 'Goodnight' to Abigail and then we can sit together for a while. And if you still think it's a booty call, we can take sex off the table."

Bethany thought about that for a moment. "What if I want to put sex back on the table?"

"Then I don't want to eat off that table, literally, ever again," said Davey, flatly.

Bethany laughed, hard. Davey, too. And they were good again. She stood on her toes and kissed Davey. A great kiss. One of the 10 best kisses in the history of the world. Then she pushed him away.

"Go take a shower, stinky man." Bethany shut the door and left Davey smiling happily to himself.

• • •

When Davey arrived at Get Shorty's for the next Tuesday's Ladies Night, things had calmed down somewhat. Not normal, or even nearly normal, but maybe some sort of new normal.

There was a scattering of Bubble Talkers around the bar, which was typical. Davey decided to sit down next to Carly. "Hey," he said, by way of greeting. "Hey, stranger," Carly answered with a smile and a hug. "Davey, this is my boyfriend, Jens," Carly introduced the Nordic-looking blonde man sitting to her right.

"Hallo," said Jens, shaking Davey's hand. He had a bushy blonde beard and bright blue eyes.

"Jens is from Holland," Carly offered without further explanation.

"Only now, I am from the Florida Keys," Jens added with a smile. "Such a beautiful place to be from."

"Glad to have you," Davey said, as though citizenship in the Keys were his to convey. And then to Carly, "Thanks for getting me home the other night." He shrugged; he didn't want to make a big deal of it.

"We take care of our own," Carly announced, firmly. They smiled and raised their glasses. Jorge had already brought Davey his first beer, just as if he had never had any other drink in his life. At that precise moment, Davey could have hugged him.

Greg and Mark were nowhere to be seen. Things seemed to be more normal every minute.

"Back on beer, huh?" Binky was like black mold: he wasn't there and then, suddenly, he was. "Well, that's okay, I guess." Still Binky even as his aberrant self was normal in a way.

Davey wondered what Bethany was doing but then quickly tried to put her out of his mind. They had agreed to keep things as they were and that's what he was trying to do. Davey went to Happy Hour alone, always had, and anyway Bethany had Abigail to take care of. She couldn't go gallivanting off to the bars whenever the spirit moved her.

So, this was good: a vestige of Davey's prior life in the Keys preserved for the present and future.

Still, he wondered if her hair was up in a ponytail or splayed around her shoulders, reflecting the light like a shimmering wave whenever she turned her head.

"Davey Jones, you motherless missing trope!" Di had arrived. "Why you don't bring that cute girlfriend of yours over here? Why you hide her away like a selfish fuck?"

Di was loud enough for the people in Tavernier to hear him.

"I told you, she's a friend. She isn't my girlfriend." Davey felt slightly unfaithful the moment he'd said it. He'd never had to lie to anyone down here before. Why was he suddenly on the defensive now?

"Well, if she isn't maybe she should be." It was Carly. Davey looked at her, questioningly. "I have eyes," she said. "I wasn't that drunk."

This was getting out of control. Things needed to get back on track and now.

"You have any more mouthy divemasters on your boat this week?" Davey asked Carly. Di signaled Jorge and got the first of what would certainly be many Captain and tonics.

"Not this week," answered Carly. "We've had other issues but not that specific one."

"I had a deaf student this week," Jens volunteered.

"Really?" said Davey, genuinely interested. "How'd that go?"

"Pretty good, actually," Jens recalled. "His dive buddy could hear and she signed for him. Once we had the dive signals learned, it was pretty easy underwater."

"I knew a deaf instructor years ago," said Carly. "And when he taught deaf students, they could do the entire briefing underwater. They never had to surface and they got much more underwater time. It was crazy. They turned a disability into an advantage."

"That makes sense," Davey agreed. He liked this better. Let's talk about diving and not ask about girlfriends, real or imagined.

But he couldn't help being a little curious about whether Bethany was wearing one of those skintight, scoop-neck tops that showed off her body so well, or an oversized man's shirt that made her look tiny and vulnerable. And incredibly cute. So cute he could barely look at her without wanting to—

"Buy me a drink! Or I buy you a drink!" How long had Di been talking? Davey wasn't sure. Had Di noticed he wasn't listening?

What the hell was going on?

Davey nodded to Jorge, who brought the captain another Captain.

The band was playing and a few desultory tourists were dancing in the light of the setting sun. Nothing like Jimmy Buffet cover bands to bring out the inner islander in the New Jersey crowd.

"So, what name did you say, that cute girl of yours?" Di wanted to know now. Davey couldn't make it stop.

"Why aren't you dancing?" Davey asked Di. "I thought Greek men all love to dance. You should be out there impressing the tourists, not sitting here annoying me."

"I left Greece when I was sixteen," said Di, as if that explained everything.

"So, you never learned to dance, really?" Jens asked.

"The Syrtaki? Every Greek knows the Syrtaki," Di asserted. "We're born knowing it. Is very simple anyway."

"Teach it to me," said Jens, joyfully. "I always wanted to do it."

"Who am I, Zorba?" asked Di. "This music is no good anyway."

"It has a beat. It has timing," Jens insisted. "What is the word... tempo! With tempo, you can do any dance. Come on, show me."

"You think I can't?" Di it took up as a challenge. "I show you something, you can bet!"

Carly was amused and eager to cause more trouble. "I think Davey should go, too. It was his idea."

"That's a hard no," Davey insisted.

"Yes, Davey, too. You cannot say no," Jens declared. Davey was pretty sure he could say no and, what's more, he thought not getting up from his seat would be pretty effective, as well.

But Di and Jens picked him up under his arms and carried him along with them until the three of them stood in a line on the dance floor, arms on each other's shoulders, facing Carly.

A few of the other dancers moved slightly, clearly annoyed by the intrusion.

"Okay, we go half speed," instructed Di. "Slide right one step. Stand. Pause. Slide left one step. Stand." With Di in the center, Jens and Davey on the sides, watching Di, the three of them moved with him. They did the steps a couple of times.

They were an improbable sight but not altogether ridiculous.

"Now forward, on your right leg and slap the floor," Di commanded. "*Opa!*" Davey and Jens were younger and in good shape but it was nothing short of a miracle that Di could do this without falling over. And yet, he did. When dancing, Di was as light on his feet as a teenager.

"Now backward one step, kick the right leg forward. Right leg, *your other right!* That's good. Backwards one step, kick the left leg forward. Cross steps turning right then left, one, two, back to the starting position and repeat."

The three of them repeated the steps, getting more relaxed each time. They weren't bad. "Slap hands!" Di called out. He spun to the right and high fived Davey with his left hand. He spun to the left and high fived Jens with his right. "*Opa!*"

"Now again!" They repeated the entire routine. Most of the tourists were drifting off the dance floor. Carly was almost doubled over with laughter and the rest of Bubble Talk had stopped talking to watch. To gape might be a more accurate description.

The band gave up on Jimmy Buffet and the base player started plucking out the Zorba theme. How on earth did he know that?

"From here you do many, many variations," Di instructed. "Step, slide, knee." Following Di's lead, Jens and Davey went down on their right knee. Up, other direction, down on their left knee.

"If we were in my village tavern, the floor would be covered with broken dishes by now." Di looked like a man transported. He moved effortlessly, having returned to the land of his youth and memory.

The keyboard player picked up the melody, slow and insistent. These guys were real musicians! What the hell were they doing at Get Shorty's? The three dancers repeated the routine, a little faster.

Suddenly, an olive-skinned woman in her mid-40s jumped up and joined the end of the dance line next to Jens. She didn't need to follow Di; she knew the steps and danced instinctively, with confidence. Di watched her with sudden fascination.

"You know this dance, my darling mystery woman?" Di asked.

"I do," she answered with a sly smile.

"From the old country?" Di prompted.

"Piraeus," she answered. Without missing a beat, Di disengaged his arm from Jens and pushed the Dutchman away. "Beat it. *Beat it!*" he hissed.

Jens drifted to the side then went back to the bar.

Di raised his chin at Davey, indicating the bar. *"Go away!"* he instructed.

"What?" Davey asked. "Wait… what?"

"If I wanted to dance with men, I'd have stayed in Greece," Di whispered harshly.

Davey disengaged and Di locked onto the dancing woman before Davey was two steps away. "You think you can keep up with me?" Di challenged. "I am Di; I am a Greek god!"

"Bring it, Dionysus, if you think you're man enough," answered the woman with a grin.

Davey wandered back to the bar where Carly and Jens sat, laughing and clapping. "You guys were great!" Carly gushed, which was pretty much out of character for her.

Di and the woman were running through their steps at a much faster tempo. The band stayed right with them. How? How were they doing that?

Davey smiled. He wished Bethany were here to see this.

Okay, that's enough! This was getting ridiculous. What the hell, anyway? They weren't teenagers. This butterflies-in-the-stomach nonsense was for high-school kids.

"So, I understand you and Jerry at Scuba Doo are becoming friends," Carly said, bringing Davey back to the present.

"We know each other," Davey agreed. "Not real close, I guess."

"I was in Publix the other day," Binky interrupted. "And I seen Jerry stocking shelves."

"Stocking shelves? That doesn't sound right," Davey said, shaking his head.

"He took off when he seen me but I *know'd* it was him," Binky asserted. Davey was absorbing this when Carly spoke again.

"I heard yesterday that the husband of the dead diver is suing for negligence," she said. "Court date is set for next month."

"I'm sorry to—"

"—Well, that's the final nail in his coffin!" Binky declared.

"*Binky, shut the fuck up!*" Davey exploded. He felt bad as soon as he said it. The little man's face registered shock then he looked hurt, pathetic actually. "Sorry... just..." Davey apologized, holding his hands up. "Just stop, okay?" Binky lowered his eyes and pouted.

Carly and Jens stared at Davey. "It's not going to go well for him," Carly said. "He was way out of standards."

"It's just a damn shame all the way around," Davey said finally. "I guess we all knew it was coming, though."

"Pretty much," agreed Carly. "Someone's got to take the blame."

Right, thought Davey, that's all that matters. Someone to take the blame.

Davey nodded. "Well, look I'm outta here," Davey said. "Great to see you." He hugged Carly. "Jens, nice to meet you. Welcome to the Keys." They shook hands.

Davey signaled Jorge for his tab. He'd only had two beers.

Davey paid it, handed Jorge a folded five-dollar bill, and waved to Carly and Jens. As a conciliatory gesture, he slapped Binky on the shoulder. Then he walked out of the tiki bar.

Di and his dancing woman were still at it, as if locked in some kind of mortal combat.

The evening air was cool and smelled slightly of the ocean.

It was just after sunset when Davey knocked on Bethany's door. He heard her footsteps running up.

"Hey," Bethany said. "I wasn't expecting you."

"Neither was I," Davey admitted. "Is it okay? I don't want to invade your space?"

"I don't need space from you," she said as she hugged Davey around the waist. "We're watching Brave, if you want to join us."

"Love to," Davey said.

When Davey sat down next to Bethany, Abigail hardly seemed to notice, she was so intent on the movie. But after a minute, she crawled across both their laps without taking her eyes off the TV until she was sitting next to Davey. She scootled close to him and tucked her shoulders under his arm.

Sitting between the two of them, Davey understood that his attempt to minimize the change in his life was a total failure.

Still, he wasn't as upset as he thought he ought to be. In fact, he wasn't upset at all. Abigail was just doing what came naturally. She liked Davey; there was no calculation in it. Kids were like that.

And her unaffected affection touched him in a place that had been dormant for a while. Years, in fact.

As for Bethany, well, no one could be less calculating than she was. She wore her heart on her sleeve. This was almost… almost too easy.

When Abigail went to bed and they were alone on the couch together, Bethany said, "I thought you were going to hang out at Get Shorty's tonight."

"I did. I left early. The whole time I was there, I was thinking of you. And wanting to be here," he said softly.

Bethany snuggled in a little closer. "That must have been awful for you," she commiserated.

"You're enjoying this," Davey said, accusingly.

"Not the worst day of my life," Bethany answered with a smile.

Davey pressed his face into Bethany's hair, breathing her scent and feeling the silky strands against his cheeks. "Yeah," he said, "mine either."

"Once Abigail's asleep, we can go over to your place if you want," Bethany offered.

"You sure it's okay?" Davey asked.

"I'm sure."

Bethany put her arms around Davey's neck and gave him a slow, deep kiss. It was a good kiss. Even though Davey knew that at that very moment that he was kissing his carefully constructed, anonymous life in Key Largo goodbye. Gone forever. Bye, bye.

Still, it was a great kiss.

I have a girlfriend, Davey thought to himself. How did that even happen? After all the years, all the pain, all the denial. After all the isolation and purposeful distancing. I have a girlfriend and I don't even feel like packing my bags and running away into the night.

I have a girlfriend.

Chapter 14

"Look up the word 'deader' in the dictionary," Davey told Larry.

Larry looked puzzled. "I don't think 'deader' is a word," he said.

"Exactly," Davey agreed. "Which is why when you initiate the rescue of a non-responsive diver, you simply can't make things worse. Because in all likelihood, that diver is already dead."

Larry tried to process what he'd just heard.

"You can't make them deader," Davey concluded.

Larry was taking the Rescue Diver course. From his paperwork, Davey knew he was 45 years old and he lived in Miami. Larry had nearly 100 dives in his logbook and now he'd decided to take his skills to the next level.

Larry was a fit and avid scuba diver with curly, brown hair, piercing eyes, and an inquisitive mind.

They'd started that morning with the classroom session for Emergency First Responder (EFR) and First Aid Provider.

"The thing that differentiates Rescue from the courses you've already taken is that, for the first time, we're training you to look outside of yourself," Davey had told him. "Open Water and Advanced Open Water focus on making you a better diver. Those are inward-looking courses. Rescue increases your situational awareness. It focuses on learning how to spot an emergent situation and to intervene, if you choose to do so. It's an outward-looking course."

The classroom session had covered bleeding wounds, CPR, providing oxygen and using an Automated External Defibrillator (AED). Now they were practicing in-water scenarios at the lagoon.

The lagoon was Key Largo Undersea Park, a curtained-off section of one of the canals that was used as training facility for both confined and open-water dives.

The lagoon had training platforms at various depths, downlines attached to the bottom, and hoops to swim through. Its deepest depth was 25 feet. The water was dark and silty, like a quarry, but it was warm and comfortable, and provided an excellent training site.

On arrival, Davey had pointed out the location of the lifeguard ring, the closet where emergency oxygen was stored and the exit points from the water.

Greg was acting as the "rescue dummy" for the course and while they were setting up their dive kits, he fell off the seawall into the water and started to drown.

Larry looked at Greg, then at Davey.

"What are you going to do about that?" Davey asked.

Larry thought for a moment but didn't move.

"You're a rescue diver. What's your plan?" Davey prodded.

"Do I jump in?" he asked.

"Do you?" Davey asked in return.

Larry took a step toward the edge. "I'm jumping in," he said.

Davey held his arm. "No fins, no mask, no air. He'll drown you as well as himself."

Larry stopped and thought some more.

"He's drowning," Davey prompted.

"Should I put on my fins and mask?" Larry asked, getting a little anxious.

"Should you?" Davey asked.

"I'm putting on my fins and mask," Larry said, turning to grab his equipment. Again, Davey grabbed his arm.

"What is your very first course of action?" Davey asked.

Greg was doing an excellent job of drowning right in front of them. Occasionally he yelled, "Pizza!" because no one wants you yelling "Help!" during an exercise, even to add verisimilitude.

Larry looked around and his eye landed on the lifeguard ring.

"I throw him a floatation device, if available," Larry stated.

"Go do it," Davey agreed.

Larry ran to the lifeguard ring, yanked it off the fence and got ready to throw it.

"Talk to him. Tell him what to do," Davey suggested.

Larry threw the ring. It landed behind Greg. "Grab the rope and pull yourself to the ring," Larry ordered. Greg continued to splash.

"Grab the rope!" Larry yelled. Greg looked around.

"Talk him through it," Davey said.

"Grab the rope. And pull yourself to the ring!" Larry boomed.

Greg pulled the rope until he was hugging the ring, floating on top of it. Larry started pulling in the line.

"Where are you taking him? Is he climbing up the wall right here?" Davey asked.

Larry looked for the closest exit from the water and walked toward the stairs.

"Keep him engaged," Davey said. "You need to control the situation."

"I'm bringing you in. Are you okay?" No response from Greg. "Are you okay!" Larry boomed.

"Yeah. Yeah, I'm good," Greg answered, out of breath.

Larry pulled the line to the edge of the steps leading into the water.

Greg put both his feet on the bottom step and then raised one hand for Larry to pull him up. "Thanks," Greg said. "Thanks, man."

Larry grabbed Greg's outstretched hand. Greg tightened his grip, kicked back and pulled Larry headfirst into the water.

Davey chuckled. They all fall for that one. "Okay, guys, good job. Come on up and let's talk about it."

They sat next to their dive kits while Davey briefed the session.

"The most dangerous thing you will ever encounter in the ocean is not a shark. It's not a sea snake. It's a panicked diver," Davey said. "Never, ever trust a panicked diver. Keep your distance, maintain control of the situation, and always have a backup plan."

Larry looked a little sheepish.

"Don't be embarrassed," Davey said with a smile. "We fool everyone at first. Because they always assume the person in trouble will assist with their own rescue. But they won't. A panicked person won't make rational decisions. They'll kill you both if they can."

Once they were in the water, they practiced the self-rescue methods and tired-diver tows. Then they began the individual skills.

Again, Greg pretended to panic at the surface.

Larry approached him but kept his distance. "Diver, are you okay?" he called. "Diver, are you okay?"

"He's not okay," Davey suggested.

"You need to calm down," Larry called out. "Focus on me and listen to what I say."

Greg shot forward and tried to grab Larry, but Larry had his legs pointed toward Greg and he was able to kick backwards in time. Good, thought Davey, that was good.

"Diver, listen to me! I'm trying to help but you need to calm down," Larry entreated him. Greg kept flailing.

"What do I do if he doesn't calm down?" asked Larry.

"There's no rush," Davey said. "Let him drown a little bit."

Larry looked at Davey, startled.

"You control the situation," Davey added. "Never get within grabbing distance of a panicked diver who still has energy. He can't keep this up forever. Let him wind down."

Obligingly, Greg began to show fatigue. His arms stopped flailing.

"Diver, can you hear me?" Larry asked. Greg didn't answer.

"Diver, inflate your BCD!" Larry commanded. Greg didn't.

Larry circled around Greg, while continuing to stay out of his reach. Greg didn't move and Larry got behind him.

"That's good," encouraged Davey.

In one quick motion, Larry grabbed Greg's tank stem and pulled it back, while placing his knee in the small of Greg's back. Now Greg had no leverage. Larry inflated Greg's BCD and got him floating on his back.

"I got you," Larry offered soothingly. "You're okay. I got you."

"Okay, great. That was perfect," Davey applauded.

Greg went back to floating upright and the three of them bobbed on the surface.

"Nice work," Davey said. "You kept out of reach. You engaged the diver. You modified your plan in real-time based on circumstances. And you controlled the situation. You tagged every base."

They descended to the bottom of the lagoon.

At 25 feet underwater, Greg pretended to become disoriented and began to thrash around, raising silt off the bottom. Larry got to him quickly, yanked his BCD strap hard to get his attention and made eye contact. He pulled him out of the silt and brought him over to a rock where he could hold on.

Davey gave the OK signal.

When they were back on the surface, Davey continued the briefing. "Always remember that your voice can have a calming effect so narrate the entire rescue effort. 'I'm Larry. What's your name? I'm inflating your BCD. We're headed back to the boat now.' Talk to the other people, too. 'I've got a tired diver. I'm bringing him back to the boat. Throw me a line!' Whatever."

This was actually one of the hardest things for people to grasp. Most got the skills down okay but they were reluctant to maintain a dialog, which was critical to the process.

"When you're narrating, you're controlling the situation. It puts you in charge. Don't worry about whether you're the most qualified person or not. If you've got a diver in the water that you're rescuing, you're in charge."

Larry nodded, not totally convinced but getting there.

"So, you get the diver back to the boat and another diver says, 'Hey, I'm his dive buddy. I'll take it from here.' What do you do?"

This caught Larry completely off-guard.

"Um... ask if he's a rescue diver, I guess."

"Nope. This is no time for a conversation."

"Well, if he seems very sure... if they have a relationship," Larry was stumbling.

"No time for that. You're in charge; you stay in charge," Davey said flatly.

"But... what do I tell his dive buddy?" Larry was really concerned.

"Don't get into a debate with him. Give him a job," Davey instructed.

"Not sure I understand."

"You be the dive buddy. I just brought your friend up the ladder."

"Okay, thanks, I'll take it from here. I'm his dive buddy."

"Great, get his dive gear, okay? It's right next to the swim platform."

"Okay, I got the gear, now I want to take over again."

"Thanks, that was terrific. Check and make sure the gear is secure, okay?"

"Did that."

"What's your friend's name?"

"Ah… I don't know. *Bob!*"

"Is Bob here with his family? Is there anyone on shore waiting for him?"

Larry stopped and thought about what Davey was doing.

"Meanwhile, I'm continuing the rescue and I'm still in charge," Davey instructed.

"Got it," Larry acknowledged. "That's really clever."

"If the boat captain, the mate, or one of the instructors employed by the dive shop offers to take over, let them. But not one of the other guests. *Ever.* You don't have time to assess their qualifications. It's your rescue. You're in charge."

"Seems like I'm in charge an awful lot," Larry demurred.

"The moment you're not in charge, chaos will occur. On your watch."

That was a sobering thought. "Do I have any liability here?" Larry asked.

"No, you're protected by the Good Samaritan laws as long as you're operating within the limits of your training."

"Good to know," Larry seemed somewhat mollified.

"You're under no obligation to become involved in a rescue. None whatsoever. But once you do, keep going up to the limits of your training. When that runs out, stop."

"Wow. That's a lot of responsibility," Larry mused.

"What's the worst that could happen?" Davey asked.

"Well, I suppose… he could die?"

"That's why I told you to look up 'deader' in the dictionary."

"Right. I get your point." Larry nodded.

"If he dies, he was going to die anyway. You didn't kill him. You just failed to bring him back to life."

Larry considered this carefully.

"With an unresponsive diver, your chance of success is maybe one in 20. One in 30. There's nothing to be afraid of. You can't make it worse."

The next exercise was rescuing an unresponsive diver at the surface. This exercise combined some of the previous skills they'd already covered. Greg floated face down on the surface as Larry approached, cautiously.

Larry splashed some water over Greg. "Diver, are you okay?"

No response.

"Diver!" Larry splashed some more water. "Are you okay?"

Larry crossed Greg's arms and rolled him onto his back. He inflated Greg's BCD fully, so he floated high on the water.

Larry quickly removed Greg's mask and regulator, and listened for breathing. Hearing none, he pretended to administer two "rescue breaths." That consisted of raising Greg's chin from his chest to clear the airway, holding his nose closed and doing mouth-to-mouth resuscitation.

"I have an unresponsive diver here!" Larry called out to the imaginary boat crew. Davey smiled. He was learning.

"I'm bringing him in. Throw me a line!" Larry called.

On a count of five, he faked another rescue breath. Then he reached down to undo Greg's main BCD buckle.

"Do the shoulder straps first," Davey instructed.

Larry unclipped one of Greg's shoulder straps.

"Maintain that five count," Davey reminded him.

On the count of five, Larry faked another rescue breath. He tried the second shoulder strap but his finger slipped. He struggled to get it unclipped.

"Watch your five count," Davey advised.

Larry faked another rescue breath. Then he tried the second should strap again and it unclipped.

"Now the main buckle but not the cummerbund," Davey counseled.

"Okay, I've got the line. Pull me in!" Larry instructed the imaginary mate. Davey ended the exercise.

"That's good. Well done," Davey said. "Do you know why I had you do the shoulder straps first?"

"No," Larry admitted.

"Once you undo the main buckle and cummerbund, the diver's going to slip off his BCD and you lose a lot of floatation. But it's very hard to get him out of his shoulder straps at that point. So, you undo everything else first, then do the cummerbund last, when you're ready to pull him onshore or up onto the boat."

"Makes sense," Larry agreed.

"It's a lot, isn't it?" Davey commiserated.

"Yeah, it sure is," Larry said with a smile.

"Well, tomorrow we're doing the whole thing in the ocean and there will be even more to think about. So run everything through your mind tonight, while you're relaxing."

"I will," Larry promised.

"You're gonna sleep soundly tonight, I promise you."

Davey's prediction turned out to be completely accurate.

The next morning *Calypso* headed to Elbow Reef to complete the Rescue course. Mark had eight snorkelers in his group. Greg was still the rescue dummy.

Davey intentionally left out some details from the boat briefing.

He sat down next to Larry. "You ready for this?" Davey asked.

Larry nodded. "Yeah, I think so," he answered.

"Good, now tell me where the emergency oxygen, man-overboard ring and throwable buoy are?"

Larry was silent. He looked around.

"You can't rescue anyone if you don't know where the rescue equipment is stored," Davey instructed. "If you're serious about being a rescue diver, you need to know those things before you get in the water."

"Wasn't that supposed to be in the boat briefing?" Larry asked, plaintively.

"It was supposed to be. But it wasn't."

Larry looked undecided. "If you don't hear the information you need in the briefing, ask," Davey said finally. Davey stood up.

"Okay guys, *guys*, if I can have your attention again for a moment, a couple of things I forgot in the boat briefing. We have emergency oxygen and first aid in the V-berth. All of the crew–– and Larry, our newest Rescue Diver––are trained in it use. And we have a man-overboard ring attached to the railing up on the flybridge. If you see someone fall overboard, point and shout. Do not jump overboard to save them. Keep pointing until one of the crew throws the life ring to the person in the water."

Davey sat down next to Larry again.

"In addition to that equipment, we have a throwable buoy on the current line, which is about 100 feet long. And up on the roof, next to the life rafts, we have an ADRU with a float on a 500-foot line. Now you know everything," Davey said.

"ADRU?" Larry looked confused.

"Asshole Diver Retrieval Unit," Davey said with a smile.

The water at Elbow Reef had mild chop but very little current. Captain Di tied off on the Hannah M Bell wreck because it had nice shallow corals for the snorkelers and it was a perfect site for the rescue course.

Javier was still attaching the bow line to the mooring ball when Greg fell off the side and started drowning.

This time, Larry didn't hesitate. He grabbed the current-line buoy from under the bench and stood on the swim platform.

"Hey swimmer, can you hear me!" he shouted to Greg.

Greg didn't respond; he just thrashed around in the water.

"I'm throwing you a line. *Grab the line!*" Larry yelled.

Larry threw the buoy and it landed just behind Greg's head.

"Grab the line!" Larry instructed. Greg didn't.

Larry quickly put on his fins and jumped in the water. He swam toward Greg, who was winding down now.

"Grab the line," Larry instructed, still about 10 feet away from Greg.

Greg grabbed the line and pulled till he reached the buoy. He clutched it.

"Great. Now hold onto the buoy. We're going to pull you to the boat," Larry said, still keeping his distance from Greg.

"Pull him in!" Larry yelled to Davey. "We got you, buddy," he narrated to Greg. "Just hold on. We got you." Davey pulled in the current line.

As Greg and then Larry climbed the ladder onto the boat, Mark's snorkel group applauded. Davey smiled.

"Impressive," Davey said to Larry. "It's getting harder and harder to fool you."

Once Mark's snorkel group was in the water, Davey and Larry put on their dive kits. Greg had already geared up and disappeared over the side.

"Okay, I just came back to the boat and announced that I lost my dive buddy," Davey told Larry. "The last time I saw him, we were near the mooring line. I looked around for a minute and couldn't find him so I surfaced. He wasn't there and we don't see bubbles."

"Got it," said Larry.

"Of course, there actually are bubbles because otherwise Greg would drown," Davey added with a smile. "But you need to set up a search as if there are no bubbles."

Davey and Larry splashed in and Davey followed Larry to the mooring line. Visibility was good, about 50 feet. Larry began to swim a circular search pattern around the mooring line, swimming up and over coral ridges looking for Greg.

After a five-minute search, they found Greg lying face down behind a coral head. Larry shook Greg's wrist. No response. He checked to see if the regulator was in place (which of course it was) and looked inside Greg's mask to see if his eyes were open.

Holding Greg's BCD strap with his right hand and keeping Greg's regulator in place with his left hand, Larry started for the surface.

Davey swam slow circles around both of them to observe.

As they ascended, Larry vented air from his and Greg's BCDs to avoid positive buoyancy and control the ascent. One foot per second, Davey noticed. Perfect.

At the surface, Larry inflated Greg's BCD and positioned him on his back. *"I have an unresponsive diver!"* he shouted to Javier.

Larry removed Greg's mask and regulator and checked for breathing. He faked two rescue breaths and towed Greg toward the boat.

"Throw me a line!" Larry called to Javier. Javier threw the current line and buoy. Larry grabbed it

"Watch your five count," Davey suggested.

Larry faked another rescue breath.

As Javier pulled the line toward the boat, Larry unsnapped Greg's shoulder straps. He stayed right on his five count.

At the swim platform, Larry undid Greg's main buckle and cummerbund and slipped the dive kit off to the side.

"Grab his dive kit for me, will you?" Larry commanded.

"Got it," said Davey. He was still holding Greg's mask. "What method are you going to use to get him on the boat?"

"I think I can manage the ladder carry," Larry answered.

"Do it," Davey agreed.

"I'm going to need the O2 and the AED!" Larry shouted to Javier.

Larry carried Greg up the ladder and performed simulated CPR and defibrillation flawlessly.

From start to finish, the combined scenario took 35 minutes.

"Well, what do you think?" asked Larry, when it was finished.

"I think he's dead," Davey said, but on Larry's disappointed look he added, "But you did everything perfectly."

"Thanks," Larry said.

"You have to set your expectations," Davey advised. "This diver was missing and presumed unresponsive for 10 minutes before you found him. It took another 12 minutes to get him on the boat and begin CPR. A guy who's down for 22 minutes isn't coming back."

Larry nodded, shrugged. "Then why do we do all this?"

"Because sometimes miracles happen," Davey answered.

Later that morning, when they were heading back to the dock, Larry asked, "So what do I do now?"

"Now," answered Davey, "you remember everything you've learned and hope like hell you never have to save use any of it."

Chapter 15

Abigail knitted her eyebrows and pushed out her lower lip.

Abruptly, she served the volleyball and it sailed into the opponent's court. A girl in the back row stopped the ball, hitting it upwards. A second girl in the back row tapped the ball softly toward the tall girl in front of her, who spiked it across the net, hard.

But a girl in front on Abigail's team was waiting for it and she blocked it back over the net. Two of the opponent's players collided going for the ball and Abigail's team won the point.

The parents cheered. There weren't that many of them but they made up for it with enthusiasm.

Davey sat in the bleachers watching the play. Abigail was bigger than most of the other girls and a lot stronger. She still had a bit of tomboyishness about her while the other girls looked like they were starting to experiment with make-up and boys.

There weren't many dads at the game. It was mostly stay-at-home moms, and they watched the game and watched Davey with just about equal attention and about the same level of competitiveness.

Davey could see a lot of Bethany in Abigail. Same eyes, for one thing. Same chin. Abigail's hair was darker and she hadn't grown into her features yet but someday she'd most likely be a beautiful woman, just like her beautiful mother.

Davey had no idea what Abigail's father looked like. Bethany never spoke about him except to say he was a druggie and an alcoholic, and to hint that he might have been abusive at times.

But as far as Davey could see, her father was as absent from her genes as he had been from her life.

The volleyball game wasn't evenly matched. Abigail's team owned the other side but they were graceful winners, shaking hands and slapping shoulders as if it had been a close contest. As the teams ambled to the sidelines, Davey walked down the bleacher seats like steps to congratulate Abigail.

"Great win!" he told the grinning girl. "You killed them."

"Davey!" Abigail hugged Davey around the waist, which got the attention of at least two of the mothers. "This is Brittany. And Chelsea. My two best buds!" Abigail gushed.

The two girls smiled shyly at Davey. "Hi best buds!" he greeted them. As if by magic, two mothers appeared at the girls' sides. But before they could speak, Davey heard a man's voice behind him.

"Mr. Jones, I believe, or do my eyes deceive me?" It was Ken Duplay. Davey hadn't noticed him before. "How nice to see you here cheering for your… for Abigail." His expression was what on him passed for a smile. Davey still wanted to wring his little chicken neck.

"Gotta cheer for the home team," Davey said, politely.

"Should we expect the pleasure of your company regularly at our matches?" asked Duplay.

"No promises," Davey answered. "Depends on my work schedule. Is there paperwork I need to do to be here?"

"No, our athletic events are open to the public. We still miss Abigail's mother, though," Duplay offered, smarmily.

"She wishes she could be here but putting food on the table takes priority," Davey said, with as much restraint as he could manage.

Duplay turned and walked away, off to spread his particular brand of sunshine somewhere else.

"I'm Crystal," said one of the mothers, putting her hand out to Davey. "Brie," said the other. Davey shook their hands. "I'm Davey."

"Davey's a friend of my Mom's," Abigail said, as if he were a world-famous rock star. "He's a dive instructor. He saved a woman's life last month!"

"Let's not make it a bigger deal than it was," Davey said, trying to avoid the subject entirely.

"Oh… I remember reading about that," said Brie.

"Me too," said Crystal. "Sounded like kind of a big deal to me."

"It was a good outcome," said Davey, as if he were talking about the weather. "A lot of people were involved, not just me."

"Davey can do anything," Abigail gushed. "He's like a superhero."

Brittany and Chelsea looked a bit skeptical but Crystal and Brie seemed to agree with Abigail. The group was all looking at Davey.

"Are all your matches easy wins?" Davey asked the girls.

"The Homestead team is pretty tough," said Chelsea.

Brittany nodded, "Yeah, they practice, like, all the time."

"We're proud of our Tornados, though," said Brie, brightly.

"Indeed, we are!" seconded Crystal.

"It was a great match," Davey agreed. "I got a few pictures for your Mom." Davey held up his smart phone.

At the mention of Bethany, Brie and Chrystal shifted slightly and looked at Davey differently. He could feel the change and it creeped him out a little.

"So, what do you guys do to celebrate a win?" he asked, changing the subject.

"Ice cream!" shouted Abigail. The other two girls nodded and their mothers smiled in agreement.

192

"Let's go," Davey responded. "I'm buying."

• • •

"Captain Rocky is driving the boat today. My name is Arnie, I'll be your first mate. And we have Davey from Captain Dan's with us today on a boarding pass. So, if you have any questions at all about anything, ask Davey."

Arnie got a laugh with that one and Davey smiled along with him.

"So, you're a celebrity here, too," said Peter, Davey's private dive guest for the morning.

"Not really," Davey answered. "He's just messing with me."

Calypso mostly went to the shallow reefs unless there was a request for the deep wrecks and enough divers to fill the boat. Peter had paid for a private tour with Davey and he'd requested to dive the *Duane*, so Davey took him on a boarding pass with *Reef Rider*.

A boarding pass was one of the ways the smaller dive shops supported each other. If one shop didn't have enough divers to send out a boat, or there was a request for site that wasn't on the schedule, the dive guide/instructor took the guest or guests on another shop's boat on a space available basis. The originating shop split the guest fee with the boat operator and the instructor rode free. Everyone got a little; no one made a fortune.

But no one made a fortune in the dive business, anyway.

Peter had booked his private tour with Davey back when the buzz about Erin's rescue was at fever pitch. He was traveling to Key Largo the following month, he had said, and he wanted Davey the Hero all to himself. It was the sort of booking that made Davey cringe but so far Peter seemed like a pretty good guy.

And he also seemed to be a knowledgeable diver.

The *USCG Duane* was a deep-water wreck, like *Spiegel Grove*, but not nearly as large. At 327 feet, she was a decent-sized vessel although not as high off the bottom, which similar to the *Spiegel Grove* site was down around 130 feet. There were three mooring lines on the *Duane* and the most popular one, amidships, tied off on the wreck at about 80 feet.

A former Coast Guard cutter, the ship was scuttled in 1987 as an artificial reef. It was heavily encrusted with coral and filled with marine life. A Goliath grouper weighing about 600 pounds was a common sight on the wreck. The *Duane* was a popular dive site, although slightly less popular than the *Spiegel Grove* because it was smaller and often had more current.

"We have less superstructure here, so there are fewer places to hide from the current," Davey briefed Peter. "The thing to remember is that the current isn't as strong if you're close to the deck or close to the wall. If you see me make this signal... " Davey pointed his right thumb down at his left palm, then changed it so his left palm was vertical. "...or this one, I'm telling you to get closer to the deck or the superstructure. Don't try to swim against the current when you're out in the water column. You'll just use more air and get tired."

Peter nodded. He seemed to understand and wasn't intimidated at the prospect. "Sometimes I may drift with the current to find a better shelter. Just follow me and do what I do." Peter nodded again.

"In the event that we get blown off the wreck," Davey looked very serious now. *"Which we do not want to do.* But if it happens, we stay together and I'll inflate my SMB." Surface Marker Buoy. "We'll use the SMB line for a safe ascent and wait on the surface to be picked up. It may be a couple of hours because the dive boat can't leave the mooring until all the other divers are aboard. So, let's not get blown off the wreck."

Davey didn't like to scare divers but he also felt that if they knew the actual risks, there was less chance of something going wrong.

"I'll just stick with you," Peter said. He seemed pretty up for it.

When they arrived at the site, there was no current at all. That's how it went sometimes. The conditions you prepare for aren't the ones you encounter. No current on the *Duane* is a rare and very welcome occurrence.

Peter and Davey splashed in off the bow, holding onto the granny line. The Corinthian offered bow entry and side ladders for exiting the water, so it was a little bit easier than *Calypso* for deep wrecks.

They pulled themselves along the granny line to the mooring ball and Davey signaled for descent. Both divers pulled themselves down the mooring line, equalizing the pressure in their ears as they descended. About half a dozen divers were ahead of them on the line and a dozen more strung out behind them.

They were on the line amidships so they encountered the wreck at 80 feet, where the funnel had once been. Dropping below to the deck, they were tucked behind the upper superstructure on the starboard side.

There was a mild current coming from the port bow. Davey signaled Peter that they would swim into it on the lee side of the wreck. Davey dropped down to the lower deck, 106 feet of depth and swam forward staying close to the deck and wall.

There was a huge loggerhead turtle sleeping in the cut-through. Davey pointed him out to Peter and took a picture.

Swimming out of the passageway, they encountered the current coming off the port bow at about eleven o'clock, a little stronger than expected. They were close to the bow, around 100 feet now. Davey swam to the port gunwale and looked over the side. A southern stingray flew lazily along the bottom heading north.

Davey signaled for Peter's air pressure. Twenty-three hundred psi was the answer. Davey checked his own and it was 2,400 psi so Peter was doing pretty well. Fourteen minutes NDL time remaining.

Davey swam out over the sea bottom, hovering at 100 feet, and let the current carry him toward the stern. The drift was slightly toward the wreck so getting to shelter would not be a problem. Peter and Davey glided slowly astern and Davey ducked behind the superstructure once they were abaft of the radar tower.

Swimming over to the starboard side just at the gunwale, Davey pointed out three bull sharks swimming lazily along the bottom. Peter gave the OK signal. A shadow passed overhead and Davey turned just in time to see the Goliath grouper passing slowly above their heads from the stern in the direction of the radar tower.

A 600-pound grouper is a really big fish. Davey got a shot of Peter with the Goliath grouper just behind and above him. That would be a keeper, for sure!

Eight minutes of NDL time at 106 feet. Davey signaled Peter for his air pressure. Fourteen hundred psi. But just to be safe, Davey checked Peter's gauge. Fourteen hundred was right. Davey had 1,600 psi. They swam up to the superstructure deck at 90 feet and got back six more minutes of NDL time.

Davey swam up to the wheelhouse on the starboard side and swam through. Peter followed. Coming out on the port side, Davey drifted aft and checked Peter's air behind the superstructure. He was at 1100 psi. Davey shot a picture of the radar tower against the sunlight on the surface and signaled to Peter to go up. They ascended to the mooring line above their heads.

Davey didn't have to tell Peter to fully inflate his BCD at the surface or to take off his fins before he climbed the ladder.

"Good skills," said Davey when they were back onboard the *Reef Rider.* "Thanks." The compliment didn't surprise Peter.

"You've been diving a while," Davey observed.

"Yeah, a few years," was the answer. "I had still 10 minutes NDL time when we started up," Peter observed.

"But you had 1,000 psi when we got on the line," Davey answered. "That's our benchmark for ascent. NDL time won't do you any good without air."

Peter nodded. "How long have you been a dive instructor in the Keys, Davey?" he asked.

"About five years now," Davey answered.

"I imagine you've seen a lot in that time. I mean, a lot of different circumstances and conditions," Peter probed.

"I've been through a few things," Davey smiled.

"Must have stories to tell," Peter added, hopefully.

"I don't really tell stories," Davey said, guardedly. Red flags were starting to pop up.

"Come on, sure you don't want to share?" Peter prodded.

"I really don't," Davey answered. "Here, let me switch over your tank for the next dive." Peter moved out of the way and Davey turned off the air valve and bled the regulator.

"Can you tell me, in your own words, about the time last month when you resuscitated that diver?" Peter asked directly.

Davey looked straight at him. "Nope," he said, flatly.

"Why not? I'd be very interested," said Peter.

Davey finished switching over Peter's tank and started on his own. "Because I think you're a reporter, which you've neglected to tell me."

"Miami-Herald," Peter admitted. "I wasn't being dishonest. Sometimes you learn more if people don't know who you are."

"How is that not being dishonest?" Davey asked.

"It's not like we're the police. We don't need to identify ourselves," Peter was becoming defensive.

"And I don't need to talk to you," Davey answered. He finished switching his tank and unzipped his wetsuit.

"It'd be a good story. Very upbeat and positive. Most people enjoy a little good publicity," Peter pushed.

"Guess I'm not most people," Davey said.

"Katherine would probably like some positive press. Be good for the business," Peter persisted. He'd said Katherine but he probably meant Kate.

"You want to write a story about diving at Captain Dan's, how we treat our guests, what I'm like as a dive guide, I'll answer any question you got," Davey said, finally.

"That's not a story," said Peter.

"Neither am I," said Davey. And that was that. Stalemate.

"We've got a one-hour surface interval before our second dive," said Davey. "You'll be a lot warmer if you take off that wetsuit, at least down to your waist. Right now, your body is losing a lot of heat trying to warm a cold wetsuit, which it can't do."

Davey looked at Peter, shook his head and bit his lip.

"I'll be up on the bow in the sunshine," Davey said.

When Davey got back to the shop, he rinsed his gear and hung it up to dry. Kate was sitting in her space near the front door.

"How did it go today?" Kate asked without looking up.

"Did you know he was a reporter?" Davey asked her, flatly.

"I'm sorry, what?" Kate asked. She stopped what she was doing and looked at Davey.

"Did you know that Peter was a reporter with the *Miami-Herald*?" Davey asked again. "Was this whole thing a set up?"

"I don't know what you're talking about," Kate answered. She seemed genuinely confused. "What the hell happened?"

"Would it kill you to help us get a little good press?" Katherine shouted from her repair bench. "There's a lot of people from Miami come down to the Keys."

So, Peter *had* meant Katherine. Well, that answered that.

"If this happens again, I'll be looking for a new dive shop," Davey said, bluntly, and he walked out the door.

"What the *hell* did you do?" he heard Kate yell back to Katherine.

But before Katherine could answer, Davey was halfway to his car.

• • •

Davey signed for the registered letter and stared at the letterhead as he closed his front door. It was from the same lawyer in Kenosha who had sent the document from Patricia five years ago.

This time it wasn't a notarized legal form with a post-it note; it was a letter from the lawyer himself, William R. Lockwood, Esq. The letter said Mr. Lockwood, Esquire had important business with Mr. Jones that really shouldn't be conducted over the telephone. If Mr. Jones would be so kind as to come to Kenosha, Mr. Lockwood, Esquire felt sure that he, Mr. Jones, would agree it was worthwhile.

It was the sort of lawyerly formality Davey hated but since it obviously concerned Patricia, whom Davey had not heard from in over five years, he decided to go and find out what was happening.

Davey needed to take three days off since he couldn't fly for 18 hours after diving, and he actually preferred to make it 24 hours. Decompression sickness was nothing to mess around with. Kenosha was a pretty short ride from O'Hare Airport in Chicago and Davey arrived at the lawyer's office at 2:30 PM, the agreed upon time.

It was a nice enough office suite, unassuming, situated in a low-rise professional building overlooking a storm-water pond. Davey was ushered into the inner office by a bleached-blonde secretary (they still called them secretaries in Kenosha), who announced:

"Mister Lockwood, this is Mister Jones," and promptly left.

William R. Lockwood, Esquire was around 35 years old and Davey quickly sized him up as a country-club kid who'd gone to good schools and now made a decent living doing as little as possible. There was a tennis racquet next to the bookshelves. A golfing award hung on the office wall next to his diploma.

"Mister Jones, Will Lockwood," the young man said affably, rising to shake Davey's hand. He was comfortably dressed with a light sweater and an open collar shirt. He had a kind face with a quick smile and slightly thinning hair. It was the face of a man who'd always been sheltered from life's harsh realities.

"Please," he indicated a chair for Davey to sit down. "Tell me," Lockwood asked, "what if anything have you heard from your wife over the last five years?"

"Aside from the document I received from you, nothing," Davey answered. "I assumed as much," Lockwood stated, nodding.

The lawyer put his hands on the desk on front of him. "I'm afraid it is my sad duty to inform you that your wife is dead. She died last January." Both men were silent for a minute.

"I assumed it was something like that," Davey said, finally. "I'm still not sure why I needed to come all the way up here, though."

"Yes, I'm sorry about that," Lockwood continued. "I hope you'll agree with my decision when we're done. Would it surprise you to learn that you are your wife's sole beneficiary in her Will?"

"I guess I never really thought about it," Davey answered. "Yes. But in a way, no."

"It's not a big estate, mind you. Patricia had a trust fund from her parents and in the last few years she attacked the principal several times," Lockwood said.

They were silent again. "You aren't curious as to how much there is?" Lockwood finally asked.

"Not really," said Davey, still trying to process the news. It was strange, he'd never really thought about Patricia. She had always been so competent, so sure of herself. He'd never actually wondered what became of her even though he'd seen how crushed she was.

Patricia was Patricia. She went her own way without any help from anyone. That was how it had always been. End of story.

"As I said, it's a relatively small estate," Lockwood. "After fees and recording costs, you should net around $120,000 plus change."

"Fees and recording costs…" Davey repeated, absently.

"There's probate, court costs. And my fee as executor is twenty-five percent."

"Twenty-five percent seems like a healthy bite," Davey said.

"All due respect, Mister Jones, you're not my client. Your wife is… or was," the lawyer said.

"I'm sorry, I didn't mean… What can you tell me about Patricia?" Davey asked. "I guess not much, right? I mean, you're her lawyer."

"Well, I did legal work for her but confidentiality, if that's what you're referring to, is largely left to my discretion at this level," Lockwood offered. Davey waited for him to continue.

"I didn't know Patricia well but I was, what shall I say, touched by her plight. She was so obviously broken. When we first met, she was showing early signs of alcoholism and that deepened significantly over the years. She had difficulty holding a job in spite of a brilliant mind. Even I could see that. It was really quite tragic."

Davey nodded. "What was the cause of death?"

Lockwood didn't answer right away. "Patricia took her own life, I'm afraid." He let that sink in for a moment. "Pills on top of alcohol. I guess it all just became too much for her, Mister Jones."

"Please, call me Davey. I don't know who Mister Jones is," Davey pleaded. "Are there arrangements that need to be made?"

"Everything was specified in her Will. I didn't know how to reach you so I contacted Patricia's parents," Lockwood said.

"How'd that go?" Davey asked.

"Not the way I would have expected, I won't lie," Lockwood said breathlessly. "I was… well, let's just say I was taken aback. Her father made it abundantly clear they had no further interest."

"Sounds about right," Davey agreed.

"I may owe you apology," Lockwood added, tentatively. "When Patricia first came to me, it was so obvious that she'd been hurt, terribly hurt. Under the circumstances, I may have wrongly assumed that you were at fault. But after I spoke to her father, well, I no longer have any doubts whatsoever as to where the problem lay."

Davey didn't respond. He sat, silent, as if lost in thought.

"If you're interested, Patricia was laid to rest at the cemetery in Rockford, next to her daughter."

"Next to our daughter," Davey corrected him.

"Yes, sorry… next to your daughter. In case you want to visit."

"I don't," Davey said. The lawyer remained quiet for a moment. "Sounds like you more than earned your fee," Davey added.

"I did what I could. I said that I didn't know Patricia well but I was always struck by how principled she was, even in her reduced state. I found it admirable."

Davey smiled ruefully. "She didn't have principles," he said. "She had ideals."

Lockwood frowned slightly. "That strikes me as a distinction without a difference."

"It's a huge difference," Davey said and he looked up at the lawyer.

"Principles are easy. You want to be honest, be honest. Success is guaranteed. You want to be loyal all you have to do is be loyal. You may be tempted to make exceptions but in the end, it's up to you." Davey shook his head sadly.

"Ideals on the other hand are unattainable. They're states of perfection. With ideals, you're guaranteed to be a failure your entire life." Davey fell silent.

Lockwood looked around uncomfortably. He was probably late for a tennis match and Davey was just harshing his glow.

"Well, you knew her better than I did, I suppose," Lockwood said, standing. "I'm very glad to have met you, Mist-- I mean, Davey."

The two men shook hands.

"I'm sorry I didn't contact you sooner but I had no forwarding information. Online searches produced no results until that article in the *Miami-Herald* popped up last week," Lockwood explained.

Peter had written the article anyway, with no input from Davey. There were no quotes from Kate or Katherine, and Kate swore that neither one of them had co-operated with the reporter. She didn't want to lose Davey; she was adamant. There was an exterior photo of the dive shop and interviews with the paramedics.

The fact that Davey had been an ER nurse was also included for the world to see. So that was public now. There was no mention of Stasie or Patricia; maybe they just didn't fit in with the story. But it was clear that Peter had done some research and Davey's privacy had been irrevocably shattered in the process.

Who said, "No good deed goes unpunished?" Davey's carefully constructed anonymity had been destroyed in the blink of an eye. He was a public figure now. His past life was everybody's business.

And he had a girlfriend! Part of the same continuum of events, if you really thought about it. He had obligations, and attachments, and zero privacy, and mounting expectations.

Everything he hadn't wanted.

For someone like Davey, for the person he'd tried to be over the last five years, it was a crushing defeat. Everything he'd built wiped out by a single event.

And now this! It wasn't the background noise pounding in his ears. This was something entirely different.

Davey suddenly realized that Lockwood was still talking.

"These matters are best handled in person of course but, to be honest, after speaking with Patricia's father, I really just wanted to meet you." Lockwood looked almost apologetic. "I'd be willing to reimburse your travel expenses out of my fee. Seems only fair."

"That won't be necessary," Davey replied. "Thank you, Will."

"For what?" asked Lockwood, genuinely confused.

"For being Patricia's advocate when she had no one else to turn to," Davey answered.

They shook hands again and Davey left.

Chapter 16

"I'm pretty sure I'll be better at this when we're out on the reef," Arthur said, nodding his head vehemently, as if to convince himself.

"I'm sure that's true," Davey answered, although it was a preposterous idea. If Arthur was getting freaked out by his mask in the pool, he wasn't going to suddenly get calm five miles offshore in the ocean. Sure, you'll be better on the reef. What are you, *high?*

But Davey stuck with his policy of being affirmative. They'd deal with the reef when they got there. Meanwhile Arthur and his girlfriend Trish, and their friends Ken and Pidge, were booked on a one-day Discover Scuba course and Arthur was blowing it, bigtime.

The mistake Arthur was making was not uncommon. He kept trying to breathe through his nose. You can't really breathe through your nose with a dive mask on but, to the extent that you can, you're going to be breathing in water. And choking.

"Your brain wants to do things the way it's always done them, which means it wants you to breathe through your nose," Davey explained. "So, try this. Pretend you have a cold. When you're congested, you don't walk around trying to breathe through your nose. It doesn't work. So, you breathe through your mouth. Try that."

Davey liked this explanation and he used it frequently but he couldn't really be sure if it actually worked or not. Some people overcame the problem and some didn't.

When they got to the deep end of the pool, Arthur stood up on the bottom like he was waiting for a bus. The others managed a decent neutral buoyancy hover but Arthur was either glued to the bottom or blasting to the surface. He displayed no understanding of the physics of scuba diving. The reef was going to be a goat fuck.

Of the four of them, Pidge and Ken were the most proficient. They were horizontal while swimming, they maintained neutral buoyancy and their finning technique was a thing of beauty. Trish tried to keep up with them but only succeeded in outdoing Arthur.

They were all young, probably just out of college. They were just at that point in life when you discover that the people you were friends with in school don't necessarily have anything in common with you in the real world.

On *Calypso* that afternoon, conditions were basically ideal. The ocean was calm. There was no noticeable current and the visibility was about 80 feet at Molasses Reef.

The low seas and lack of current was especially lucky since Davey needed to take his divers down the mooring line. Under adverse circumstances, they'd get exhausted swimming against the current before they even got to the line.

Davey's briefing had been specific and pointed: stay close to your buddy, stay in a group, and stay behind Davey. Slow and easy does it.

The four of them followed Davey down the mooring line, equalizing the pressure in their ears as they went. At the bottom, which was 30 feet down, a strange thing happened: three of the divers immediately swam in different directions. Davey grabbed Arthur's wrist to keep him from bolting, too.

Even with the excellent visibility, it wouldn't be long before the other divers were out of sight. Davey signaled Arthur to stay where he was and he chased after Ken, who was holding onto a coral ridge and looking under the ledge. Davey pulled his hand off the coral.

Ken looked up in surprise. Davey slapped his own hand to indicate "NO TOUCHING." (It had been in the briefing but, yeah, right.) Then he put his index fingers parallel to one another and bumped them together, asking Ken where his dive buddy was. It took a moment for the message to sink in.

Davey indicated for Ken to follow him and he swam toward Pidge, who was watching two queen angelfish swim in and out of the coral. When Davey touched her shoulder, Pidge almost jumped out of her skin. Davey made the sign for dive buddies and shrugged.

"SO, WHAT WERE YOU THINKING?" the signs asked. Davey wagged his finger at Ken and Pidge in remonstration.

He could see that Arthur was still holding onto the downline. So that was something.

Trish was about 15 feet away hovering near a coral head looking at a sleeping turtle. When she saw the other three approaching, she waved and pointed excitedly. Davey cocked his head to the side and made the buddy signal but Trish was too distracted to understand.

Davey decided it would be easier to bring Arthur to the group, so he indicated for the other three to stay where they were. Everyone agreed; they were fascinated by the turtle. And Davey swam to the mooring line to collect Arthur.

The 80-foot visibility was a two-edged sword. On the one hand, it was much easier to see and keep track of everyone in the group. On the other, they were more likely to be emboldened and not stay as close to Davey as they should.

Arthur swam alongside Davey and, for reasons beyond understanding, he was much better here than he had been at the pool. Good trim, good finning, no mask problems.

Once the group was together, Davey signaled Trish and Arthur: dive buddies, OK? They signaled OK. Ken and Pidge, dives buddies, OK? But at that moment, the turtle started swimming away and they all bolted after it. Davey finned hard to get ahead of the group.

Thank God for slow turtles! If they'd been chasing a stingray, Davey would never have seen them again. He got ahead of them, got the pictures everyone wants, and then signaled them to stop.

STOP! Both hands. They stopped. The turtle disappeared.

Time to regroup. Davey organized the dive buddies. *Again.* Indicated they should follow him. *Again.* And off they went.

The sand channel from Racetrack led to Winch Hole. With the prevailing conditions, you could see almost all the way across the large open area, which was always rich with sea life. Davey took pictures in front of the winch. A Caribbean reef shark swam lazily by, which freaked out Trish for a second but she recovered.

No one felt like chasing the shark, so that was one good thing.

A free-swimming moray eel slid out of a hole in the coral, immediately regretted its decision and swam nervously from coral to coral looking for a new place to hide. All four divers hovered like pros as the eel swam under and around them.

At 30 minutes into the dive, Davey headed back for *Calypso* with four tired and excited divers in tow. They spent the last 10 minutes under the boat and then surfaced.

"Great dive, guys!" Davey encouraged them once they were back on the boat. "I saw some things I liked down there.

The four 20-somethings were all smiles. "Thank you, Davey," said Trish. "That was so cool!"

"Yeah, thanks Davey!" said Ken.

"Arthur, I got to hand it to you. You were better on the reef than in the pool. Just like you said you would be," Davey slapped Arthur on the shoulder. Arthur beamed.

Look at them, Davey thought, so happy, so trusting. *So stupid!* What the hell were they thinking swimming off like that. First time underwater? Anything could have happened. Damn crazy kids.

"That shark was sick," said Pidge, shaking her head.

"How about the turtle. The turtle was *crazy!*" Trish gushed.

"No, what was crazy was swimming away from each other like that!" Davey was surprised as soon as he said it. That wasn't his style. He didn't go off on his students. He was affirmative.

"Yeah, I guess… " said Trish, chastened. "But--"

"--No buts!" Davey interrupted. "What if your dive buddy had an emergency? You weren't anywhere near him to help."

The smiles were gone but now Davey couldn't stop himself. Greg and Mark stopped talking to their groups and looked over at Davey.

"And you were all too far away from me! Look, you guys aren't certified. I'm responsible for the four of you underwater and three of you were more than 30 feet away from me. No one was with their dive buddy. *People die underwater!*"

Javier started singing a little reggae but his heart wasn't in it and he stopped.

"The only one who seems to have listened to my briefing at all is Arthur and he was such a basket case in the pool I almost didn't let him come out to the reef!" Now Davey knew he'd gone too far.

This was way over the line and Arthur looked stricken.

Davey couldn't understand why he'd talked to them that way. Sure, they'd been bad divers but he worked with a lot of bad divers. Now he had four sad and slightly angry people with one more dive to do and not a lot of can-do spirit between the lot of them.

Things sure had turned a corner since all the "Thank you, Davey!" comments five minutes ago.

"Anyone want a mint candy, get the saltwater taste out of your mouth?" It was Mark doing damage control. He passed a container of candy in front of everyone but no one took one.

"Let's get your gear switched over guys," said Greg, jumping in. "We're happy to do it for you but it would be good if you watched so you can learn the drill." Greg was leading a group of snorkelers today who were looking at Davey with wide eyes.

In a couple of minutes, everyone was switching gear and talking about the dive but there was a long way to go before they'd get back to happy.

Davey tried to make small talk with each of them; he knew it was his fault. He'd blown it, lost his cool. It was up to him to make it right.

But he also knew it was going to be a long boat ride home.

● ● ●

"I don't know what came over me today," Davey said, stroking the soft skin between Bethany's shoulder blades as the two of them lay beside one another in his bed.

"I'm sure it wasn't that bad. You're too hard on yourself," Bethany answered.

"It was bad," Davey insisted. "I never talk that way to students. You should have seen their faces."

"Don't obsess," Bethany said, kissing Davey lightly as she got out of bed. Davey watched as she walked, naked, toward the kitchen, her perfectly formed butt swinging like a metronome. How did I get so lucky, he thought to himself.

He heard the refrigerator door close and Bethany walked back toward the bed holding a glass of wine. Davey didn't keep any alcohol in the house usually but since he and Bethany had started sleeping together, he kept a bottle of that California Chardonnay she liked in the fridge for when she came over.

Bethany walked back into the bedroom.

Her hair fell below her shoulders, just barely brushing her nipples, which were pink and hard. She had a stud in her navel and a nice flat tummy between slender hips. They had just made love but watching her move, Davey suddenly felt aroused again.

Bethany stood by the nightstand and took a sip of wine. Davey rolled toward her and kissed her right where she was standing.

"Oh. *Oh!*" Bethany squealed. "Okay, etiquette question: Am I supposed to curl my little finger when I'm holding a glass of wine and a man's tongue is in my vagina?"

"All the best people do," Davey said as she put down the wine glass, tossed her hair back, and snuggled next to him again.

"You're feeling frisky tonight," she said, running her hand down his stomach and stopping when she had him firmly in hand. Davey pressed his face into her hair and breathed in the scent of her.

He stroked the soft skin between her shoulders again.

"Are you happy?" she said, after a few moments of silence.

"What, you mean right this minute?" Davey asked. "Yeah, I'm delirious."

"No, I mean in general. With us?" There aren't a lot of answers you can give to that question when a woman is playing with your penis.

"How am I not the luckiest guy in the world?" Davey asked.

"I don't mean because the sex is good," and then she was suddenly serious. "It is good, isn't it? I mean for you, too?"

"Bethany, every time I think of you, I get hard," said Davey, raising her chin so he could kiss her. "Which is not very helpful on the dive boat, I can tell you."

"It's just that I'm so happy. And it scares me a little," Bethany was serious but trying hard not to be too serious.

"Why would being happy scare you?" Davey was stalling, playing dumb. Because he knew the answer and he knew she was being smart and protective by questioning him.

"It's just that, well... I wanted my world to change and this is exactly the change I wanted," she kissed his chest. "So, I didn't lose anything, I got something and what I got was what I wanted."

Bethany had really good hands and it wasn't easy for Davey to stay focused on the conversation.

"But you, in all the time I've known you, you keep yourself apart in your own little world, and I don't think you were looking for it to change," she stopped for a bit, stopped talking at least.

"So, I guess I'm wondering if you're happy it did? Change, I mean."

Davey took a long breath. This woman lying beside him was one of the great treasures of the earth and she deserved an honest answer. He just wasn't sure he knew what that answer was.

"I'm happy we're together. I'm happy you're here right now and I can feel you next to me, and smell you, and have the warmth of your body against my body."

"Is there a 'but' coming, 'cause it really sounds like there's gonna be a 'but'," Bethany's voice had suddenly dropped an octave.

"No, there's no 'but.' I can say all of that without reservation." Davey stroked her hair and ran his fingers down her spine.

"But there are things in my life —"

"That's a *'but'!*" Bethany exclaimed. "How is that not a 'but'?"

"It's not a 'but' about you. It's a different 'but.' About other stuff."

"Okay, let's hear it," Bethany said, not at all convinced.

"I guess I feel like my life has a lot of moving parts," Davey said, trying to make things sound as unthreatening as possible. "I don't know, I used to be strong and sure of myself but in the last few years, I feel as if I'm just barely hanging on."

His hand stroked her back again.

"My life is like this fragile Jenga tower and every time another piece gets moved, I feel like the whole thing is going to come down," he said.

"Not sure I like my role in your little metaphor, there," Bethany said quietly.

"Okay, I can't concentrate if you keep doing that," Davey said, reaching for her hand and then clasping both of her hands in front of him. Bethany smiled and arched her eyebrows.

"Every part of my conscious brain knows that you're wonderful and I in no way deserve someone as good as you in my life," Davey said, looking deeply into Bethany's eyes. She felt a little better.

"But I do struggle," Davey said. "And I don't know *why* I struggle. I don't always know the reason I feel the way I do. Sometimes, I'm angry, sometimes I'm terrified."

"Maybe I can be a thing that's added to your life instead of something that's taken away. Maybe I can make your little Jenga tower stronger again." She tried to move her hand but Davey held it.

"It's not about you because everything you are, everything you do, is beyond wonderful," said Davey. "It's me and I just have to work on me. I need to understand why I would go off on people like I did today."

"Maybe they were just assholes," Bethany said with a shrug.

"Working with assholes is part of my job," Davey answered. "I'm supposed to be able to handle assholes."

Bethany looked into Davey's eyes for a long moment and seemed satisfied by what she saw there.

"Okay, well you work on you," she said, throwing the covers off the two of them. "Meanwhile, I know what will make you feel better right now."

Davey watched her long hair slide down his chest as she moved her head downward along his body. But when she began, at first it seemed like the moment might have passed.

"You're going to have to help a little here," Bethany said, and she started again. Davey breathed in deeply and his fingers gathered her hair in his hand. "There we go," she said, triumphantly.

Just about a minute later, Davey completely lost his mind.

• • •

A lot of people brought fast food or pizza to the potluck dinner, which seemed a little like cheating since Bethany had spent the afternoon making homemade meatballs.

Most of the parents there were mothers, Davey noticed, just like at the volleyball match. Fathers were in short supply. It wasn't that these families were without fathers. It was more a matter of it being a perfect evening for fishing.

Bethany put her meatball dish on the long table with the other food offerings, and she and Davey stood next to Abigail while she scanned the crowd for her "best buds."

"Why do I feel like a skunk at a picnic?" Bethany asked, looking around.

"Don't worry, they don't bite," Davey reassured her. "Usually."

"Chels!" Abigail shouted, waving. Her friend Chelsea from the volleyball team ran over with her mother, Brie, tagging behind. Within minutes, Crystal and Brittany were there, too, and introductions had been made all around.

"This is my Mom, Bethany," said Abigail proudly. Was it Davey's imagination or were Brie and Crystal slightly disappointed to see how pretty Bethany was? They all shook hands and chatted idly about the nothing they had in common.

"I'm so glad Abigail has such great friends," Bethany said, kindly. "She talks about you guys all the time!" Bethany made talking hands.

"It's great to finally meet you," Crystal said with a pretty good attempt at a smile. "We miss you at the games."

"I wish I could be there," Bethany responded. "Right now, my work schedule won't allow it. But Davey will come when he can."

"Well, we certainly enjoyed meeting Davey," Brie said with a little too much enthusiasm.

"So how do we do this? Do we, like, eat? Or is there a time?" Bethany indicated the long table filled with food and no one eating.

"It's pretty informal," Crystal offered, helpfully. "People hold off till they feel like everyone's here, then they hit the pizza first. After that, you're lucky if you get any food at all."

Everyone laughed at that and it felt like things were going pretty well. Abigail and her friends ran off to find their other teammates. Pretty soon Davey could see the six of them confabbing excitedly about whatever teenage girls talk about.

Davey watched them. Two of them reminded him a little of Stasie. That was weird. Just little things. Like the way they held their heads when they talked. And their hand gestures.

As he watched, he realized that all of them reminded him of Stasie. They even started to look a bit like Stasie. *Bizarre*.

"Oh, oh, we have our first customer," Brie said, pointing at the food table. Ken Duplay was helping himself to a piece of chocolate cake at the far end.

"That's so typical," Crystal added. "Marjorie knows he's got a sweet tooth and she always brings the chocolate cake from Publix. Then she makes sure he knows she brought it."

A blonde woman with far too much make-up touched Duplay's arm and pointed at the cake on his plate. They laughed together, as if the funniest thing in the world had just happened.

"Who's Marjorie?" asked Davey.

"She's one of the Moms," said Brie, with a slight edge. "Daughter's a bit of a bully. Popular, though."

"Is her name Marjorie Downey, by any chance?" Davey asked.

Crystal looked at Davey like he'd just bent a spoon with his mind.

"How on earth would you know that?" she asked.

Davey smiled. "Lucky guess." But Bethany was looking at him crooked, too. "The girl Abigail got into it with," Davey said by way of explanation. Bethany made an *"Ah!"* face and nodded, knowingly.

"Mister Jones, again we have the pleasure of your company," Duplay approached the group from behind Davey. He was a ridiculous figure under ordinary circumstances but with chocolate frosting stuck in his teeth he was a comic opera.

"It's a pleasure to be here," Davey answered, fairly certain he might have to kill this little prick someday.

"Do I dare trust my eyes, is this Abigail's mother?" Duplay asked looking at Bethany as if she were a stray dog.

"You know I am," Bethany answered without hesitation. "We've met before."

"It's been so long—"

"I'm at every parent/teacher conference here for seven years," Bethany interrupted, and Davey wondered why he would ever think she needed him to defend her. "I miss some things because I work."

"Well, we feel honored to have you here with us tonight," Duplay oozed and he strolled away with his plate of cake. Davey wondered how he could walk so straight when he'd just had his balls cut off.

The moms were silent until Duplay was out of earshot. "He's such a little worm," Brie said, breaking the silence.

"He's all about being this self-righteous Christian man, all God and family, and everything. But I guarantee you he's banging Marjorie," Crystal said, and Brie hit her on the arm.

"*Crystal!*" she exclaimed and they both laughed, conspiratorially.

"Mom! *Mom,*" Abigail ran over with the other girls. "Can I spend the night at Brittany's?"

Brittany looked at Crystal. "Is it okay, Mom? Chelsea, too?"

"Sure, sweetheart," said Crystal. Bethany smiled, "If it's okay with Brittany's Mom, it's okay with me."

The girls jumped up and down and slapped each other's hands.

"It's Friday night so it's okay if they stay up late and sleep in tomorrow," said Brie.

"I'll go pack an overnight bag for Abigail," Bethany said.

"Leave Abigail with us and we'll swing by on our way home for her things," said Crystal. From the look of things, Davey thought, Brie might be coming over, too and wine might be involved.

"That sounds perfect!" said Bethany, now fully inducted into the Mom Clan.

Twenty minutes later, as she and Davey climbed the stairs to their second story apartments, Bethany was still in wonder.

"Do you know how often Abigail has been invited to spend the night at a friend's house?" she mused. "*Never. Tonight is the first time.*"

Davey nodded. He was thinking about all the little Stasies he'd seen at the Pot Luck tonight. They were jumping, and dancing, and waving to him. "Come on, Daddy! Over here." *So many Stasies.*

"She's such a little buddy to me, I never even think about it," Bethany continued. "It happened because we went to the Pot Luck. I've got to do more of that. I need to find a way, for Abigail's sake."

Bethany opened her front door and Davey followed her inside.

"Are you hungry? I can make us dinner," Bethany offered. "You didn't get much at the school."

"There wasn't much to get," Davey said absently. "Once the food was fair game, it looked like locusts clearing a field."

"At least they finished my meatballs so I could bring home the dish," Bethany said, putting the empty bowl in the sink.

She walked up to Davey and put her arms around his neck. "Once Abigail picks up her stuff, we'll be all alone for the whole night. Whatever will we do, say, an hour from now?"

"Are we on a timetable?" Davey managed to say.

"That's what you do when you're a single mom," said Bethany. "You schedule sex."

"Over here, Daddy! We're here!" the group of Stasies shouted. There were dozens of them now. And one right in front of him, tugging on his hand. *"I'm right here, Daddy. Right here!"*

Davey fell back against the wall behind him and slid down into a fetal position. He was shaking uncontrollably.

"What's the matter?" Bethany cried, crouching on front of Davey. "What's wrong? Davey, what's *happening!*"

Davey shook harder. He couldn't see; there were bright spots in front of his eyes. Bethany's voice seemed far away.

"I can't do this," Davey said. *"I can't do this!"*

"Do what? Davey, you're having a panic attack."

"I can't do this." Davey struggled to stand up. "I have to leave!"

"Don't get up," Bethany pleaded. "Sit down. Let it pass. Davey, it's a panic attack. You need to sit down."

Davey pushed himself up against the wall. He elbowed Bethany away. He stood, uneasily, and looked around for the front door.

"I'm sorry. *I'm so sorry,*" he said, wildly. "I have to go. Have to go! I'm sorry."

Davey staggered out the front door and almost bumped into Abigail and her two friends coming up the stairs.

"Hey!" said Abigail. "Where are you going?"

"I can't ... talk now," Davey mumbled as he stumbled past them. "Gotta go!"

"Davey!" Abigail shouted plaintively. Her voice changed suddenly, like she was near tears. "Why are you leaving?"

"Where are you going, Daddy?" Was it Abigail or Stasie? He heard Stasie's voice. He was sure he did. And she was crying.

Crystal and Brie sat in their cars in the parking lot, chatting through their open windows. They stopped talking as Davey ran past and jumped in his car and fired up the engine. Davey backed out of his parking space and gunned it for the exit.

There was very little traffic on Overseas Highway at this hour. In seconds, Davey had pulled onto the road and was heading south.

Driving down the Route 1 he had to force himself to concentrate, as if he were driving drunk. He stayed in the right lane and drove at the speed limit, which meant other cars were speeding past him.

I am the worst kind of person, Davey was thinking to himself.

I am a coward. I'm a phony. She deserves so much better than me and now I've hurt her. I'm a bastard!

I can't do this, Davey thought to himself. *I can't do this, I can't do this, I can't do this.*

He pulled over at the Caribbean Club, drove to the northeast end of the lot and parked there, looking across the darkening bay.

I can't do this, Davey thought and he closed his eyes.

Chapter 17

Davey didn't want things to end like this. He didn't want to be That Guy. She deserved better than a man who walked out on her with no explanation. She deserved someone who could be, at the very least, decent and trustworthy. She deserved the best possible man, the most loyal and dependable man. She deserved better.

But he couldn't face Bethany tonight and, what was even more likely, he couldn't face himself either. He felt guilty and ashamed. He stayed out until past midnight then crept silently into his apartment.

The next morning, he left early so there was no chance of running into her.

After two days of sneaking in and out, Davey stopped being careful and when he still didn't see Bethany, it belatedly dawned on him that she might be avoiding him, too.

By Tuesday, it didn't really matter anymore. Things *had* ended like this, whether Davey wanted it that way or not. He'd missed his chance. He *was* That Guy.

He knew he had hurt Bethany more than he was willing to admit. This wonderful, fragile girl had trusted him and he'd abused that trust. Well... not fragile. No one would say Bethany was fragile but that was really just a cover, because underneath it all she was still vulnerable and soft. She'd let him in and he'd betrayed her terribly.

Conflicting thoughts flooded Davey's mind. He knew he hadn't acted rationally. Any clear-headed assessment plainly showed that Bethany was the best thing that had happened to him in years. He'd had an uncontrollable reaction to dramatic changes in his life.

But losing Bethany wasn't going to bring back the world he'd lost. Nothing would do that.

Still, rational thinking had little to do with this. Every time Davey tried to think about the situation dispassionately, his mind raced in circles and his heart pounded in his ears.

He couldn't get outside of it. Couldn't be objective. Couldn't calm the storm. Couldn't see any way out of this trap he'd made for himself.

He found himself slowing down to examine the beer section in the Winn Dixie. But Davey had never been a drinker, not really. It wasn't his thing. He did go to work early and stay late, as a way of losing himself in it, and he also spent a lot of time trying to pretend that Bubble Talk was more interesting than it actually was.

So, he found himself alone at Get Shorty's on the next Ladies Night, which was busy as always. Tourists packed the tables and locals sat at the bar where they'd be able to get their cheap drinks faster. Davey surveyed the crowd and noticed something unusual, at least he thought it was unusual.

Everyone at the bar was a couple tonight.

Are there more sad songs on the radio when you're sad or do you just hear them more? Was everyone a couple on a typical Ladies Night or was Davey just more aware of it tonight?

Carly and Jens sat at one corner of the bar, very much into each other. Like they should get a room. Roald was sitting between two women who were openly competing for his Nordic favors and might even have been willing to share him. Di – *even Di!* – was huddled with his Mediterranean dancing woman, faces nearly touching, alone in the world except for each other.

"Not dancing tonight?" Davey asked. Their heads bobbed up like he'd touched them with a cattle prod. "Davey, you fine upstanding guy!" shouted Di. "You remember Ellie!"

The woman looked at Di adoringly. "It's Elpis," she said, holding her hand out to Davey. "He can never remember. Elpis, it means Hope."

"Pleasure to meet you, Elpis," Davey said with a smile, then to Di, "Fine upstanding guy? Who *are* you?"

"I am transformed by love," Di claimed, with his hand pressed over his heart. "From now on, I see only good things. I reject darkness in my life."

Di held Elpis's hand to his lips. "Apollo has sent me a goddess."

"Apollo!" Elpis objected with a wave. "I was sent by no man. It is Athena, my darling, who has sent me to you. Athena the Warrior!"

"Athena the Wise," countered Di. "Then my heart is even more full." Di grabbed Davey's arm and pulled him toward them.

"Come, join us! Where is that girlfriend you keep hiding away from us?" Di exclaimed but Davey pulled away.

"No," he begged off, "three's a crowd."

Moving down the bar, the only person who wasn't part of a couple was Binky. Davey sat down next to him. It's come to this, he thought, ruefully.

"How's it going, Binky," Davey said as Jorge brought him his first beer. Binky didn't answer. Davey was being snubbed.

Snubbed by Binky!

"You gonna bite my head off again?" Binky asked sullenly.

"Sorry about that," Davey apologized. "I just hate to see a man get kicked when he's down."

"I wasn't kickin' no one. It don't make no nevermind to me," Binky protested.

"Enough said. No need to explain," Davey said. "Sorry I blew up."

Binky snuffled a bit and wiped his nose on his sleeve.

"No one thinks I know anything. I know stuff."

"It's okay, Binky. Just let it go."

"Been around a long time," Binky couldn't let it go. "Seen plenty. Know plenty."

Davey nodded. He hoped this would be over soon.

"You're 'bout the only one never jumped all over my shit before."

Now Davey felt really terrible.

"So, I'm just goin' to say this an' if you blow you're stack, well then, you blow your stack," Binky said purposefully.

Davey looked at the sad little man.

"Court case starts tomorrow," Binky pronounced solemnly. "So's whatever's gonna happen, it's gonna happen tomorrow."

"Court case...?" Davey said, not following.

"The husband? The one suin' Jerry *fer negligencing?*" Binky said as if explaining to a child. "They go to court tomorrow."

A hollow-eyed woman with limp blonde hair and a lot of body art sat down next to Binky. "Hello, Babe," she said and hugged Binky. "Hey," Binky responded casually, as if having random women hug him was a daily occurrence he'd simply learned to accept.

Davey stared in disbelief.

Even Binky was with a woman tonight! It was the ultimate irony. Davey was now the only single man at the bar. He shook his head in awe, stuck six dollars under his plastic cup of beer and left.

• • •

The Monroe County Courthouse on Plantation Key was an unprepossessing structure that might easily have been mistaken for a low-end professional building or municipal recreational center.

Its two-story architecture and low sloping roofline made it blend into the landscape and Davey almost missed it as he was driving south on Overseas Highway.

He wasn't sure exactly why he had come. *Calypso* was scheduled for its annual Coast Guard inspection prior to the busy summer season and Davey certainly didn't want to hang around his apartment where he might run into Bethany. Plus, if he was honest with himself, he was more than a little curious to see how liability issues were resolved when there was a diving accident.

Every scuba instructor had nightmares about losing a diver or being accused of negligent procedures. Most didn't even like to talk about it for fear of tempting fate, as Di would say.

The deputies at the entrance instructed Davey to put his cell phone in a locker and ushered him through the metal detector. From their critical glances at his clothes, Davey understood that his shorts, sandals and polo shirt qualified as the bare minimum for "appropriate attire" in their professional assessment.

One of the deputies, his name tag identified him as HARDESTY, handed back Davey's car keys, looked at him closely, smiled and said, "Hey, I know you. You're the guy!" He slapped his partner on the shoulder and pointed at Davey.

"He's the guy!" said Hardesty.

"What guy?" asked Davey. "I'm what guy?"

"You're the guy that saved that diver a couple of months back," Hardesty said as if he'd just solved a mystery. "I was one of the deputies who took her gear into evidence. I remember you. Cool as ice."

"He's *that* guy?" the other deputy asked.

"Yeah," said Hardesty, nodding, "he's that guy."

It was like a curse he just couldn't escape; it followed him everywhere. Davey shook his head, wondering when would it ever end but the deputies were done with him now and had focused their attention on the next person who came into the courthouse.

Feeling a little self-conscious, Davey hoped he'd be able to hide among the crowd of spectators in the back row of the court. But this plan blew up when he entered the courtroom and found there were fewer than 10 people in the entire room.

As Davey closed the door behind him, the judge looked up and everyone else turned around to stare. Sitting in the back row would have been ridiculous at that point so Davey found a seat about midway up toward the rail and everyone went back to normal.

"Please continue," said a man in a suit to the man on the witness stand, as if Davey's entrance had been a distracting diversion.

"We were swimming southeast from the *Benwood* wreck on a course of about 140 degrees..." the man stated unemotionally.

The judge was an older man with a white beard who looked a great deal like Santa Claus except for his black robe. He was flanked by flags and "In God We Trust" was emblazoned in gold letters on the wall behind him.

He sat on an elevated platform behind an imposing desk where a plaque identified him as the Hon. Edmond Wallston.

Davey figured that the man testifying was the plaintiff and the man standing at the podium was likely his lawyer. Jerry was sitting at a table on Davey's left with his attorney. Jerry's lawyer was young and eager; he looked like a typical suit. Jerry was dressed casually in a Scuba Doo logoed shirt.

Good for you, Davey thought to himself. Show the flag till the bitter end. No need to dress up for a hanging!

Jerry gave a bit of a smile and a two-finger wave as Davey sat down. Davey nodded and smiled unobtrusively, not wanting to draw any further attention. A court reporter sat to the left of the judge and a bailiff stood to the right, looking stern and impassive.

There was a woman sitting by herself a couple of rows behind Jerry. From the back, she seemed attractive, possibly in her early 40s. She wasn't close enough to provide any meaningful support to Jerry but she was in his general vicinity, so Davey assumed it was Jerry's wife, Henrietta. Interesting, under the circumstances.

On the other side of the aisle, a few rows behind Davey, a lone man sat taking notes. He was casually dressed with a loose tie and ratty jacket, his glasses up on his forehead. Probably a reporter for one of the local Keys newspapers, Davey thought. He hoped the man hadn't recognized him.

"Did there come a time," the lawyer was speaking again, "when you began to feel uneasy about the dive plan?"

"Well... when we got down to 90 feet, we all circled around Jerry, the instructor, and there were just too many people--"

"--Objection!" Jerry's lawyer stood up. "The witness is making a judgment, not stating a fact."

"Your honor, the witness--" the plaintiff's lawyer started.

"--Sustained," the judge interrupted. "Mister Gaffney, you will restrict your testimony to your observation of the facts, not conclusions you may have reached independently."

The lawyer, frustrated, started again. "Mister Gaffney, in your mind--"

"--Same objection," Jerry's lawyer snapped.

"Sustained." The judge raised his eyebrows. "Mister Moran, are you unclear about my instructions here?" he asked Gaffney's lawyer.

"Your Honor, my client is an experienced diver and, as such, his conclusions are relevant to the matter before us," Moran insisted.

"Is counsel claiming that his client qualifies as an expert witness? Because if that's the case, if he's an expert, we can all go home right now. Case dismissed!" Jerry's lawyer argued.

"He's right, Mister Moran. You can't have it both ways," said the judge.

"Allow me to re-phrase," Moran backpedaled. "Please describe what happened when you reached 90 feet of depth."

"Well… we formed a semicircle with Jerry at the center, as we had been briefed to do before the dive," Gaffney explained.

"And your wife, Melissa, was by your side at this time?" Moran asked.

"Yes, we were arranged in buddy teams and my wife was next to me on the sand," Gaffney answered.

"Now, when you say 'on the sand,' you weren't floating above the bottom at this time?" the lawyer asked.

"No, we were all kneeling in the sand, as we'd been instructed to do," Gaffney answered.

"Is that a standard practice--"

"--Your Honor!" Jerry's lawyer objected.

"I'll re-phrase," Moran corrected himself. "Have you ever been asked by an instructor to kneel on the bottom before?"

"Yes, when I was certified for Open Water, we did skills on the bottom in a kneeling position. When my wife got certified two years later, her instructor also practiced skills while kneeling on the bottom," Gaffney said with certainty. "I have no idea what is standard for the advanced course in deeper water," he added, as if showing off his compliance.

"And while you were all kneeling on the bottom, did that have any effect on the visibility? How well you could see one another?"

"It was fine at first," Gaffney stated solemnly. "Jerry, our instructor, swam around to each buddy team and showed us a color card. Then he shined a flashlight over the colors so we could see how much they darkened at depth from the refraction of sunlight through water. And then back to normal under the flashlight."

"Anything else?" prompted Moran.

"Yes, we compared depth gauges on our computers to check for slight variations from one to another," Gaffney stated.

"And how was the visibility during all of this?" Moran asked.

"It began to get very poor," Gaffney answered. "People were kicking up sand and silt from the bottom. With that many people, all moving around. Some were having trouble maintaining their balance and buoyancy. It became much harder to see."

"What happened next?" Moran asked.

"When we'd completed those tasks, our instructor, Jerry, over there," Gaffney pointed at Jerry. He seemed preoccupied with making sure the judge knew Jerry had been his instructor. As if there could be any other reason his being in the courtroom.

"Jerry indicated that we should all follow him and continue the dive," Gaffney stated.

"And did you?" Moran asked.

"Yes, everyone rose up off the bottom and started to swim after Jerry. That kicked up a lot more sand from the bottom. My wife and I were at the end of the line. By the time we started to follow the group, we were in zero visibility."

"What did you do then?" Moran asked, as if this were all brand new and fascinating to him.

"It was confusing, disorienting. I didn't know which direction to swim."

"Could you still see your wife, Melissa, at this point?"

"I couldn't see my hand in front of my face at this point!" Gaffney raised his voice dramatically but it was still pretty obvious he'd rehearsed his story many times before.

"How did you react to that?" Moran probed.

"I put my hands on the bottom so I wouldn't get vertigo and I basically hand walked and swam until I came out of the sand cloud and I could see again."

"How long did that take?"

"It's hard to say. Time gets tricky when you can't see. It seemed like a long time but it was probably only a minute or so."

"And when you could see again, what was the situation?"

"The wall where we'd descended was pretty far away. I'd been swimming in the wrong direction and I'd moved pretty far from the group. I could just make out some fins kicking at the far edge of my visibility and I swam toward them," Gaffney stated.

"Did you have Melissa in sight at this point?" asked Moran.

"No, I hadn't seen her since we got silted out," Gaffney said, reliving the moment. "I assumed she was with the other divers and I'd find her when I joined up with the group."

"And did you? Find her?"

"No, she wasn't there. I swam up the line a little ways and couldn't find her. Then I went back to the end of the line again to see if she'd shown up there. But I never saw her again, alive that is."

"Where was Jerry during this time?" asked Moran.

"I assume he was leading the line of divers. I couldn't see him," said Gaffney.

"And if you couldn't see him, it's safe to assume he couldn't see you either," Moran stated flatly.

"Objection!" Jerry's lawyer called out. "The witness cannot testify as to what Mister Delblaine could or could not see." Then he pointedly added, "And neither can his lawyer."

"I agree, Mister Tenley. The objection is sustained," ruled the judge.

"Mister Gaffney, how many students were there, total, in your dive class?" Moran asked with a flourish.

"Your Honor…" Tenley started with a sigh.

"I'm asking for a fact, not an opinion," Moran interjected.

"I'll allow it. It's a legitimate question," said the judge.

"There were sixteen students," Gaffney stated. "Eight buddy teams."

"I have no further questions at this time," Moran concluded.

"Your turn, counsel," the judge raised his eyebrows at Tenley.

"Thank you, Your Honor. Mister Gaffney, you testified that you were certified two years earlier than your wife. Is it fair to say you're a much more experienced diver than she was?" Tenley was aggressive but his manner was subtle and ingratiating. He'd invited the witness to brag about himself, which Gaffney promptly did.

"Yes, I was already an experienced diver when she got certified," Gaffney preened. "That's why I felt qualified earlier to comment on the number of—"

"—How many dives were in your logbook prior to the dive in question?" Tenley interrupted.

Moran was whispering to a stylish young woman at his table, a second chair or paralegal. They both glanced at Davey. The woman rose and walked back toward the exit, looking directly at Davey as she passed by.

"I had 60 logged dives," answered Gaffney with obvious pride.

"And aside from your initial training dives, were you supervised during any of these dives?" Tenley asked.

"No, not really. I mean, there were guides on some of them but there was no real supervision," Gaffney stated.

"So, you're actually quite capable and qualified to dive safely without an instructor's direct supervision, isn't that right?" Tenley asked, palms held upward for divine judgment.

"Well, I..."

"Objection, immaterial!" Moran interjected stridently.

"How so, Mister Moran?" asked the judge.

"You Honor, counsel is trying to establish that Mister Gaffney didn't require supervision during the dive. But the issue at bar is that Mister Delblaine was legally required to provide direct supervision whether Mister Gaffney needed it or not. Mister Gaffney's qualifications are not material to the *res gestae*."

The judge nodded. "He has a point, Mister Tenley. Sustained."

"Mister Gaffney," Tenley continued without missing a beat, "you testified you were your wife's dive buddy, is that right?"

"Yes, we decided to take the advanced course together," Gaffney answered.

"So, you're her dive buddy, and we've already established that you're a much more experienced diver than she. Isn't being a dive buddy a role that comes with certain responsibilities?" Tenley asked innocently.

"Same objection, Your Honor." Moran stood up. "Both Mister and Missus Gaffney were enrolled in this course as students. Their instructor bears the sole burden of responsibility for both of them during training. It wouldn't matter if they had invented scuba."

"I agree, Counselor," said the judge. "Sustained."

The young paralegal came back to the table and whispered something in Moran's ear. Moran glanced quickly at Davey and sat back down.

Tenley collected his thoughts for a moment and went right back on the attack. "Mister Gaffney, you testified that once you rejoined the group, you swam part way up the line of divers looking for your wife. Why not swim all the way up to the instructor and let him know right away that there was a problem?"

"Because that's not the accepted procedure," Gaffney protested. "If you lose sight of your dive buddy, you're supposed to look for your dive buddy."

"For how long?" Tenley asked. Gaffney paused, as if caught out and not wanting to answer.

"For one minute," he said, reluctantly.

"And after a minute, what?" asked Tenley.

"Surface, and see if your dive buddy is there," Gaffney stated.

"And is that what you did?" Tenley prompted.

"No... but we were down at 90 feet. I didn't know if that was still the procedure at that depth. I'd never been at that deep before," Gaffney protested.

"Your Honor, this entire line of questioning is immaterial," Moran stated, tiredly. "The only question before us is whether Jerry Delblaine acted negligently in his conduct of this class."

The judge seemed to weigh the matter in his mind. "Are you saying that your client's actions have no effect on the matter?"

"No, Your Honor, but counsel has made it clear he is unwilling to accept my client's opinion as expert testimony. Yet now, he's trying to establish my client's experience as a mitigating factor."

"That's a good point," the judge nodded. "Mister Tenley..."

"Your Honor, I--"

"--As it happens, Your Honor," Moran interrupted, "We have an expert witness who can testify as to the defendant's procedures during the dive in question and save us all a lot of time."

The judge looked at some papers in front of him. "I don't see anyone on your witness list," he stated.

"It was unexpected," Moran explained. "We didn't arrange for the witness; he just showed up."

Davey felt the hairs on the back of his neck stand up. Moran had turned and was looking right at him.

Jerry turned and looked at Davey with a puzzled expression. Tenley looked confused and upset. "We've not been informed of any expert witness, Your Honor."

232

"What gives, counselor?" the judge asked Moran. The paralegal scrawled something on a legal pad, which Moran read.

"Your Honor, David Jones, who is present in the courtroom today, is a certified scuba instructor who successfully resuscitated an unconscious diver two months ago. He's a local hero among dive professionals! He's very well qualified to testify regarding the procedures employed by the defendant just prior to this tragic accident."

"Is that this gentleman here?" the judge asked, pointing at Davey.

"Yes, Your Honor," replied Moran.

"Mister Jones, could you stand up, please?" the judge lifted his hand, palm up. Davey stood, slowly, wondering what fresh hell he'd just fallen into. "Are you here to testify?" asked the judge.

"No, judge... I mean Your Honor," Davey stammered. "I'm just here to observe. I'm a spectator."

The man Davey assumed was a reporter had taken a sudden keen interest in Davey and was scribbling notes on his pad.

"But why not take advantage of this unexpected resource to clarify all of our questions? Defense can hardly object. I believe they're friends," Moran insisted.

"Your Honor, I just came to watch. I'm not a witness," Davey insisted.

The judge shrugged. "You are if I say you are," he said flatly.

"Don't I have anything to say about that?" Davey complained.

The judge pushed out his lower lip, which made his beard bristle. "Not really, no," he stated.

"Your Honor," objected Tenley, "we've had no notice, no opportunity to interview this witness. No idea what he'll say."

"I don't think any of us has any idea what he'll say," the judge said with obvious anticipation. "Let's find out together."

The judge looked at Gaffney on the witness stand. "Mister Gaffney, you're excused for now, subject to recall if defense counsel wishes. Mister Jones, please take the stand."

"Your Honor, this is completely unprecedented!" Tenley complained.

"My courtroom, my rules," the judge stated evenly. "Let's get a move on. I want to hear this."

Chapter 18

"As a certified scuba instructor, are you familiar with the Training Standards which are defined by the certifying agency?" Moran asked.

This was the nub of it. Everything else was window dressing.

Davey felt like he himself was on trial. It was strange because he really didn't have anything at stake personally but just being on the witness stand was intimidating, and he hated Moran for putting him in that position.

He'd been sworn in, taken the oath to tell the truth, the whole truth, and then it started. He said his name was David Jones. He said how many years he'd been an instructor. He said where he worked. He said that most people called him Davey.

"What is your level of certification, Davey?" Moran asked.

"I'm an MSDT, a master scuba diver trainer," Davey answered.

"And is that the highest level of certification?" Moran probed.

"No, the highest level is Course Director, which is what Jerry is," Davey responded. Moran pursed his lips.

"Over the years, how many students have you certified?" asked Moran.

"I don't know the exact count," Davey demurred.

"In the hundreds?" Moran asked.

"Yes, certainly hundreds," Davey answered.

"Ever had a student die in your class?"

"No."

"Close call?"

"No."

"Any accident that required you to file a report?"

"I had a student rupture an eardrum a couple of years ago."

"How did that happen?" Moran wanted to know.

"The student indicated that he was OK throughout the descent every time I asked if his ears were clear. But it turned out he just wanted to please me, make me think he was cooperating. One ear never fully equalized and the eardrum ruptured at 40 feet," Davey recounted. The memory still rankled. What was the point of hand signals if students weren't going to give you honest answers?

"But, even in that case, you never ceased to have the student under your direct supervision, is that right, Mister Jones?"

"That's correct," Davey answered.

"Ha!" the judge laughed suddenly. *"Davey Jones!"* he chortled. "You're Davey Jones. I just got that!"

Moran frowned at the interruption but the Bailiff broke character and smiled.

But now they had come to the important part: the standards.

Davey steeled himself. He had to be truthful but he didn't want to hurt Jerry, if he could avoid it.

"Please tell the court, in your own words, what the Training Standards are," Moran instructed casually.

"They're guidelines for instructors to use during training." Davey testified. "And, they're the limitations beyond which liability insurance no longer covers you."

"Really?" Moran asked, dumbfounded. "You really think the standards are created for insurance purposes?"

"I don't know if that's their purpose but it's one way they're used," Davey equivocated.

"You also referred to them as guidelines. Does that mean you think they're intended to be optional?" Moran asked.

"The standards can't anticipate every situation. A good instructor needs to be able to use his own discretion," Davey answered.

"Do you seriously believe that the Training Standards are intended to be optional?" Moran repeated with extra emphasis. He wasn't going to accept an evasive answer.

Davey hesitated. "No. I guess not," he said.

"Thank you," Moran said with relief. "That was more difficult than it needed to be."

"You Honor," said Tenley, "Counsel is badgering his own witness."

"Yes, he is," said the judge, with a warning look at Moran.

"Do you know, off the top of your head, what is the instructor/student ratio for Advanced Open Water dives? I can provide you with an Instructor Manual if you need to refresh your memory."

"The ratio is eight students per instructor," Davey stated calmly.

"Very good Mister Jones! Impressive," Moran crowed. "So, it would be fair to say, would it not, that Mister Delblaine was outside of the accepted safety standards by a factor of one hundred percent."

"It would be accurate," Davey stipulated. "I don't know that it would be fair."

"Isn't it true that the standards are there to provide the generally accepted safety margin for students being trained? Yes, or no?" Moran asked pointedly.

"I believe that is their intention," Davey answered.

"Isn't it true that the instructor is required to provide direct supervision for all students on a deep dive, and that the standards define the limits established for direct supervision? Yes? Or no?" Moran asked, again pointedly.

"You can't define direct supervision with an instructor/student ratio," Davey insisted. "In practice, it just doesn't work that way."

"That's twice you've answered a yes or no question with an answer that was neither yes or no," Moran complained.

"Let's keep things moving along, counselor," urged the judge.

"Your Honor the witness is obfuscating his answers to protect his friend," Moran said with a shrug.

"Then ask him a question he can't obfuscate," the judge suggested. "You called him up here."

Moran walked back to the table where his paralegal was sitting. He looked casually at the Instructor Manual on the table in front of him. He turned back to Davey.

"Mister Jones, you were aware of the instructor/student ratio for deep training dives without referring to the manual. You had that number committed to memory, correct?"

"That's right," Davey agreed.

"Yet Jerry Delblaine, a man with years more experience than you have, a man with, by your own testimony, a higher certification level than you have, took twice that many students on a deep dive, where one student was lost and subsequently drowned, is that right?"

"I… I guess so," said Davey, reluctantly.

"No further questions," Moran snapped, and he sat down.

"Your Honor, this isn't fair," Davey said to the judge.

"What's not fair, son?" the judge asked, not unkindly.

"The way he's asking these questions, I'm not getting to tell the whole story," Davey said.

"That's how this works," said the judge. "He gets to ask the questions he wants to ask in the way he wants to ask them."

"But I swore to tell the whole truth, not some edited version of it," Davey asserted.

"Your Honor, I have some questions for this witness," Tenley spoke up.

"Have at it," the judge agreed with a sweep of his arm.

"Mister Jones, what if anything is the court missing from your prior testimony?" Tenley asked.

"Objection, Your Honor, the question is hopelessly broad. The witness can say anything he wants."

"Yes, he can," agreed the judge, looking at Davey with a smile. "He certainly can." Davey thought carefully about what he wanted to say.

"Well, for one thing, there's this whole concept of direct supervision. It's a unicorn. It doesn't exist underwater," Davey asserted in a confident voice.

"Can you expand on that for us, please?" Tenley prompted.

"Well, take the student who blew his eardrum on me," Davey began. "I had my hand on his arm the whole way down. But he was still injured because he gave me wrong information."

The judge seemed to weigh this.

"Direct supervision implies control. But there is no control underwater," Davey testified.

"Is there anything else the court should know?" Tenley asked, hopefully.

Moran threw his head back and gestured his frustration by raising his arms to the heavens.

"Well, I guess I'm going to tell on myself a little bit here," Davey started. "A week ago I had four students doing Discover Scuba. Having four students is well within standards. But they all swam away from me in different directions. Until I herded them all back together, I couldn't have handled any emergency that happened. They were on their own."

"Sounds frightening. Was that unpreventable?" asked Tenley.

"They had been briefed to stay with me, but they chose not to. They had been briefed to stay together as buddy teams, but they didn't do that either."

"Even after you had briefed them?" Tenley pretended to be incredulous.

"We brief people all the time. Extensively. It doesn't have much impact," Davey said. "They get underwater and they forget."

"So, you're stating, just so I'm clear here, that even with direct supervision as defined by the Training Standards, you cannot be assured of maintaining control of the situation, is that right?" Tenley asked with a flourish.

"That's correct," Davey said. "There is no control underwater."

"In fact, every time you go underwater you are taking an unavoidable risk, which is why there are detailed waivers that all students sign agreeing not to sue their instructors in the case of an accident, isn't that right?" asked Tenley.

"Yes, that's right," said Davey.

"Thank you for your honesty. And for your expertise. I have no further questions for this witness, Your Honor," and Tenley sat down.

"Counsel," the judge looked at Moran, eyebrows raised, "any re-direct?"

"Just one question, Your Honor. After listening to that flight of fancy that took us to the moon and back, I have only one additional question for this witness." Moran walked the few steps up to the witness stand and bore into Davey with his piercing blue eyes.

"Would you, David Jones, take 16 students on a deep dive on the *Benwood* wall? Yes? Or No?"

Davey hesitated. "I think I'd--"

"--Yes? Or no, Mister Jones?" Moran's gaze was relentless. Davey repositioned himself on the uncomfortable wooden seat.

He took a deep breath. "No," Davey said, finally.

• • •

"Thanks for torpedoing our case," said Tenley later, when the three of them were talking privately in a side room. "Thanks a lot!"

"He was under oath, he had to answer honestly," Jerry said in Davey's defense. "Don't blame Davey, blame me. I'm the one who took 16 students down the wall."

"Jerry, I know we're all alone here but I wish you wouldn't say things like that," Tenley complained.

"Mark, we all know how this is going to end," Jerry said, resignedly. "The only thing left to decide is whether the judge is going to award Gaffney both ears and the tail."

Tenley didn't look like he got the metaphor.

The voice in the back of Davey's head started up again, that intangible feeling that something obvious was being overlooked.

"There's something wrong here," Davey said, thoughtfully.

"What do you mean?" asked Jerry.

"He swam away from her," said Davey, thinking out loud. "Gaffney testified that when they got silted out, he abandoned his wife and swam away."

"So what?" Tenley asked.

Davey looked at Jerry. "If you got silted out, what would be the first thing you'd do?"

"Reach out and grab my dive buddy before I lost her," Jerry said, almost without thinking.

"Exactly," Davey affirmed. "But Gaffney swam away. Why?"

"Could be anything. He panicked. He's stupid. Doesn't really like his wife that much," Jerry counted on his fingers. "Why do any of these people do anything?"

"What are you saying?" Tenley was finally interested.

"It just doesn't make sense. That he'd swim away like that," Davey insisted.

"He isn't all that great of a diver, I can tell you that," Jerry said with a shrug.

"Yeah, but it's natural. It's instinctive," said Davey.

"For you, maybe. Or me," Jerry agreed. "But these inexperienced divers, you never know what they're gonna do."

"Maybe he was trying to find his wife and couldn't," Tenley proposed.

"But that's not what he said," Davey insisted. "He said he put his hands on the bottom to avoid vertigo and swam until he was out of the silt. He never mentioned trying to find his dive buddy."

Tenley thought for a moment. "Well, it makes no difference to our case what he did. The judge pretty much accepted the idea that Jerry has a supervisory responsibility regardless of the other divers' experience or qualifications."

The three men were silent for a moment.

"It just doesn't feel right," said Davey, shaking his head. "Something's wrong."

Jerry reached across the table and shook Davey's hand. "Thank you, Davey. It was a dirty trick, putting you on the stand like that but I think you did us some good. The judge was impressed by what you said."

Davey shrugged. "I don't know. I hope so. Good luck to you, Jerry."

"We'll see what happens," Jerry said sadly. "Hey, nice save with that diver, by the way! That was a good piece of work."

Et tu, Jerry? Davey just couldn't get away from it.

On the drive home, Davey thought about Jerry's case and what he'd seen of the trial and it made him sad. Jerry was technically at fault; there was no doubt about that. But he wasn't evil and he was going to lose everything. Everything he'd built over 30 years. Gone.

It was a done deal.

And what about Gaffney? He was a little too slick for a guy who'd abandoned his dive buddy in an emergency. Where did he get off being so self-righteous?

If anyone could have saved his wife, it was him!

Davey came out of his reverie when he saw police lights coming up behind him and heard the siren. *"Shit!"* he said, slowing down to the speed limit. The Monroe County Deputy's police car pulled up alongside Davey. The cop behind the wheel was Deputy Hardesty. He waved and laughed, pointed at Davey.

Hardesty switched off the lights and siren, laughed and waved again, and sped off up Route 1.

"Asshole," Davey said out loud.

It was that kind of day. It had been that kind of week. It was turning out to be that kind of life. Davey pulled into his apartment parking lot and shut off his engine.

He sat in his car for a couple of minutes, just thinking.

Okay, now it was the moment of truth.

When she opened her apartment door, Bethany stood there in front of Davey looking up at him wordlessly with sad eyes. Everything he had thought he might say flew out of his head like bees from a shaken hive. He was momentarily struck dumb.

She didn't look angry, or surprised, or even guarded. There was just something beaten down about her.

"I wouldn't blame you if you never wanted to see me again," Davey said in an uncertain voice. "I'm pretty sure I'll never forgive myself for what I did."

Bethany's expression didn't change. She called behind her, "It's Davey." And to Davey, "Come on in. We have company." Then she turned and walked back into the apartment. Davey followed.

Abigail was sitting on the couch with a man Davey didn't recognize. He had longish hair and a disheveled appearance. His skin was sallow and his body seemed thin and frail.

He was sitting very close to Abigail but her arms were crossed defiantly and she was leaning away from him.

"What are *you* doing here?" Abigail demanded, looking hard at Davey.

"Groveling," Davey answered. Abigail's expression didn't soften.

"What's groveling?" she asked.

"Google it," Davey said, lightly.

"Who's this guy?" asked the man on the couch. "Walkin' in here like he owns the place."

Bethany said, "This is Davey. He's my... he's our friend. He lives next door." It was clear Davey had walked into the middle of something but he had no idea what.

"This is Tony," said Bethany, tonelessly. "He's Abigail's father."

So that was it. Davey's first impulse was to turn and run. But his second, stronger compulsion was to stay and defend Bethany and Abigail from whatever in life made them sad or afraid.

"I see," said Davey, slowly. "This is a surprise."

Bethany leaned against the kitchen counter. "More like a shock," she said.

"Why shouldn't I want to see my daughter?" Tony asked belligerently. "Child of my loins. Heir to all I possess. I miss her."

Tony put his hand on Abigail's shoulder and she shook it off.

"You've missed her for eleven and a half years. Doesn't seem to have bothered you much," Bethany said, sternly.

Davey was still trying to assess the dynamic in the room. Bethany and Abigail were clearly not happy about Tony being there. But they didn't seem angry or hostile, exactly. More like catatonic.

Tony was a scrawny thing, very likely the result of habitual drug use, Davey thought clinically, but he held his head up, defiant, as if everyone should defer to him.

How were he and Bethany ever a couple? Davey wondered. But then he mentally removed thirteen years and saw that Tony might have been better looking as a young man, before the ravages of substance abuse shriveled him.

The bad boy every good girl falls hopelessly in love with.

"How's the parental bonding going?" Davey asked Abigail.

"Terrible," she complained, twisting herself a bit further from Tony's reach.

"*Hey,* what did I tell you about being respectful?" Tony said menacingly. "I gotta teach you manners?" He swung his hand back, as if he might hit Abigail.

"You touch that child and you'll never use that arm again," said Davey, staring darkly at Tony, "I promise you that."

Tony leaned away from Abigail and looked thoughtfully at Davey. "Tough guy, huh? You got yourself a white knight here, Bethy!"

"Your friend Duplay thought Abigail should have both parents in her life," Bethany said to Davey. "He called Tony to ask if he wanted a school pass for the coming year. Let him know you'd probably have one."

"Called me right up, he did," Tony smiled. He had addict's teeth.

"I'll have to remember to thank him," Davey said. He couldn't believe the nerve of that little prick. Judgment Day was coming.

A duffle bag lay on the floor next to the couch and Davey noticed there was a folded sheet by the armrest and a few shirts and socks lying around. So, Tony had been staying here, had he?

Where was I when they needed me? Not here, nope. Hiding, like a fucking coward. Davey cursed himself for the hundredth time.

"What are your plans, Tony?" Davey asked directly. "You here for long?"

"Well, that all depends, I guess," Tony answered, rubbing his jaw. "I might find fatherhood agrees with me. Could be here a while, maybe, become quite a nuisance." Tony smiled again. "I can be, you know. A nuisance."

"I'm sure you can," Davey answered. This was obviously some sort of negotiation. But where was it going?

Tony was hardly a menacing figure yet it was clear that Bethany and Abigail were afraid of him. For two strong women, that was surprising. Which meant Tony was unpredictable. Unpredictable people are scary no matter who they are.

Especially the ones who like to hit women and children.

"'Course, if I had some incentive to go, I might just take off. Not bother nobody ever again," Tony said thoughtfully.

"He came for money," Bethany said, disgustedly. "I already told him I don't have any but he refuses to leave."

"Maybe the white knight's got a little green he can spare." Tony smiled at Davey. "You making it with my old lady, huh? Pretty tasty dish. Right? So how about it, white knight?"

Tony stared straight at Davey, serious now.

"I can be very reasonable under the right circumstances." Tony smiled.

Davey was pretty sure he'd seen all of Tony's cards and they didn't add up to much of a hand. He looked at Bethany.

"When was the last time Tony paid child support?" Davey asked.

"Let me think," Bethany said. "Oh yes… *never!*"

Davey clucked his tongue. *"Uh, uh, uh.* Deadbeat Dad is a serious offense in Florida. And my new best friend, as of today, is Monroe County Sheriff's Deputy Hardesty. We're very close."

Tony flinched as Davey strode toward him. Davey grabbed the duffle bag and stuffed the loose shirts and socks into it.

"Hey, hey! That's my *stuff!*" Tony protested. "You can't just come in here and mess with my stuff."

"Just because you were a bad choice twelve years ago does not give you the right to barge in and make yourself at home," Davey said, pulling the ties on the duffle bag tight. Tony grabbed at the bag. Davey pushed him, hard, and he fell backwards onto the couch.

"Come on, *man!*" Tony yelped.

Davey walked to the front door and looked over the railing. There was a piece of shit Toyota with a rear bumper missing and a wrong color replacement door on the passenger side backed into the spot below Bethany's apartment.

It looked like Tony might be living in it.

Tony followed Davey out the front door. "Give me my stuff, man. This is really uncool," Tony sniveled.

"The police are always happy to get a lead on a Deadbeat Dad," Davey mused. "Then, if they have any other outstanding warrants, well that's automatic jail-time."

Tony looked concerned for the first time.

"Your car?" Davey asked, looking over at the Toyota.

"Look, be cool. We're not even talking about that much, here. A couple hundred bucks."

Davey threw the duffle bag over the railing and it landed on the Toyota's hood with a *clunk*. Something heavy and solid was in there but it was broken now. Spreading liquid darkened the duffel bag.

"Tomorrow morning, my close personal friend Deputy Hardesty will have your name and license plate number. So, you've got a little over 12 hours to get your sorry ass out of Monroe County. Far, far away!"

Tony made a quick assessment of his options, looked up at Davey one last time and scurried down the stairs to his car.

"You ain't seen the last of me, *man!*" Tony yelled, shaking his bony finger at Davey. "I'll get you for this, you'll see." He jumped into the driver's seat, started the car, and was gone, tires squealing.

Bethany and Abigail stood in the doorway, watching.

Sometimes life hands you a moment of perfect clarity, a single instant in which all of life's biggest questions coalesce into one, unified answer. And that's what happened to Davey right now.

Abigail threw her arms around Davey's waist and hugged him, tight. "Just because I'm hugging you doesn't mean I'm not still really pissed at you," she sobbed into his shirt.

Davey rubbed her back with his hand. "I know, Sweetie," he said. "I'm sorry. I mean Abigail."

Abigail snuffled. "You can call me that if you want to. That can be the exception."

This was where he belonged; these were his people. His life had purpose and meaning with them. There was no safe place in the world, not really. But this was the place he must never abandon.

Ever again.

Bethany put her hands on Davey's shoulders and hugged him from behind. Because that's what you do when you're a single mom. You take the hug any which way you can.

Davey pulled Bethany around in front of him and they all stood there, clinging to each other. "I just hope... I hope I haven't lost you by being such an idiot," Davey said into Bethany's ear.

"Don't talk. Just hold me," Bethany said softly.

"I think we should move in together," Davey said.

Nobody said a word. But he felt their arms tighten around him.

Chapter 19

"You can't quit. You were born to do this," Davey insisted.

"Time to move on," Mark shook his head sadly. "I can't hack it anymore."

Mark had quit the dive shop and Kate had asked Davey to try and talk him out of it.

Mark hadn't really been himself since the unresponsive diver incident. Everything about his attitude had changed. The confidence, the extraordinary skill with people, it had all gone away.

"You can't let this one thing throw you like that," Davey pleaded. "You know what the odds are? I mean, we see crazy stuff every day. But when was the last time anyone had an unresponsive diver?"

Mark started to speak.

"Not counting Erin," Davey added quickly.

Mark was silent.

"The odds are a thousand to one against that ever happening again." Davey held his hands wide in supplication.

"But it did happen," Mark said, shaking his head slowly. "And it happened to me."

They were sitting at the bar at Captain Ed's, overlooking the sound. Neutral territory. Not a place either of them went normally. It was down Route 1 past the stoplight where the road divides, halfway to Tavernier.

"If you hadn't been there. If you hadn't taken over, she'd be dead. On my watch. A dead diver, not an unresponsive diver," Mark was shaking his head again. "How do I come back from that?"

"I understand; you're upset," Davey said supportively. "Anyone would be. But it's behind you now. The next time something happens––if there even is a next time––you'll be ready for it."

"Not a risk I'm willing to take," Mark insisted.

Davey was beginning to realize it was hopeless to argue.

"What will you do?" he asked his friend. "You've invested years in this. You're one of the best I've ever seen."

"Buddy of mine is a bartender down at Barracuda's. He's going to teach me how and they'll let me double on the early shifts with him."

Davey shook his head in disbelief.

"Once I learn the ropes, they'll give me my own shifts," Mark said.

"Terrible waste," Davey said, sadly.

"For the best, I think," Mark answered. "Anyway, I can do that for a while until I think of something new."

"You belong on a dive boat," Davey insisted. "You'll be a Course Director in five years."

"That's just not happening," Mark said. "Anyhow, thanks for trying. I appreciate the kind words."

Davey paused and then tried one more tack.

"It was Kate's idea. She doesn't want to see you go any more than I do," Davey said. "Katherine, too."

"Wow," Mark responded. "That was random."

"Shouldn't surprise you. They're odd ducks but you're valued. No one wants to try and replace you."

Mark smiled at the thought of Katherine and Kate.

He stood up and put his hand on Davey's shoulder.

"Thank you for saving that girl. And for saving me from having a dead diver on my conscience for the rest of my life."

"It wasn't your fault."

"It was my responsibility," Mark said, and he slowly walked away.

"Take care of yourself," Davey called after him.

"Thanks," Mark waved. "Come down and see me sometime. We have Happy Hour, too, you know."

"I'll do that," Davey promised, but they both knew he wouldn't.

Davey signaled the bartender for his tab. He noticed a grizzled man wearing a dirty, white captain's hat several seats down, looking at him with a crooked grin.

"Four twenty-five," said the bartender and Davey started to count out some bills, including a five-dollar tip.

"Dive instructor?" asked the man with the hat.

"Yeah," Davey answered, without really looking at him.

"Dangerous business, I guess, huh?" the man persisted.

"Not really," Davey said absently. "Just need to respect it, is all."

"How 'bout that woman who drowned a couple months back?"

Davey really didn't want to get into a conversation with the guy so he just pretended not to hear him.

"I's there, you know," the man said. Davey looked at him finally.

"On the dive boat?" Davey asked.

"Naw, got my own boat," the man answered, happy to have engaged Davey at last. "Center console charter fisher. Thirty-foot Contender outta Islamorada."

"The way I heard it, there were no other boats onsite," Davey challenged.

"Gone by the time they called the Coast Guard," he offered, looking at his empty glass, inviting Davey to buy him a drink.

Davey didn't bite.

"Some crazy tourist lady," the man smiled at the recollection. "We's fishing there in the deeps. Not on the dive site. She's says, 'I'm gonna go check the hooks,' and in she jumps with her scuba gear. Tells me not to raise the dive flag. Comes back 20 minutes later an' says, 'Ain't no fish here,' an' off we go back to port."

"That's odd," Davey mused.

"We get all kinds in the charter business," they man looked at his beer glass again, pointedly. "I'll tell ya all about it, if ya like."

"No, I gotta run," Davey demurred. If he wanted crazy, he could always talk to Binky.

"'Ain't no fish here,'" he repeated and laughed. "In the ocean! Kind of a looker, though. Had a little octopus tattoo right over her butt-crack just above her bathin' suit."

"Thanks," Davey called out to the bartender as he walked out. He didn't look forward to telling Kate that Mark wasn't coming back.

• • •

Carlos's line of hibiscus plants along the patio wall was in full bloom. There was a profusion of red flowers, making even the austere architecture of Captain Dan's Dive Resort seem festive.

"*Hola, Carlos,*" Davey said as he arrived in the morning.

"*Hola, Mister Davey,*" Carlos answered with a smile.

"All your hard work paid off," Davey said. "The hibiscus are beautiful!"

"Thank you, *gracias,*" Carlos said with a slight bow.

"You're both well?" Davey asked. "I don't see Lucinda."

"We are both very tired," said Carlos. "We are getting old, I'm afraid. But we are well, thank you for asking."

"You're not getting old," Davey said with a smile. "I couldn't do half of what you do every day." Carlos smiled at the compliment.

Davey walked down to *Calypso*. They were headed to the *Spiegel Grove* today.

When the safety briefing was completed and they were driving through the mangroves, Greg and Davey put their heads together on the dive plan.

"We got a total of eight people," Greg said. "You want to keep them together as one group?"

"That depends," said Davey. "You plan to go inside?"

"One of my buddy teams wants to see Snoopy. So yeah, we will if conditions allow it," said Greg

Snoopy was an insignia painted on the floor of a lower deck. It was about 90 feet deep and located amidships in a very dark area of the passageway. Everyone wanted to see Snoopy but the guides tended to be circumspect about who they took in there.

"I'm not taking 10 divers that far into the wreck. Not even with one of us bringing up the rear. *No way!*" Davey shook his head.

"Two groups it is," Greg agreed.

"I'm worried about my mother," Staci said, once she realized that she and her husband, Don, would be in Greg's group and her mother would be paired with another diver in Davey's group.

"She's never done a deep wreck before and she's a little scared." Staci implored Davey with her eyes.

"I'll keep a close watch on her," Davey promised. "She'll be right behind me and we aren't going to do anything exotic."

"Okay, I'm trusting you," Staci said, meaning she didn't trust him at all. Staci's mom, Angela, didn't seem all that nervous but Davey paired her with Geno, another diver he wanted to keep close tabs on. Geno had 50 dives in his logbook and he'd been deep before but Davey just had a feeling about him. He wanted Geno close by.

His other two divers were less of a concern. They were husband and wife, Christo and Marion, with lots of deep dives. They'd been on the *Spiegel* before. Davey told them to stay behind Geno and Angela but stick close to the group. He gave all four a very detailed briefing about how he planned to conduct the dive and what he expected from them.

"Don't worry about us," Christo said. "We know what to do." And Marion nodded.

Calypso moored on Ball 6, the line that tied off amidships at the highest point of the superstructure. When they got to depth, Davey made sure his group looked closely at the point where the line met the wreck.

Conditions were ideal. About 80 feet of visibility and no current.

Greg's group descended down the portside hull to the entry point for the lower deck. Always do the deepest part of the dive first.

Davey got his group together on the first deck and headed for the ship's bridge. Angela and Geno swam right behind him. Christo and Marion brought up the rear, looking good.

The *Spiegel's* bridge is a beginner's swim-thru. It's a straight line, about 30 feet across with good light all the way through. Like a lot of guides, Davey took divers through the bridge before he attempted any other swim-thrus, just to see how they reacted.

Davey pointed at the entrance and indicated swimming into it. Angela and Geno signaled OK. Davey looked at Christo and Marion. OK? OK. Davey swam into the open hatchway.

Swimming from port to starboard, there are two open doorways to the right and several open windows to the left. The wheelhouse itself was well lit. Davey swam straight through, checking behind himself to make sure his divers were following him. He came out the starboard side, turned, and took the pictures.

The pictures everyone wants.

Davey checked his computer: 16 minutes No Decompression Limit time. He signaled his divers for their air pressure. Angela was at 2,000 psi, not great, not bad. Geno had 2,200. Christo and Marion both signaled 2,400. Impressive. Christo didn't even need to look; he knew.

That's advanced diving, Davey thought to himself. He's been keeping track of his air pressure on his own.

Davey led the group aft along the deck. At the railing they descended to the second-level deck and headed for the crane operator's cabin. There was an American flag on a pole on top of the cabin. It hung around the flagpole in the slack current.

Davey signaled for Angela and Geno to pose next to the flag. He'd take a picture. They swam forward but overshot. Then they fumbled with the flag for a bit. It took about a minute to get them in position, while Marion and Christo hovered in place over the deck.

Davey got the picture. When visibility is good, this is everyone's favorite shot.

Davey checked everyone's air. Angela, 1,500; Geno 1,700. Marion, 1,800. Christo looked at Marion and signaled 1,800.

All good, Davey thought. They had 10 minutes NDL time but they'd be back on the line sooner than that. Angela was the fastest air-user and he had to get her on the line with 1,000 psi in her tank.

Christo wanted to go inside the superstructure but Davey wagged his finger: NO. He pointed to the flag and pointed to his camera. Christo and Marion swam up to get in position. Christo held the flag out. Marion hovered next to the flagpole and Christo hovered on the other side holding the corner of the flag.

Davey moved into position to frame the shot. Just in time to see Christo give the out-of-air signal. Then Davey saw Christo's big eyes.

And he watched Christo spit out his regulator.

Christo was headed for the surface but Davey got to him at around 60 feet. He shoved his alternate air regulator into Christo's mouth and hit the purge button. Then he dumped the air out of Christo's BCD and shook his shoulder strap, really hard.

He did that twice.

Christo was choking on water but Davey held the regulator in his mouth. They were descending slowly because Davey had emptied both BCDs. Davey had a death grip on Christo's BCD strap. Christo was still coughing but at least he had stopped trying to swim up.

The other three watched in awe mixed with horror. At least they'd stayed where they were. Good for them. Davey signaled for everyone to follow him toward the mooring line and they did. Christo had stopped coughing. Davey made eye contact and saw that he was calmer. He signaled, OK? Yeah, OK.

Now they had to get to the surface.

Davey checked his air. He had 1,500 psi, enough to get two divers to the surface. He asked for everyone else's air and they were all over 1,000 psi. He looked at Christo's submersible pressure gauge and, sure enough, it was on zero.

Okay, we'll figure that one out later.

Davey moved slowly up the mooring line, one foot per second. He watched all four divers to make sure no one was getting ready to do something stupid. Angela, the one he was supposed to watch out for, was calm and perfect for God's sake! Geno was fine. Marion was upset, probably about Christo, but everyone signaled OK.

Davey looked into Christo's eyes: you, OK? Yeah, I'm OK. Christo was totally calm now. In a few minutes they'd be back on the boat.

They went up the line slowly and waited out the three-minute safety stop.

When they were finally onboard had their gear off, Christo couldn't look Davey in the eye.

"What the hell happened to your air, man?" Davey asked. There was an unmistakable edge to his voice.

"I dunno," Christo mumbled. "That's never happened before."

"Last time I checked, you had 1,800 psi," Davey said.

"Yeah, that was probably wrong," Christo admitted.

"You think!" Davey asked, incredulous.

"Marion and I use the same amount of air, pretty much every dive," Christo said. "So, I just figured if she had 1,800, I had 1,800."

Davey was stunned. He could barely ask the next question.

"And you didn't check your own SPG?" Davey asked. "Like, ever?"

"I know, rookie mistake, right?" Christo was hangdog.

"Yeah, the kind that kills people," Davey said, with resignation.

Control! There is no control. Anyone who thought they had control over other divers underwater was high.

But there was no point in making it worse.

"Good dive, everybody," Davey said, upbeat. "Angela, great job! Superstar. Tell your daughter to stop worrying about you."

Angela beamed.

"I'll be right back down and we can switch over our gear," Davey said. "Hang loose and hydrate."

Working with assholes was part of the job, Davey reminded himself. No need to get worked up about it.

"We can't double dip the *Spiegel,*" Davey said to Di when he got up to the flybridge. "Why not," Di wanted to know.

"Because I got a diver who can't do a second deep dive. Not with me, anyway. Either we keep him on the boat or we go shallow."

Ultimately, it was Di's decision. He was the captain. But he respected Davey's judgment.

"Benwood good for you?" Di asked.

"*Benwood* is perfect," said Davey. "Thanks. You're a lifesaver."

• • •

The crowd at Get Shorty's was pretty big for a Happy Hour that wasn't also a Ladies Night. Davey stood at the entrance with Bethany and Abigail.

"First time in a bar, huh?" Davey asked.

"It's a patio dining room," Abigail answered. "How is this any different from where my Mom works?"

Davey shrugged; she was right.

"So, this is the infamous Bubble Talk," Bethany said with a smile.

"Part of it anyway," Davey said and he led them to the corner of the bar where Di was sitting next to Roald.

"Davey Jones, you motherless f--!" Di stopped short when he saw Abigail. "You wonderful guy, you."

"Where's Elpis?" Davey asked.

"She broke my heart, man," Di moaned. "Athena betrayed me! All women are harpies." That seemed to be as close to an answer as he was going to get so Davey moved on.

"This is Bethany," Davey made the introductions. "And this is Abigail. Di and Roald. I expect you all to be on your best behavior."

Di kissed Bethany's hand with great ceremony. "He has been keeping you to all himself. He is a selfish, very bad man."

"I am happy to meet you," offered Roald. "Bethany, Abbie."

Abigail didn't correct Roald, which surprised Davey.

Jorge looked at Davey with anticipation. "It's okay if Abigail sits at the bar, Jorge?" Davey asked.

"So long as she don't dance on it," Jorge answered, and Abigail smiled and blushed.

"You know mine," Davey said, "plus a Coke and… a Chardonnay?" Bethany nodded. "Yeah, a Chardonnay," Davey said.

Jorge went to get the drinks. Davey noticed that Abigail was staring at Roald with undisguised teenage infatuation. Okay, well that was something that was coming down the pike.

So… look forward to that.

"You hear what happened to Scuba Doo?" Di asked Davey.

"No, did the judge rule already?" Davey asked.

"Jerry loses everything," Roald offered. "The husband is winning a settlement up to a half millions dollars."

"Up to…?" asked Davey.

"Jerry has no money. And insurance doesn't pay, just as you said it would not," Roald announced.

Jorge brought the drinks and Davey handed the girls theirs.

"So, the judge cut the baby in half," Di jumped in. "Jerry's only asset is the dive operation. His bitch wife… Excuse me," Di caught himself and bowed his head to Bethany and Abigail. "His darling helpmate and life's partner agreed to sell. She gets half and the husband gets half, up to a half million."

"Will that cover it?" Davey asked.

"It will be close," Di nodded. "But Jerry's wiped out."

"Is this the court case you went to last week?" Bethany asked.

Davey nodded. "Poor guy. His wife will be out the door next."

"Already happened," said Di. "She filed for divorce over a month ago."

"The course of true love," Davey mused. "Present company excepted, naturally." Bethany smiled and kissed Davey.

"You're killing me," Di lamented. "My heart is broken in pieces and you do this right in front of me."

Bethany smiled at Di, tilted her head and kissed him on the cheek. A quick peck. Di brightened and turned scarlet, all at once.

"I am also very much heartbroken," Roald said happily. "Did I mention that?"

"Okay, okay, this isn't the Kissing Booth at the county fair," Davey protested.

"I'm ready to turn the hose on all of you," Abigail said with a grimace and everyone burst out laughing.

"What's so funny," asked Carly pulling up a barstool with Jens at her side.

"Hey, I know you!" said Bethany.

"We met," said Carly with a nod at Davey, "that one night."

"And I am Jens." Bethany shook hands.

"You are hearing about poor Jerry?" Jens asked, after he and Carly ordered drinks.

"We were just talking about it," Davey answered.

"A terrible outcome," Roald offered.

"Terrible," Di concurred.

"He knew it was coming," Davey volunteered. "Not that it helps."

"Well, he ain't goin' to raise no money stockin' shelves at!" How the hell did Binky do it? He arrived on the scene like smoke. Suddenly, he was just there.

Davey chose to ignore him.

"I almost lost someone on the *Spiegel* this week," Davey offered thoughtfully.

"Really?" Bethany was surprised.

Di had already forgotten. "You! You bring divers back from the dead! You don't lose divers."

"What happened?" Carly asked.

"Ran out of air at 80 feet," Davey said.

"Did he then spit out his regulator?" Jens asked.

Davey nodded. "They always do."

"And probably bolt for the surface?" Roald asked.

"Fortunately, I was right there," Davey said. "Two seconds farther away and it would've been a different outcome." There was a moment of silence.

Then, being instructors, they started to re-live the event.

"Was he making the big eyes?" Jens asked.

"You know he was," Davey answered.

"Rapid ascent from 80 feet," Roald pondered. "DCS, that is for certain." Decompression sickness.

Jens jumped in. "Extreme barotrauma. Air embolism. Because he probably holds his breath also."

"Or all of the above," Davey agreed. "Take your pick."

"How does he run out of air on the *Spiegel?*" asked Carly. "New diver?"

"No, experienced diver," said Davey. "He was one of the ones I *wasn't* worried about."

"The *fu--*" Di started, but swallowed what he was about to say when he glanced at Abigail. "--fun never stops," he pivoted.

"Never looked at his air gauge. Can you believe that?" Davey added.

Based on all of their expressions, none of them could.

"He figured he was using the same air volume as his wife."

It took a moment for that to sink in.

"But how, then, did he use so much air?" Jens wanted to know.

"No idea," Davey said, holding his palms up in wonder. "Best guess is he never turned his air off after he assembled his dive kit. Forty-minute boat ride. Slow leak. If he never checked his gauge, he might have gone into the water with 1,500 psi."

"You are saving his life," Roald said, respectfully.

"I was lucky," Davey demurred.

"*Stupid diver* was lucky!" Di said with disgust.

"Nice work," Carly said quietly. No one really liked to think about how close to disaster they all were at all times.

They raised their glasses but no one spoke.

• • •

Lying in bed later, Bethany asked, "So how do you want to do this? You move in with us? We move in here?"

"I should probably move in with you guys," Davey said. "That way Abigail gets to stay in her own room."

Bethany nodded. "That makes sense. Yeah, that's good."

"I do some of my best thinking when you're lying naked next to me in bed," Davey agreed. Bethany poked Davey in the ribs and then climbed up on top of him, her forearms on his chest, her long hair spilling over his face.

"Look at us being all practical and domestic," she said with a cute little smile.

"Since we're combining resources, we could also think about finding a nicer place. Nothing fancy, but nicer."

"Or," Bethany kissed Davey lightly. "We could think about saving some of that money. I've been broke so long I don't even know what it would feel like to have a little something in the bank."

Bethany brushed her breasts against Davey's lips, playfully.

"That's not the way to have a meaningful discussion," he protested. Bethany lifted herself up on her hands.

"I didn't say you should stop," Davey complained.

"You want to hear something incredibly boring?" Bethany asked, lying down beside Davey again. "Before I got pregnant, I was studying to be an accountant."

"Really?"

"Yup, that's me: Betty Bookkeeper. My father's an accountant. It seemed like a nice, safe thing to be." Bethany sighed. "The best laid plans, right? Now look at me."

"Okay," Davey raised the covers and stared at Bethany's naked body.

"You know what I mean," she said, swatting the covers back down. She turned and snuggled closer.

"What happened?" Davey asked.

"Abigail happened."

"Couldn't your family have helped out?"

"No, they pretty much drifted away when I decided to keep the baby. It wasn't a popular decision."

"So, you were on your own," Davey said softly.

"Pretty much," Bethany sighed. "But I wouldn't trade her for anything."

"Hell no!" Davey agreed.

"No pressure but... she absolutely adores you," Bethany said gravely.

"Yeah, no pressure..." Davey said and left it at that.

"So, when you talk about moving into a nicer place, my accountant brain thinks, no, let's save some money."

"Not something we have to decide right now," Davey said. "I'll move in with you guys at the end of the month. And I'll pay the rent."

"Half the rent," Bethany said, poking Davey's chest for emphasis. "Let's be fair about this."

"I already pay that amount here. I can afford it," Davey offered.

"So, you save half and I save half. Betty Bookkeeper has spoken!"

It's very hard to argue with a naked woman. And Bethany was about to make it a lot harder.

• • •

There was an ambulance at Captain Dan's when Davey arrived in the morning. Lights were blazing and two paramedics were hovering over a gurney.

Carlos stood nearby, wringing his hands. The old man was in tears.

"What happened?" Davey asked, putting his hand on Carlos's shoulder.

"Lucinda, she fell," Carlos moaned. "Coming down the stairs with the laundry."

Davey held both Carlos's shoulders and looked directly into his eyes. "Please let me help with those heavy baskets. She can leave them at the top of the stairs. I'll carry them down when the boat comes in."

"She is a proud woman," Carlos answered, nodding. "Even I am not allowed to help. Now they are taking her to the hospital."

Carlos looked around at the motel property.

"Someone needs to watch the front desk."

"You go," Davey insisted. "Someone else will cover the desk."

"I cannot go," Carlos agonized. "Miss Kate would be very angry with me."

"Go," Davey pulled a twenty-dollar bill from his wallet and stuffed it into the old man's hand. "When you know she's okay, take an Uber back here."

Carlos stood paralyzed by indecision. *"Go!"* shouted Davey. The old man climbed into the ambulance next to the gurney as the doors closed. The siren wailed and the vehicle pulled out of the driveway.

When Kate and Katherine arrived, they were in uncharacteristically sunny moods. They were actually laughing together as they got out of the car. That changed quickly when Davey told them what had happened and further informed them that he'd sent Carlos to the hospital with Lucinda.

"Who's watching the front desk?" Katherine asked plaintively, as if someone had stolen food from her plate.

"I'm happy to do it," offered Davey. "But then you'll have to guide two non-swimming snorkelers on the reef."

"I'm not going out on the reef and that's for *damn* sure!" Katherine stated abruptly.

"Well, then you'll have to watch the front desk because I've got PICs to process and you don't know how to do that," said Kate.

Davey knew she was lying. The PICs could wait but Kate didn't want to be pulled out of her comfort zone. Neither did Katherine.

"Why does everything bad always happen to me?" Katherine whined, pursing her lips and shaking her head at the injustice of it all.

Neither one of them asked how badly Lucinda was hurt.

Chapter 20

"I want to learn to scuba dive," Abigail announced excitedly.

Bethany gasped but before she could say anything, Davey said, "That's a great idea. When do we start?"

"What do you mean, 'When do we start?'" Bethany sputtered.

"I thought it was pretty self-explanatory," Davey answered.

"She's only a child!"

"I've certified kids as young as ten."

"But… it's dangerous!"

"I dive every day. It's not dangerous," Davey asserted.

"The stories you tell. They scare me to death."

"Diving is only dangerous when people are stupid," Davey insisted. "It's risk management. I'll teach her how to manage the risks."

Abigail knew when to keep quiet so she let the argument run its course.

"You have no idea what you're asking," Bethany said, shaking her head.

"Do you honestly think I would *ever* let anything bad happen to Abigail?" Davey asked. "Serious question." This was moving into a slightly different territory, upping the stakes. Abigail watched the two of them like a spectator at a tennis match.

"No, but your opinion is biased," Bethany replied. "And you can't control everything that happens underwater. You said so yourself."

"She's smart, she listens, she's an athlete," Davey insisted.

"I'm her mother. I have to be the responsible one who makes the hard decisions." That was match point and Abigail knew it.

It was move-in day for Davey. A couple of hours earlier he had showed up at Bethany's door holding some hangers of clothes and a box of personal items. There were three boxes behind him

"I can't believe this is all the stuff you have," Bethany said, honestly astonished.

"My dive gear is at the shop. These are my clothes. That's my scrapbook. And this is my TV, which I never watch."

"Abigail has more things than you and she's twelve!" Bethany protested.

"I sold everything when I left Illinois," Davey explained. "I rented a furnished apartment and I didn't decorate." He shrugged.

"You're a vagabond," Bethany said, with a laugh.

"I don't have stuff," Davey announced, flatly. "And I really don't need it." Davey followed Bethany into her bedroom.

Davey watched as Bethany pushed her clothes to the right side of the closet and started to combine drawers in her dresser.

"I'll tell you what, though." Davey had a sudden inspiration. "I'll go get a cheap dresser at K-Mart so you don't have to give up any of your drawer space."

"You don't want to get in my drawers?" Bethany said with arched eyebrows.

"Mom!" Abigail shouted from the living room.

"Don't listen to private conversations!" Bethany shouted back.

Davey and Abigail shared a guilty smile and stifled a laugh.

"Okay, put all your stuff back. I'm going to K-Mart." Davey kissed Bethany. "Abigail, you want to take a ride?"

Abigail considered the invitation. "Sure, I'm down."

There was an Ikea in Miami, which would have had a much better selection, but that was a long haul and Davey didn't care much about functional things. Whatever K-Mart had would be fine.

"That one's nice," said Abigail, pointing at a six-drawer, side-by-side dresser as they strolled down the furniture aisle.

"I don't think your mother's room has the floor space for that," David answered. "I don't even think the box will fit in my car."

They walked along, looking at the other choices.

"I like that one," Abigail pointed.

"So do I," Davey answered. "And the next time I'm in the market for a turquoise-colored dresser, that's the one I'm going to get."

"Okay, I get it," Abigail said. "Too girly."

Davey stopped in front of a black, six-drawer upright dresser and examined it critically.

"So... sometimes when there's a really big storm, or I have a bad dream, I go in and sleep with my Mom," Abigail said hesitantly.

"That happen a lot?" Davey asked, pulling one of the drawers open.

"I guess not," Abigail answered on reflection. "More when I was a little kid."

"I don't want you to change what you do because I'm there," Davey said, looking at Abigail.

"Yeah but, I mean, you guys will be in bed together," Abigail said. "So, how's that gonna work?"

"Come here," Davey said, and he led Abigail to one of the floor sample couches. They both sat down.

"You know, it's not just me and your Mom moving in together. We'll all be living together," Davey said. Abigail was looking down so he raised her chin. "I don't want it to be weird for you. And I don't want your life to change in ways that make you feel like you've lost something. Does that make sense?"

Abigail nodded.

"If you don't think this is a good idea, I can probably get my old apartment back." That was a risky because he knew he couldn't, but he wanted to hear what she'd say.

"Actually, I feel a little safer with you there." Abigail made a face.

"Well, okay then, if you have a bad dream and need to sleep with your Mom, you do that."

"But you'll be…"

"Knock on the door, because we deserve our privacy. If we say come in, come in. If we don't answer, we're asleep. Come in and sleep right between us. Bring your blanket. Sleep on top of ours."

"You've thought about this?" Abigail was surprised.

"Totally making it up as I go along. And if you help, I'm sure we can work out everything that needs to be worked out."

Abigail nodded, slowly.

"I like that one," Davey said, looking at the black upright dresser.

Abigail made a face indicating that she didn't share his preference.

While they were loading the box into Davey's car, they talked about Abigail's school and her friends, and one thing led to another.

Ten minutes later, they'd added one more errand to their outing.

"Okay, don't be mad at us," Davey said to Bethany, lugging the box with the dresser into the apartment when they got home.

"Do *not* be mad at us," Abigail repeated with emphasis.

"What's going on? What are you two up to?" Bethany asked.

Davey balanced the box on its end.

"Do you know why Abigail does all her homework at school?" Davey asked.

"Because she's a great student?" Bethany answered.

"Because she doesn't have a computer at home," Davey stated the fact. "You know who else doesn't have a computer at home?"

Davey paused for effect.

"Stone-age tribes in Borneo! Everyone else on the planet has a computer at home," Davey asserted.

Bethany's eyes narrowed. "What did you do?" She was suddenly very serious.

"I got a laptop!" Abigail shouted and she held up the box.

"Davey, really you can't--"

"She needs a computer to keep up with her workload. It's only going to increase. And by doing all her homework at school, she's missing out on social opportunities with her friends. That's not fair."

"Then we should have talked about it. Had a discussion. You can't just come home with a computer, like it's not a big thing. You can't buy her love!"

Bethany was wearing her Mom Hat; this wasn't going to be easy.

"I am *not* buying her love," Davey insisted. "Renting it... maybe..."

Silence.

"Yeah... that didn't come out right," Bethany said, shaking her head.

Davey agreed. "It sounded better in my head."

"*Ewwwww*," said Abigail.

"I panicked. You can be intimidating at times." Bethany was still flushed with anger. Then suddenly, she burst out laughing.

"Me?" Bethany yelped.

"Yes, you!" Davey laughed. It seemed somewhat safe to laugh now.

"I intimidate you!" Bethany said and squinched her face.

"You can be scary. *Sometimes.*"

And that was the end of the argument. For now.

"Well, why don't you take that dresser into the bedroom while I go scare up some lunch."

"Go set up your computer!" Davey whispered to Abigail and she scurried off toward her room.

"And let me be perfectly clear about one thing!" Bethany announced flatly, turning around to confront the two of them. "This isn't over. This is not the way we're going to do things in this house."

"Okay, Mom," said Abigail.

"Okay, Mom," said Davey.

Bethany walked up to Davey and poked him hard in the stomach three times. "Don't. Get. Cute." Davey decided just in time that this was a good opportunity not to be a smartass.

Twenty minutes later, over lunch, the whole Abigail-taking-scuba-diving conversation came up so their first half-day of living together was pretty eventful.

After lunch, while Davey was assembling the dresser, Abigail asked him, "Do you think she'll let me do scuba?"

"I think so," Davey answered. "Give her some time. We hit her with a lot today. That was my fault."

"I really want to, you know," Abigail persisted.

"I know. You just need to be patient right now." Davey put the first drawer on its runners and tested it. It slid smoothly back and forth. "You're not the only one whose world has changed a lot."

"I know," Abigail nodded. "Thanks for being on my side."

"There are no sides, Sweetie," Davey said seriously. "We're all in this together. Let's keep that in mind, okay, always."

"So... are you going to call me that a lot? Or just sometimes?" Abigail asked softly. Davey stopped and thought about it.

"Just sometimes," he said. "And never in front of your friends."

Abigail smiled. "Speaking of friends, I mean, what do I tell people about you?"

"You tell people I'm your Mom's boyfriend. And I'm your friend."

Davey put the second drawer in place and slid it back and forth.

"If that's how you think of me, I mean." he added. "That's up to you. I think of you as my friend. I'd be very happy if you felt the same way about me."

Abigail stood up. She put her hands on Davey's shoulder and kissed him on the cheek. "Thank you, Davey," she said.

"What was that for?" Davey asked, smiling.

"It was a friendship kiss," Abigail said simply and she left the room.

That first night, as they were getting ready for bed, Davey set out his toothbrush and shaving kit in the bathroom for the morning.

"Does it feel weird?" Bethany asked, "Being here instead of your place?"

"A little," answered Davey. "Good weird, though. I feel really good about this."

"So do I," Bethany said, hugging Davey from behind.

"So... are you going to wear pajamas... or..." Bethany hesitated.

"I don't *own* pajamas," Davey said.

"Well, she comes in sometimes. And..."

"I know. We talked about it."

"You and my twelve-year-old daughter talked about you and me sleeping together? How is that not the most terrifying thing I ever heard?"

"Well, we didn't talk about what I'd be wearing. Or not wearing."

"That's a relief. I guess." Bethany looked like she might start hyperventilating.

"I suppose I could wear my sweatpants when we're sleeping."

Bethany nodded. Everyone loves the romance but the logistics take them by surprise.

"She showed me how she got her computer set up already," Bethany said with wonder in her voice. "She's got all these files on her desktop, all labeled. How does she know how to do that?"

"She's twelve," Davey said. "She could probably build a computer from parts."

"That was incredibly generous of you. Too generous. But how is it even going to help? We don't have any internet here."

Davey stopped and looked at the big, blinking red DANGER sign flashing in front of his eyes.

"Yeah, we should probably talk about that," Davey said, as casually as he could manage. "I was thinking maybe we'd get Xfinity."

"It's really expensive!" Bethany responded. "I'd love to but last time I looked into it, there was just no way."

"I'm saving half my rent money. How about if I pay for it?" Davey offered.

"No, you can't. It's too much. And you shouldn't pay for my daughter's broadband."

"It won't just be for her. It's part of the basic cable package. It'll be for all of us."

"I don't know. It's a lot of changes all at once."

"I'm homeless. That's a big change. You don't see me complaining," Davey said, getting into bed, looking up at Bethany.

"You're not homeless. This is your home," Bethany said, dropping her robe onto a chair. Every time Davey saw Bethany naked it sent a little shiver up and down his body. Maybe in 50 years it would be different; he'd be used to it.

But he doubted it.

"Well, if this is my home, I want basic cable," Davey said as Bethany climbed into bed next to him and swung her hair behind her shoulders. Her head lay on the pillow beneath Davey's face.

"Okay, okay. We can get the cable," she whispered.

"Good, they're coming Thursday to install it," Davey said, kissing Bethany. She pushed him away.

"Hey! That's cheating!"

"What? We had a discussion and you agreed to it."

"It's not a discussion if you've already ordered it."

"It felt like it was a discussion."

"Is that right? Well, how does this feel?"

It felt like Bethany wasn't really all that mad, is how it felt.

It felt good.

"So, welcome to the first day of our new lives together," Davey said, kissing Bethany deeply as she moved her body under his. She was warm and firm. Her skin was soft in his hands.

How did I get this lucky? Davey asked himself. How did I ever deserve this girl?

What terrible vengeance is waiting for me just around the corner?

But those thoughts and others melted into the darkness around them as they made love in a world in which they were the only two people who existed.

Afterwards, Bethany lay on Davey's chest and tapped her fingers lightly on his chin.

"So, you have to be honest with me," she said, finally. "If I let Abigail take scuba lessons, will she really be safe? And I don't want your standard happy-face answer."

"She will," Davey answered. "I'll make sure of it. But you have to be totally comfortable with the idea."

"Well, I trust you. You know that. But she's everything to me."

"She's the right age, she's got the right attitude. Plus, I won't let her in the ocean unless I think she's ready."

"I can't believe I'm even considering this," Bethany frowned.

"You'll be facing a lot of new challenges in the next few years as Abigail grows up. She already knows you love her. She needs to see that you trust her, too."

"And you'd be right there, the whole time?"

"She can only dive with me, or a parent, or another certified dive-professional until she's fifteen. So, it's a safe bet she'll always be diving with me," Davey told her.

"Really? Well, that makes me feel a lot better," Bethany said.

"It'll be a fun thing for us to do together. It would actually be a lot of fun for the three of us..." Davey just let it hang there.

"Oh, no. No way! Someone has to survive this." Bethany was shaking her head vehemently.

"So, what... if Abigail and I both die, at least you'll get my car? Is that your secret plan?" Davey looked expectantly.

"I'd be too afraid. I know I wouldn't like it," Bethany said.

Davey pushed Bethany's hair away from her face and stroked her back with his fingertips.

"That's a discussion for another day," Davey offered. "No pressure."

"Yeah, no pressure," Bethany said with a snort.

"Meanwhile, Abigail's ready now. But whatever you decide, I'll support you."

"Right, it's up to me," said Bethany, feeling strangely like nothing was up to her anymore. Not really.

"It's up to you," Davey said. "Goodnight." And he kissed her.

• • •

When Davey arrived at Get Shorty's without Bethany, it felt weird to him. But then, everything felt weird these days. Good weird, but still. It was as if he'd woken up on a different planet.

A nice planet with people he loved, but not Earth.

Definitely not Earth.

There was a light breeze out the northwest wafting the salt smell of Blackwater Sound in toward the tiki bar.

The band was playing and the tourists were dancing the Macarena. Their world was unchanged, the same as it always had been yesterday and the day before

Carly and Jens were at the bar next to Di, and Elpis was there by his side. They were staring into each other's eyes adoringly.

"Elpis, you're back!" Davey said, brightly.

Elpis smiled and held Di's face in her hands. "He is such a baby! I go visit my sister in Greece for 10 days and he thinks I've abandoned him. Such a child."

"I am a passionate man," Di protested, palms up in supplication. "When my heart breaks, it breaks."

Di looked deeply into Elpis's eyes and smiled. "When Pandora closes her box, after she releases all the evils into the world, the only thing left inside is Elpis: Hope. Hope is all we have left. Hope is our salvation."

"Hey Davey," said Carly, with a hug. "I hear you're a householder these days."

"You hear right," Davey answered. "Wonders never cease."

"Told you," Carly said with a knowing smile.

Jorge brought Davey his first beer as he pulled up a barstool.

"So where is your girl? You think we want to stare at your ugly face all by yourself?" Di asked.

"She's being a mom," Davey answered. "Someone has to be the grown-up."

Carly smiled and shook her head. "Pretend all you want. I'm not buying it," she said, and laughed, softly.

Elpis cupped Davey's chin in her surprisingly strong hand. "You have a beautiful face, Davey Don't listen to him. He knows *nothing!*"

"Dudes and dudesses! What up?" Theo hopped up onto a barstool and engulfed the group with his *faux* hipness. He signaled Jorge for a Happy Hour beer.

He was wearing a wool cap over his dreadlocks, which made him look more Jamaican than Javier, except not really.

"Dudesses? What is that?" asked Jens, earnestly.

Davey waved his hand dismissively. "It's nothing. Not a real word."

"Real enough," insisted Theo, taking his beer from Jorge. "So, I've got a tasty morsel for all of you to chew on."

"What's he saying?" asked Jens, totally lost again.

"Don't get cute," Di warned. "You got something to say, say it."

Theo took a long sip of beer, aware that everyone was looking at him.

"You're overplaying your hand," Davey suggested.

Theo put down his cup. "Scuba Doo just got sold," he said and wiped the beer off his upper lip.

"The hell!" Di challenged.

"Really, so soon?" Carly asked. "It's only been, what, six weeks?"

"Bought by a couple from Texas. Or maybe it was Montana," Theo asserted.

"So really, you know nothing," Di said, decisively. Theo was unfazed.

"I know what I know," he insisted. "You don't have to believe me."

"I am hearing also the same story," said Roald, who sat down at the hightop next to Theo.

"From who?" demanded Di. "That woman who was the roommate of the brother of the mate's uncle, or whatever she was?"

Roald made a grim face and sucked air in through his teeth. "No, she and I are not talking so much anymore."

"I bet there's a story there," Carly said with delight.

Roald looked honestly perplexed. "I like her very much. But she is beginning to think she is owning me and I'm not so good with that."

Carly leaned over and gave Roald a hug because, why not? "Poor man," she commiserated. "Get used to having that problem."

"I don't give a crap about your love life," Di interjected. "I want to hear more about Scuba Doo."

"I am hearing that it sold," Roald repeated. "I did not hear any amounts."

"I heard they got a million and a half," Theo piped in, trying to regain control of his story.

"Ridiculous!" said Di, shaking his head. "No way they got that."

"They got a nice boat. That's worth something," Theo objected.

"It's an old boat," Di reposted. "I would pay for that boat $75,000 at most."

"Don't forget he owns the parking lot next to the shop," Carly added. "On a canal."

"After a fatality?" Di asked, incredulous. "It's a distress sale. No one pays that much right now, today."

"It sold for $825,000."

Everyone turned toward the speaker. When did Binky get here?

"*Bullshit!*" said Di, after a pause, but only because it was Binky. The figure was very realistic.

"What does it matter?" asked Elpis. "Who cares what the price is? It's not your money."

"We have to know. It's our business," insisted Di, defensively.

"My darling, it is very much *not* your business," Elpis stroked Di's chin. "You are gossiping, that is all."

"We are being concerned. About our community. And our colleague." Di nodded his head decisively.

"So, what is that meaning for Jerry? Does he pay off his judgment?" Roald wanted to know.

"How would we know that?" Di asked. "Does he have a mortgage? Is the judgment a dollar amount or whatever he gets for half the business?" Di counted out the variables on his fingers.

Then, as if on cue, they all turned to Davey, expectantly.

"How would I know?" Davey protested. "I don't know any of those things."

"You're his friend, yes?" asked Jens.

"Hardly friends. We talked. He came diving once."

"You testified at his hearing," Theo added.

"Purely by accident. I just got called because I was there. And it was awful."

No one spoke. After a moment, Roald broke the silence.

"At least you are knowing him better than any of us," he said.

Davey shrugged. How could he explain to these people that he didn't have any facts to add to what they'd already heard?

"Well," said Elpis finally. "Your friend was in trouble because of money. And now he has money. So at least he is in less trouble today and maybe no trouble at all. Be happy for him."

"Poor son of a bitch," Di said solemnly, raising his glass and taking a drink.

"Why? Why do you say that?" Elpis wanted to know.

"Owing someone money you don't have, that's one problem," answered Di. "But losing everything you've spend your whole life earning, that's a bigger problem, I think."

Everyone was silent with their own thoughts.

Some nodded. Yes, they could see it.

Having a judgment against you, well, that was a terrible thing.

But giving everything you had in the world to a total stranger and having nothing left over.

Yeah, that was worse.

Chapter 21

Two eagle rays swam by in a tandem ballet, large, graceful, wings in perfect unison. Davey watched in fascination, as if there and yet not there. He hovered, motionless, in the water column.

Two nurse sharks were swimming together. Almost unheard of; they always hunt solo. But these two were side by side. They nodded at Davey as they swam by. Did he see that right?

"I'm a better diver than he is," said one of the sharks. No surprise there. Sharks tend to brag.

The visibility was perfect, a hundred feet at least. In fact, it didn't seem like there was water at all. It seemed to Davey that he was flying, floating on thin air. But still able to swim.

Two southern stingrays passed in front of him, majestic, stately. Not as large as the eagle rays. One was missing its tail.

"I'm a better diver than he is," said the stingray without a tail.

Davey started to feel short of breath and realized he hadn't been breathing. He needed air. He tried to breathe but couldn't. No air would come. Was his regulator jammed? He had no regulator!

He was underwater without a regulator. He needed air!

Davey sat straight up in bed, gasping for breath.

It was a dream!

A dream and he'd been holding his breath. It took a few seconds before he stopped gulping air.

"What?" asked Bethany, groggily. "What's the matter?"

"She was a better diver than he was," Davey said, still not totally awake. "That's what Jerry told me. She was a better diver."

"*What?*" Bethany wasn't following. Didn't really want to follow.

"Nothing," Davey answered. "Just a dream. It was just a dream."

"S'posed to sleep when you're dreaming," Bethany complained.

He leaned over to kiss the side of her head. "Go away! Sleeping," Bethany said. She pushed him away and her hand brushed against his bare legs.

"You need to put on your sweatpants," she said, her face still crushed into the pillow. "Case Abigail comes in."

"Sorry I woke you," Davey said, grabbing his sweat pants off the chair.

"You didn't," Bethany answered and she was asleep again.

• • •

"Okay, you're signed in," said Davey. "And you see there, you're registered under Captain Dan's Dive Resort, so you're our student."

Abigail gave Davey a sideways, teenager look.

"You know how to do all this without my help, don't you?" Davey realized, nodding.

"Yep," answered Abigail, popping the "p" with her lips.

"Okay, there are five separate modules. You could probably do one per night. If you get hung up on anything, I'll be out in the living room." Davey kissed Abigail on the top of the head and walked away.

He'd never done that before; it was a first. But she'd kissed him on the cheek that time before. And he didn't want to rush anything, but still, they needed to figure out who they were to each other.

It was a process.

"If I get *hung up* on anything?" Abigail asked, a little sarcastic.

"Look, I know you're smart. But this is all new stuff and some of it's a little complicated." Davey smiled and left the room.

"How's she doing?" Bethany asked when Davey sat down on the couch next to her. She was sipping a glass of Chardonnay.

"She'll be fine. Right now, she's trying to figure out how to be cool and casual about something brand new and a little scary."

"Her friend Brittany told her she's the luckiest girl in the world to be doing scuba. Literally, the luckiest girl in the world!" Bethany said. Davey smiled.

"That's good," he said. "That's social capital. Very important for a kid her age."

Bethany leaned into Davey and he put his arm around her.

Bethany bit her lower lip. "You aren't..." she started, then stopped. "I mean, you're not..." Bethany stopped again.

"What? I'm not what?" Davey asked.

"I don't even know how to ask," Bethany said, shaking her head.

"Then I don't know how to answer," Davey said.

They were both quiet for a minute.

"It's just that... your daughter was about Abigail's age when... I can't even say it." But she didn't have to. Davey knew what she meant.

Davey touched Bethany's face with his fingertips, serious for once. "Stasie is gone and she's never coming back. I'll never see her again. She's gone. Forever."

A tear ran down Bethany's cheek.

"Abigail is a totally different person; she's herself. I'm not confusing the two of them," Davey promised.

"I'm sorry," Bethany said, burying her face in Davey's shoulder.

"Don't be sorry," Davey said. "It was a fair question."

He kissed her forehead and inhaled her scent.

This was a brave new world.

Who knew what traps or treasures lay around the next corner?

• • •

When Davey arrived at the dive shop, he saw the new maid carrying a basket of clean sheets up the stairs to the linen closet.

Lucinda had fractured her fibula in the fall. She'd be on crutches for three months because of her advanced age. She still kept the books but she couldn't do any of the housekeeping, which had Kate in a fury because she was paying extra money to keep the rooms made up.

Davey went to set up the boat while he waited for the dive shop to open. Later, when he was checking the morning's manifest, Davey said to Kate, "Abigail finished her knowledge development. The next time I get an open water class we can just add her to it."

"This is our busy season," said Kate, sternly. "I need all hands focused on our regular business."

"Which is why I'm adding Abigail to a regular class instead of giving her private lessons," Davey said. "It doesn't take me out of rotation and it doesn't cost you a thing."

"It doesn't make me anything, either," said Kate, a little sourly.

"We already had this conversation, Kate," Davey said quietly but firmly. "Do we need to have it again?"

Kate had agreed not to charge Abigail for the Open Water certification, the part Davey was teaching, and Davey agreed to pay the certifying agency directly for the online course and C-card.

"No, we're fine," Kate said, sullenly. "You've got an Open Water class next week. We'll slide her in there."

"Is everything okay, Kate? Are you alright?" Davey asked.

"Yeah, yeah," she said, distractedly. "There's a lot going on. Come talk to me after the afternoon boat."

Both tours were uneventful. It was one of those rare days when the ocean is as calm as a lake: Lake Atlantic the locals call it. Visibility was so crystal clear you could see 150 feet in every direction from the current line at French Reef. Swimming through the sand channels on the bottom you could still see the dive boat on the surface, which was not possible when there were any waves.

Davey was guiding experienced divers, morning and afternoon, and even though he kept his guard up, no one needed intervention during any of the four dives. The biggest challenge was keeping up with the pictures because there were so many opportunities in the crystal-clear water.

A lone bull shark swam by on the eastern edge of the reef and everybody waved and posed because they thought it was a reefie.

"That was a *bull shark?*" Darren gasped when they were back on the boat.

"Yep. Pretty rare sighting for here," said Davey. "It was cool."

"I'm a lot less excited knowing it was a bull shark," Darren answered.

"Bull sharks are fine. You don't bother them; they won't bother you," Davey assured him. But Davey could tell Darren was more apprehensive on the second dive.

Later, after all the tanks had been filled and put away, Davey went up to the shop to talk to Kate.

"What's up?" he asked.

"So..." Kate said, closing a couple of files and locking them in her desk drawer. "How long have you known that Carlos and Lucinda are Cuban?"

"I didn't know," Davey answered, honestly. "I thought they were from Belize."

"That's what they said. Turns out they've been lying to us for over 30 years, if you can believe that," Kate said, bitterly.

"You think you know people!" Katherine shouted from the back. "You trust them, treat 'em like family, and this is what you get!"

"Would your Dad have hired them if he'd known they were Cuban?" Davey asked.

"Hell no!" said Kate. "Cubans will rob you blind! *Every time!*"

"Have Carlos and Lucinda ever stolen from you?" Davey asked.

"Well... no, I don't think so. But we never knew they were Cuban!" In the face of this ironclad logic, Davey decided to cede the point.

"So, what did you want to talk to me about?" he asked.

"When Lucinda broke her leg, they took X-rays. There was a small tumor on her fibula. The biopsy showed it was cancer. Lucinda has bone cancer."

"That's terrible!" said Davey.

"It's bad news for us, that's for sure!" shouted Katherine.

Davey was still having trouble seeing what any of this had to do with him.

"They don't have any health insurance, naturally," Kate continued. "So, they can't afford treatment in the United States. But Cuba has universal healthcare. So, they're going to go back to Cuba."

There was the headline.

Kate had a real problem getting to the point but Davey suspected they were at least in the vicinity of what she wanted to talk to him about by now. So, he waited, silently.

"Didn't you say your girlfriend was an accountant or something?" Kate asked, as if she were just making conversation.

"That was her major," Davey agreed, without bothering to add that she hadn't finished her degree.

"Well, with Carlos and Lucinda leaving, we have an opportunity that might be perfect for the two of you," Kate said, brightly.

Davey got ready for a whole lot of shoes to drop, all at once.

"It comes with free living quarters and we'd pay you guys exactly what we've been paying Carlos and Lucinda, even though they were with us for decades." Kate finished with what she felt certain was an extra, added inducement. "Plus, you can still work as a dive instructor and make some extra cash, if you want to do that, too. As long as it doesn't conflict with your other responsibilities."

"I hope you see this as a sign of how much we trust and care about you!" Katherine shouted from her repair bench. Davey suspected Mister Vodka had made his first appearance of the day.

Davey wasn't sure exactly how to respond so he started to laugh. And once he started it was pretty hard to stop.

"This isn't the reaction I was hoping for," Kate said, a little miffed.

"You're joking, right?" Davey asked, incredulously. "I mean you have to be joking."

"It's a good offer!" Kate sputtered, indignantly.

"It's a terrible offer and you know it!" Davey stated positively. "You've been taking advantage of these two poor immigrants for 35 years because they didn't have any better options. And now you think I'm going to take a turn in the barrel because they're going back home? Not a chance!"

"I think I kind of resent your tone." Kate was defensive. "We have a good opportunity here and we thought of you first. It's a compliment. And that's how you should see it."

"Okay Kate, I won't debate the point. But here's the reality: I'm not going to live on-site and be your 24-hour maintenance monkey. That's just never going to happen."

Katherine stepped outside of her safe cubicle, glass in hand, so she could listen better.

"I'm a dive instructor and that's what I'm going to continue to be," Davey went on. "If you want to hire Bethany to do your bookkeeping--and she'd be an inspired choice, by the way--that's a salaried position at market rates, not abused-immigrant rates."

Kate was clearly not happy with the way things were going.

"I'm sure there are a lot of bookkeepers out there," she said sullenly.

Davey nodded. "And I'll bet a lot of them know how to skim off the top without anyone being the wiser. So go ahead and hire a stranger for less money, by all means."

"I need to think about this some more," Kate said, disappointed that she had not been able to advantage of Davey the way she'd hoped.

"Take all the time you need. By the way, I get an average of two offers a week from other dive shops. I've been loyal to Captain Dan's because you hired me way back when and I like the team here."

"What are you saying? That you'll leave if we don't hire Bethany?" Kate was a little concerned at this point.

"Not at all. But it would be a nice selling point if we were both working at the same place," Davey said evenly.

"We're going to need to think about this," Katherine drawled in her whiskey voice from the back. "Y'all need to hang by the phone and we'll get back to you."

Davey nodded to Kate and headed for the door.

"No, we don't need to think about it," Kate folded like a house of cards. "Davey, you're good for the shop; I don't want to lose you. Especially with Mark gone. And if you think Bethany's a good choice for us as bookkeeper, I'm willing to trust your recommendation."

"We need to think about this!" Katherine insisted.

"No, Katherine. We don't," Kate said flatly. "It's decided. Have Bethany come talk to me. We'll work something out."

Yeah right, a negotiation between a lion and a lamb. Not going to happen.

"Before I tell Bethany to come talk to you, let's discuss general parameters." Davey suggested a figure for Bethany's salary. Kate's eyes nearly popped out of her head and she countered with one just over half of Davey's.

"She makes more than that as a waitress," Davey shook his head.

Davey took fifteen percent off his first number. "If that doesn't work, then there's really nothing for you and Bethany to talk about."

Kate reluctantly agreed and Katherine looked as if she might die on the spot. "Of course, I can't speak *for* Bethany," Davey said as an afterthought. "But I think she might be interested in this. You'll hear back from her." And he walked out of the shop.

Later, over dinner, Bethany was saying, "Well, whatever secret *juju* you laid on Ben, it seems to be wearing off."

"Is he giving you a hard time again?" Davey asked.

"Just a lot of little digs. And an overall bad attitude," Bethany said. "It may be because he knows we're living together now."

"How does he know that?" Davey asked.

Bethany pretended she hadn't heard the question. Davey stared at her, waiting.

"Oh, for heaven's sakes, nobody has any privacy down here. It's like a small town," Bethany sputtered.

289

"So, you told him?" Davey asked.

"No, but I may have mentioned it to Kirsten and she possibly said something to Ben," Bethany said with her most innocent eyes.

"Can I have some more mac and cheese?" Abigail asked. Davey held up the bowl just out of her reach. "Please," she added.

"Well, this actually works well with something that came up at the shop today," Davey said, smiling. He told Bethany about the bookkeeping job and told her the salary he and Kate had settled on.

"Are you kidding me right now?" Bethany shrieked.

"Not kidding. It's a solid offer," Davey answered.

"When were you planning to tell me about it," she challenged.

"It just happened today," Davey protested. "I was going to tell you tonight and this seemed like the perfect time."

"I still can't believe it."

"Believe it. It's a real offer."

"But I'm not qualified. I never got my degree."

"You've already got the job. That's how qualified you are."

"I don't know tax-law, I'm not certified in the state of Florida…"

"All you need to know now is how to run QuickBooks," Davey interrupted. "Everything is all set up already, what do you call it the Chart…"

"Chart of Accounts," Bethany said.

"Right. And once a year the file goes to their CPA and he files the taxes. That's not your job."

"So, I'm just doing order entry, basically," Bethany said.

"If you say so," Davey answered.

"I can do that," she said, a little more confidently.

"I know you can do that. You can do anything." Davey leaned over and kissed Bethany.

"People are eating here," Abigail objected.

Davey and Bethany looked at each other and laughed. "My apologies, Miss. We'll try to conduct ourselves with more propriety in *fewt-chah!*" Davey barked.

Bethany stifled a smile.

"Kate will definitely try to beat you up, so don't settle for a penny less," Davey said.

"I won't," Bethany promised.

"She's tough, I won't lie. But you have to hold the line," Davey insisted.

"I will," Bethany promised.

Two days later, Bethany came home from her meeting with Kate. She'd taken the job for ten percent more than Davey's original ask.

"That's even more than I asked for," Davey said.

"I know," Bethany said cheerfully.

"She turned me down flat. There wasn't even any discussion about it."

"She mentioned that."

"And you got her to agree to even more."

"We had a very productive discussion," Bethany observed. "I think we're going to get along very well."

Bethany gave her two-week notice at Pompano Grill, spent one long day with Lucinda, and started work at Captain Dan's the week after Carlos and Lucinda went back to Cuba.

When would Davey learn that he didn't have to prop up this amazing woman? That she could take care of herself? Maybe never, he wasn't sure.

But he knew she'd probably prove it to him again and again.

Chapter 22

"How'd you find me?" Jerry asked. He didn't sound happy.

"I asked out front. The manager said you were on a break," Davey answered. That wasn't what Jerry meant and Davey knew it but he didn't want to explain how he learned Jerry was working at Publix.

"Welcome to my world," Jerry said, his hands spread wide to indicate the warehouse that sprawled behind the store.

The two men were silent for a moment. Davey wasn't sure where to start. Jerry was sitting on a pallet of soda cartons.

"Don't they have a break room?" Davey asked.

"Over there. But I prefer to be by myself," Jerry answered. "In case you were wondering," he added, pointedly.

"Look," he said at last, "I know what's happened--"

Jerry cut him off. "--No, you know what you heard at Bubble Talk."

"Okay, that's fair," Davey conceded.

There was another awkward silence.

"So, what's on your mind?" Jerry asked, finally.

"I had the craziest dream the other night--" Davey started.

"--*Oh, my God!*" Jerry was shaking his head.

"Okay, not the best place to start. But it got me thinking. Hear me out." Davey held up his hands, like they were diving: STOP.

"I got five minutes. Then I gotta get back to work," Jerry said.

"You said she was a better diver than he was," Davey said.

"Yeah, what about it?"

"So, if she's a better diver than he is, why does she drown in a silt-out that he swims out of like it's nothing? It doesn't make sense."

"Things don't always make sense," Jerry shrugged. "You been doing this long enough to know that."

"Yeah, but my point is: what if it wasn't an accident?" Davey raised his eyebrows, provocatively. "Have you ever considered that?"

Jerry looked at Davey the way you'd look at a crazy person. "Are we back to your dream again?"

"Forget the dream. Just indulge me for a second here. What if it wasn't an accident?"

"Two people got silted out at 90 feet and one of them drowned. It's a tragedy, not a mystery."

"You see another boat at the site?" Davey asked.

"Yeah, a little fishing boat was a ways off when we got there. Maybe a hundred fifty yards southeast. Gone when we came up."

Davey wasn't surprised, not really. You didn't teach big classes successfully for years without having a good eye for detail.

"They were fishing, not diving," Jerry added.

"One diver, no flag," Davey said, softly. "Down about 20 minutes."

Jerry paused. He seemed to be considering the new information.

"Hard to build a conspiracy out of a coincidence," he said, finally.

"Melissa," Davey said softly.

"Huh?"

"His wife's name was Melissa."

Jerry shrugged. "So?"

"The only reason I know that is because his lawyer said her name several times during his testimony," Davey said with grim determination. "Gaffney himself never said her name. Not once."

"I don't see what—"

"—His dive buddy, his *wife*, dies... just a few feet away from him, and he never says how sad he is. Never says he feels guilty. Never says he's lost the love of his life. He never even says her name."

"Not a great husband, I guess," Jerry commented, thoughtfully.

"His entire testimony, his sole focus, was on your liability. Nothing about his tragic loss," Davey said. "Doesn't that strike you as... odd?"

Jerry pursed his lips. "The hearing was about money, not love. He stayed on-message."

Jerry looked at his watch. "Break's over," he said. "Gotta get back to work."

"I met the captain of that fishing boat," Davey said quickly, as Jerry was standing up. "Down at Captain Ed's. He was trying to peddle his story for some free drinks and I wasn't into it, so I blew him off." Davey waved a hand dismissively.

"But then I started thinking about it. And I think there could be a connection."

Jerry stretched his neck and shoulders. "Look, I wish the whole thing didn't happen, but it did. And I'm not gonna go chasing unicorns trying to change what can't be changed."

"We both agreed that the natural reaction to a silt-out is to grab your dive buddy," said Davey. "Everyone knew right where to look for her but still she wasn't found for days."

"Doesn't prove anything," Jerry said.

"There was air in her tank when they found the body." Davey had read the Coast Guard report.

Jerry shrugged. "Diver loses her regulator, panics, drowns before she can recover it and drifts away on the current. Makes perfect sense to me."

"I know it's a long shot but where's the harm? We could find the charter captain, get the police to interview him," Davey insisted.

"Police already closed the case," Jerry reflected.

"We could track down this mystery charter guest, find out if she has any connection with Gaffney…"

"She?" Jerry asked, absently.

"It was a woman. 'Kind of a looker,' the captain said," Davey smiled at the memory. "Little tattoo of an octopus on the small of her back."

"Octopus, you say? That right?" Jerry's eyes met Davey's for the first time. Then he looked away, turned his head left to avoid eye contact, the way he had that first night at Get Shorty's.

"My boss here is a twenty-seven-year-old kid. Eager type. Ambitious. Wears a pocket protector so the pens in his shirt pocket won't bleed ink onto his white, short-sleeved shirt." Jerry tilted his head. "I sure don't want to get on his bad side." At least Jerry still had his sense of humor.

"I'll help," Davey pleaded. "Go to the cops with you. Help find the boat captain."

"I appreciate it, Davey. I really do. You're a good guy," Jerry patted Davey's shoulder. "But I'm ready to call it a day, put this whole business behind me."

"It's a chance! You could get your life back. What've you got to lose?" Davey pleaded as Jerry walked through the swinging doors back into the store.

"Those shelves aren't going to stock themselves," Jerry said, and he waved without looking back over his shoulder.

• • •

Abigail took her Open Water class with three other students. During the initial gear set-up, she was the first one to get it right.

The other students were in their 20s. Tim and Martha were a couple, and Bobby was their friend. When Bobby saw that he was going to have a 12-year-old dive buddy, he rolled his eyes.

They did their pool session at the Jacobs Aquatic Center behind the Divers Direct warehouse store.

Tim and Martha were cute and in love. They were so into each other it was hard to get them to concentrate on scuba. But they made it through the skills reasonably well and Davey had few real concerns about taking them out for the Open Water dives.

Bobby was another story. He was kind of a natural-born klutz. When he and Abigail were doing the alternate air sharing exercise, Bobby gave the out-of-air sign and immediately spat out his regulator, even though he'd been briefed to keep his regulator in his mouth until his buddy's alternate air was presented to him.

Before Davey could intercede, Abigail had shoved the regulator back in Bobby's mouth and hit the purge button.

Abigail looked at Bobby. Bobby looked at Abigail. Abigail held out her hands toward Bobby to indicate he should start again.

Look at her, thought Davey, acting like a Divemaster.

This time Bobby did it right and the exercise was flawless.

When the pool work was completed, Abigail seemed proud of herself but not to the point of being cocky. On the ride back to shop she peppered Davey with questions.

"Did I do okay?" she asked.

"You did *great!*" Davey answered.

"When we get out to the reef, is there going to be current?"

"We won't know till we get there."

"Am I going to be okay out there?"

"You're going to be fine. I have no concerns about you."

"But you'll to be right there, right?"

"I'll be right there. But I'll be watching the other three, too, and frankly I'm more concerned about them than you."

"Why do you care more about them than me?"

"I don't *care* more about them. I'm more *concerned* about them. They weren't as good as you were."

Abigail sat back and grinned ear to ear.

Horseshoe reef had one- to two-foot waves and mild current out of the southwest. A lot of boat captains liked to tell their guests that the reef got its name because the Spanish cast their gold in the shape of horseshoes and then painted them black to fool privateers. Four golden horseshoes had been lost at this site and only three were ever recovered.

It was bullshit, of course, but the tourists enjoyed the story.

Calypso was moored on the north ball, which was anchored near a circular sand patch that Davey called the *cul-de-sac*.

He got his four students kneeling in the sand in the *cul-de-sac* and went through the dive skills. Bobby struggled a bit with the mask clearing but that was to be expected. Everyone else blew through the skills and was ready to do the rest of the dive.

There are cube-shaped blocks of coal at Horseshoe reef which are surprising to see if you're not expecting them. They're clearly not natural formations but it's hard to identify what they actually are. Because of the mild current, some sand had settled in the debossing on one block's face and a Crown logo with the words PATENT and CARDIFF below it were readable, like a tracing.

Davey pointed that out to his students and took a picture.

Technically, Davey wasn't supposed to have a camera when he was teaching. But with good students, he did sometimes. It was a GoPro attached to his BCD on a retractable coil so his hands could be free quickly if he needed them.

As they were swimming down the sand channel with the reef on their right, a large southern stingray passed them on the left. Davey saw it first because he'd just turned around to check on his divers, and he got a beautiful picture of Abigail with the ray right below her.

At 20 minutes, Davey asked for everyone's air pressure and made sure they were all comfortable in the water column.

Before he could turn back to the front, he spotted two reef sharks coming up behind them, swimming quickly. Their pectoral fins were angled down, so they were hunting. The sharks darted ahead of the divers, turned and swam into a coral channel, came back out again and swam away to the southeast.

Davey got pictures of the whole thing.

"You had her in the water with *sharks!*" Bethany protested, pulling a slice of pizza from the box and dropping it on her plate.

"Mom, it was so cool!" Abigail enthused. "You should have seen them. They were *amazing!*"

"They're not dangerous," Davey assured Bethany. "We see them a lot. These two were hunting so they were swimming a little faster."

"*Hunting!*" Bethany was aghast.

"They eat fish, not people. There's nothing to worry about."

"For you, maybe," she was wearing her Mom Hat again.

"She did well," Davey said, changing the subject. "You'd have been proud of her."

"I'm always proud of her," Bethany replied, wiping a little pizza grease off Abigail's chin.

The next morning on the reef, Abigail finished the course and got her temporary C-card. She'd aced it from beginning to end. There was no limit to what this kid could do.

Davey and Abigail were headed home; Abigail was basking in the glow of her accomplishment. Davey was very proud of her. She was going to become an excellent diver in no time. He was already planning to take her through the advanced course next summer.

Then Davey saw police-car lights in his rear-view mirror. The cruiser came right up behind him and hung there.

"What the hell," Davey said and he pulled over on the roadside. He was pretty sure he hadn't been speeding. He rolled down his window as the officer approached.

"What's the problem, officer?" Davey asked.

"Good afternoon, Mister Jones, how you doin' today?"

Davey looked at the officer's nametag: HARDESTY.

"I'm good. What's up?"

"Maybe you wouldn't mind joining me in the cruiser for a just a short minute," Hardesty requested.

"Stay here," Davey said to Abigail. "I won't be long." Davey got out of the car.

It was a tight fit getting into the passenger seat of the police car, wedged below the computer.

"You can call me Jim," said Hardesty.

"Okay, Jim. I'm Davey," answered Davey.

"Last night, the Sheriff's Office answered a call in Big Pine Key. It was a pretty unusual call for us: double murder and suicide. Not your typical Florida Keys event."

"Sounds horrible," Davey responded, not knowing what else to say.

"Worse than you can imagine. I saw the report when I came on shift this morning. The offender broke into a private residence and killed a couple that was living there. Used a shotgun. Pretty messy. Then he turned the gun on himself."

"Oh God, that's awful."

"The offender was unrecognizable, if you know what I mean. But from the driver's license recovered off the body, they were able to tentatively identify him. It's your friend,

Gerald Delblaine, the fella you testified for down at the courthouse."

The reality of it hit Davey like a body blow.

Jerry was dead. Not just ruined, not just disgraced and out of business. *Dead!* Suicide by shotgun!

"Who were the victims?" Davey asked, his mind racing

"That's where it gets interesting," Hardesty said, as if the narrative so far hadn't warranted Davey's attention. "The man was a fella named Gaffney. He was the plaintiff in that same case. And the woman was Henrietta Delblaine, the offender's ex-wife. Appears like the two of them had set up housekeeping down there a while back."

Davey's mind had trouble embracing the enormity of it all.

Jerry, a murderer! His wife and Gaffney living together! What was that about? How had any of this come to be? This wasn't life in the Florida Keys. This was some far-flung fantasy out of a cheap murder mystery.

Hardesty recited the details, a little at a time so that Davey could absorb them. When he was done, he asked if Davey had any questions but Davey just shook his head, dumbly.

He looked out the windshield of the police cruiser toward his car. He could see Abigail sitting in the passenger seat, waiting as she'd been told to do.

Davey stared at her. He didn't know why, he just needed to confirm that in a world gone crazy Abigail was still safe at that moment in time.

"I wanted you to hear it from me so you didn't just get the rumors and gossip," said Hardesty. "I don't know how close y'all were but I guess he was some kinda friend a yours."

"Thank you, Jim," said Davey, still in a daze. "That was kind of you."

"Happy to be of service," Hardesty said.

"Actually, I do have one question, if you don't mind," Davey said as a sudden thought occurred to him. "Did the woman have any identifying marks? Like an octopus tattoo on the small of her back?"

Hardesty looked perplexed by the question. He tapped the keyboard on his computer, looked at the screen, and furrowed his brow. "Now, how would you know a thing like that?"

Davey sighed. "Lucky guess," he said. "I... I should get back..."

Davey pointed to his car and Abigail.

"Yeah, sure. You take care now." Hardesty said. "Sorry about you friend and all."

"Thank you," mumbled Davey. He didn't know what else to say.

Davey walked slowly back to his car. When he got into the driver's seat, Abigail asked, "What was that about?"

"Nothing," Davey replied absently. "Nothing for you to worry about. I just got some bad news."

"You look like you saw a ghost," Abigail observed.

Davey smiled wanly. "I imagine I do."

Abigail looked at Davey; it was her penetrating look. After a few moments, she asked, "It's something about my Dad, isn't it?"

That brought Davey out of his reverie.

"Your Dad? No. *God, no.* He's gone, I promise you," Davey said reassuringly. "We're not going to see him again."

"Well, it's something. I can see it in your face."

Davey squeezed Abigail's knee reassuringly.

"A friend of mine died," Davey explained. "It happened last night."

"Oh..." Abigail said, and immediately she went quiet.

Davey started the car and put it in gear.

"I'm sorry," Abigail said in a soft voice. "About your friend."

Davey smiled at her. "Thank you."

He checked traffic behind him and pulled out onto the road.

Davey shared the story with Bethany, eliminating a lot of the gory details. No one needed to have nightmares over this. She was sympathetic even though she'd never met Jerry.

"I feel like I should head over to Get Shorty's," Davey said. "This will be all over Bubble Talk and I'm pretty sure I'm the only one who knows the facts."

Bethany understood immediately.

"You're standing by your friend," Bethany said, nodding. "It's important to you."

Davey smiled. She was right, as usual. "If you asked me why, I couldn't tell you," he admitted.

• • •

Di was hunkered down at the bar with a somber group already huddled around him. Elpis had her arm around Di's shoulder. Roald sat next to them with a long face. Theo was at the hightop, his usual spot, uncharacteristically restrained.

Davey guessed they had heard already.

"Davey, come here," Elpis called with her arm outstretched. "We have such sad news."

"I know," Davey nodded. "I heard it, too."

"How would you hear?" Roald asked. "He got the letter only an hour ago."

"What?" Davey asked. "What are you talking about?"

"Di's father died," Elpis said, leaning her head on his shoulder. "He got a letter. From Mykonos. It is very sad."

Davey was stunned. Di never talked about his family back in Greece.

"I'm so sorry, Di. Sorry for your loss," Davey managed to say.

Di raised his head. "He was a prick *bastard!* I cursed his life years ago. I'm glad he's dead."

"You don't mean that. He's your father, whatever else happened," Elpis said softly.

"I mean every word," Di insisted.

Roald blanched. He was unaccustomed to such blunt candor.

"Dude, what did he do to you?" Theo wanted to know.

"You want to know? My father? *My blood!*" Di's face revealed sadness mixed with anger.

He sat up and Elpis's hand slid off his shoulder.

No one said a word.

"I come to this country, I am nineteen. Have very little English. Mykonos is a tiny spot on the map. No one cares. Artists and hippies live there. Most are very poor."

Davey watched his friend transport himself back to another time and place. He was a different person, with different hopes and dreams.

"Every week, I send money home. 'Buy land.' There are places on the island that have no electricity. No one lives there. I want to have an olive grove someday. 'Buy land,' I tell my father. Every week I send money for this valueless land."

"He stole your money? Davey asked, quietly.

"*Oh no!*" Di announced emphatically. "My father honors his son's request. He buys land exactly where I tell him to buy." Di took a meditative drink from his cup. "Every year, he sends a map showing my land, how it grows."

"I don't think I see you as an olive farmer," Roald commented. "Is that how it's called, an olive farmer?"

"Makes no difference what you call it. Because my father, he buys the land but forgets to put *my* name on the title. Ten years later, the beautiful people have discovered Mykonos. The Jet Set. There is no valueless land on the island. My father, he sells the stremmas he bought with my money and he is rich. My whole family is rich."

"That's awful," said Davey.

"They are gypsies. They rob from their own blood and they are rich." Di spat on the floor.

"Man, that's harsh," Theo offered.

"Will you go home for the funeral?" Davey asked.

"Years ago, I swear an oath I will never step foot again in Greece!" Di slapped the bar for emphasis. Then he waved his hand. "Anyway, he was buried last month." He shrugged. "Even if I wanted to... "

"Then why the letter? Why now?" Davey asked.

Elpis was stroking Di's shoulder again.

"The letter is from his father's lawyer," Elpis said. "He leaves one hundred Euros each to his other two sons and his second wife."

"Second wife...?" Davey asked.

"My mother died ten years ago," Di said, without emotion.

"Everything else – his fortune, his house, everything – he leaves to Di," Elpis added. "He begs forgiveness on his deathbed, his lawyer says."

"*Forgiveness!* For a lifetime of cheating me," Di growled.

"The others will fight it in the Greek courts, the lawyer says. But they cannot win. The Will is legal," Elpis said, with her cheek on Di's shoulder again. "So, what was rightfully his is his once more."

"My God," said Davey. "This is right out of Greek tragedy."

"Aristophanes, not Sophocles," Di objected. "It is a comedy and I am a clown."

A respectful silence fell over the group. Carly and Jens entered the bar and casually joined the others. There were no smiles or hugs.

"You must hear this amazing story," Roald said to the couple.

"Jerry Delblaine is dead," Carly announced quietly, sitting next to Theo at the hightop. Jens pulled up a chair from another table.

"Wait… *what?*" Theo was incredulous.

"You will never believe how it happened," Jens sounded astonished.

"Jerry…?" Elpis looked puzzled.

"Scuba Doo Jerry," Carly clarified. "He's dead. And that's not all."

"The hell you say!" Di sat up abruptly, pulled out of his mourning by this news.

"It's true," Carly asserted. "It happened last night--"

"--Did he… kill himself?" Di asked, with a sudden insight.

"No." Carly answered. "Well, yes… but not right away."

"First he kill the man who sue him!" Jens jumped in.

"My goodness," Elpis hand went to her mouth.

"This cannot be true," Di shook his head vehemently. "That's not Jerry. He would never--"

"--It's true!" Carly insisted. "It was a double murder. The man who sued him and some woman who was there. It happened on Big Pine Key."

"Who was the woman?" Di asked.

"I bet it was the wife!" Theo surmised. "She never really died in the accident. It was all a scam!"

Davey wanted to stop them right there, to tell them what he knew but for some reason he couldn't speak. The words just didn't come.

"Her body was recovered by the Coast Guard, you *nitwit!*" Di spat. "Do you think they were also part of your *scam?*"

Chastened, Theo contemplated this.

Roald asked, "How did this happen?"

"I heard he used a machete," Carly said, grimly. "There was blood everywhere! It's incredible."

Di was unconvinced. "How did he kill himself then?" he asked.

Carly shrugged. "I don't know. I didn't hear all the details."

"I am still wondering who the woman was?" Roald mused.

"I question the whole story!" Di asserted, but it was clear his resolve was wavering.

Davey had to stop it. He had to stop it now. This was Bubble Talk running amok right in front of his eyes.

"The woman was Jerry's ex-wife," said Davey, finally. Everyone turned toward him, eyes wide.

"What?" Di asked, incredulous.

Davey shrugged. "It was Henni. She and Gaffney were living together. And it was a shotgun, not a machete."

The group was stunned. Di groped for words.

"I know Jerry for maybe twenty years," Di said at last. "This is crazy talk. This is not the man I know."

It was clear the others felt the same way.

The fact was no one really thought too badly of Jerry for running over-large classes. Standards, well, people respected them (mostly out of fear) but no one revered them.

And there'd been a certain amount of sympathy for Jerry when he lost everything over one bad outcome, however tragic the results may have been for Melissa Gaffney.

But now he was a murderer, a mad killer, a man who took out the consequences of his own actions on other people.

Even Davey struggled with his new revelation about his friend.

"It's not what you think," Davey said, trying to make sense of it. "That missing diver, the woman who died, it wasn't an accident."

"The hell you say!" Di repeated.

"Don't ask me to explain it," Davey pleaded. "I can't prove anything. But I know it's true. It was no accident."

"But..." Carly started. "If it was no accident, then how..."

"Gaffney killed his wife and blamed Jerry," Davey stated flatly. "And Henni was his accomplice."

Chapter 23

For the first time in the five years since he'd moved to the Keys, Davey found himself ambivalent about diving. He no longer felt the awe of the ocean; gone was the sense of wonder that engulfed him every time he splashed in.

He felt empty.

The source of this insinuating malaise was difficult to locate. He and Jerry hadn't been close friends. Circumstances had thrown them together for a brief period of time but there was no real depth to the relationship.

Still, Davey found himself simply going through the motions.

He taught a 65-year-old student who overcame her lifelong fear of water and passed her certification with flying colors. He could barely find the energy even to pretend that he shared her joy.

The woman's husband, an experienced diver, was so grateful he pressed a hundred-dollar tip into Davey's palm and shook his hand with great vigor. He posted a five-star review on TripAdvisor naming him "simply the best instructor I have met in 20 years of diving." Davey took no pleasure in the accolade.

On Wednesday, he was guiding six divers at North North Dry Rocks when he realized halfway through the dive that two of them were no longer swimming behind him.

Davey silently swore at himself. Visibility was good, at least 60 feet. But he hadn't looked back to check on his divers often enough. Two of them had lagged behind or taken a wrong turn. It was careless, unforgivable - dangerous.

Davey reversed course and swam back the way he'd come. All six in the group were certified divers. Still, he was responsible.

A hundred feet back, Davey spotted a bubble trail rising behind a coral ridge. And there they were.

The two missing divers were looking at a moray eel they'd found under a ledge.

Davey swam over and took a few pictures. The other four gathered around and Davey got pictures of everyone with the eel.

Problem solved. In fact, as far as anyone knew, there had never even been a problem.

But Davey was angry with himself. You can't do this, he scolded himself. You can't let your guard down for one minute. Every time you're underwater you have people's lives in your hands.

Pay attention!

But it was a tall order. There was a void in his soul where his passion once had been.

The local papers were filled with the story of the triple murder that week. This was sensational news for the Florida Keys and the newspapers couldn't devote enough ink to it. Jerry, Henni, and Gaffney were all pictured in large photos on the front page.

Davey struggled with his own dark secret: had he caused the death of three people? After all, he was the one who told Jerry he thought Melissa Gaffney's death wasn't an accident. Insisted on it.

And he was the one who, without knowing he was doing it, identified Henni as the charter guest, the mystery woman at the accident site. The woman with the little octopus tattoo.

Jerry had looked him right in the eye on that one. What an actor! Davey had replayed it over and over in his mind. Jerry knew at that moment that his wife had betrayed him. Knew she'd conspired with Gaffney. But it never showed on his face. Not even a glimmer.

The charter boat captain from Islamorada saw the pictures in the newspapers and went to the Monroe County Sherriff's Office to tell his story. The new information caused a nuclear explosion.

Of course, nothing could be certain. And the police weren't pursuing the investigation because all of the principals involved were deceased, so what would be the point?

But Bubble Talk went into overdrive and new theories emerged, some fairly lurid and others completely ridiculous.

Davey was pretty sure that only he knew what had really happened.

When they got silted out, Gaffney had reached for his dive buddy, just as Davey thought he should--and turned off her air!

Gaffney didn't have a lot of time. If he was missing for too long, someone might turn back and look for them. So, he needed to leave Melissa quickly and rejoin the group.

That's where Henni came in. She knew right where Jerry's class would do their deep-water skills. And while the large group swam in the opposite direction, she located Melissa's body, turned her air back on, and towed the body away from the site.

It wouldn't have to be far. Just far enough so no one would find her and the current would carry her off.

That guaranteed there wouldn't be an investigation for several days. And when the body was found, it would look like a simple drowning.

Who could say it wasn't?

It was classic misdirection. Everybody was focused on the "standards" and Jerry's lack of "direct supervision" but no one was looking at what actually killed Melissa Gaffney.

It was no accident; it was murder.

But what part had Davey played in all this? Did Jerry already know he'd been set up? Would he have found out about his wife, even if Davey hadn't told him? Why didn't he let Davey help him unravel the mystery and get at least part of his life back?

It didn't have to play out like this.

"Maybe life ain't run over you yet like a big goddamn Mack truck," Jerry once said to Davey. Well, then again, maybe it had. Davey had been there and so he knew.

He understood how it felt to be so far down that any effort at all was too much to expect. He'd hit bottom; he knew what it felt like.

And now he was stuck with this terrible secret, this gnawing realization so horrible he couldn't even share it with Bethany. Someday maybe, but not now. For now, it was his burden alone.

Davey couldn't stop visualizing those last few minutes in Big Pine Key. Had the couple woken up, startled, maybe even scared, when Jerry broke the back window to get inside?

Did Gaffney feel a moment of regret for killing his wife and blaming Jerry once he realized that he, himself, was about to die?

What did Henni think when she saw her husband pointing a loaded shotgun straight at her? Did she make the big eyes, the panic sign every dive instructor recognizes? Did she beg for her life?

What was Jerry's final thought as he turned the shotgun on himself?

"When you put a shotgun in your mouth," Di said. "You don't shoot yourself in the head. You don't have no head no more."

"I *tolt* you it was the husband the first day it happened!" declared Binky, filled with righteous indignation.

Davey looked at Di. "He did say that. Even before he knew there was a husband."

But Di wasn't having it. "A broken clock says the right time twice a day," he said, dismissively. Still, Binky had been right for once and the world would have to learn to accommodate to that reality.

For a couple of weeks, nearly every conversation on the island centered in some way around the sensational story. Bubble Talk spoke of little else. Every action and revelation was parsed and rehashed.

And then in the natural course of things, people moved on, and the missing diver and the terrible events that followed began to take on a more historical feeling, a remembered episode in the distant past.

Bubble Talk returned to more prosaic themes.

"When are you getting your inheritance?" Roald asked. "Must we now genuflect in your presence? King Di, the rich!"

"*Oh*, like that king who had the Midas Touch," offered Theo. "You know the one I mean. Who was that?"

Nobody spoke; everyone looked at Theo. One, two, three...

"Oh, right," he got it at last. "*Ha, ha!*" he laughed at himself as if he'd made the joke on purpose. "Yeah, *him*."

Di snorted and took a long drink.

"He declined his father's fortune," Elpis added, after a moment. "Gave it back to the family."

"What?" Davey was astonished.

"They will fight over the money among themselves," Di observed, somberly. "I hope they kill each other for it."

"But that was your money," Davey insisted.

"I lose that money years ago, in another life," Di groused. "This is the life I have made for myself."

Di smiled at Elpis. "This is the life I keep."

No one spoke but they all exchanged confused glances.

Di shrugged philosophically. "They are spoiled after 30 years. They would not know how to be poor."

"Maybe not so much of a misanthrope after all," Davey mused.

"Hey, *hey*, you watch what you say, okay?" Di barked.

But Davey smiled. Everyone has secrets, he thought, things they hide inside themselves and rarely share with others.

• • •

For Davey, the empty feeling he'd been unable to shake dissipated as mysteriously as it had arrived. He was able to breathe again. The passion he felt for diving returned.

People come to the Florida Keys for many reasons: to retire, or to run away from their past, to build new lives, or to recover from old wounds. They come to escape and they come to rejoice in the sheer mindless pleasure of it all.

They come to float on the tropical breezes. Or they come, like Jerry, to create something, to build a legacy that will hopefully sustain them for the rest of their lives.

After 30 years of hard work, Jerry's dream had slipped through his fingers like sand. And then, finally, he'd even lost himself.

Where were the standards that protected good people from the vast unfairness of life?

Apparently, there were none.

One day a week later, when Davey didn't have an afternoon boat trip, he came home early and found Bethany working on Abigail's laptop.

"Working from home today?" he asked.

Bethany was entering data from a pile of invoices and receipts she had stacked on her left.

"Katherine's getting in the habit of leaving me to watch the front desk while she goes and does God knows what," Bethany said without stopping. "I told Kate that's not my job and if I'm going to end up bringing work home, I might as well work from home to begin with."

"How'd she take it?" Davey asked.

"Just about the way you'd expect. And Katherine had a *shit-fit*," Bethany answered. "But I told them it's my way or the highway on this one. They need to staff that front office anyway. Katherine's terrible at it. She's awful with people."

"She doesn't relate to the species," Davey mused.

"They can afford to do it right. They make a buttload of money off those rooms," Bethany insisted.

"So, you're working on Abigail's computer?" Davey asked.

"That's right," Bethany agreed. "But I'll be done by the time she gets home."

Davey stood there without saying anything. Bethany turned and nailed him with a look.

"Don't," she said simply. "Don't even think about it."

"What?" Davey shrugged as innocently as he could manage.

"I've got a good job now and next week I'll go out and buy my own computer," Bethany stated. "With my own money."

Davey acted like it had never entered his mind to buy her a computer but they both knew that's exactly what he'd been thinking.

Student orientation for Abigail's senior year at Key Largo School came with one additional and very welcome surprise.

Ken Duplay was gone. Disgraced.

Crystal could hardly wait to supply all the details.

"He got pulled over in August and the officer thought he smelled alcohol on Duplay's breath. So rather than cite him for DUI, the officer called his wife at home and asked her to come pick up her husband," Crystal relayed, breathlessly.

That decision brought unforeseen consequences because Duplay had Marjorie Downey in the car with him and, try as he might, he was unable to come up with an acceptable reason why that was so.

"The cop thought he was doing Duplay a favor but it didn't turn out that way," Crystal chortled. Brie thought the whole episode was pretty amusing, as well.

So Duplay's wife had kicked him out of the house and was filing for divorce. He was a pariah at his church. No one knew where he was living but it wasn't with Marjorie Downey because she was having nothing to do with the little rat.

Marjorie was embarrassed and humiliated and as far as she was concerned, it was all Duplay's fault.

The school board seemed to agree with that assessment and Duplay had been fired for having an inappropriate relationship with the parent of a student. So, he was toast.

All in all, it was the most satisfying school event Davey had ever attended.

The mail came early the next morning and they were still sitting around the breakfast table enjoying the end of summer vacation together. Bethany was expecting some paperwork from Abigail's school, so she got up and went to the mailbox in the parking lot.

"What the heck's Florida 529?" asked Bethany, holding up an official looking envelope as she came back through the front door. Davey took the letter, folded it and put it in his pocket. "Oh, that's nothing," Davey said with a shrug. "Nothing to worry about."

"Why is it addressed to you with my daughter's name on it?"

"It's just a thing I sent away for," Davey hedged. "Not a big deal."

Bethany continued staring at Davey.

"Anything else?" he asked, hopefully. "Did you get the school stuff?"

"You get an official document from the State of Florida with my daughter's name on it and I shouldn't be concerned?" Bethany was skeptical.

Abigail watched from the breakfast table. It didn't look like something she wanted to get in the middle of.

Bethany put her hand out. "Give it here," she said firmly.

"It's nothing," Davey pleaded. "Not a big deal."

"Give it to me," Bethany insisted. This wasn't going away.

Davey handed her the envelope.

"Okay, look, the 529 program is a prepaid college savings account. It's never too early to plan for these things. I opened an account for Abigail and that's why her name is on it."

Bethany looked at the letter and looked up at Davey.

"I'm opening this," she said.

"Before you do, I want you to remember that a college degree opens doors."

Bethany put her finger under the flap and tore the envelope open. She looked straight at Davey as she did it.

"You've got a smart kid there. She should be allowed to go as far as she can go without being held back for lack of tuition money."

Bethany took out the letter and examined it. Her mouth dropped open and she fell back on the couch.

"Let's not make a big thing out of this," Davey cautioned.

"I can't… we can't accept this… Davey this is crazy!"

"What am I going to do with it? I have everything I want. There's nothing I need that costs money."

"There's $120,000 in this account!" Bethany said, breathing heavily.

"Who knows what things will cost by the time she goes to college." Davey sat down on the couch a few feet away from Bethany. This wasn't a good time to crowd her.

"With this, she can go anywhere she wants and do anything she's capable of. Whatever school she gets into. Graduate school. If there's only one program in the country, she can apply for it."

"But I can't let you do this!" Bethany was anguished.

"Look, you and me, we didn't have a lot of advantages when we were young. We missed opportunities that could have helped us in our lives, our ambitions. But we got where we got, so good for us."

Bethany was holding the letter like it was the Shroud of Turin.

"Don't we owe it to Abigail to see that she has every advantage we can give her? To see that she has every opportunity to earn a better place in the world? Don't we owe her that?"

Tears streaked down Bethany's face.

"No strings. It's done and done. Whatever happens between us happens. If anything happens *to* us, her future is taken care of."

Bethany folded the letter and put it back in the envelope. She handed it back to Davey.

She didn't speak, just shook her head from side to side.

"We don't need to think about this or look at it ever again. When the time comes, it'll be there," Davey said.

Abigail walked over to Davey and sat silently in his lap. She put her arms around his neck and lay her head on his shoulder.

Davey wrapped his arms around the twelve-year-old.

"Anything you want to be, be that thing," Davey whispered in her ear. "Any dream you want to have, dream that dream."

For several minutes, no one said anything.

About the author

Thomas Simmons is a full-time scuba instructor and dive guide at Sail Fish Scuba in Key Largo, Florida. Prior to living the privileged life of a dive bum, he was an advertising creative director for four decades and he isn't even sorry about it, although he probably should be.

Made in the USA
Coppell, TX
31 July 2021

59749544R00184